Augathella Short and Sweets

Books 4-7

An Augathella Christmas

An Augathella Wedding

An Augathella Easter

An Augathella Masquerade Ball

ANNIE SEATON

ISBN 978-1-7638747-6-3

AUGATHELLA SHORT AND SWEETS

An Augathella Surprise

An Augathella Baby

An Augathella Spring

An Augathella Wedding

An Augathella Christmas

An Augathella Easter

An Augathella Masquerade Ball

Following on from:

THE AUGATHELLA GIRLS

Book 1: Outback Roads –The Nanny
Book 2: Outback Sky – The Pilot
Book 3: Outback Escape – The Sister
Book 4: Outback Winds – The Jillaroo
Book 5: Outback Dawn – The Visitor
Book 6: Outback Moonlight – The Rogue
Book 7: Outback Dust – The Drifter
Book 8: Outback Hope – The Farmer

An Augathella Christmas

ANNIE SEATON

Augathella Short and Sweets: 4

Chapter 1
Sophie

Sophie Mason leaned back in the swivel chair that had been delivered a few days before Ruby Rose was born. A pale dove-grey colour matched the doona cover, and the two plump red cushions made the soft chair perfect for breastfeeding. Its position—tucked into the corner of their bedroom between the two picture windows—provided a pretty outlook over their front house paddock. Sophie had continued Kent's mother's gardening when his parents had moved to Brisbane, and the front garden was full of early summer blooms. During Ruby's night feeds, Sophie sat with a dim nightlight beside her and looked out at the star-studded outback sky.

She smiled when she saw Kent loading the baby bags she'd packed earlier for him to put into the back of her SUV.

The gentle movement against her breast made Sophie look down. Even though it was two weeks since their little girl had been born, Sophie's heart still flooded with emotion each time she looked at her baby's face. A contented sigh escaped Ruby Rose's mouth as her lips slipped off Sophie's breast and her little rosy cheek rested against Sophie's skin. She was a perfect baby and had fed like a charm from the first hour of her life.

Callie shook her head the first time she came to visit.

'She's been feeding for six minutes,' Sophie said as she supported Ruby on her lap with her fingers beneath her chin and rubbed her back gently. 'She'll stay asleep now.'

'My God, Sophie, do you know how lucky you are?' Callie reached down and ran her fingers lightly down Ruby's cheek. 'The first week Munro and Megan were born, they were taking over an hour for each feed. An hour each! Two hours of feeding and then they were awake in another three hours and it all started again. I don't know what I would have done without Braden there helping with the double nappy changes and the burping!'

'Our Ruby Rose is a champion.'

Sophie smiled when Kent, the proudest dad in the world, chimed in. 'She knows what she wants, and she goes for it and fills her little tummy in a couple of minutes.'

Sophie swapped Ruby to the other breast to see if she wanted more, but her eyes stayed tightly shut, and her lips pursed. If she stuck to her normal routine, it would be five hours before she woke with a soft little cry, had a quick feed and then went back to sleep.

Sophie had worried at first that there was something wrong with her newborn because of all the horror stories she'd heard about feeding. Laura Adnum, the midwife who delivered her had been satisfied with Ruby's progress when Sophie and Kent had gone into town last week.

'She's gained half a kilogram, Sophie.'

'Is that enough?'

'That's perfect and shows that she's feeding beautifully.' Laura said. 'Now, how are you?'

'I'm remarkably relaxed and getting good sleep every night,' Sophie said. 'It's so much easier than I expected!'

'Keep it up.' Laura smiled as she handed Ruby back to Sophie. 'We'll see you here after Christmas for your six-week check-up.'

Now Sophie leaned back into her chair and ran her finger over Ruby's fine blonde hair. Her lips were pursed in a beautiful rosebud; she and Kent had come up with the middle name of Rose even before they had noticed her little rosebud lips.

Rose had been Braden and Sophie's grandmother's name, and Sophie wanted to have that connection to the Cartwright side.

'How long before you're ready?' Kent appeared in the

doorway. 'Looks like she's finished feeding.'

Sophie looked up. 'I'll get ready now if you can take her. She can go in the car carrier as soon as I get changed. Won't take me long.'

'The car's packed.'

'Yes, I saw you loading it while she fed.'

Sophie buttoned up her shirt and then placed Ruby on her shoulder, giving her a little pat. A soft belch came from Ruby's lips, and her head flopped down on Sophie's shoulder.

'She's sound asleep already.' Sophie smiled up at Kent.

'I'm happy to hold her while you get ready,' he said with a wide grin. 'Take your time.' Kent hovered beside the chair, and Sophie smiled up at her husband.

'Okay, I'll get ready. I had my shower when I got up this morning when you were out in the shed.'

'Come to Daddy, beautiful girl.' Kent took Ruby Rose from Sophie and pressed his lips against her forehead.

Sophie stood. 'I think we have a little girl who is going to be spoiled rotten by her daddy.'

Kent's smile said it all. 'We're staying at Kilcoy for dinner, aren't we?' he asked as he settled in the chair.

'Sorry, didn't I tell you? Yes, Callie said we'll have an early barbie. It'll be good to catch up with them all.' Sophie glanced back from the door before she walked into the hallway. The look of love on Kent's face as he looked down at Ruby Rose brought another tear to her eye. It was the only after-effect of pregnancy and childbirth she was having. She was always so damn emotional, but with a husband like Kent and a perfect baby, she had a good reason to be.

Chapter 2
Callie

'So, what date can we go to the Gold Coast?' Braden reached in and took out the tray of meat from the bottom shelf.

Callie lifted Munro to her shoulder and patted his back.

Braden smiled when a satisfying burp emitted from the three-month-old's lips. 'That's my boy,' he said. Callie handed Munro to Braden and reached for Meg, who was in the double pram beside the table.

'Your dad still doesn't know how to burp you, does he, sweetheart?'

Callie smiled and looked at her husband as a delicate puff of wind came from between Meg's lips. 'That's my girl.'

'Do you think I've got enough meat out of the freezer?' Braden asked as he held Munro with one hand and, with the other, put the tray of almost defrosted meat on the sink tray.

'Give me a couple of minutes. I'll just put them in the cot, and we'll talk about dates,' she said. 'And yes, that's heaps of steak.' She reached over and took Munro from Braden and nursed him as she pushed the pram up the hall to the nursery.

The three boys were playing outside, and Callie could hear them giggling as she walked up the hallway. The twins both went down very quickly, and she stood there for a moment, looking at their plump cheeks as they drifted off in the cot beside each other.

When she walked back down the hall to the kitchen, Braden had made a fresh pot of tea, and she sat beside him at the table.

'What on earth are those boys doing?' she asked. They

were still giggling, and occasionally, there was a happy scream followed by loud laughter.

Braden shook his head. 'I don't know. I was going to go and have a listen because Nigel's almost hysterical with laughter. Something's amused them.'

Callie put her hand on his arm. 'It's good to see, isn't it? Nigel's been so good these last few months.'

'Especially since the twins arrived. He seems to have grown up a little bit,' Braden said. 'And he's so much happier.'

They both looked at each other and smiled as another shriek of laughter drifted up the back steps.

'What *are* they doing?' Braden poured Callie's tea and added two spoons of sugar to his black tea. He got up and, walked across to the back door, and looked outside.

Callie watched her husband as he stood there. Braden said that Nigel had been happy, but since the twins had been born, there had been a shift in him too. He had been happy enough when she first met him, but now that they were married and had Megan and Munro, as well as Petie, Nigel, and Rory, who she considered as hers now, Braden had shed the worry and angst that had sometimes dogged him. These days, he was always smiling and whistling; his shoulders were straight, and he didn't even worry about the property as much now. Fair enough, the rains had been good through the winter, and they had nothing to worry about financially, but even though that had been the case before, he had always managed to find a problem when there was none.

Now, a grin spread across his lips as he tipped his head to the side. He listened to the boys for a while longer, then shook his head as he walked back across the kitchen.

Callie held her hand up and caught Braden's hand as he moved past her to sit down.

'I love you, Braden Cartwright.'

He paused before leaning down and brushing his lips over hers.

'And I love you too, Mrs Cartwright.' His eyes held hers as he sat down, and he picked up his mug. 'What brought that on? Not that I'm complaining.'

Callie smiled. 'Nothing special. I'm just happy. And I'm very content.'

'So am I.' Braden grinned. 'Even if our sleep is being interrupted every night.'

Another scream and more laughter came inside.

'What are they doing?' she asked curiously.

'I believe from what I overheard that they are writing a play.'

'A play?' Callie's eyes opened wide. 'Ah, I know what they're doing. Kimberley's got a contest running at school as part of the literacy program.'

'A contest?'

'Yes. She's invited all the students from Prep to year six; if they write a play for the Christmas concert in the last week of school, one play will be chosen to be performed by some of the children.'

'And it sounds like the boys are right into it.' Braden chuckled. 'Although I don't know if what I heard would be suitable for a school audience.'

'Oh dear. I hope no swearing?'

'No. But I'm sure they'll tell you about it. I won't spoil the surprise. You can judge for yourself.'

'Okay, Kimberley has given them some great motivation. Whoever writes the winning play will be able to choose the cast.'

'So, it's supposed to be a nativity play?' Braden asked.

'Well, sort of. All they have to do is have Joseph and Mary and baby Jesus in it, and they can do what they want with the story. It doesn't even have to be in the stable. They don't have to have the three wise men. They just have to write a story, an original story that teaches of the joy of Christmas.'

Braden laughed. 'Does there have to be a donkey in it?'

'A donkey? Why?'

'Yes, there's always a donkey at the manger. I think the boys have picked that up.'

Callie frowned. 'From memory, I think Kimberley did give them some examples and she did tell them that some nativity plays have been written from the donkey's point of view. Is that what they're doing?'

Braden's eyes gleamed with mirth. 'Not exactly, but you'll see.'

'Tell me, Braden. Do I need to censor it before they hand it in?'

'Um, how about a farting donkey at the manger? I heard some of the sound effects from Nigel when Petie screamed before.'

'Oh, my goodness, maybe I'd better read it!'

'No, let them go. They're boys, and they're having fun and working together without fighting! Besides, we could be away for the concert. Now, what day have we got all the Christmas stuff over and done with?'

'Well, we've got the school dinner at the pub on the ninth, and then we've got dinner with all our friends the next night. I've got an afternoon tea at Jenna's tea room on the fourteenth—the last day of school. And then we're free.'

Braden rolled his eyes. 'That's going to be a big weekend with two nights out.'

'Yes, it is, but I've already lined Ruth up. She's happy to have the twins. We can take the kids to the Sunday night family one, but Ruth's happy to have the boys on the Saturday night as well as the twins.'

'Isn't that a bit much to ask?' Braden asked. 'Looking after the *five* of them?'

'Ruth said Fallon and Jon will be there, and they'll help out. Apparently, she's minding Emily's Ophelia too.'

'We're so lucky to have Ruth in town, aren't we?' he said. 'I wouldn't have asked Sophie. Not for a while anyway.'

'We are, and no. Sophie is busy with Ruby Rose. Okay, so we're clear from the sixteenth of December, the end of the last week of term.'

'Good. That works out well. If I book the apartment from the nineteenth, it gives us time to get down there for four days and still be home for Christmas Day. How does that sound? We'll have to leave on the Saturday morning after your do at the tea room.'

'Yeah, that sounds okay,' Callie said slowly.

'But?' Braden said. He knew her well, Callie thought.

'The only problem is that Saturday is the day the play will be on at the school hall. The boys would probably want to be there.'

'I don't think a farting donkey story will be chosen though, do you?'

'Probably not.'

'Okay, that's the date sorted. I'll book the unit online after Sophie and Kent leave after dinner. I've already put a hold on it for that week. I just have to pay the deposit.'

'I guess Sea World, Dream World, and Movie World will sweeten missing the concert for them, plus we'll be home for Santa Claus presents on Christmas Day.'

'Saves lugging the presents to the coast.' Braden nodded. 'The boys will be fine. We'll have to tell them that's the only option.'

Callie drained her tea and stood up. 'Well, that's your job, Daddy. You can tell them. I'm not getting involved in that discussion.'

'I'm happy to.' Braden stood and picked up both mugs, and rinsed them in the sink. Are you right if I go out to the shed until Kent and Sophie arrive? Or do you want me to set the table or something?'

'You've put the table out near the barbeque, haven't you?'

'Yes. It's up.'

'You go to the shed and send the boys in on your way. They can set it while I put the salads together. Sophie and Kent won't be far away.'

Braden stood and caught Callie in a quick hug as she

passed his chair. 'Why don't you go and have a quick lie down while the boys are setting the table? I can do the salads while Kent cooks the meat.'

'I'll think about it.'

Braden dropped a kiss on the end of her nose and chuckled before he let Callie go and headed for the door.

'What? You don't trust me with a salad or two?'

Chapter 3
Sophie

Sophie waved back as Braden poked his head out the shed door and gave her a wave.

She turned to Kent. 'It's so good to see Braden so happy these days. He's been a different guy since he and Callie got married, hasn't he?'

'The best thing we ever did, all of us,' Kent said, squeezing her hand. 'Getting married.'

'And Ruby. She's the best thing, too,' Sophie said, nodding her head toward the back seat where Ruby Rose was sound asleep in her car seat. 'I feel so silly now. All those doubts I had.'

'I think they're both pretty much an equal number one. Marriage and family.'

'They are, aren't they?' Sophie replied. Kent squeezed her hand again, and Sophie smiled as a wave of contentment washed over her. All those doubts she had about motherhood, about giving birth, about her ability to look after a baby, had disappeared the instant Dr Harry had placed Ruby Rose in her arms. A wave of love unlike anything she had ever felt before, had consumed her as she looked down at the perfect little face of their baby girl. She'd looked up at Kent, and tears filled her eyes as she saw tears streaming down his cheeks. He gripped her hand and then leaned down and pressed his wet cheek to hers.

'We've done well, Kent.'

'*You've* done well,' he said.

And to think she'd been terrified of the labour. Ruby Rose had been born in just under two hours and Dr. Harry had been kept busy running between the labour ward where she was, and next door where Amelia Riley was giving birth to their little boy, Sebastian.

'I must catch up with Amelia this week,' she said as Kent parked near the back fence of the house yard of *Kilcoy Station*. 'We've had a couple of quick phone chats and texts, but I must go into town for a visit.'

Kent honked the horn as he turned the motor off.

'Kent! You'll wake her up. And Megan and Munro!'

'Oops sorry, didn't think.' His smile was apologetic. 'I'm learning. This is only our second outing with her.'

A smile tilted Sophie's lips too as she heard the squeals and whooping as her three nephews ran over to the car.

'That's a welcome and a half,' she said.

Nigel was almost beside himself. His face was red, and he was jumping and punching the air with both fists.

'I'd see they're excited to see their new cousin for the first time.' Kent hurried out and came around to open Sophie's door. She held her hand out to him and smiled as he helped her out of the car.

Kent had always been a gentleman, but since her pregnancy had been confirmed, he'd been extra attentive. He squeezed her hand again before letting go and opening the back door. Ruby Rose was still sound asleep.

'Are you right to get her out while I give the boys a hug? And I'll tell them to be a little bit quieter.' Sophie whispered.

'I think I'll be right.'

Nigel rushed over and wrapped his arms around her legs. 'Aunty, Soph, it's so good you're here today.'

'It's good to see you too, Nigel,' she said quietly. 'Let's whisper so we don't wake Ruby Rose up. I guess you're all excited to see her.'

'We'll see her later. We need to talk to you. It's urgent.' Nigel dropped his voice to a loud whisper.

'Urgent?' Sophie frowned. 'What's wrong?'

'Don't you dare tell, Nigel!' Rory came racing behind, but

his grin was as wide as his little brother's.

Petie brought up the rear, hugging his precious Apricot. Wherever Petie was, his dog, Apricot wasn't far away. Everyone had gotten used to the name Petie had chosen when they all got new pups when Callie first arrived at *Kilcoy Station*.

'We're really, really glad you're here,' Nigel said.

Rory put his finger to his lips. 'Shush, it's a secret, remember?'

'It's not a secret,' Nigel said with a smile. 'Don't be silly, Rory.'

Sophie raised her eyebrows.

'Okay, Rory said what *we're* doing is a secret; the project isn't. Everyone knows about that.'

'A secret?' Sophie asked. 'You three know I love secrets. Come on, I won't tell.'

Rory's grin grew wider. 'We just can't say what it is exactly, Nigel,' he said.

'Yes, but we still have to ask Aunty Sophie for permission. And the others.'

'Okay, you three come over here and sit on the swing with me and tell me what's going on.'

Kent was waiting by the car nursing Ruby. 'And then I'll have to help Uncle Kent get the stuff out of the car.'

Kent was cradling their baby close to his chest. 'When you're done, I'll come back out and get the stuff out of the back.'

'Not a problem. I just need to talk to the boys for a moment. I'll be in, in a while.'

Kent smiled and walked across to the back door. Callie must have heard the horn beep; the screen door was open almost immediately and Kent disappeared inside.

'We've set the table for Mum,' Petie said proudly. 'We even put some candles out.'

'Good job,' Sophie said as she led them across to the swing set near the fence. It always warmed her heart to hear the boys call Callie "Mum". She was the best stepmother ever, not to mention a wonderful sister-in-law.

Rory sat beside her on the double swing, while Nigel and Petie stood next to them. 'You're pretty good at keeping secrets, Aunty Soph, I know that. But this one is a *special* secret.'

Petie started giggling, 'Aunty Soph, it's so funny, especially when the donkey farts.'

'A donkey?' Sophie burst out laughing. 'Have you got a donkey now? I didn't think your dad would ever agree to that.'

Braden had never been a lover of horses, but when Julia, his first wife and the boys' mother had died in a horse accident, he'd switched the property to aerial and motorbike mustering.

'No, it's an imaginary donkey,' Petie said. 'You know that.'

'I don't know what's going on at all. I don't know what this project is. And I don't know what the donkey's got to do with anything, but I think you need to tell me.'

'You have to promise,' Nigel said.

'Okay, guys, I cross my heart. I won't tell anyone what's going on.' Sophie wondered if she was promising too readily. Knowing these three, they could be up to all sorts of mischief.

'Well,' Nigel and Rory both tried to speak at the same time.

'No, Nigel. I'm the oldest so I get to ask.' Rory shoved Nigel as he leaned close to Sophie.

'Settle down,' she said.

'Alright.' Nigel's lip dropped, a mannerism that was very familiar to Sophie from when she'd looked after the boys for eighteen months after Julia had died.

Rory rushed on. 'Mrs Jansen and Miss Riordan have got us—'

'Writing,' Nigel interrupted.

'And it's for Christmas,' Petie said, not to be outdone.

'One at a time,' Sophie said. 'Rory, you go first.'

'Well, Miss Riordan, she's my teacher. You know her.'

'Yes, I know her very well. She's a good friend of mine, and I know she's a very good teacher. So, she's given you something to do, has she?'

'Not exactly,' Nigel said. 'Now it's my turn. Mrs Jansen, *my* new teacher who is really super-duper, had the idea and Miss Riordan made it a project for the whole school and she's given us the same project. It's a competition and anyone can enter.'

'What do you have to do?' Sophie asked.

Nigel rushed in to speak before Rory could answer. 'You have to write a play. You can write it by yourself, or in a group, but it has to be controversial. But still be about Christmas. And Mary and Joseph and joy and all that sort of stuff.'

'And the donkey. Don't forget the donkey,' Petie chimed in.

Sophie raised her eyebrows. 'Controversial?'

Rory shook his head. 'No, no. You know what the nativity play is, don't you?'

'Yes, I do. I was in one every year I was at your primary school.'

'Well, we have to write a nativity story, but it has to be different. Mrs Jansen and Miss Riordan said it can be the nativity stuff that we always do, or it can be set now. It doesn't have to be in the olden times when Mary was on the real donkey.'

Sophie said, 'Maybe she meant contemporary.'

'Yes, that's exactly what it was,' Rory said. 'I remember that word. She wrote it on the board. So, see, Nigel, you got it wrong, you have to let me explain.' Rory nodded, like the grown-up ten-year-old he was. 'It has to have a theme.'

Nigel pouted and kicked his bare foot in the dirt underneath the swing set.

'Stop pouting, Nigel,' Sophie said from habit. 'And what

does the theme have to be, boys?'

'Okay,' Rory said. 'It has to be something special about families, something special about love, and something about Christmas.'

'About joy,' Nigel added.

'That leaves it pretty open.' Sophie couldn't help the grin that crossed her face. 'Again, now tell me, boys, so that's where the donkey is. It's not a real one. So, tell me how you're going to do the story with love and happiness and joy in it?'

'Well, we thought we'd keep the original story about a man and a lady getting married and having a baby,' Rory explained.

Nigel rushed in. 'Because everybody in Augathella is so happy, and we know it's all because they found who they wanted to marry. And we could still have Joseph and Mary and the baby and the donkey too.'

'It sounds very creative.' Sophie nodded slowly. 'Yeah, I get your drift.'

'There was Dad and Callie first.'

Nigel chimed in. 'And then you and Uncle Kent. And Fallon and Jon.'

'My turn,' Petie said.

Sophie turned to Petie. 'Do you want to add anyone?'

Little Petie beamed. 'Yes. Ben and Amelia and Chilli Girl.'

Sophie nodded, getting into the swing of their idea. 'I like it.'

'And then there was Nurse Bec and Matt, who saved me at your wedding,' Petie said. 'Mum said they're getting married soon.'

'And then there was Miss Riordan and Mr Calthorpe.' Nigel squealed as his excitement built. 'And Dr. Harry and the nurse who gave Mum the twins.'

'And don't forget Aunty Jacinta and Uncle Ryder,' Rory chimed in.

'Well, you've certainly got a handle on things,' Sophie said. 'We have a busy town, haven't we? And you're right, everybody's happy. So how are you going to show this in the Christmas play?'

'Nigel had the best idea,' Rory said, grinning at his little brother.

'Well, I thought we could have Mary near the manger, and then the narrator—'

'What narrator?' Sophie asked.

'Well, because we've only got a week, there's no lines for the cast to learn. The narrator, probably Mrs Jansen, will do all the talking.'

'Except for the donkey,' Nigel squealed.

'Anyway,' Rory continued, 'she could read our script about joy, and some of the kids could play all the happy people we said before. They don't have to talk, just walk through on the stage, and Mrs Jansen would say their name.'

'It works for me, except do you mean a real donkey or a pretend one?'

'A pretend one. Rory and I want to be the donkey.'

Rory, Nigel and Petie all screamed with laughter.

Sophie shrugged. 'I guess it would be funny being a pretend donkey.'

The boys kept laughing.

'So much fun,' Rory screamed. 'And I get to be the back end of the donkey.'

Sophie nodded slowly, enjoying the boys' mirth. 'Sounds good to me, but you know you'll have to check with all those friends to make sure they're okay with being in a play?'

'Yes, we can do that at the pub next weekend. We've made a list,' Rory said. 'And we can ring up Aunty Jacinta.'

'Well done, guys. It sounds good to me.' Sophie jumped off the swing. 'Now, come and meet your new cousin.'

The boys looked at each other.

'Um, there's one more thing,' Rory said.

'This is what we really, really needed to talk to you about.

And remember, it's a big secret. You don't know anything we told you,' Nigel reminded.

'Okay, so what do you need me for?'

'Well, seeing we've got a new cousin, we thought she could be in our play.'

Sophie's eyes widened. 'I only know of one new cousin that you've got. And Uncle Kent just carried her inside. How do you expect Ruby to be in your play? She's a bit little.'

'We thought when they ride us—I mean, the donkey—into the hall, she could be in the basket of straw on the stage. And if somebody poked her, she could cry because if she's in the basket of straw, they won't be able to see her from down in the audience. We haven't really figured that one out yet,' Rory explained.

'We could put her near the curtain, and you could stand behind it and reach around and poke her, Aunty Soph,' Nigel said.

'Hmm, I'll have to have a good think about that, boys. Now I'd better go and say hello to your mum and dad.'

'And remember, it's a secret,' Rory said. 'Everything.'

'Okay, but seeing Uncle Kent will be in the play, can I tell him I gave you my permission.'

Rory put his finger to his lip.' What do you think, Nigel?'

Sophie kept a straight face while Nigel considered the question for a moment.

'I think you can tell him. We can trust Uncle Kent.'

'Thank you. I'll swear him to secrecy, too. I think what you guys need to do is get this written down, and then I can have a read of it. And then we'll talk about Ruby Rose again. Got a deal?'

She held up a hand for a high-five and got a high-five from Rory and Nigel while Petie grinned.

'Looks like you've got a deal, Aunty Soph,' Petie said.

Chapter 4
Sophie

Sophie smiled as she opened the screen door and walked into Callie's kitchen. Kent was over at the sink filling the kettle, and Callie was sitting at the table nursing Ruby Rose.

'Hi, Cal,' Sophie said with a wide smile as Callie looked up.

'Hi, Soph. How are you? You look amazing.' Callie had shadows beneath her eyes.

'Really good.'

'I hear she's sleeping well.' Callie looked down at her new niece.

'Has Kent been bragging? He's a besotted new dad. But yes, Ruby's the opposite of what I was expecting. She's slept through from eight till six the last three nights.'

Kent switched the kettle on. 'I'll leave you pair to chat. I'll go and see if Braden's got any cold beer in the shed.'

'Half your luck,' Callie said with a tired smile. 'The twins are still waking twice each night at different times.'

'I don't know how you do it, Callie. And you've gone back to work one day a week.'

'That's my holiday. It's the day when Braden deals with all the nappies and, the washing and the feeding, and the bottle sterilising. I quite enjoy my Mondays at school,' she said.

'Well, if you ever need a hand, yell out. I'm happy to come over.'

'I might hold you to that when the mustering starts,' Callie said. 'What did the boys want? You looked like you had some secret business going on out there. The huddle on the swings.'

Sophie tapped her nose. 'Definitely secret business. I promised I wouldn't tell.'

'Sounds like they're up to mischief again,' Callie said. 'They've been hyper and laughing all afternoon.'

'No, the opposite, actually. They were talking to me about a school project, and that's all I can say.'

'Ah, the nativity play,' Callie said.

'You know about it?'

'I know what the topic is. It's Emily Jansen's idea.'

'They said Mrs Jansen. Do I know her? I guess she's the new teacher at school. She's not been in town long, has she? Or is she the one with the little girl with the pretty name?'

'Ophelia, and yes, Emily is the best, one of the best teachers we've ever had, and the kids absolutely adore her.'

'That's good to hear.'

'Anyway, Nigel's had her this term, and he's absolutely smitten. He comes home every afternoon he has her: "Mrs Jansen said this" and "Mrs Jansen did that." Makes me feel quite inadequate as a mum and a teacher,' Callie said.

'I think I met her at dinner at the pub.'

'Yes, she joined our group one night. She's living at Jenna's place. She knows Luke Elliot, the guy from— oh, hang on, you know Luke. He works with Kent at your place too, doesn't he?'

'Yeah, I know Luke. I thought he and Jenna were going out.'

'Where have you been for the last few weeks?'

Sophie chuckled. 'At home with a newborn baby. I've only been to town once so far, and I was inundated. Every second person wanted to see her, poke her and talk to her, cuddle her, kiss and hug her.' She shook her head. 'She's little. I'm staying away from crowds.'

'It doesn't actually get that crowded in town,' Callie said.

'No, but you can still get germs from one or two people. Let me get her to a few months older, and then I might start socialising a bit more.'

'Are you coming to the pub for our Christmas dinner next Sunday?'

'I'll think about it,' Sophie said. 'Okay, tell me what's going on. What have I missed?'

'Well, Jenna's left the tea rooms for a while. She put it in Ella's care for a couple of weeks, and she's gone away with—wait for it—Amelia Riley's brother.'

'Amelia's brother? Do I know him?'

'No, he came to town, and he and Jenna . . . wow. Do you believe in love at first sight? It was instant,' Callie said. 'So, Jenna's gone back to North Queensland with him for a visit. I hear she's coming back soon, though. And I've heard that he's buying a place around here.'

'Poor Luke,' Sophie said. 'I thought he was quite taken with Jenna.'

Callie shook her head. 'We all thought that, but I think we were wrong. I don't think "taken" was the word. I think if you saw him with Emily, you'd understand what I'm talking about.'

'He's certainly a quiet guy. He hasn't said a word about any of this when he's been out with Kent. Very private.'

'So, back to Emily, anyway. She's a lovely person and a lovely teacher. She's very quiet too. She often doesn't look happy. I think she might have a bit of a past that's sent her flying out here. Anyway, it's none of our business, so let's get back to this nativity plan. Emily and Kimberley have set the topic, and whoever writes the best play gets to pick the cast, but even if it is set in the present, there has to be a Mary and Joseph.'

Sophie chuckled. 'And a donkey.' Callie looked at her curiously. 'I don't know anything about donkeys. I just know that when the guys have been out there making up the story, they have been in absolute hysterics.'

'I can understand why,' Sophie tapped her nose. 'You'll see.'

Chapter 5
Emily

As Emily Jansen walked across the playground of the primary school, her name was called.

'Mrs Jansen, Mrs Jansen!'

She turned with a smile, which grew as the three Cartwright boys ran across the grass towards her.

'Good morning, Rory, Nigel, and Petie. You're having another orientation day here today, Petie, I believe.'

'Yes, Mrs Jansen, we're going to do some Christmas decorations today, Miss Kimberley said. But I already know how to make them because Mum teaches us at home, so I'll be able to help the other children.'

'That would be a good help, Petie.' Emily nodded as she walked towards her classroom. 'Now, was that just a good morning you were calling out to me before, or did you want something?'

She stopped walking as Rory put his finger to his lips.

'Can we ask you a private question?' he said.

'As long as it doesn't break the rules,' Nigel added.

'What rules, Nigel?' Emily asked.

'Well, it's about the play project and the rules.'

She nodded and looked at them. 'Yes?'

'We've started to write the play, and it's really, really good.' Rory nodded seriously.

Petie was jumping around. 'It makes me laugh, it's so funny. I've got two very smart brothers.'

'That's wonderful to hear. So, what's your question about the rules, boys?'

Nigel looked around again to make sure there were no

other children near them, and Emily smiled. Many children were taking this play competition seriously, with groups sitting together in the playground with pencils and paper every lunchtime since she and Kimberley had announced the competition.

'Our literacy engagement has really improved,' Kimberley had said the other day. 'All thanks to you, Emily. You've certainly hit the sweet spot with this one.'

'No, I'm sure you've done it before, and literacy here is good already. I've looked at your data, and the school is already above the benchmark for rural schools. And I've worked in other schools where there hasn't been the enthusiasm that the teachers here have,' she said.

Kimberley had already spoken to her about work next year, and Emily was seriously considering it. It was a wonderful school, with well-behaved children and fabulous staff.

Ruth had indicated she was available to mind Ophelia next year, and Jenna was happy to have them stay in the apartment for as long as she needed it.

Emily frowned; the sticking point for her was Luke, but she'd think about that later. She turned back to the boys.

'Okay, we don't have many rules, but is there one in particular that you want to ask about?'

Rory put his hand up as his brothers both started to talk.

'Petie, you're not in this; you're just the audience. Nigel, I'm the oldest, so let me check with Mrs Jansen.'

Nigel's face fell. 'But it was my idea.'

'Doesn't matter if it was your idea; if it doesn't fit the rules, we can't use it.'

'I'm not sure if I can answer you. If your question gives you an advantage, it might be unfair to the other children. How about I just go through the rules with you, and then you can make up your mind if you still need to ask me?'

'Yeah, that's what Mum said too. It's okay,' Nigel said. 'She read the rules last night, so we're just gonna have to wing it. If we do it wrong, that's our bad luck.'

Emily smothered a smile and nodded. "Wing it" sounded good.

'Well, I'm really looking forward to reading your play when you get it finished, boys. And as long as you are aware of the rules—which it sounds as though you are— and follow them, you won't be disqualified. I'm sure it will be a very good story.'

Petie burst out laughing. 'It sure is, Mrs Jansen, it is the funniest story. You see, there is this donkey—'

Nigel leaned over and put his hand over his brother's mouth. 'Petie, shut up. Don't talk about it, and don't you dare tell any of the other kids today anything about it. If you do, I'm going to go and see Mum, and she'll put you in the car, and you can sit there all day.'

Emily shook her head. 'I don't think that would be wise, Nigel, putting anyone in a car. And I'm sure Petie won't tell.'

'You better not,' Nigel's eyes narrowed, glaring at his little brother.

'Well, boys, you have a good day. I'll see you in class, Nigel. I'm going to get our classroom ready for the day. I can't wait to read your play. Remember, it's due this Friday.'

'Yes, we know that. We're just tidying up now. We've got our story done. It's just a question we had about the characters and permissions,' he said. 'But we won't ask you. We won't get an advantage over the other kids.'

They ran off to the playground, where their friends were already playing on the equipment in the soft-fall area.

Emily smiled as she headed towards the classroom. Gladys was walking down the corridor and looked at her with a frown.

'Good morning, Mrs. Tingle, can I help you?'

Gladys Tingle usually volunteered in the canteen a couple of days a week. 'It's alright, Mrs Jansen. Sylvia is sick today, so I've been doing the cleaning for her. Your classroom is ready, and may I say what a beautiful classroom you have. I didn't have to pick up any paper or sweep the floor like I have to with—'

Emily put up her hand and interrupted before she had to listen to a "name and shame" session. 'Thank you for that. I'm so pleased that you found it easy. Anyway, I have to get ready for the day so I need a few minutes. It's only twenty minutes to the bell time. Thank you so much for coming in and helping out; we really appreciate it.'

She turned before she could get involved in one of the gossip sessions Gladys Tingle was notorious for; she had often tried to waylay Emily when she was on playground duty or canteen.

As she put out the pencils and writing pads for the first numeracy session this morning, her mind turned to Luke; she'd been stunned when she first came to town to discover that he was working in Augathella, flying in and working on a lot of the properties. Since he'd learned she was now here for the three months of next term as well, he based himself in the town and was flying out to his other Queensland properties and Northern Territory jobs with his base at Augathella. She hadn't told him yet that it was likely she would be here for the whole of the next school year.

The last time he came around to the apartment, Emily had found it hard to resist him and had to remind herself why she wasn't resuming a relationship with Luke Elliott. No matter how much she wanted to, no matter how attractive she found him, and no matter how much she knew deep down that she loved him, and she always had, she couldn't trust herself.

The loss of her husband and their strained relationship had left Emily with doubts that she would ever be able to maintain a relationship.

No matter what a lovely person Luke was, she still knew that the chance she would stuff it up was there, so no matter how much he pushed, she was not going to listen to him.

A pang of envy had hit her chest when she'd seen the boys tumble out of Callie's car. Ophelia was never going to have any brothers and sisters, and she would always be the only child of a single parent.

Emily vowed to herself that she would be the best single mother in the world. Ophelia would *not* suffer because of her determination to remain single. She would resist Luke Elliott, no matter how hard he tried to convince her that they were meant to be together.

Perhaps they were, but Emily would never be in a position to commit.

Chapter 6
Emily

Emily stood in front of the mirror, focusing her attention on the hair curler as she curled strands of hair on each side of her face. It had been three years since she had last been to a Christmas party, and she was looking forward to it.

Thank goodness that she found Ruth.

Ruth was the most wonderful woman, and Emily was sure that Ophelia was already starting to think of her as her surrogate grandma. A pang of sadness ran through her. Her parents had both passed away when she was in her teens; she had been a change-of-life baby to parents in their forties. When Ophelia was born, Troy's mother, now living in America with her second husband, had shown little interest in her new granddaughter, having already had another three grandchildren from Troy's step-siblings. Emily closed her mind to Troy's reaction to his child; she couldn't bear to go there.

If Ruth was prepared to fill the role of grandma for a few months, Emily was more than happy to let her.

'Mama, mama,' a little voice called from the living room.

Emily put the hair curler down, picked up her lipstick, and gave her lips a second coat of the pastel pink colour. She pulled out the new summer dress. New from the ops shop, anyway.

Tonight, she almost felt like a princess as she dropped the soft silk dress over her head and slipped into the strappy sandals she'd bought at the same op shop in Charleville.

She walked into the living room, where Ophelia was playing happily on the floor, making a tower of blocks and knocking them down. 'Mama, pretty,' she said.

'Thank you, my sweetie, and so are you,' Emily had dressed Ophelia in the new dress she'd picked up at the bargain store in Charleville. Surprisingly, it was a kids' label brand and fitted perfectly.

Since Emily was going out for dinner, she had decided to dress Ophelia up for her visit to Ruth's house. She'd also packed some shorts, T-shirts, and her sleeping suit into the bag along with her bottles.

'Come on, bubs, it's time to go and see Auntie Ruth.'

Ophelia's little face lit up as Emily reached down and scooped her off the floor. She put her bag in the back of the car and headed two streets away to Ruth's house.

##

As the school had quite a large number of staff, the group tonight, including partners, cleaning staff, and teachers' aides, filled the private dining room at the hotel. Emily sat at the side of the table, her heart thudding.

When she'd walked through the bistro to the private dining room, her eyes had widened as she spotted Luke Elliott sitting at a table for four with an unfamiliar woman.

Luke had his back to her, but Emily would recognise him anywhere. She put her head down and hurried through the bistro into the dining room, wondering why Luke was there and who he was with. She had gotten to know most of the people in town in her few weeks here, but the woman was unfamiliar.

She shrugged and focused on staying calm; it didn't matter. She had made her intentions clear to Luke; no matter how much he insisted they should resume their relationship from several years ago, Emily had stayed firm. It didn't matter what she felt. It didn't matter that she wanted to accept Luke's offer and ride into the sunset with him for a happily ever after because she knew there wouldn't be one.

Anyway, she wasn't going to think about Luke Elliott being there tonight or who he was with. She was here to have a good time in the company of her new workmates. She really liked the staff at Augathella Primary School, and when Bob Hamblin called her in last Friday and raised the possibility of a whole year of work next year, Emily accepted readily without even having to think about it.

Only a couple of the staff had arrived before her. Emily liked to be early because she could pick where she was sitting. So now, she sat with her back to the door where she wouldn't be tempted to look out to see if she could see Luke.

Kimberley Riordan was sitting opposite her, looking at her phone. After a few seconds, she put it down and smiled over at Emily.

'Sorry, Emily. Just reminding Quinn to get here as soon as he can. Don't you look gorgeous! Amazing how we all brush up for Christmas, isn't it?' Kimberley reached into a bag beside her chair and pulled out a circle of green tinsel. 'We decided not to inflict Christmas hats on the staff this year, so we've got tinsel circlets for the ladies and tinsel ties for the gentlemen.'

Emily reached over with a smile and carefully placed the circle of tinsel on her head. 'Your hair looks gorgeous,' Kimberley said. 'Such a pretty colour.'

'Thank you. It was fun getting dressed up tonight. I haven't done that for a long time.'

Kimberley looked at her curiously, and Emily knew that the whole town wondered about her background. She'd trusted Luke not to tell anyone, and she hadn't shared it with anyone. She and Ruth had had a bit of a talk one night, and she told Ruth that she was now a widow, but she asked Ruth to honour her privacy and not tell anyone, and she knew she could trust the older woman. She hadn't shared any of the details with Ruth; it was hard enough to carry them, let alone verbalise them.

Gradually, the rest of the staff arrived, and soon, the dining room was a hubbub of noise, laughter, and conversation. Bob Hamblin took pride of place at the head of the table, and at the far end sat Gladys Tingle, who had been doing some casual cleaning; as far as Emily could see, Gladys didn't miss a trick.

Emily smothered a smile. The older woman had tried over and over again, calling into Kimberley and Emily's classroom, to pry out some details about Emily, but Emily was an expert at deflecting her questions.

Callie and Braden Cartwright took the two chairs on Kimberley's left and smiled at Emily as they sat down. 'Hi, Emily. It's good to see you. We saw Ophelia at Ruth's when we dropped the boys and the twins off.'

'Ruth is amazing, isn't she?' Emily said.

Callie nodded. 'She sure is, but we won't be having a late night.'

'Neither will I,' Emily agreed. 'Although sometimes I think Ophelia would be happy to live with Ruth. She gets upset when we leave now. I think our room is pretty boring. Ruth has so many toys at her place.'

'She's minded so many children over the last twelve months she's gathered quite a collection of toys,' Callie said.

A man who Emily hadn't seen before walked along the other side of the table, stopped, and put his hand on Braden Cartwright's shoulder. 'Gidday, Braden. Good to see you.'

Braden looked up, and his smile was wide. 'Hey, Quinn! Haven't seen you for ages. Good thing our girls work at the school, and we see each other at least once a year.'

Kimberley leaned over towards Emily and caught her attention. 'Emily, this is my fiancé, Quinn. Quinn, this is Emily Jansen, the new teacher at the school.'

'Hello, Quinn. It's nice to meet you.' she said. He was a nice-looking guy, and Emily smiled when she saw him take hold of Kimberley's hand.

How sweet.

A pang of envy lodged in her chest, and Emily pushed it away. She was here to have a good time. Not to brood on what could have been.

Or what could be, an insistent little voice said in her head.

'Emily, we're not going to talk work tonight,' Callie said. 'But I just wanted to ask you whether Rory and Nigel caught up with you. They've been asking me so many questions about the Christmas play. I told them to go and see you at lunchtime yesterday.'

Emily nodded and smiled. 'Yes, they came to be before school but then decided not to ask me the question because they didn't want to have an unfair advantage.'

Callie shook her head. 'They're taking this so seriously.'

'I mentioned the rules of the task to them, and they both said they understood. That you'd told them.'

Braden rolled his eyes. 'How do you do it, Emily? They rarely listen to a word I say.'

'Right,' Callie said. 'That's it. No more work talk.'

Kimberley turned to Callie. 'I hear you guys might be going away for a trip before Christmas.'

Emily was surprised to see alarm cross Callie's face as she shot a swift glance at Braden.

'Yes, we're going down to the Gold Coast for four days to take the boys to the theme parks before Christmas. They don't know yet. How did you hear?' Callie asked.

'Um, Gladys.' Kimberley lowered her voice. 'Are you taking them out of school?' Kimberley asked.

'For the last couple of days because the term ends in the middle of the week,' Braden said. 'Callie will be finished for the year, and we've got such a busy schedule that we've decided to go down and be home for Christmas.'

'Does that mean that you won't be in town for the play, Callie?' Kimberley asked glumly.

'Looks like it, but we haven't broken the news to the boys yet.'

'Oh dear, they will be a bit disappointed,' Emily said. 'But the appeal of Sea World and Dreamworld should make up for it.'

Callie shook her head slowly. 'I'm starting to wonder. We haven't mentioned it yet, so we'll see what the reaction is.'

'Petie will be fine,' Braden said. 'He's absolutely fixated on Nemo.'

The conversation drifted from one topic to another as the entrees were served. Emily's ears pricked up when Kimberley asked Callie a question.

'Who's that out there with Jenna and Josh?' Kimberley asked.

'Jenna? I didn't see her out there,' Callie replied. 'I didn't think they were back. I thought they were up in the Gulf of Carpentaria at his parents' place.'

'No, they flew in this afternoon,' Quinn said. 'I was out near the airport getting some Avgas for my plane, and Josh flew in. He had another two women with him, too. So, they've obviously got guests.'

Kimberley chuckled. 'Nothing is private in this town, is it?'

'No, we've got a pretty good grapevine going.' Callie rolled her eyes and gestured down towards the end of the table where Gladys was chatting to two of the teachers' aides. 'With some help.'

'And that grapevine has certainly had a hold on the school for the last couple of weeks. How on earth did she know about your holiday?' Kimberley said.

Callie rolled her eyes as well. 'No idea. She's one for gossip, that's for sure, but she's got a heart of gold. I hope Gladys hasn't been pestering you, Emily.'

Emily gave an absent smile. 'I can handle myself,' she said, wondering who Jenna's guests were, and if it was the woman she had seen sitting with Luke.

Putting down her fork, she picked up her napkin and dabbed at her cheeks. It was awfully hot in here, but there was no way she was going to walk out and draw attention to herself. She swallowed a few times as the conversations around her merged into an unbearable noise; by sheer will, she forced back the building panic attack.

Chapter 7
Emily

Later that night

It was a lovely, warm evening with a cool breeze blowing from the northeast. So far, the weather hadn't been as hot as she'd expected out here, even though it was the beginning of summer.

The weather had been under discussion tonight, and everyone had agreed that it was pleasantly cool for this time of the year. Emily didn't mind the heat. In fact, she welcomed the dry heat of the west after living in the humidity of the northern tropics for three years. That was the heat she couldn't cope with.

Pushing the stroller to Ruth's had been a good idea, and Emily had been able to have two wines—one before dinner and a champagne to toast Christmas with the girls after they finished their meal. The wine had relaxed her, and she had enjoyed herself, and again, she thanked her luck in getting a position at a school with such kind and caring staff.

The only difficult part of the night had been knowing that Luke was sitting outside the dining room. She'd managed to get over the panic attack before it took hold and had focused on talking to everyone at the table as they moved around between courses. At dessert, she found herself sitting on the other side of the table looking out into the bistro, but to her relief, there'd been no sign of Luke and the group he was dining with.

It would have been much better if she hadn't had him in her thoughts as she sat back and listened to the conversations wash around her. If she was going to make a success of her new life, it would be better if Luke hadn't encountered her that first night at Jenna's unit.

With him in town for long-term stays and the chance of bumping into him—not to mention the three occasions he had knocked on her door in the last two weeks—made it very difficult for Emily to move on, and she needed to move on.

She turned the stroller around the corner into Jenna's, not surprised to see the light on in the front room of the apartment block. Listening to the talk at the table, she suspected Jenna would be home by the time she'd picked Ophelia up and walked home.

As long as Luke wasn't there, too.

Ophelia had been asleep when she arrived at Ruth's to pick her up, and she had managed to transfer her from the small cot into the stroller without her waking. 'She's had a lovely evening,' Ruth said. 'I hope it was alright to let her stay up till seven thirty because she was having so much fun playing with the Cartwright boys. She was fascinated with Ryan, too, and kept pointing at him, saying "Bubba". She's really started to talk since you've been in town.'

'Yes, I've noticed that too. Her vocabulary has expanded in the last three weeks.'

Emily walked slowly along the street, enjoying the fresh air, the crescent moon hanging low in the east, and the stars brilliant in the indigo sky. Three doors up from the apartment block, she heard footsteps crunching on the gravel path behind her but wasn't overly concerned. She already knew that Augathella was a safe place to be out at night.

'Emily, wait up.'

She kept walking and briefly closed her eyes, ignoring Luke's request as she gripped the handles of the stroller.

'Emily, it's me, Luke. I didn't mean to give you a fright.'

There was no need for him to say that; she knew very well who it was. Huffing a sigh, Emily stopped walking but kept pushing the stroller backward and forwards; the last thing she wanted was for Ophelia to wake up. If she woke up this early in the night, she'd be up for hours wanting to play, and after having a couple of wines, Emily was more than ready for her bed.

'Luke,' she said, keeping her voice expressionless.

'Hi, Emily. I was watching for you to leave the pub, but I missed you. By the time I saw the last of your group leave and the lights went out in the dining room, I realised I hadn't seen you walk out.'

'Yes, you must've missed me,' she said, not letting on that she'd slipped out through the back door of the dining room, which led directly onto the street, for this very reason; she hadn't wanted to have a conversation with Luke tonight.

'Did you have a good time? There was lots of laughter coming from the dining room. I was in the bistro with Jenna and Josh and some of his family.'

'I did. I went down to Ruth's to pick Ophelia up.'

'She's sound asleep,' Luke said, looking into the front of the stroller.

'Yes, and I don't want to wake her up, so I'm going to have to be rude and keep walking while we talk.'

'That's fine. I'm pleased you enjoyed yourself, Em,' His voice was like a warm caress, but Emily refused to react.

'How long are you in town for? Have you been away?' she asked

'Yes, I flew home for a couple of days last weekend just after I saw you. I was hoping that you'd come out and have dinner with me one night next week.'

'I'm pretty busy at school,' she said.

'Please don't make me beg.'

'Luke, I'm sorry. There's no point in us seeing each other all the time. It's good to have you here, but I told you I just want to be friends. I want to put all of my energy into my job and establishing myself at the school and in town.'

Luke's face closed, and he was quiet for a moment. 'Very well. I won't hassle you. Good night, Emily.' He turned on his heel and began to walk away, and a surge of guilt rose into her throat.

'Luke,' she called after him. 'Come back.'

Luke stopped and walked towards her slowly. She stopped walking, and Ophelia didn't move or make a peep.

'I'm sorry, Luke. It's too soon. I know you want to pick up where we left off, but I've told you all we have is friendship.'

Luke's voice was ragged, and it took all of Emily's self-control to stay strong.

How easy would it be to step into the safe haven of Luke's arms and let him care for her?

'That night when I came to you three weeks ago, that night that you let me hold you in my arms, you said we'd talk.'

'I know I did, Luke. The time's not been right. Like I said, I'm trying to sort myself out and settle down in town and at school. Perhaps you could be patient with me.'

'When will the time be right?'

Emily shrugged.

'How about if we go out for dinner as friends and we just have a conversation about what's happening in town and about your new job? Would that be acceptable to you?'

'Let me think about it, and I'll have to see if Ruth is available too. She's pretty busy with all the Christmas shows on at the moment, minding children from all over town.'

'I don't mind if you bring Ophelia. In fact, I'd love you to bring her.'

Well, there goes my last excuse, Emily thought. She bit her lip. 'What night would suit you best?'

Luke's eyes lit up; hope gleamed in his moonlit eyes. 'You choose whatever would suit you best. I'm in your hands,' he said.

'Okay, well, this is my only Christmas function, apart from the picnic we have on the last day of school in just over two weeks, and I'll be tired that night. How about Sunday night of next weekend?'

'It's a date.' Luke reached over and squeezed the hand that was gripping the stroller. 'I look forward to it.'

Emily was tempted to repeat his words because she would look forward to it, too, but she shook her head. There was no point in giving Luke any encouragement at all. 'I'll meet you at the pub that night at six o'clock, okay?'

'Six o'clock is fine. How about I pick you up?'

'No, I'll walk and meet you there. Ophelia will need a baby seat.' Emily frowned. 'If you're flying in and staying at the pub, how are you getting around?'

Luke pointed to his feet. 'I fly out to the properties and walk everywhere in town. Sometimes, I bunk out at the properties, but Sean at the pub has been great. He's taken a permanent booking from me for a couple of months. I meant I'd come down and walk you to the pub.'

'Oh, okay. If you want to.'

Luke was whistling as he turned and walked back in the direction of the pub.

Emily wondered whether it was wise to have dinner with Luke; she'd see how that night went, and she could make it clear to him that it was their one and only night out together.

Parking the stroller at the bottom of the steps, she undid the clasp on the front, gently lifted Ophelia out and put her on her shoulder. She stood there until her little girl settled again.

As she waited for Ophelia's head to go back down to her shoulder, the noise of several different voices drifted out of the open window at the front of Jenna's living room.

Jenna and Joshua had been gone for two weeks, going home to Joshua's family station up in the country of North Queensland. Emily had been envious; Josh and Jenna had fallen hard and fast for each other, and Emily was so happy for them. It had been a delight to watch their relationship bloom over a few days.

She had enjoyed the last two weeks in the apartment by herself, and she had decided, once she signed a contract for the twelve months' work next year—and Bob Hamblin, the principal, had assured her that it would be ready early next week to sign—she would start looking for an apartment of her own.

At the moment, especially with Jenna and Joshua coming home, she felt like a bit of a third wheel. She was sure Jenna would now prefer to have her apartment to herself, even though she told Emily she was welcome to stay as long as she wanted.

She pushed the stroller underneath the side of the carport; it didn't look like it was going to rain, and there was no fear of anyone taking it in the short time it would take to put Ophelia down.

She walked up the stairs, and the front door was open as she turned left off the porch. She hesitated for a moment, unsure whether to knock and then decided just to open the screen door and go in. It was her home, too; she was paying rent to Jenna. She opened the door and walked quietly to the large archway that opened into the living room.

Jenna and Josh were sitting on the sofa, and an older woman and a young woman were sitting on the other double sofa facing them. Jenna jumped up, but Emily put her fingers to her lips and nodded to Ophelia, sleeping on her shoulder.

'I'll come back out in a few minutes,' she said quietly. Jenna sat back down, and Emily walked down the hall, opened her bedroom door, and rocked her daughter for a little while until she was sure she was sound asleep. She put her in the cot, felt her nappy to make sure she was dry, and then lightly pulled the sheet up over her little shoulders.

Emily looked down, and a wave of love for her child ran through her as she ran her fingers gently through her soft curls. She took a quick trip to the bathroom, and when she was in there, she fluffed up her hair and reapplied her lipstick. If Jenna had guests, she might as well look presentable.

She walked down the hallway, hearing laughter, and her spirits lifted as she realised how she had heard very little apart from laughter in the weeks she'd been in town. Everything had been happy, and laughter surrounded her every day. The children at the school had been wonderful and accepted a new teacher at this late time of the year without a problem. Her class was delightful, and she'd taken to it like a duck to water.

She walked into the living room, and Jenna smiled. 'Come and join us, Emily, come and meet Josh's family.'

'Josh's family?' she asked curiously.

The older woman waved to her from the sofa. 'Hello, Emily. We've heard all about you. I'm Josh's mum, Lucy Foley.'

'Hello, it's nice to meet you, Lucy.'

The young woman jumped up. 'I'm Molly. Molly Foley.' Emily frowned. She didn't think, from what Jen and Josh told her, that Josh had any sisters. But the young woman rushed on to explain. 'I'm Josh's brother's wife. We live in Darwin, and Josh brought Jenna up to meet us, and seeing Amelia has had her baby, Mum and I decided to come down and surprise her.'

She shot an affectionate glance at her mother-in-law. 'But the surprise was on us. Would you believe that Ben and Amelia have gone down to Charleville for the weekend? His mother went down with them, visiting some of Ben's family down there. They're just away for the night, and apparently, they'll be back tomorrow afternoon.'

'That will be a lovely surprise for them. I'm sure they'll be absolutely delighted to see you. I know Amelia misses being home. I had a good chat with her at the spring fair. She was really sad her family wouldn't be here for her new baby.'

'We're here, and we're looking forward to seeing Amelia. I'm not going to sleep a wink tonight,' Lucy said. 'Family is the most important thing there is.'

Chapter 8
Amelia

'I'll have to mow the lawn this afternoon,' Ben said as he changed back a gear and turned into their driveway.

'Sounds good, we might put the Christmas lights up. What's your mum up to for the rest of the weekend?'

'She's got the CWA Christmas party tonight. She's still busy putting out the last of the Christmas cakes for the CWA. I think they've got a stall in town a couple of mornings this week. Why do you ask?'

'Oh, no reason. I know what a busy life she leads. It was lovely of her to come to Charleville with us to see your extended family.'

It had been nice to meet Ben's cousins and aunts and uncles, but it had brought home to Amalei how much she missed her family.

Ben reached over and squeezed her hand as he parked in the carport, picking up on her mood as he always did. 'You're a good daughter-in-law, Amelia. You're very thoughtful.'

'I love your mum,' she said. 'She's a great mum-in-law and your dad too, of course.'

They had only been inside for a few minutes, and Amelia had changed Seb's nappy. She was about to put him into the cot when she heard steps come up the front stairs and voices at the door.

'Ben, can you get that? There's someone at the front door. I'm just about to put Sebastian down in the cot.'

'Don't you dare put him in the cot yet.' Josh's voice called from the front door.

'Josh, Jenna, come on in. Okay, I'll bring him down. He can go for a little snooze after you have a cuddle.'

Amelia walked down the hall with their new little boy cradled in her arms. Jenna and Josh were standing inside the front door, both smiling widely.

'Hi, guys. It's good to see you. You didn't stay away long.'

'No, I was keen to get back to the tea room. I felt a bit guilty leaving it with poor Ellie,' Jenna said, 'and Josh has got some big news. In fact, he's got three lots of big news.' Jenna turned and smiled at Josh, and Amelia thought how happy he looked.

'Hang on, I'll call Ben.'

'Don't worry, he's out at the shed. We saw him on the way in. He said he'll be in soon.'

Amelia frowned. She could swear she'd heard Ben talking outside.

'Guess what.' Jenna interrupted her thoughts. 'Josh has bought a property out on the Old Charleville Road.'

Amelia's eyes widened. 'You've bought a property? Here?'

Josh folded his arms and smiled at his sister. 'I am, Melie. Good enough for you to move here, sis? I thought I might come here too. There's a lot here to attract me.' He put his arm around Jenna's shoulders.

'Oh, that's wonderful news, Josh. I'm going to have some family here. And what are the other two bits of news?'

'Well, it's pretty special,' Josh said. 'It's like a bit of an early Christmas present for you.'

'Can I nurse Sebastian while you put your hands over your eyes?' Jenna asked with a wide smile.

'What is it? What have you brought back? Have you brought me something from home, or tell me you didn't bring me my horse, did you?'

'No, she wouldn't get in the plane.' Josh chuckled. 'It's a better surprise than that.'

'You've got me intrigued.'

Amelia handed Sebastian over to Jenna and smiled as she

looked down at him with an envious look on her face.

'Now put your hands over your eyes,' Josh said, 'and don't peek. I have to go outside and get something.'

Amelia laughed. 'I guess I can do that.'

She did as she was told, and there was absolute silence in the room, apart from the door opening. After a minute or so, it closed again, and there was a rustling noise.

Josh came over and put his hand on her arm. 'Amelia, leave your hands on your eyes. Rightio, on the count of three, two, one. Okay, you can look now.'

Amelia lowered her hands and looked at Josh. With a frown, her gaze moved to the left of him. Her eyes widened, and tears sprang to her eyes as she recognised the two women standing behind him.

'Mum?' Her voice squeaked. 'Oh my God, Mum, what are you doing here?' The tears rolled down her face as her mother stepped forward and put her arms around Amelia.

'Hello, darling. I've missed you so much.'

'Oh, Mummy, I've missed you too.' Amelia couldn't stop crying as her mother held her close, and it was a full minute before she reached out her hand to Molly. 'And Molly, you're here too. How long are you staying for?'

'Well, Dad and the boys are out mustering,' her mother replied. 'They bought some land up in the Gulf and have a really big bush block up there now. So, they're out for a couple of weeks. Molly and I are going to stay till Boxing Day.'

'And where's Matt?' Amelia stepped out of her mother's arms and hugged her sister-in-law.

Molly's grin was wide. 'Matt's mustering with your dad and your brothers.'

Amelia's eyes were wide as her mother took her hand. 'We didn't tell you, but Dad had a bit of a turn about two months back, and he sat down and had a good long think after the muster. When I go back, he's going to leave the property in your brothers' charge, and we're going away for a while.'

'Away?' Amelia frowned. 'Is he alright?'

'Yes, we're going to do a bit of travelling; we've bought a campervan and guess where the first stop is?'

'Augathella?' Amelia said tentatively.

'Spot on. I just came ahead to suss it out first,' she said, her smile teasing. 'Now let me hold my grandson.'

Chapter 9
Callie

It seemed that everyone in Augathella had decided to choose the second Sunday night in December for their Christmas party. The rural fire service had booked half the dining room, and the Country Women's Association were in the other half.

Braden and Callie Cartwright and their friends took up the street side of the bistro with three long tables joined together. In the middle of the bistro, there was a table for the children, and between those two tables, they left room to park four prams.

Braden grinned as he walked in. 'Looks like we've taken over the pub tonight, Callie.'

'Sure does,' she said, 'but how sad is it to walk in that door and not see Reg sitting there? He would've loved this tonight, wouldn't he, Braden?'

'He would, but I think it's such a wonderful mark of respect that Sean and the staff have taken his table and chair away and put that pot plant under the plaque.'

Braden's eyes widened as he saw the tables. 'Holy heck, how many of us are here tonight?'

'Well, you think of everyone that we know and socialise with, and they're coming tonight. Saves a lot of individual visits. There wouldn't be enough nights before Christmas to catch up with everyone.'

'I'm pleased to see that Ruth and her husband are here too; it gives her a bit of a break. We'll make sure that she doesn't run after any of the kids tonight.'

'Yes, he came back from Brisbane,' she said. 'He's

finished his contract there now, so she'll have someone in the house with her all the time.'

'But she's still going to babysit next year, and she—'

'Yes, Fallon's got part-time work next year, and Ruth will have Ryan, the days that Fallon goes to work.'

'I'm behind on the times; the twins have kept us so busy.'

'They surely have,' Callie said, looking down at the two sleeping babies in the pram. They'd started sleeping a little better a couple of nights ago. 'They had a big feed before we left home, stayed awake in the car for most of the trip and now they're sound asleep.'

'Hopefully, the noise won't bother them.'

'They need to get used to it.'

'I asked Sean specifically to arrange the tables like this so the kids could sit at the table behind us and be near the door. They can go out to the lawn and play after they eat. And we can put the prams in the middle here. If Amelia and Ben, Sophie and Kent, Jon and Fallon, and you and I sit along here, we can just turn around and reach the prams. They won't be jammed in the corner.'

Braden put his arm across Callie's shoulders. 'You think of everything, Cal. What did I ever do without you?' He reached down and brushed a kiss on her cheek, and Callie smiled into her husband's eyes. Life couldn't get much better.

The only thing they hadn't done yet was talk to the boys about the trip to the Gold Coast. She and Braden had talked about it when they got home last night and decided to wait until after tonight.

Mind you, she thought, the boys had been closeted in Rory's room most of the day, and the hilarity hadn't been as loud as it had been the other day. *Maybe they'd lost interest in the project,* she wondered.

Sophie and Kent walked in, pushing the pram.

'I'm so pleased you decided to come, Soph. It wouldn't have been the same without you.'

'Yeah, I couldn't miss Christmas at the pub,' she said.

'How's that little girl?'

'Perfect as usual. How are the twins?' Sophie asked hesitantly.

'Actually, sleeping a bit better,' Callie said.

'Look, here's Amelia and Ben,' Callie said as a third pram rolled into the bistro. She waited until they got closer and gestured to the space for the prams. 'This is the parking lot for the prams, guys. We can turn to the prams and the children easily without having to navigate the crowds.'

'That's fabulous,' Sophie said. 'Now let me have a look at this little boy of yours, Amelia.' She hadn't seen little Sebastian yet.

An olive-skinned face topped with jet-black hair beamed up at them, his dark eyes wide open.

'Oh my God, Amelia, he's absolutely gorgeous.'

Amelia looked up at Ben. 'We think so too.'

Ben smiled at his wife and then turned to Callie. 'We're only going to stay for a quick dinner because we had a wonderful surprise waiting when we got home at lunchtime today.'

'I heard you had some unexpected visitors.'

'Yes,' Amelia said with a laugh. 'Mum flew down from Granite Station, and Molly, my sister-in-law, came with Josh and Jenna from Darwin.'

'That's wonderful; you should've invited them tonight.'

'Jenna and Josh are coming, but Mum and Molly said they didn't want to impose on our Christmas night because they didn't know anybody.'

'They would've been most welcome,' Callie said.

'I know, but we'll just stay for dinner and then head back home. So good to see Mum, and she's absolutely smitten with Seb. Mum wanted to babysit, but he's due for a feed. So, if he has a feed, then goes to sleep, we might run him home and come back.'

'That sounds like a plan,' Callie said. A large group of people walked into the pub at the same time, and soon, the dining room was full, and their table was noisy as all their friends arrived and settled in. Callie glanced across at the children's table, where Rory and Nigel were in deep conversation. Petie was standing at the prams, moving from one to the other, looking at all the babies.

He wandered over to Callie, and she pulled him up to sit on her knee. 'You look very serious, Petie.'

'Mum, where do babies come from? And why did they all come at the same time? Was it like at a shop sale or something?'

Callie bit back her smile and hugged him close. 'That's something that we'll sit down and talk to you about in a while. All you need to know is that babies come when people love each other, but we all love you as much as we love our new babies.'

'But where do they come from?' Petie persisted.

'I think you need to talk to Daddy. Wait there.'

Petie nodded and waited.

'Braden,' Callie called over the noise. 'Petie needs to talk to you.'

Chapter 10
Callie

It was a fabulous night at the pub. Friendship, love, laughter and the satisfaction of perfectly-behaved twins enveloped Callie, as well as three well-behaved little boys. Sean had excelled himself getting the waitresses to decorate the Christmas tables for them. Gift-wrapped presents were exchanged, as the friends talked and laughed.

As they waited for dessert to be served, Callie sat back and reminisced about the last Christmas she spent in Brisbane. She had been alone in her house by the river, thinking of her family and feeling sad. Jen and the kids, along with her husband, Darren, had travelled north to Maryborough to celebrate Christmas with his family. Jen had always made sure that Callie was looked after during Christmas. They had been friends for a long time, and that particular Christmas had been very hard. Now, she looked around at her husband, her three beautiful stepsons, and her two adorable twins.

Fallon caught her eye across the table and smiled, and Callie could tell by the look on her face that her thoughts were taking a similar line.

Ruth had been the star of the show that night; she was such a lovely person. Everyone had looked after her very well, and she'd been a little bit tipsy.

Callie put a hand over her mouth and smiled as Ruth looked at her. 'No more drinks. Ben wants to buy me a dessert wine.'

'You deserve to have a good night, Ruth. Enjoy yourself,' Callie added, winking at her.

The only thing that Callie hadn't been sure about that

night was the three boys. Even though they had behaved well and eaten their meal without complaint—even vegetables with their baked dinner—Nigel and Rory had been subdued. Each time Callie looked over, they were writing on a piece of paper and seemed to be crossing off items. Every so often, they both got up and walked to each end of the table to talk to the adults.

She was proud of them. It was lovely of them to make sure they wished everybody a Merry Christmas. At one point, Nigel walked past, and she grabbed his hand. 'Are you having a good time?'

'I am, Mum. Thank you. Have to go. Rory's got a job for me.'

She wondered what they were up to, but whatever it was, they were behaving, and they weren't fighting. Petie spent most of his time at the four prams, looking at the babies quietly and smiling at her every time she caught his eye. Braden had fobbed him off with a promise to talk tomorrow. Callie sat back, a wave of contentment and love filling her.

The night was in full swing when Rory came up to her and asked if he could say a few words to everyone.

'I think that's okay. What do you want to say?'

'It's alright. I just want to say Merry Christmas and thank you to everybody.'

She put her arm around his waist, and he snuggled into her.

'That's lovely, Rory. Dad and I are really proud of you boys tonight. You've all been so well-behaved.'

Rory grinned, and she wondered about the look on his face. 'Nigel is going to talk with me too.'

'Braden, can you get the attention of the table? The two boys want to say something.'

Petie turned her face. 'Me too.'

Callie and Braden looked at each other, and Braden shrugged. He stood and tapped his dessert spoon on his beer glass.

'Can I have your attention, please, everyone?'

It took a couple of minutes, but eventually, there was silence.

'First of all, I want to say thanks, everyone, for coming tonight. What a great night we're having, and I hope you all have a Merry Christmas. Got a couple of boys here who wanted to say Merry Christmas as well.'

There was a little round of applause. Nigel stood beside the table next to Braden. Rory stood straight with his shoulders back, and then Nigel moved behind him with a wide grin on his face.

'Thank you, Dad.' Rory looked over and saw Petie over by the prams. 'Nigel and Petie and I want to say Merry "Christmas to everybody too.'

A chorus of "Merry Christmas, boys" filled the room. 'Hope Santa brings you everything you want.'

'Thank you,' Rory said. 'We also want to wish Mum and Dad a happy Christmas.'

Callie blinked back a tear.

'But most of all, we want to thank everyone we've spoken to tonight for letting us use them.'

Callie frowned. 'Use them?'

'We just have to finish it off tomorrow before we go to school and hand it in. Then on Friday, we'll know if we've won.'

There was a big round of applause, and Callie and Braden looked at each other. 'What are they talking about?' Braden asked.

'I don't know,' Callie said. 'But they're up to something with that play.' She shrugged. 'No one seems upset about it, so we can ask them when we get home.'

'Good luck with that,' Braden said. 'If Rory and Nigel decide to keep a secret, you can't pry it from them. Not even with torture,' he said with a grin.

'Don't be like that.'

'You'll see.'

Dessert was a flaming Bombe Alaska for the tables. Sean had excelled himself, and the children's eyes were wide as a miniature version was put on their table and then the flames extinguished. Petie leaned over to Callie. 'Can I just have ice cream, please, Mum?'

'You can have whatever you want, sweetie.'

The night came to an end, and there was much hugging and wishing of Merry Christmas as Christmas paper, wrapped gifts, and bon bon scraps were put in the bin. Rory, Nigel's and Petie's presents remained wrapped on the table.

'Do you want to open your presents, boys?'

'No, we're going put them under the Christmas tree,' Rory said.

'You're growing up fast,' she said, giving him a quick hug before she stood and went over to the pram; the twins were still sound asleep. 'What's the chances of you staying asleep till we get home for a feed?' she asked aloud.

'They'll be good. They'll learn off their big brothers how to behave,' Braden said.

'I'm sure they will. Come on, family, it's time we hit the road.' Braden put his arm around Callie's shoulders as they pushed the pram together towards the door, and their three boys forged ahead.

A few minutes later they were out of the township and headed along the dirt road to Kilcoy Station.

Callie smiled at Braden. Nigel and Rory were talking quietly in the backseat, and she turned around to check on them. Petie was already asleep. She turned back to the front and put her hand on Braden's thigh. 'That was nice of the boys to wish everyone a Merry Christmas,' she said.

'It was.' Braden raised his voice a bit. 'Tell us a little bit more about your play, boys. You were talking about using some of our friends in the play, weren't you? When you wished everyone Merry Christmas. That was a good thing to do. I was proud of you.'

Callie waited for the reply from the back, but it didn't

come.

'Yeah, the play's going well,' Rory said finally.

Braden looked at Callie and raised his eyebrows.

'Can you tell us what it's about?' Callie asked.

'It's a nativity play about joy, happiness, and Christmas, and it's got a donkey in it,' Rory replied.

'A special donkey?' Callie inquired.

She looked over the back, and he said, 'No, just an ordinary donkey.' His face was a picture of innocence.

'The winner's going to be announced this week, is that right?' she asked.

'Yes, it is. At Presentation Assembly,' Nigel said. 'I reckon we're going to win.'

Braden frowned and glanced across at Callie.

'Boys, we have something to tell you.' Braden's voice was loud enough for the boys to hear, but not enough to wake the twins. 'We're going to go down to the Gold Coast and visit Dreamworld and SeaWorld and Movie World.'

'Yay!' both boys yelled together.

Callie turned in her seat and looked over into the back seat. 'There's only one problem. If we go to the Gold Coast before Christmas, we won't be here for the Christmas play.'

Nigel's mouth dropped open as he put his hands on the back of Braden's seat, his eyes wide. 'Not gonna happen.'

'You mean you don't want to go away and do all those fun things?' Callie asked.

'No, we don't want to,' Rory replied. 'Not if it means missing the play. Mum, we've worked so hard on our story.'

'What if your play doesn't get chosen? Would you be happy to go away then?' Callie questioned.

Nigel shook his head quickly from side to side. 'That's not going to happen, either. We're going to win.'

'So, you wouldn't mind missing out on the theme parks so you can produce your play?'

'Yes, we want to do it. We can go to Dreamworld and those places any old time, can't we?'

Braden shrugged, and Callie stared at him.

'So, when do we find out who the winning entry belongs to?'

'This Friday, Dad. And really, even if we don't win, I think it's poor form if we leave the school and don't see whoever's play wins, that is. It might look like we're bad losers. You know what I mean. If we don't win, then we will leave town. That's pretty rude, you know.'

Braden frowned and met Callie's eyes.

'We don't have to worry about that, Rory. We're going to win,' Nigel repeated.

All was quiet for a while as the vehicle headed along the dirt road towards home.

Finally, Braden spoke quietly. 'I think we may have to reconsider our trip. What do you think, Cal?'

'Sounds like it. I hate to think that the boys would be considered sore losers if we leave town. We know they're not, but they don't want others to get the wrong idea.'

'Okay, I won't book the apartment till Friday,' Braden said. 'I'll email them and say that we've had a change of plans. You disappointed?'

'To tell the truth,' Callie said hesitantly, 'not really. I was dreading packing up the babies and all the assorted paraphernalia in the Land Cruiser. Maybe in the June school holidays, when it's cooler out here, we can pack up and take them down to Brisbane and stay at my house. We can do day trips to the Gold Coast. How does that sound?'

'Whatever suits you best, my love.'

Callie pulled a face at him. 'You didn't want to go away either, did you?'

Chapter 11
Emily

Between assessments, reports, and Christmas preparations, as well as teaching her class in the daytime, Emily's three-day school week flew by. It was Wednesday night after she had put Ophelia down before she got a chance to read the seventeen Christmas play entries.

Kimberley had been overwhelmed by the response to the literacy competition, and the whole school, staff and students had been talking about it. Not to mention the number of parents who mentioned it as they picked up their children at the school. Excitement was buzzing about Augathella Primary School's Christmas play.

Rory and Nigel Cartwright had tagged behind her when she did playground duty a couple of days this week and tried to engage her in conversation about when she was going to read them. But Emily didn't let on that she hadn't started. She smiled and nodded. 'Yes, boys, going well.'

As she sat at the small desk in her room that night, she looked over at the cot. Her daughter was sound asleep; Ophelia had been sleeping well since she'd been spending her days at Ruth's. Even though Emily had the next two days at home to read the plays, she decided to complete them tonight. Christmas shopping in Charleville was a possibility for tomorrow. She wanted to get some gifts for the staff at school, and now that she had a regular salary, she was in a position to spend some money. Plus, she needed some Santa presents for Ophelia and something for Jenna. She wanted to get a very special gift for Ruth. Although she paid Ruth to look after Ophelia, Ruth's care of her little girl went above and beyond the money she would accept. She was a wonderful woman, and Ophelia adored her.

Some of the plays had been typed up and printed out, and Emily wondered, maybe unfairly, how many parents had actually helped the students with the project. She was sure she'd be able to pick it up by the language and the setting out. She flicked through the papers until she came across the one from the Cartwright boys.

Their entry was handwritten in pencil, and some of the pages had what looked like food stains and dirty fingerprints on them. Emily smiled; one crinkled page looked like it had been screwed up and then flattened. Plus, there were some drawings and diagrams on the back of the paper that looked like genuine works in progress. She laughed as she saw the rough drawing of a donkey costume and a cushion.

She put their entry at the bottom of the pile; the boys were so keen she should see what the competition was like before she got to that one. But no favourites.

Emily pulled out her marking criteria and sat it on the desk beside her pencil.

Out of the entries she read in the first half hour, it was disappointing that some children had obviously been assisted by parents.

The next five entries were obviously the work of the students, but they did not meet the criteria for theme. There was no mention of the nativity scene, no Mary and Joseph in several. It was mainly about Santa Claus coming to Augathella, going down chimneys with assorted presents, with a bit of "Christmas brings joy to everyone" at the end. She did smile, however, when in one story, Santa did manage to get a donkey down the chimney.

The three entries she read after that were possibilities, and she put them aside. With a bit of work and creativity, they could be turned into a play. That was something she would have to work on over the weekend once she decided on the winning entry. When it was announced, she could work with the student or group that created it.

Finally, Emily reached the stained and crumpled entry of the Cartwright boys and suppressed a smile. The entry was just like the boys—full of passion, enthusiasm, and creativity. She switched the desk lamp on before she started and then decided to go make a cup of tea before she read the last entry.

She headed out to the kitchen; Jenna and Joshua were out for dinner for the night, and it was almost as if she had an apartment to herself. It would be nice to have her own place, especially if the work next year came through, as Bob had said.

Her gut told her it was a certainty, but until she signed on the bottom line, Emily wasn't sure. She also needed to sort out Luke on Sunday night when they went out for dinner, to tell him that if she did stay in town next year, he would have to realise they were just friends and for him to give up the foolish hope that they could rekindle their relationship of years ago.

Not that it needed rekindling. Emily knew she had never stopped loving Luke Elliott.

She reached up to get a chamomile tea bag out of the caddy and then stood at the kitchen window as she waited for the kettle to boil. The sun had long set, and darkness had stolen over the back garden. For the first time in a long time, Emily felt content and secure. She was starting to make some good friends, and she loved the children at the school. Jenna was the best landlady that she could ask for, and Ruth was almost like a grandmother to her daughter and, in a way, a surrogate mother to Emily.

Ruth always engaged her in conversation at the end of each day when Emily picked up Ophelia, wanting to know how her day was, what she was planning for dinner, and always giving her some sort of treat—a small container of biscuits, a slice of homemade cake or some fresh fruit that she'd bought at the supermarket.

'You spoil me, Ruth.'

'You deserve spoiling, Emily. I worry about you.'

'There's no need. I'm used to looking after myself.'

Ruth had looked at her intently. One day, Emily thought she would share her story with the older woman. Troy's suicide had traumatised her, and she could recognise that. Maybe one day she'd get past it, maybe one day she'd have confidence in herself to have a relationship.

As she poured the hot water over the chamomile, surprise stole over her. For the first time, she had started to think positively in terms of healing. She wouldn't tell Luke what she was thinking; he might get his hopes up high.

Reaching for one of the peanut butter biscuits Ruth had packed in a plastic container for her to bring home today, Emily put it on the saucer and headed back to her room.

Ophelia had kicked the sheets off, and Emily pulled them halfway up over her. It was too hot to be completely covered up tonight. Maybe when they went to Charleville, she'd find a fan to put in their room.

Her daughter lay on her back, her face set in a contented pose. Her dark lashes framed her rosy cheeks, and her tiny fingers were curled up in fists resting on her tummy. A wave of love so strong it almost hurt ran through Emily, and tears filled her eyes.

'Troy, oh Troy, couldn't you see what we could have had?'

Her grief counsellor in Cairns had told her that Troy would have felt that suicide was the only way to end an unbearable pain he was feeling as the result of trauma in his life, and it could have come from many years ago.

Emily had shaken her head. 'I don't know what it would have been. I need to understand why.'

'Emily? You need to understand you may never know. When you accept that, your healing will start.'

She had known that Troy hadn't been in a good place for a long time, and she had to accept that and move on. It wasn't healthy for her to dwell on the whys when she had no chance of discovering the cause. She had tried to talk to his mother and had had no success.

Emily sighed, put the teacup and saucer on the desk and switched on the lamp above the computer as she settled down to read. Halfway through the play penned by Nigel and Rory Cartwright, she was laughing out loud.

It was balm for her soul. She was laughing so much she almost choked on a crumb of a peanut butter cookie, and she had to put the teacup down so she didn't sputter tea all over the already stained play.

This was the winning entry; there was absolutely no doubt she knew by the time she reached the end. Her laughter had turned into tears, and she marvelled at the insight those three boys had. She knew they had suffered tragedy; they had lost their mother, and then their Aunt Sophie had cared for them for eighteen months as Braden had dealt with his grief.

Braden had married Callie almost a year after she had come west from Brisbane to be a nanny to the boys. That scene in the play had made Emily laugh and cry; it gave her a whole new picture of Braden and Callie.

Callie had not hesitated to tell Emily her story. Now they had their twins, and they were so happy together. The amount of love that these boys were obviously given showed through in every word they wrote, and Emily sat back, tears rolling down her face.

They understood the power of love at eight and ten. How could she not understand it at twenty-nine? Emily pushed the play to the side of the desk, put her hands over her face, and began to sob.

Chapter 12
Callie

Callie attended the school assembly on Friday. She didn't work Fridays, and neither did Emily, but she knew Emily would come in to announce the winners of the play. The boys had driven her and Braden crazy all week—breakfast, dinner, bedtime, first thing in the morning, and feeding the animals. The topic of conversation had been the play, who was going to be in it, how they were going to produce it, and what props they would need.

Callie was going to Charleville to shop on Saturday, and the boys had extracted a promise that they could come too. There was a bargain store in town that had everything they could possibly need. However, Callie had to promise that they could shop by themselves as everything was to be a surprise.

'You have to win yet,' she reminded them after dinner on Thursday as they made a secret shopping list.

'We'll win,' they both said together.

Later that night, when the three boys were in bed, Callie sat in the living room beside Braden as he flicked through Netflix.

'You do realise they are going to be devastated if they don't win this competition.'

Braden frowned, 'Yeah, I know. And to top it all off, they'll have to watch someone else's play performed, and we won't be going down to the coast. Maybe we could go after Christmas if they're miserable.'

'Well, let's not jump to conclusions. You never know; they've put so much work into it, maybe they'll win.'

'With a farting donkey?' Braden said, 'I don't think

they've got a hope in hell, sweetheart.'

Now, Callie pushed the double pram into the assembly hall. There were four rows of chairs for parents at the back, and she took a seat in the back row so there was room for the double pram beside her. Petie sat in the chair on the other side, and she wondered how he'd last for the full hour. Meggie and Munro had had a broken night and were now sound asleep.

'That'd be right,' she thought as she covered a yawn.

There was still the grocery shopping to do after the hour here. If the twins behaved, she'd call into Jenna's and have a cup of coffee at the Vintage Tearoom and feed the babies before she headed for the grocery store.

It was a long assembly today because it was the day when the children received their class awards.

Emily walked down the space between the two groups of children in the centre of the hall and sat with the staff at the side of the stage.

Bob Hamblin stood at the lectern on the stage and welcomed the parents. The next half hour was filled with two performances by students from prep and grade four, and then the school choir singing Christmas carols with Kimberley conducting. Craig Anderson's son recited a Christmas poem.

Callie's eyes got heavier, and she had to force herself to stay awake. It was hot in the hall despite the large fans circulating air overhead. Meggie began to stir, and she reached into the pram and gently patted her back.

Finally, the certificates were presented to each year from prep to grade six. Meggie settled, and Callie leaned back in the chair and closed her eyes. After a minute or two, she forced herself to wake up as they got to Nigel's class. She sat up straight, clapping as he was presented with his certificate and a merit award for being a good class monitor.

Finally, it was Rory's turn, and he received a merit certificate for his work in mathematics, his improvement in writing, and his knowledge of geography. She cheered and clapped, full of pride. A full fifty-five minutes had passed since she'd sat down, and she glanced into the pram, the twins were still sound asleep. Knowing her luck, they would wake up for a feed soon, and she'd miss the contest announcement.

Ruth had said to drop them in any time she wanted to, but Callie relied on her too much. She'd have to learn how to cope.

Relief shot through her as the twins slept on, and Petie sat quietly, taking it all in, and Bob called Emily to the stage.

'Now, I'm going ask Mrs Jansen to come to the stage and announce the winner of our Christmas play competition.' The principal beamed. 'Congratulations to all who managed to write a play. That's a big achievement. Mrs Jansen tells me that they were all great stories, but of course, there's only one winner. We're looking forward to starting rehearsals next week, and this play will be performed on Saturday of next weekend here in the primary school hall. I'm sure you'll all be here, and boys and girls, someone told me that there might be a visit from a man in a red suit after the play's over.' As Emily made her way to the stage, the children clapped and cheered at the thought of Santa Claus coming to the primary school.

Callie sat there, her fingers crossed. She could see Rory's head in the group of children, and Nigel was a monitor, so he was standing at the side.

Emily took the microphone. 'Thank you, Mr. Hamblin. I must say it's been an absolute pleasure reading all your stories, but we have a winning entry, and I'm looking forward to talking with the authors this afternoon and taking them through the script I've written from their story. The winner of the Christmas literacy competition and the authors'— Callie's heart gave a little skip at the plural—'the authors of this play have done a fine job.'

Emily nodded slowly. 'Not only did they capture the spirit of Christmas and the theme of love and joy with the Christmas story in a contemporary setting, they made me laugh, and I must admit, they made me cry.'

Callie's hopes sank; she couldn't imagine a story with a farting donkey would make anyone cry unless it was with tears of laughter.

'Now, I would like to ask the winners of our competition to come to the stage so Mr Hamblin can give them a special certificate for winning the Christmas play competition.'

Callie held her breath as Emily looked out over the children. Bob Hamblin took the microphone from her and made a drumroll sound while Emily waited.

Emily hesitated as she waited for the microphone, and Callie's heart raced.

'Gosh, what must the boys be going through?' she wondered. She glanced across at Nigel and saw the instant his expression changed.

Emily smiled. 'Rory and Nigel Cartwright, please come up and receive your certificates.'

The hall erupted in an uproar of yells and screams, clapping and cheering. Callie blinked back tears as Nigel and Rory made their way to the stage. Petie leaned over with a big grin. 'See, I knew they'd win, Mum.'

Braden was waiting at home to hear. Callie pulled out her phone and sent a text:

They won!!!!!!!!!!!!!

Chapter 13
Luke

Strong crosswinds buffeted Luke's plane as he brought it to a quick landing at the Augathella aerodrome. He'd had every intention of getting back to town early and having a leisurely shower while planning what he was going to say to Emily over dinner tonight.

As he taxied the aircraft and then came to a stop near the hangar, he looked at his watch. By the time he secured the aircraft and called a taxi to take him back into town—because he wasn't going to walk the distance from the aerodrome this afternoon like he usually did—he'd barely have enough time to have a shower and head down to Emily's to pick her up at six o'clock.

It was all Braden Cartwright's fault; Kent Mason had come over from his place, and they spent a couple of hours yakking about plans for next year. Luke had lost track of time until he looked at his watch and saw how late it was.

'Gotta go, guys. I've got a date.'

Braden grinned. 'Let me guess, Emily Jansen?'

Luke nodded and smiled. 'Send me positive vibes and wish me luck tonight; I'm trying to make a breakthrough.'

The taxi arrived quickly, and Bert, the driver of the only taxi in town, looked at Luke when he said he was going to the pub.

'You could've walked there, mate.'

'Yeah, I know, but I'm in a rush,' Luke said.

He paid the fare, raced up the steps to his room, jumped in the shower, and stood there, trying to catch his breath as he planned what he was going to say to Emily.

He knew deep down that she cared about him, and he had

no doubt that he loved her. He was going to tell her that tonight, and if she wasn't interested, well, he wouldn't come back to Augathella after Christmas. He was committed here until Christmas Eve, and then he was due back in Narrabri.

He had a month of leave then, and he had to figure out what he was going to do. If Emily stayed here next year—and she said that she was going to be offered work—with any luck, he wouldn't come back here. It was time to spread his wings, literally and figuratively and travel more widely with his job. If Dwyer Holdings weren't prepared to let him go to Western Australia to work, he could resign and do contract work. He had the reputation that would get him work. It all hinged on Emily tonight. Luke had decided that he was going to be totally honest, even if she didn't want to talk. He was going to force her to. It might be cruel, but it was the only way they could come to some sort of understanding. He jumped out of the shower, quickly dried off, and then ran a razor over his face to make sure it was clean-shaven, just in case.

***

Emily got ready in a daze; she knew she wanted to look her best. But she stood at her wardrobe for a good two minutes, trying to choose between the black dress or the floral dress she bought in Charleville when she went down to buy Christmas presents for Ophelia last week. The floral dress won out because it was a close match to her sandals, and once she was out of the shower, she slipped it over her head.

Ophelia was sitting on the living room floor, playing with those beloved blocks. She had bought a new set for Christmas, but she wondered if she'd wasted her money because Ophelia loved the brightly-coloured set they had had for the last six months. She picked them up and began stacking blocks.

Her hand shook as she tried to apply her makeup. She was terrified of talking to Luke tonight, but that's what she was going to do; it was time for honesty. Those two little boys, the Cartwrights, would never have any idea of what they'd done for her, how she saw the error of her ways. She realised that the path she'd been on was not the right one.

She'd always loved Luke Elliott, and she knew that he cared about her. What had happened was in the past, and the examples that those two little boys had given, and how they related it to happiness in the town, had opened her eyes. It was time that she moved on. She couldn't carry that burden for the rest of her life because it would taint Ophelia's upbringing. She needed to look at the positives and think about what was the best for both of them, what was the best for the three of them.

'Hello, Emily.'

'Hello, Luke,' she said. She stood at the door, her fingers gripping the door handle. Jen and Joshua were still out, and she'd had the house to herself. Ophelia was sitting in the pram, gripping her little ragdoll, and she smiled when she spotted Luke at the door.

'Hello, Ophelia. How's the prettiest girl in the world today?'

Emily tipped her head to the side and put on a coquettish smile. 'The prettiest girl in the world?'

'After her mother, of course,' Luke said with a smile.

It was going to be alright. Emily knew it was going to be alright. She locked the doors, and Luke manoeuvred the stroller down the steps.

It was a lovely evening. The wind from earlier had dropped, a gentle breeze blowing, keeping it cool. Jenna's front garden was a riot of colours—petunias, lobelia, and geraniums spilled out over the garden edge. The fragrance of the single rose she had growing in a pot next to the gate drifted on the evening air.

Emily opened the gate as Luke pushed the stroller out, and she swallowed. She followed him. Luke kept the stroller on the grass of the footpath as they headed towards the pub, and Emily walked beside them. Neither of them spoke. It appeared that Luke was lost in his thoughts as much as she was.

She swallowed again. 'Luke,' she asked quietly.

'Yes, Em?'

'Would it be okay if I held your hand as we walk to the pub?'

The smile that broke over his face filled her with joy, the same joy that the boys had written about in their play.

'It sure would.' He held out his hand, and Emily laced her fingers through his, and their eyes met. It was going to be alright.

Ophelia sat happily in the high chair the bistro provided.

'Would you like a drink, Emily?' Luke asked.

'I would, please. I'll have a glass of bubbles.'

Luke raised his eyebrows. A lump stuck in his throat as he thought about the talk he wanted to have over dinner. Was he doing the right thing?

'Yes.' His conscience nagged at him. They had to talk. He had to know whether he was wasting his time. Emily asking if she could hold his hand on the way to the pub had filled him with hope, but he didn't want to get his hopes up too much.

He came back to the table with two glasses of champagne and put them in front of his place. 'I feel as though we should be toasting a celebration.'

'We should be, shouldn't we?' Emily held his gaze, her heart starting to beat faster.

'Did you want to order yet? Or just sit and have a drink for a while?'

'Let's have a drink and chat before we order,' she said.

'Thank you for coming out with me tonight, Emily. I really appreciate it.'

'My pleasure,' she said. 'Thank you for inviting me.' Every time he looked at her, he saw her eyes on him, and Luke's hopes began to build even more. So, he decided to take the plunge.

'Emily, I hope it doesn't upset you, but I really want to talk tonight.'

'So do I, Luke. What did you want to talk about?' Her eyes snagged his and held them.

'I want to talk about Troy,' she said.

Luke had to consciously stop his mouth from dropping open.

'Yes, the elephant that's in the room between us, the one that I refused to talk about.'

'You want to talk about Troy?'

'I realise that I've been wrong, Luke. I've been wrong for three years. I'll never regret it because I have my beautiful little girl from that relationship. I had decided that it was my fault, that I was responsible for what he did. But something happened this week that made me think deeply and long and hard, and I know it wasn't me. Troy had issues, and we hadn't really been a couple since the first year we were married.'

Luke reached over and took her hand, and her fingers brushed his. 'It was never your fault, Emily. Troy has always carried his demons. You know what caused it, don't you?'

He was surprised when Emily shook her head. 'No, I have no idea. I just knew he had black moods. At first, I blamed myself, and then I realised it wasn't me.'

'You don't know what happened?' Luke said.

'No,' she said again.

'Did you know about his father?'

'No, I just know that his mother lives in America with her second husband.'

'How old were you when you came to Narrabri High?'

'We moved there when I was in Year Eight.'

'Yes, I couldn't remember what year it was.'

'Why do you ask?'

'Because when we were in Year Seven . . .' Luke paused. Her eyes were holding his, and they were wide. 'When we were in Year Seven, Troy discovered his father had been embezzling money from his work account, and rather than face investigation, he killed himself.'

'I never knew that,' Emily said.

'The worst part is that Troy found him; his father hung himself in the garage.'

Emily's eyes filled with tears, and Luke wondered if he had gone too far in telling her.

'You didn't ever know?'

'No, I didn't. He would never talk about anything in the past.'

'I can understand that. He had a terrible childhood. He was pretty much left to do his own thing, and when his father killed himself, his mother fled. She left Troy with a neighbour to finish off his Year Seven, and then, by the time you came to town, care was finalised for him. He moved in with his aunt and uncle.'

'That's right; they never told me what it was like either. I had to make the call to tell them when he crashed the helicopter.'

Luke's fingers grasped his glass. 'I'm sorry, Emily. I should've told you when I could see you falling for Troy. I thought you'd be good for him, but I upset that you'd moved on.'

'I was never good for him; Troy never loved me. I don't know why he married me.'

But she reached over with her other hand and touched her fingers to his cheek. 'Maybe he knew that I needed something, and look, I've got a beautiful little girl.'

'You've just got to look at Ophelia and remember that she's a good part of Troy.'

'She is; she does look a little bit like him, but you know Troy was never interested in her.'

'He didn't have much confidence, Emily; I don't think he had any idea of how to have a relationship after his father died. I was stunned when he started asking you out. You know why he did, don't you?'

'I do. Because he was jealous of you and that I was starting to care about you. We were good mates, Luke, good friends. I've had an experience this week that has taught me to be honest, so I will be. If it means you get in your plane and leave tomorrow, I'll still be honest. I'm sorry for the way I've treated you over the past couple of weeks, and that I didn't tell you how many times I thought of you after we left Narrabri to go north. I missed you every day, and I knew I'd made a mistake, but I was going to commit to my promise. To the wedding vows I made. But it just got harder and harder, and then when he died, I just shut down. I blamed myself, and I tried to push you out of my thoughts. When I saw you in Augathella, I couldn't believe it, and it all came rushing back, and I knew I was in trouble. That's why I fought so hard.'

Emotion flowed through Luke, and his eyes pricked with emotion. 'Emily, I can't believe what you just said. You've made me the happiest man in the world tonight. I was going to be honest, too. If you just wanted to be my friend, I was going to let you have your year here and fly somewhere else and leave you in peace.'

Emily's eyes opened wide, and she held his. 'I love you, Luke Elliott. I always have, and I know I always will.'

'And I love you, Emily and I love your little girl. Can you see a future with me?'

Emily's eyes filled with tears as she looked at him. 'I can.'

Chapter 14
Callie and Braden

The Play:

Love and Joy come to Augathella

Written by Rory and Nigel Cartwright

There was standing room only in the hall at Augathella Primary School half an hour before the Christmas play was due to begin. Luke was on chair duty, and he'd called to Kent to help as the carpark filled and the queue outside the hall lengthened.

Emily and Kimberley Riordan were standing at the front door selling tickets.

'We can't let any more in,' Bob Hamblin said as he hurried past. 'It would be a fire hazard.' He stopped when he spotted Braden and Callie waiting at the door with Sophie and Petie. Nigel and Rory were already backstage.

'Welcome, Braden and Callie,' he said. 'There are three reserved seats for you at the front, for you and Mr. Mason.'

'What about Petie and Sophie?' Callie frowned.

Bob tapped a finger on the side of his nose. 'They don't need seats. They have some special duties.'

Callie turned to look at Sophie. 'You've got a special duty?'

Sophie nodded. 'I sure do. You'll see. So does Ruby Rose.'

Callie turned to Petie, but he'd already gone. Sophie grinned up at Kent. 'Enjoy the show.'

Callie shook her head as Sophie took off after Petie,

pushing the pram.

It had been a week of secrets. She'd taken the three boys to Charleville on Saturday after they heard they'd won, and she waited with the twins in the coffee shop next door while they did their shopping. Rory looked very grown-up when Callie handed over her credit card and told him the PIN.

'Mum,' he said, 'you're not allowed to look at your online bank stuff until after the play. You're not allowed to know what we've bought, okay? Do you promise?' he said.

'Yes, I promise.' Callie was intrigued. They had carried out two big parcels wrapped in brown paper and had asked to drop them off at the school on the way home.

'Mrs Jansen will be there, and we're going to rehearse.'

'Have you picked all the cast already?' Callie tried for some information with no luck.

'You'll see. Dad can come back in and pick us up later.'

'Okay.'

Rehearsals had been on all week. The children involved had been pulled from class—apparently, Rory and Nigel had already chosen them at the writing stage—and rehearsals filled the day. Callie had worked on Monday and had been banned from the hall. When she'd walked past a couple of times, all she could hear was laughter.

The twins were with Ruth, who'd called and insisted, 'You won't be able to focus on the play if the twins wake up.'

'But you should see it too,' Callie had insisted.

'No, I'll see the video.'

'The video? Callie asked.

'Yes, Jon is filming it. It's one of the hobbies I didn't know my son-in-law had.'

'Talk about a production and a half,' Callie said to Braden when she took his cup of tea out to the shed halfway through the week. 'The play's being filmed.'

Braden nodded absently. 'What did you need your red suitcases for? Did you get them out before we decided not to go away?'

Callie stared at him. 'I haven't touched them. Why?'

'I was looking for my kit bag to take mustering next week, and they're not there. I wondered how you'd reached them up there.'

'I have no idea where they are. I haven't had them out since you put them there after they dried.'

'That was a long time ago.' Braden leaned over and kissed her. 'That's one of my best memories of when we met.'

'I'm not a city slicker any more. I'd know not to hide luggage in an irrigation channel these days, plus I know a lot more than that.'

'You sure do. Anyway, they'll turn up.'

Callie didn't give them another thought until Emily stood at the front, and the play began.

She tapped the microphone that was on the stand in front of the closed curtains. 'Welcome everyone, parents, children, family and friends. We have a special presentation tonight. Also, after the play has finished, there is a special supper being served in the quadrangle, jointly catered for by Jenna's Vintage Tearooms and the CWA. If you'd like to purchase a cuppa and cake, all proceeds are going to our branch of the rural fire service.'

The audience applauded.

Emily continued. 'If you think back to the 1920s when films were all action with dialogue unspoken, you will understand the gist of the Cartwright brothers' play. I think we can look forward to seeing playwrights or filmmakers of the future.'

'Like Smiley Creevey,' someone called from the front.

Emily nodded. 'So, this evening, I am going to be the narrator, and the action will unfold in front of you.' She smiled. 'We need you to know that no children, babies or animals will be harmed in this production.'

'Thank goodness for that,' Braden whispered as he reached over and squeezed Callie's hand. Pride emanated from him as he stared ahead.

'I give you, *Love and Joy come to Augathella*,' Emily said to thunderous applause.

'And now to begin.' As Emily spoke, the lights dimmed, and the curtains opened.

A contemporary play. Callie smiled. One criterion ticked off.

Two children sat on the stage beside a manger, and it was clear that they had to be Joseph and Mary, although they were dressed in jeans and T-shirts.

'It took Joseph and Mary a long time to reach Bethlehem. It was like a trip travelling from Brisbane to Augathella.'

Callie and Braden smiled at each other. She knew that trip well.

'When they arrived, Mary was very tired. They needed to find somewhere to stay, but the town was crowded with lots of people, and every motel was full. A kind pub owner took pity on them and let them stay in his stable down the back.'

Callie frowned as a young girl dressed in red walked onto the stage carrying her two red suitcases.

'My suitcases, Braden,' she hissed. 'That's my suitcases!'

'And look to the left,' he said. 'A cardboard cutout red sports car. I'm nervous,' he said.

'Hmm,' Callie said as Emily began to speak again.

'And now we move to the love and joy in our town. Once upon a time, a lonely man with three little boys rescued a damsel in distress.'

Braden chuckled along with the rest of the audience.

'And the power of love—and water—' Emily paused. A collective gasp sounded from the audience as a bucket of water was tipped over the girl in red from above. Her hair was stuck to her face, and she turned as a grade six boy walked onto the stage, followed by three boys from the prep class. He kneeled in front of the young girl, and his hands went into a beseeching position in front of his chest.

'The power of love,' Emily continued, 'ensured that true

love followed its course. resulting in joy for a very sad family in the town of Augathella.'

The girl nodded and took the boy's hand, and they exited the stage on the left side with the three small boys skipping happily after them.

Callie looked at Braden as tears rolled down her cheeks. 'That's us and the boys.'

Braden's mouth was set straight, and she could swear a tear glinted in his eyes. 'It is.'

Before they could think about that scene, a donkey shuffled onto the stage. Callie leaned over to Braden and whispered. 'That's Nigel and Rory, I recognise their shoes.'

Emily continued. 'During the night Mary gave birth to Jesus. She put him in his baby clothes and laid him in a manger full of hay.'

As they watched, the curtain at the back of the set moved, and a hand appeared. It reached down, and a short baby cry came from the manger.

'A huge thank you to our youngest star, Ruby Rose Mason, who is playing Baby Jesus in the manger,' Emily continued with a wide smile. Callie gasped as Sophie poked her head through the curtains and smiled.

The donkey turned and ambled out, it paused near the exit and a loud noise emitted from the side of the stage.

Braden cackled out loud. 'Oh, Cal, they were allowed to have the farting donkey.'

'Were they?' she asked, wiping tears of mirth from her eyes. 'Or was that unscripted?'

The answer came as Emily returned to the microphone. 'A special thank you to Petie Cartwright for the sounds effects, courtesy of a whoopee cushion, sponsored by the Charleville Bargain Store.'

Emily looked to the right of the stage as a boy ran in, holding a large plastic helicopter.

'Soon, the power of love and wind'— Emily smiled— 'at this point, I may need to remind you that wind also powers helicopters before there is further need of sound effects . . . yet.'

By this stage, everyone in the hall was laughing and smiling.

'Again, the power of love,' Emily continued, 'ensured that true love followed its course. resulting in joy for a lonely pair in the town of Augathella.'

Ben and Amelia were next, with a special appearance by Chilli Girl on stage.

Braden whispered, 'I can see where that reminder of "no babies or animals being harmed" came from!'

The donkey reappeared from the side, crossed the stage and the same sound effect brought the house down.

'Look at that pair of rascals, Cal, they're laughing so much, the costume is going to slip off if they're not careful.'

Callie let out a sigh of relief as the donkey left the stage. 'Hopefully, no one else will know it's our boys.'

Braden's eyes met hers, and he smiled. 'I love you,' he mouthed. 'Here's the next scene.' They laughed as a doctor ran across the stage to sit beside a demure young lady who had sat on a picnic rug.

'How did they know all this!' Callie exclaimed. 'That's Dr Harry and Laura!'

'Your boys don't miss a trick,' Kent said.

The scene that brought the house down was the three boys dancing to *YMCA*.

'If only Ryder and Jacinta were here,' Kent said.

'We can show them the video.'

'It'll probably go viral.' Kent chuckled.

Sophie and Kent were portrayed next, followed by Petie lying on the stage being attended to by characters representing Matt, the singer, and nurse, Bec Hunter, followed by Quinn and Kimberley, each scene being interspersed with the farting donkey and Emily's words, 'Again, the power of love ensured that true love followed its course resulting in joy for this couple and the folk of

Augathella. It doesn't need to be Christmas to feel the joy in life.'

The curtain finally closed after a final appearance by the donkey and a hungry cry from Ruby Rose. Thunderous applause and whistles filled the hall.

'More, more,' the crowd called. 'More donkey,' a boy's voice called from the front.

Emily took the microphone. 'We would like to invite all the cast to the stage to take a bow. Including the donkey.'

Braden leaned over to Callie. 'Do you realise what a high the three boys are going to be on tonight?'

'But how proud are you, Dad?' she asked.

'Absolutely bursting,' Braden said as the cast came onto the stage.

To their dismay and mirth, the donkey took centre stage as Rory and Nigel were revealed respectively as the front and rear end of the donkey. Petie ran out and held up the whoopee cushion to much laughter.

'Well, it sure is a different take on the nativity play,' Braden said.

'But absolutely beautiful,' Callie said as they stood to make their way to the stage.

Epilogue
Callie

The catered supper was a huge success, and the crowd stayed until the food was gone, and Jenna began to pack up. Braden went down to collect the twins and brought Ruth back, and she'd already watched the video on Jon's camera, while nursing Ophelia.

As Callie stood watching Ruth laugh, a gentle hand touched her elbow.

'Callie?' She turned and smiled. Luke and Emily stood beside her. Luke's arm was around her shoulders, and Emily's face was alight with joy.

Callie shook her head. 'You are one amazing woman, Emily.'

'She is, isn't she?' Luke's smile was as wide as Emily's and Callie's heart filled with joy for them.

'It's certainly been a joyous night,' she said.

'Thank you. 'Emily's cheeks flushed pink as she looked up at Luke. Her eyes switched back to Callie. 'I wanted to thank you and Braden but he's busy stacking the chairs away, and we have to go now.'

'Thanks to your boys, Luke and I are going out to dinner to celebrate our engagement. If we don't hurry, the bistro will be closed.' Emily held out her hand. A single diamond on a gold band graced her ring finger.

'Oh, my goodness, that is such good news.' Callie hugged Emily and then Luke too. 'You have made my night, and what a night for it to happen!'

'Love and joy in Augathella,' Emily said. 'And we're engaged because of your boys.'

Callie frowned. 'How? What have they been up to?'

'It's a long story, Callie, but I've been carrying a lot of grief, and when I read their story last week, it made me realise what I had been missing all the time. Rory and Nigel showed me the power of love. I will be forever grateful to them.'

'And so will I.' Luke's arm went around Emily again and he pulled her close.

'Congratulations. Now, you two scoot, and I'll help Bob lock up.'

'One more thing. We'd like the three boys to be page boys at our wedding. We're getting married in January, so we can go away before term starts. Would you ask them?'

'With great pleasure.' Callie stood back and smiled widely as Luke and Emily headed out for their special dinner.

It looked like next year was going to begin with more love and joy in their town. Callie headed over to Braden, her heart bursting with love for her husband and their five beautiful children.

An Augathella Wedding

ANNIE SEATON

Augathella Short and Sweet: 5

86

Chapter 1
Rosie
March

'Are we crazy moving so far away to a place we've never even been to?' Rosie Renouf reached over and placed her hand on her husband's knee as he changed back a gear in the truck.

'There's not one bit of crazy between us. Just great choices.' Lex shook his head. 'And a lot of luck.'

'I don't call it luck, sweetie. It was all Chloe. And I totally trust her.'

'I do too, and I guess I have to accept that, but my logical brain says it was luck. It actually scares me a bit.'

'What does?

'How she is. What she knows.'

'Chloe has a gift.'

'She sure does. Anyway, we're only about ten kilometres from Augathella so get ready to see your new home.'

A quiver of anticipation ran through Rosie and she tried to stay calm. They were almost there; three months of planning, purchasing, and organising and Lex was about to get his farm.

And they were getting a new start in life. If anyone had told her that they would be moving to the Aussie outback within two years of emigrating from London, she would have said they were crazy. But they hadn't met Chloe and Greg then.

Now they were the crazy ones.

The highway from Charleville to Augathella had a couple of slight hills, but the road had been fairly flat most of the way since they'd left Brisbane three days ago. Lex had enjoyed driving the big truck and had even suggested that he might take up truck driving—with a grin and a glance at Rosie—as a new career. She didn't take the bait. Her husband knew what he wanted to do here in Augathella. They all did, and there were exciting times ahead.

Rosie enjoyed looking around; the landscape was so different from what she had expected. She must admit she'd had her doubts when they'd chosen this town because she envisioned it being in the middle of the red, dusty outback.

However, here, along the edges of the highway just south of their destination, thick, silver and pale green trees filled the paddocks. Some of the trees reminded her of the forest near her childhood home in England.

When Rosie called her mum and dad to tell them that they were moving from Brisbane to the outback, her mother was horrified. 'Oh dear, darling, I don't know that we'll ever be able to come and visit you there now. I don't think I could cope with the heat. You'll have to come home and see us every year.'

Her mum's request to visit would have been impossible up until recently—airfares had been out of reach— and even though they could now afford to go back to the UK for visits, Rosie hoped her parents would come and visit. She knew they'd love it here.

Even in the outback.

Her parents were stuck in their ways, and she vowed never to let herself get like that.

She kept her voice even. 'That's why air-conditioners were invented, Mum, and we will have one in every room. We're going to build our beautiful family home out there on a small property. I'd so love you and Dad to come and visit. We'll book your tickets for you.'

There was a long silence, then, 'You know your dad won't fly.'

'I'll book you on a cruise ship.'

'He can't swim either.'

Rosie's eyes swam with tears, and she gave up. 'Okay. We'll come home for a visit once we get settled.'

'I still can't understand what's happened to you,' her mum

said. 'First, you leave home and move to London. Next thing I know you're heading off to another country with Lex. And now he's dragging you out to the dangerous outback. It's about time you settled down and had children instead of going off on mad adventures. You read way too much Enid Blyton when you were a child.'

Rosie had stifled a giggle at that, but she knew if she told her parents what had caused this "adventure", they would have been even more shocked. She shook her head as she thought back to that fateful night in December. She and Lex still had to pinch themselves to believe it wasn't a dream.

Their adventure had all started when her best friend, Chloe, told them what she wanted to do. She and Chloe had met in the local supermarket the week after Lex and Rosie had arrived in Australia to start their new lives. Rosie had a casual job there. They had struck up a conversation and had quickly become firm friends. Lex and Chloe's husband, Greg, had hit it off, too, and soon, their friendship group expanded. They had more friends in Australia than they had ever made in London.

Chloe's suggestion was delivered at a barbeque at Rob and Suzanne's place in early December; it had certainly got a response.

'What?' their friend, Leah, had exclaimed. 'You're crazy, Chloe!' Leah, a teacher, was a very sensible, straight-down-the-line sort of friend.

'Crazy?' Chloe shook her head. 'No, I'm not. I know this. All we need is fifty dollars from each of us. One hundred per couple. So, we'll have five hundred dollars to invest.'

Leah shook her head again. 'Are you sure it will have a return?'

Chloe's smile was sweet and gentle. 'It's okay, Leah. If you don't want to be a part of it, that's fine. When you commit, I'll tell you.'

Mick, Leah's husband, lifted his beer glass and chuckled. 'We're in, babe. Nothing ventured, nothing gained.'

Leah rolled her eyes at Mick. 'Okay. I guess we're in.'

'We are, aren't we, Lex?' Rosie had gone along with Chloe, even though she was as sceptical as Lex and the rest of the group.

'Yep, we'll be here with bells on,' Lex agreed. 'In for a penny, in for a pound.'

Mick scratched his head and grinned at Lex. 'You're such a pommy, mate. Half the time, I don't understand what you're saying. Pennies and bells?'

Lex grinned back at him.

'If you're not willing to risk the unusual, you have to settle for the ordinary.' Rob held up his beer. 'We're in.'

'Us too,' Peter said, but Gemma frowned; Rose knew Peter and Gemma did it tough with a big mortgage.

'Okay, no pain, no gain.' Chloe's husband, Greg, smiled. 'And if I say no to my lovely wife and if what she says is going to happen does happen, I'll be in the doghouse for the rest of my life.

'If?' Chloe said, her delicate eyebrows raised.

'*When* it happens,' Greg corrected.

'But what's going to happen?' Suzanne asked. Everyone waited for Chloe to answer.

'Change,' was her enigmatic reply.

Rosie and Lex, Chloe and Greg, Leah and Mick, Rob and Suzanne, and newer to their group, Peter and Gemma, had become a very tight friendship group even though they were all very different personalities. Some of them were dissatisfied with their public service careers. Life during COVID-19 had made them rethink their work and home priorities.

'A change would be nice,' Gemma said, 'but Chloe, we have to eat, and we've got a mortgage to pay. One day, I'd love to own a hairdressing salon.'

Rosie nodded. 'I know, and we've talked about this over the last couple of years. Lex would love to have a farm like he grew up on at home.'

'This is home now, love,' Lex corrected.

'It is. But some of us are trapped in jobs we don't enjoy anymore. True?'

Everyone nodded slowly, except for Rob and Suzanne.

'We're content,' Suzanne said. 'Aren't we, Rob?'

Rob nodded. 'Pretty happy with our lot, but we'll throw in a hundred bucks. What are we investing in?'

Rosie couldn't help looking around the deck of their luxury apartment. Of the five couples, Rob and Suzanne had the highest income, and they were the only ones with children. Whenever they socialised, their kids were sent off to babysitters.

'Change. We're investing in change.' Chloe said. 'Trust me.'

Rosie and Lex exchanged glances. Chloe was always impulsive and positive.

 But she was always right. If she said there was going to be a change, they needed to listen to what she was saying because it was likely to happen.

'On the Thursday before Christmas, you're all coming to our place for dinner,' she said.

'Should be right with us; I'll have to check my roster,' Mick, who was in the water police, nodded. 'I could be on night work that week.'

'Why not the weekend, Chloe?' Lex asked.

Chloe stood. She spread her arms wide as though embracing them all. 'Because that's the night we're going to win Powerball,' she said.

Rosie smiled as she noted the variety of pulled faces and eye-rolls. 'Sounds good to me,' she said, not wanting to put a dampener on Chloe's enthusiasm despite quietly believing that this time, her best friend was wrong.

Chloe had had the toughest time of all of them recently. Not financially, but emotionally. When she was working at home during the COVID-19 lockdown, she and Greg had decided to start a family.

'I can stay at home and work and look after the baby,' she'd said excitedly.

Now, with Chloe just coming out of another failed round of IVF, Rosie knew Greg would do anything to make Chloe happy. He might be as sceptical as the rest of them, but he adored Chloe.

'I'll buy the champagne,' he said, putting his arm around Chloe's shoulder. 'Dan Murphy's got a sale on this week.'

##

Two weeks later, they were crammed on the small deck at the back of Chloe and Greg's rented house, enjoying a pre-Christmas barbeque. It was a very different venue from Rob and Suzanne's deck, overlooking the Brisbane River.

'Okay, you lot.' Chloe stood and pointed to the door. 'Come into the living room, it's ten minutes until the draw.' She turned to Greg. 'Is the champagne cold, sweetheart?'

'Sure is, love.'

Rosie's heart went out to Chloe. She was pretty sure the rest of the group had forgotten they were here for the draw. It hadn't been brought up in conversation yet.

But as they waited in front of the television, dreams were thrown around, and the conversation turned to their futures and what they would do if they won.

Chloe sat there quietly, her face alight with her ever-present sweet smile.

'We're certainly not going to go back to the UK, no matter what your mum says,' Lex said with a glance at Rosie. 'We'd probably move to somewhere out west where we can have a bit of land.'

Greg nodded. 'We'd be in that. I'd start my own business in a small town somewhere.'

Gemma turned to her husband. 'We'd move too. We just can't afford to live in the city anymore. We've been talking about moving for a while now. And we've made the move, haven't we, love?'

Peter looked embarrassed. 'I feel like a failure, but I can't stand going into the bank every day and trying to sell products to customers who can't afford it. I've put my notice in, and we're moving. We've got enough savings to last us three months or so.'

Gemma reached out and touched Peter's hand. 'I'm leaving the salon, and we're going down the coast after Christmas to visit my sister. Then, we're going to decide where we'll move to.'

Chloe's smile widened as she switched the large flatscreen television on. 'Listen guys, after tonight, you won't need to worry. I was thinking about a tropical island or some land we could all buy together. What do you think of that?'

Mick nodded. 'That would be a dream come true for me.'

'And me,' Lex said.

The conversations continued, and the dreams became more farfetched as the ads flickered across the screen in front of them. On the dot of eight-thirty, Chloe turned the volume up. 'Okay, everyone, shush, pay attention. We have to get the right vibe going. I've written our numbers on the whiteboard in the order they'll come out. Greg, turn it around, please.'

Rosie bit her lip as Greg walked across the room and picked up the small whiteboard lying face down on the coffee table. Poor Chloe; she knew how disappointed her friend was going to be. With any luck, they might win twenty dollars and that wouldn't go far, split five ways.

As the blue and white balls tumbled in the two transparent spheres, they waited. The blue balls dropped from the left one at a time, and a tense and disbelieving stillness took hold of the five couples who were now glued to the screen.

By the time the sixth number had dropped, the room was silent. Everyone's eyes were wide. Rosie grabbed Lex's hand and held it tightly. Chloe sat back on the lounge with a smile on her face. Not one word was said. The seventh blue ball dropped out, and there was a huge intake of breath.

'Oh my God, oh my God.' Leah's voice was shaking. 'We've got seven numbers.'

'And now we'll get the Powerball because that's the number I chose,' Chloe said. 'I threw dice for the others, and as you can see, the universe was looking after me.'

Rosie looked at the board, which only held seven numbers. 'What number did you choose for the Powerball, Chloe?' she asked breathlessly. The air could've been cut with a knife as they waited for Chloe to answer and watched the white balls tumble and roll, and then one white ball rose to the top.

'Number six,' Chloe replied confidently.

They all leaned forward as the white ball reached the top.

'Is it a six or a nine?' Greg said as he dropped to the sofa beside Chloe and clutched her hand. Stunned disbelief held them in thrall as the white ball, number six, dropped to join the others, and the number flashed on the screen.

Chloe sat back and held up the printed ticket. 'Now, who'll doubt me next time?'

Rosie found it hard to breathe, and she wondered if she was having an asthma attack. Lex nudged her shoulder, and she let go of the breath she'd been holding.

Lex's arms went around Rosie as she swept her gaze around their friends. 'Am I dreaming or did we just get six numbers and the Powerball?'

'We did,' said Chloe. 'One hundred million dollars.'

Chapter 2
Rosie
The planning- January

'A cattle property,' Lex said as the guys sat around the fire pit at Chloe and Greg's new apartment; Chloe had insisted that they temporarily move somewhere nice while they made their plans. Rosie smiled at her husband as she brought out the first two bowls of salad and put them on the table.

'A cattle property with a beautiful homestead,' she agreed.

'Nope.' Mick shook his head. 'It's going to be a fishing boat for me.'

'For *us*,' Leah chimed in. 'I get to choose too. I've been looking at brochures.'

'I thought being on the water for work would make you want to escape inland,' Greg chimed in.

Mick shook his head again. 'I love being on the water. It's the only good thing about my job.'

'I think we're making our decisions the best way. Slow and considered,' Rosie said. Once the euphoria of that night had worn off, they had all agreed not to tell anyone about their amazing win; the five couples hadn't even shared the news with any of their families, although a couple of the looks Rosie had seen between Rob and Suzanne had made her wonder.

When they'd messaged the group to say that they were happy to take their fifth share and remain independent of any plans, Rosie hadn't been surprised.

The discussions between the other four couples over the past weeks had been intense, full of fantasy and farfetched dreams, and the occasional disagreement as the suggestions became more ridiculous. As always, Chloe was the voice of reason. Four weeks after the amazing windfall, she messaged their group chat and called them all together for tonight's barbeque.

'What would we do without you, Chloe?' Rosie hugged her best friend when they arrived.

'You would have all quit your jobs by now.'

'We've gone close,' Rosie said.

Their lifestyles hadn't changed since that earth-shattering moment when the Lotteries office had confirmed their win an hour after they had watched the draw. Rosie and Lex were still living in the same rented accommodation, driving the same vehicles, and under Chloe's sage advice, they were taking a considered approach to what they were going to do.

Sailing boats, overseas trips, huge homes with swimming pools on acreage; all had been discussed. This was the first time Lex had spoken of the dream that Rosie knew he had always held. Before the win, they'd discussed going out west to escape the city and live a slower lifestyle.

'Right,' Chloe said as they all sat down to eat when the barbequed meat was on the table.

'I still can't believe we're barbequing Wagyu steak,' Lex said as he passed the meat tray across the table.

'A bit different to rissoles, but I do still prefer sausages,' Rosie said with a cheeky grin.

'Well, now that we can afford the best, you can buy gourmet sausages,' Chloe said.

Rosie chuckled. 'Nothing wrong with Woollies bangers. It's what I'm used to.'

When they finished eating, Chloe stood and tapped a spoon on the side of her wine glass.

'Rightio, guys. Tonight's the night,' she said. 'Tonight, we're going to decide if we're going to go our separate ways, like Rob and Suzanne, to follow our dreams. Or will we do it together? Our tropical islands, our fancy houses, and our fancy speedboats.' Chloe paused and looked at each of them as they sat around the table, their attention riveted on her. 'Or are we going to do something that makes a difference to other people?'

'You are the most beautiful person, Chloe. You really ground us all, you know.' Rosie smiled as they all looked at Chloe. 'If it weren't for you, we wouldn't be having this conversation.'

'Well, I figure as none of us have got money worries for the rest of our lives, we *can* follow our hearts. But all the things we've talked about, the things we can buy now, do we need them? Do we need flash boats and fancy cars? Will those possessions make us happy?'

Lex and Rosie looked at each other. They each knew in their hearts what would make Chloe and Greg happy, but all the money in the world wouldn't bring that to them.

'What does your heart want? I want you all to just think about it quietly for ten minutes. Close your eyes and let your heart tell you. Feel what you want deep in your heart, what will make you happy.' Her voice trembled a little, and Rosie's heart broke for her friend. She and Lex weren't ready to start a family yet, but Chloe and Greg had been keen from the minute they married. But they had faced disappointment after disappointment in the three IVF attempts, and Rosie knew that it had been expensive.

'Rosie,' Chloe said, 'I can hear your mind ticking over from here. I know what you're focusing on. Close down your thoughts and go with your heart. What *you* want, not me.'

Rosie closed her eyes and smiled as Lex reached for her hand. They were on the same wavelength. Lex had been teaching, and she had been casual nursing, working long hours, and they both came home the same night and announced to each other they were leaving their jobs once they'd decided what to do with their share.

Greg worked at an accountant's office at Wynnum. Chloe had part-time paralegal work in the city but didn't find it fulfilling. The police force, health, law, and education; it hadn't been a coincidence how several of them had already decided to change careers before the win.

All except Rob and Suzanne; they were content with their lot—Suzanne didn't work, and Rob owned a real estate agency. They hadn't said much since the win.

Rosie had wondered if the restlessness about their various careers had been some sort of premonition Chloe had channelled. Maybe deep down, they'd known this was going to happen without recognising and acknowledging what it was.

Whoops, Rosie realised that she was thinking too much. She closed her eyes tightly and let her heart take over. The time went in a flash, and Chloe put her hands on her knees and looked around the group.

'Right, everyone, it's time. Rosie, you're first. What does your heart tell you? One sentence.'

'Moving from the city, living in a small town, doing something that makes me happy and helps other people. I don't know what, but it will happen.'

'Lex?'

'Being with Rosie in her small town and having our farm.'

'Mick?'

'Um, staying in the police force. Making a difference but not in the city, and with a boat for the holidays.'

'Leah?' Chloe prompted.

Leah smiled at her husband. 'I'll follow Mick to his small town and go back to teaching. Move into special education if I can, that's what I love to do.'

'Pete?' Chloe said.

'I'd like to start a department store in a small country town. I remember growing up in Longreach and what an eye-opener it was the times we went to Brisbane. All the shops were like Aladdin's Cave to me. I want to take that to country kids and their parents.' He glanced at Gemma. 'And of course, with a hairdressing salon and a café in the store.

Sorry, Chloe, that was more than a sentence.'

'This is all sounding fabulous.' Chloe looked at Greg. 'Sweetheart, do you want to describe our dream?'

'You go, love,' Greg said, smiling at his wife. 'After all, our life changes are due to you.'

'A toast to Chloe,' Peter said, lifting his glass and everyone lifted theirs as well. 'Thank you, Chloe.'

Chloe's cheeks were pink as she stood and lifted her hands and then brought her thumbs and index fingers together at the tips, extending the rest of her fingers. She'd told Rosie a few weeks ago that the hand gesture was called the Gyan Mudra, and its purpose was to increase knowledge and wisdom.

She was a wise, gentle soul, that was for sure. Her dark brown eyes were expressive; Lex had commented when he met her that Chloe's eyes were the window to her soul. Her eyes always expressed her calm and gentle nature. Even when her IVF hadn't been successful, she had seen the positive side to it.

'Thank you,' she said. 'Okay, now, the big question is, with all our dreams, do we all move together, or do we go our separate ways? Don't even think about it. What does your heart tell you?'

Rosie looked around at her friends, all nodding. 'Together?' she said tentatively. 'It would be nice to move to a new town, and all start our new directions together.'

A chorus of, 'Together, for sure,' answered her question.

'Okay, let's get the map out.' Chloe's voice was brisk now.

Rosie expected her to pull out her phone, but Chloe walked to the buffet along the wall and retrieved an old-fashioned paper map of Queensland.

'Boy, that's an old one,' Greg said. 'Where did you get that from?'

'It was Mum and Dad's. We used to travel around a lot when I was a kid. I found it in their stuff when I cleaned out the house last year. Something told me it would come in handy one day, and it has.' She spread the map in the middle of the table and smoothed the edges down where they were threatening to curl. 'Okay, stand up and then close your eyes. I want everybody to lean forward and put their finger on the map.'

Chapter 3
March - Laura

'Aunty Laura, look at that truck.' Petie tugged Laura's hand as they stood on the footpath outside Meat Ant Park.

'Wow, it's a beauty,' she said, smiling to herself. Spending time with her three nephews had resulted in her picking up several new Aussie phrases.

A large truck drove slowly down the street. Obviously a furniture removalist, the truck had a bright, swirly logo on it. One of the prettiest designs Laura had ever seen: swirls of rainbow with the company logo in huge purple letters: **A New Life.**

She wondered idly if it was some religious group travelling through the outback, but the truck pulled up about a hundred metres down from the park where two huge sheds had been built over the past six weeks. There had been much speculation in town as to what was going on there.

At the same time, a dozen or so houses on the edge of town had been demolished, and building work had commenced. No one seemed to know who was responsible. The builders had come out from Brisbane, and the new dwellings were going up at the rate of knots.

'It's the biggest truck I've ever seen,' Petie said. 'I wonder if Dad would do that with the cattle truck.'

'Draw pretty pictures on it?' Laura chuckled. 'I can't see your dad having a purple rainbow cattle truck.'

'I'm going to ask him,' Petie said, a serious frown wrinkling his little forehead. 'When he gets home.'

Laura held out her hand for Petie to take as they crossed the road. Her brother-in-law, Braden, was away at a cattlemen's conference in Longreach, and Callie was working extra days at the school this week because Kimberley Riordan had been off sick; Callie was taking over her classes.

It wasn't common knowledge yet that Kimberley's upset stomach was morning sickness. As the hospital midwife, Laura had talked Kimberley through the best ways to deal with it a couple of weeks ago, but Kimberley was considering leaving school early as nothing was working; she had morning sickness all day.

Laura knew if that happened Callie would be working more days. Harry was away for two days, too, and Laura had a few days off from the hospital, so she'd volunteered to look after her youngest nephew. He had a bit of a tummy upset, and Callie had been going to stay home with him. Laura had called her by chance that morning and had been happy to offer to mind Petie. Since she'd moved to Augathella, the time she'd spent with the three boys had been precious.

She shook her head, thinking back to the Laura that she had been in those days—so unhappy and bitter—and how much her life had changed. Since she'd arrived in this small outback town and met Braden, her brother-in-law, again, and his new wife and her three delightful nephews and fallen in love with Dr Harry, life had been wonderful. Assisting in the delivery of Braden and Callie's twins had been a privilege. Laura's only regret was that she hadn't come over before the accident that had taken her sister's life.

As always, when she thought of Julia, her eyes welled with tears. Julia would be so proud of her boys and Braden, the success that he was making of their property. But equally, if she knew Braden's new wife, Laura knew that Julia would have been happy to see what a beautiful woman Braden had chosen to marry and become a mother to her three boys.

Even though life was good, a tiny glimmer of worry tugged at Laura as they walked along.

Harry had been distant for the last couple of weeks, and she wondered if there was something wrong. Had he decided he didn't want to be with her anymore? No, it couldn't be that; she knew that he loved her. Was he unwell? Was he getting restless? Did he want to move away? Now that Laura had found her family, she was quite content living in Augathella. She loved her job as a midwife at the hospital, she adored Harry, and she was very content. She didn't want to go anywhere else, but if she had to make the choice, she knew what she would do. Harry was the most important person in her life, and she'd follow.

She loved him. It was as simple as that. Harry had lost his first wife to illness, and he often looked at her with a look of wonder in his eyes.

'I don't know why you picked an old guy like me,' he once said.

'Old? You're only seven years older than me, so if that's old, that makes me old too!'

Harry had smiled his gentle smile. The one that always sent that shiver of longing shooting through Laura. 'But I can see how much you love those boys, and I know you'd love to have children.'

'Harry, I love you, and I'm happy with you, and that's all I want. Besides, I'm almost forty. I've left my run too late. I'm happy being an aunty.'

But she did worry that he was thinking of leaving her to give her the chance to be a mother.

Petie tugged at her hand. 'Let's walk down and see where the truck's going and what comes out of it.' He looked up at her, his expression innocent. 'Then maybe we could have an ice cream over at the coffee shop. My tummy's good now. What do you think about that, Aunty Laura?'

Laura smiled, knowing that she'd give in. 'Hmm. I'll have to think about that.'

They walked along the footpath and stopped outside the first shed. It was built out of timber and had a red tin roof. A double set of glass doors was set in the middle of the front with a small, covered porch, but the doors were papered up so you couldn't see inside.

'Look, Aunty Laura, what do you think it's going to be?

A shop? Is it a toy shop, do you think? There's a sign ready to go up. What does it say?'

Laura shook her head. 'It says: **What You Want, What You Need – Come and See Us: A New Life Store**.'

'I need a new bike,' Petie said hopefully.

Laura frowned. It sounded like a church to her. 'Come on. We'll go to the coffee shop.'

As they reached the footpath outside the second shed, the passenger door of the truck opened, and a pretty young woman with long blonde hair climbed out. Her smile was wide as she looked at Laura.

'Good morning,' she said. 'Isn't it a lovely day!'

'Good morning,' Laura replied.

'I love your truck! Can I have a ride in it one day?' Petie dropped Laura's hand and pointed at the truck.

The young woman smiled. 'If your mum says yes, I'm sure you could.'

'That's not my mum; that's my Aunty Laura. My mum is at the school; she's a teacher, and I was sick.'

'I hope you're better now.'

'I'm okay. I just had a pain in the belly because I ate too many apricots last night.'

'I love apricots too,' the pretty woman said.

'You should've seen when I...'

Laura put a hand over Petie's mouth. 'That's enough, Petie.' He'd already given her a vivid description of what his upset stomach had done through the night, and—thank goodness—with her nursing background, she was able to cope with the graphic description. 'That's private, Petie.' She smiled at the young woman. 'Hello, my name is Laura, and as you already know, this is my nephew. His name is Petie.'

'And I have a dog called Apricot, too,' Petie said. 'And two big brothers and a little brother and sister. I'm in the middle.'

'Hello, Laura, and hello, Petie. I'm Rosie. Rosie Renouf.' She turned and spread her arms wide. 'And this is our new store.'

'You've moved to town?' Laura asked.

'We have. And we're all very happy about it.'

Laura couldn't help asking. 'Are you building one of the new houses in town?'

'No,' Rose replied. 'Our house is being built out of town a little way, but we haven't seen it yet. We've just arrived.' She glanced across at the shed as a tall, broad-shouldered man came out of the door at the side. 'This is my husband Lex; Lex, this is Laura and Petie.'

'Hello, lovely to meet you.' He lifted his hand with a casual wave. 'Come on, Rosie; come and have a look. I've unlocked both, and they're amazing.'

Laura was itching to have a look but didn't feel it would be the right thing to ask.

'I'll be there in a minute. I'm just getting to know some of the townspeople. Our townspeople,' she said, with a beaming smile.

Lex looked down at his wife with a kind smile before he looked back at Laura. 'We've just arrived and still have to unload the truck and get ourselves settled. We're going to live in the shed until our houses are ready.'

'Houses?' Laura asked.

'Our friends are a little way behind us on the road. That's their houses being built across town. We haven't had a look yet.'

Laura was intrigued but didn't want to seem too curious. 'Well, welcome to town. We sometimes have a weekend picnic in the park near the river when new people arrive in town,' she said. 'It's great to see how many new couples are moving to the district.'

'There's eight of us,' Rosie said.

'We need another picnic. Aunty Laura, can you organise one? Soon?' Petie jumped up and down with excitement. 'With another sausage sizzle and kids' races like the last one when Mummy had a baby in the toilet, but there were two!

Meggie and Munro.'

Rosie crouched down level with Petie. 'Wow, how exciting. I like this town more every minute. A welcome barbecue sounds fabulous.' She turned to her husband. 'Maybe we could have something out the back of the shop; we could have a big opening and invite everyone in town.'

'Rosie, Rosie, slowly, slowly,' her husband said, but his smile was wide.

'Come on, Petie, we'd better shake a leg if you want an ice cream. School finishes soon.' Laura reached out to take his hand.

'Can I ask one question?' he asked.

Laura nodded. 'Just one.'

Petie leaned closer to Rosie who was still at his eye level. He dropped his voice. 'Do you sell bikes in your shop?'

Chapter 4
Jenna

Jenna smiled as Laura and Petie walked up the front steps of her vintage tearoom. She picked up her order pad and hurried over to Emily and Luke to take their order before Laura and Petie settled. It had been a quiet morning. Emily and Luke were firmly ensconced in the corner, deep in discussion.

Ophelia, Emily's daughter, was being babysat at Ruth Mason's house, and Jenna wondered what they were discussing so seriously. Emily and Luke had planned to marry in January before school resumed, but the sudden closure of the pub for renovations had put paid to their plans for the reception. Braden Cartwright had offered *Kilcoy Station*, but Emily and Luke had decided to wait until the pub was open again.

When the pub had closed without notice, Jenna had quickly offered the tearooms for the reception.

'Thank you, Jenna, but no,' Emily said instantly. 'As much as it would be lovely to have it here where Luke and I met up again, I don't want you to be working at our wedding. And I know you, you wouldn't be able to help yourself.' Her smile was wide. 'Plus, I want you to be my bridesmaid,' Emily had said.

Jenna was touched. 'Oh, I'd love that. If you don't want to have it here or at Braden and Callie's place, I guess the only other place in Augathella *is* the pub.'

She crossed the room and stood beside their table. 'Ready to order, guys?' she asked.

'Just the usual coffees, thanks, Jenna. Nothing to eat,' Emily said. 'Listen, have you heard any more about the pub?

Luke heard a whisper over the weekend that it's been sold. Have you heard that?'

'No, I thought it was being renovated. It's all rather sudden and hush-hush, though, isn't it?'

'Renovations *have* started already,' Luke said. 'So hopefully it won't take too long.'

'Josh said there's a lot of building happening around town, and it all seems to be a bit top-secret too.'

'There is a lot of change in the wind. More people are moving here: a new police sergeant, a new nurse at the hospital to replace Bec, and a new teacher at the school, too. Callie was telling me last weekend.'

'Where's Bec going? She and Matt aren't leaving town, are they?' Jenna frowned.

'No, apparently Bec's been offered a job working a community role with the council. She was telling me the other day she wants to work with young people for a while.'

'She'll be great doing that. Bec's great fun. She'll be good for our town. So will more new people here,' Jenna said. 'I love living in Augie. It's great to see life being injected into it. Reg would have enjoyed what's going on.' She blinked away a tear. Jenna was still grieving for the grandfather she had known so briefly.

'And there are those two big sheds built up near the park.' Emily's face was animated. 'I'd love to know what's going on there.'

'The town is certainly coming ahead,' Luke said. 'Okay, come on, girls, let's get back to the wedding. I guess we've decided to wait for the pub to re-open?' A frown marred his forehead.

'Do you want to wait, Luke?' Emily reached over and put her hand on his.

'Not really,' he said. 'But I do want to celebrate in Augathella. We've decided to base ourselves here, Jenna. I can manage my work from here. My boss in Narrabri has agreed.'

'That's great news,' Jenna said. 'I'll go and get your coffee.'

'Hang on a minute,' Emily said. 'I've got a better idea.'

'An idea?' Luke asked.

'Jenna, could you take a day off from the tearooms?'

'Yes, Ellie can handle it by herself now.'

Emily reached over and took Luke's hand. 'Why don't we go down to Charleville next week, or as soon as we can book the celebrant, and get married there? Jenna can be our witness. And then we can have the reception in a few weeks when the pub opens up.'

Luke's face lit up. 'I think that's a great idea. How about I call the celebrant now?'

Emily smiled as he pulled his phone out of his shirt pocket and headed out to the front porch.

'Sounds like a plan's in place,' Jenna said. 'Just let me know what day, and I'll get Ellie to open up. Are you going to take some time off school to go away?'

Emily shook her head. 'No, we'll wait until the Easter school holidays. We'll take Ophelia down to the Gold Coast.'

Emily's smile was wide as Jenna made her way over to the coffee machine and put the order up. 'No food, just coffee,' Jenna said to Ellie before she made her way over to Laura and Petie, who were waiting near the door.

'Hello, you pair. Sit wherever you like, and I'll get your order going.'

'I've got a huge favour to ask,' Laura said. 'The coffee shop in town is closed, the pub's not open, and we can't get ice cream for Petie anywhere. Although I am wondering whether he should have it or not, he's off school with an upset stomach, but Petie's insisting it's all right now.'

'I got rid of the food that made me sick. Jenna, you should have seen—'

'Enough, Petie.' Laura shook her head.

'Oops, sorry, Aunty Laura.' His eyes were wide and innocent. 'But I really need ice cream to make me completely better.'

Jenna hid her smile as she held the order pad. 'Well, you're in luck, Petie. I have ice cream and lots of toppings: caramel, strawberry, lime, and passionfruit. As long as your aunty says it's okay.'

Laura nodded.

'I'll have all of them, please,' Petie said. 'Mixed up swirly on a double scoop of ice cream.'

'Obviously feeling better then. What about you, Laura?'

'I'll have a skinny cap, please, Jenna.'

'Cake?' Jenna asked.

'Tempt me. I'm starving.' Laura's smile made her even prettier. 'What have you got today?'

'Hummingbird cake with fresh cream cheese icing.'

'You're on.'

As Jenna walked back to the counter, she couldn't help but think how much she loved her job. She smiled as she stared out over the tearooms.

Almost as much as she loved Joshua Foley. He'd gone home with Amelia and Ben for a month, and she missed him like crazy.

Chapter 5

Laura enjoyed the time they spent at Jenna's Vintage Tea Rooms. Once Petie had demolished his ice cream and looked at her with big eyes, asking for a second helping, she felt mean when she told him he'd had enough. The last thing she wanted was to have him sick when she returned him to Callie after school.

As they walked along the road to the primary school, Petie skipped along beside her, chattering nonstop. 'Now that I got rid of all the apricots, I'm fine,' he assured her a couple of times.

He had got rid of all the apricots and described it to her several times. What was it with kids and toileting? Laura shook her head as they turned the corner and headed for the crossing outside the school. Not that she'd ever know; she'd never have her own.

Sometimes, a glimmer of hope rose. Perhaps Harry would want to have a child with her, but she dismissed it. It was a ridiculous idea. Harry was in his late forties. It was time that he was thinking about easing back and thinking about retirement in a few years. He certainly wouldn't want to be saddled with a child.

Laura blinked away the surprising moisture that filled her eyes as she and Petie stood outside the school gate. What was wrong with her? She'd been so emotional the last couple of weeks, worrying that Harry's aloofness was because he didn't want to be with her anymore, which was crazy. They were planning to build a house together, for goodness' sake. He was just busy with work, and she was overtired because she had picked up a few extra shifts at the hospital. It would be good when the new nurse started. Laura knew she would prefer just to be in the maternity section, but they had been so short-staffed, she had done shifts in emergency as well as the aged-care ward over the past couple of weeks, and that was why she had been more tired than usual. She covered her mouth as she yawned. Keeping Petie entertained today had added to her tiredness.

'Do you want to go and play on the swings while we wait? Do you still feel okay?'

'I'm good. I'm just hungry again.'

Laura looked at him with a smile. Her youngest nephew was growing at the rate of knots, and the older he got, the more he was starting to look like Julia.

As Petie swung himself—higher than Laura would have liked—the musical tones of the bell sounded across the playground. The couple of times Laura picked up her nephews, she was pleasantly surprised by the peaceful sound of the music. The song varied every week, and she sometimes heard it as it drifted on the wind down to the hospital.

Callie mentioned that Kimberley Riordan had suggested the music, which certainly added to the school's ambience.

'Come on, Petie, the bell's gone.' The children were well-behaved and came out to wait for their buses in orderly lines. The rowdy ones—Laura rolled her eyes—were Nigel and Rory as they came tearing out of a building. Unfortunately for them, their stepmother came out of the building on the opposite side of the quadrangle at the same time. Callie lifted one finger, and Rory and Nigel came to a sudden stop, put their bags on their backs, and walked quietly over to the fence.

'Petie,' Laura called. 'Time to meet Mum.'

'Hi guys, did you have a good day?' Laura asked when she and Pete joined Nigel and Rory at the fence.

'Sure did, Aunty Laura. We're doing another drama production.'

Laura chuckled. The performance of the nativity play before Christmas, written by Rory and Nigel, had almost brought the house down. For a week or two afterwards, everyone was talking about their performance in the play.

Their farting donkey had made them a talking point of the town.

'That sounds good. What's this one about?' Laura asked.

'This one's going to be about the history of Augathella, and it's going to have bushrangers in it,' Nigel said.

'Were there bushrangers way out here?' she asked. 'I've heard about them. We didn't have bushrangers in New Zealand.'

'You'll have to tell us about New Zealand one day, Aunty Laura. I'd like to go there,' Nigel said.

'Maybe Mum and Dad can take you for a holiday there one day, and I can come and show you around.'

A pang of sadness hit Laura. If Harry's demeanour didn't improve, maybe she was going to have to think about leaving Augathella. He had been almost dismissive of her this morning when she said goodbye. Then again, she was being unfair. Maybe he was preoccupied with something. She didn't even know the month his wife had passed away. Maybe it was the anniversary or something like that.

She needed to talk to him. Yes, she would cook a nice dinner and try to have a chat with Harry tonight.

Callie joined them, her keys in her hand. 'Hey, Petie-boy, how's that tummy been today?'

Laura chuckled. 'Well, Mum, that tummy has seen lots of ice cream and a huge lunch.'

'And I haven't even spewed or run to the toilet once,' Petie interrupted.

'Too much information,' Rory said.

'Thanks so much for having Petie for the day, Laura.' Callie held her hand out to Petie. 'I appreciate it.'

'When's Braden back?' Laura asked.

'He'll be back tonight. He said he was going to a local cattlemen's meeting on the way home, but I'm not sure what will happen now the pub's closed.'

'I wonder how long it will be closed for? Emily and Luke were hoping to have their reception there. It's put a spoke in their plans.'

'Apparently, there's a sign up on the pub door saying it's closed for three weeks.'

'Oh, yes. I've heard that, too. And there's a rumour it's been sold.'

'Gosh, what are we going to do without the pub for three weeks? There's nowhere to eat out apart from the pub. At night, that is.'

'Plus, there were a few functions booked. I don't know what will happen there. We'll have to talk to Jenna about opening up for tea.'

Callie chuckled. 'I think Jenna works hard enough. I guess we'll all be eating at home. Maybe a few barbecues around the place.'

'I know,' Laura said. 'I'll talk to Harry. We haven't had you guys over for ages. How about we have a barbeque on the weekend?'

Maybe that would get Harry out of whatever funk he was in, Laura thought.

'That sounds good to me,' Pete chimed in. 'Mum, Aunty Laura wants to take us to New Zealand for a holiday.'

Laura shook her head. 'No, that's not what I said, Petie. I said maybe Mum and Dad could take you there *one* day, and if they did, I'd come along. Anyway, Callie, I'll hand this young gentleman into your care. Now I'm going to head off and have coffee with Jenny Riley.'

Callie reached over and hugged Laura. 'Thanks so much, Laura. You were a lifesaver for the school today. We can't wait for our new teacher to arrive and we'll have an extra person on staff. I'll talk to Braden about getting together, but it sounds good to me.'

Laura nodded and pulled a face. 'I'd better check with Harry too. Who knows what he's got planned for this weekend.'

Laura decided to take her car home and then walk to Jenny Riley's house. It wasn't far from their rented place, and she could use the exercise to clear the cotton wool from her head. She knew she was worrying too much about Harry, but she had always been a worrier. Her experience with her first husband had left her insecure, and she was super-receptive and sensitive to mood changes.

She adored Harry, and they'd had a wonderful year together, but she wondered whether he was beginning to have regrets. The walk would clear her head, and *maybe* tonight, when they sat down to dinner, she would talk to him.

Maybe not, because she was scared of what he might say.

Jenny was in the front garden pruning her rose bushes when Laura turned the corner. She looked up with a smile and waved. They had become good friends over the last twelve months, serving on a couple of committees together, and even though Jenny was fifteen years older than Laura, they had a lot of common interests.

Age didn't matter with friendships, and Laura had found that to be true in Augathella, where everyone pulled together.

'Hey Laura, I was just about to go in and put the kettle on. Ready for a cuppa?'

'I'd love one.'

Jenny glanced down at her watch. 'Actually, seeing it's close enough to five, how about a wine on the veranda? It's going to be a beautiful sunset.'

'Where's Tom?' Laura asked.

'He went out to Ben's place this morning. Ben and Amelia are away, and he's doing some work on the back of the house.'

'I heard some hammering as I walked past, but I didn't see Tom or his ute.'

Jenny laughed. 'Maybe he's gone for a beer.'

'The pub's shut.'

'Oh, I didn't know that.'

'Callie was just saying that there's a note on the door that it's closed for three weeks. She heard it's been sold.'

'Wow, that went through in secret. I don't think many

people in town know. I certainly haven't heard anything. I guess Tom's not there then; maybe he's gone down to the bowling club. Anyway, no matter. Come on in, and I'll pop a bottle open.'

A few minutes later, they were both sitting in the comfortable Papasan chairs on Jenny's veranda. Laura took a deep breath, even though it was heading into autumn, and summer had taken away the soft greens of Jenny's garden, it was still pretty. Several of her native trees were in flower, and her fruit trees had beautiful glossy green leaves. Her lawn was manicured, and Laura sighed with pleasure. 'Your garden is so beautiful. I honestly don't know how you keep the water up to it and how green it always looks.'

Jenny beamed. 'I love my garden. It gives me a lot of peace. If I'm ever worried about anything, I'll always come out and sit out here. Not only the trees and shrubs but the view out over the paddocks, too. Even though they're dry and dusty, it's still a beautiful sight.'

They sat there quietly and watched as the sun lowered, the sky changing from bright blue until the setting sun picked up the few clouds along the horizon behind the mountains, and a pattern of silver and gold edged the soft apricot.

Laura sighed, and Jenny looked at her curiously.

'You don't seem yourself, Laura. Is everything okay? You're not off-colour, are you?'

'No, and I hope I won't be. I've been looking after Petie all day. He had a tummy ache from eating too many apricots, Callie suspected, and he was sick last night. So, she asked me if I could have him for the day because Braden is away.'

'And is he okay now?'

'Okay? The little terror demolished two bowls of ice cream and a massive lunch, and he was still okay when I handed him over to Callie an hour or so ago.'

'Trust me, all kids are the same. They never know when to stop. Every time Ben went to a birthday party when he was growing up, I could guarantee that he vomited when he got home because he used to eat everything that was put in front of him.'

'I hope he's better now he's grown up.' Laura smiled.

'He is, and I often wonder whether his kids will do it to him.'

'How's their new bub going?'

'Beautiful. The perfect baby. It's wonderful being a grandma.'

Jenny was silent, and Laura bit her lip. Her main regret in life was that she never had children, and unbidden tears filled her eyes. Jenny looked at her with a frown and took Laura's hand. 'Laura, what's wrong? Did I say something to upset you? Are you okay?'

'No, I'm just being a bit maudlin, thinking back on my life. I made a wrong choice at the beginning; my first husband—my ex—wasn't a very nice man, but I persevered for as long as I could. I had a miscarriage not long before I left him and New Zealand, and I guess now, I'll always regret not having children.'

'It's not too late now,' Jenny said. 'How old are you, Laura?'

'Oh yes, it is. I'm thirty-eight. And Harry's heading for fifty.'

'Doesn't stop it happening,' Jenny said.

'I know, but we've not discussed it.'

'Please know that whatever we talk about here is confidential. You know I wouldn't say anything to anyone else.'

'You're a good friend, Jenny. I appreciate it.'

'How about another wine?' Jenny said.

'No, thanks,' Laura sighed. 'I'd better get home and get some dinner on. I've had three days off work. It's been really nice. I've enjoyed cooking each night. Which reminds me, I went down the street today, and the butcher's got a closed sign on it, too.'

'The butcher? What's happening in town?' Jenny

frowned.

'I don't know. Have you seen the new buildings near Meat Ant Park?'

'I have. No one seems to know what's going in there.'

'Petie and I went past today, and a truck pulled up, and I was talking to a young woman.' Laura quickly relayed the conversation.

'Interesting. I'll have to go for a walk tomorrow and have a chat around and see if anyone knows what's happening.'

Laura shrugged. 'Whatever it is, the town is changing.'

Chapter 6

'That was a lovely welcome from Laura and Petie,' Rosie said.

'Early days yet, don't get too excited. I've done a lot of reading through the Augathella Facebook groups and had a look at the history of the region.'

'I know what you've been doing for the last two months. It's good to do some research. I hope we can make a good life. It's very different to back home, isn't it?'

'It is, but we're here with all the people who have the same philosophy as us. They want to make a difference, and we picked a pretty little place to do it. And, my dear, you have your cattle property. Are you excited?'

'Am I excited? I'm beside myself. I can't wait to go out there and see it. I was talking to the builder on the phone when you were at the rest stop, and he said it's almost ready.'

'Almost, almost,' Rosie said.

'The kitchen and the bathrooms have been finished. All of the paving around the house has been done, and he just has to get the power connected and put on the front and back doors.'

'I can't believe you won't let me see the photo,' she said.

'No, I want it to be a wonderful surprise for you.'

'It's exciting, isn't it?' They walked along and looked at the shed that was the culmination of Greg's dreams. They had decided, in the end, that they would all be shareholders in the general store business. Gemma's hairdressing salon was next door at the front of the storage shed, and Rosie had agreed to work in the store with Greg as his assistant manager.

'It's all worked out well. Don't worry, Lex, it'll be fine.' None of them had been surprised or disappointed when Rob and Suzanne had decided not to join them. Rosie had never thought they would when the group chose the outback move.

They were happy with their business and their home in the city. Rob had retired and invested the money and agreed to help them all with their investments and the real estate purchases. They intended to travel, and Rosie had been sad to hear that their children were staying with their grandparents while Rob and Suzanne were away.

When she and Lex had children—and she knew Chloe and Greg would be the same—they would be close to their children, and they would do everything together.

'You off dreaming again, Rosie-girl? What are you thinking about?'

'Nothing important. Well, it is important, but nothing important for today.' She reached out and held his hand. 'Come on. Let's go and look at this store.' She turned as they walked along the path, already edged by a pretty flower garden. The landscapers from Charleville had done a great job. They were working on the houses that the other couples had built in town, and they were putting some gardens in ready for Rosie and Lex's small farm that they had bought only five kilometres out of town.

'How far behind us do you think the others are?' she said.

'I was talking to them after the other phone call. Greg and Chloe are about half an hour behind us, and the others are not far behind.'

'Shall we wait here, and we'll all go out to look at our farm together? What do you think?'

Lex agreed. 'We do everything together. Big celebration tonight, I think. It was a great idea of Greg to put that entertainment area at the back of the storage shed and hire it out for functions.'

Rosie screwed up her face. 'The town does seem rather small. Do you think we've overcapitalised, Lex?'

'No, I'm going with Chloe's feelings. We're here to make a difference, and from what you were saying, the town has been growing, and lots of young people are moving in. I think with what we're doing, there might be a little bit more of an increase in population.'

'I think so too, sweetie. I'm so excited.' When they were almost to the back of the building, Lex stopped and put his arms around Rosie. She looked up at him and held his gaze as love surged through her. He lowered his head, and their lips met in a gentle kiss. 'Are you happy, darling?' he murmured against her mouth.

'I am. No regrets. And I'm sure there won't be any,' she said. 'Now let's go and look at our store.'

Chapter 7

The next day

Rosie and Lex had a good look inside the first building the next morning. They'd spent their first night in town in a double swag in the other shed.

'I can't believe that the shopfitters have got this all set up already. It's absolutely beautiful, isn't it, Lex?' Rosie said. 'I think Greg is going to be very happy, but I've got a lot to learn.'

'How do you think you'll go helping him as assistant manager?' Lex asked. 'Are you sure you want to do that?'

'No, I'll be fine here, working with Greg part-time, but I've got some other ideas for things I want to do—maybe start some classes for people from the aged-care facility or work with the children at the primary school, just something to give back to this community that's going to be our new home. Like the small villages where we grew up.'

'You're a good person, Rosie.'

'Shall we look at the second shed?' As they stepped out the back and walked to the second shed, which was set up as a storage facility with the function area on the back, the rumble of a truck coming down the road reached them.

'Do you think that's the others?' Rosie said excitedly.

'Sounds like it.'

She hurried down the path through the pretty gardens where the flowers were in bud. The sprinklers had come on automatically through the night, and the grass was green and lush.

'It is! It's Chloe and Greg.' Rosie jumped up and down, then skipped out to the footpath and waited for the truck to pull up behind theirs.

Chloe jumped out straight away and raced over to Rosie, hugging her. 'Oh, I love this place already. How beautiful is the landscape? It's so different from what I imagined. It's green and soft and gentle.'

Rosie chuckled. 'Yes, I thought so too. Did you see those pretty silver trees lining the road after Charleville?'

'I did, and I saw lots of interesting red dirt roads heading down to properties. I can't wait to explore this region.'

Greg climbed out of the driver's side and walked around the front of the truck. 'We're going to be too busy to do any exploring for a while, Chloe. Have you had a look inside, yet guys?'

Lex nodded. 'Sure have. We slept in the storage area last night.' He reached over and shook Greg's hand, and then Chloe kissed Lex on the cheek.

'Where are the others?' Rosie asked. 'Are they far behind?'

'No, Gemma and Peter stopped for fuel at the turnoff, and Mick and Leah are only about ten minutes behind us in their car.'

'We've only had a quick look in the first shed, but it's great. I didn't know you were getting it lined, Greg. It looks fantastic.'

Greg looked a bit embarrassed. 'Did you see the flying fox I put in?'

'Flying fox?'

'Yeah. I just love that store at Maleny, the old department store. It's got the original flying fox in it. We can just use it for messages or something when you're up in the office, Rosie.'

'Better than texting,' she answered.

Chloe linked her arm with Rosie's, and they walked out to the footpath as Peter and Gemma got out of the third truck. Leah and Mick's four-wheel-drive came around the corner and parked behind the three trucks.

'They look pretty good together, don't they? It's the first time the trucks have been in a line since we left Brisbane,' Chloe said.

'I can't believe how quickly you all caught up to us.'

Leah laughed. 'We were so excited. We just wanted to get here, so we decided to drive through the night. That's how we got here early.'

'We did stop in Charleville for a while and had a look around.'

'Pete, how'd you go driving the truck?' Lex asked.

Pete had only got his light rigid license a couple of weeks before they came away. 'Easy as.' He chuckled and looked down at Gemma. 'I even commented to Gem that I'd like to be a truck driver in a new life.'

Lex and Rosie looked at each other and burst out laughing.

'Exactly the same thing Lex said. Maybe we've got a couple of truckies here,' Rosie said.

'Hey, that's not a bad idea because rather than getting a freight company to bring our stock from Brisbane, we've got the trucks, so we can go and get it.'

Pete grinned. 'We can be truckies.'

'Don't get carried away, you pair, because it won't only be Brisbane,' Chloe said. 'Greg and I were talking on the way out, and we really want to keep the content of the department store as Australian as we can. We can have a girls' trip around some small towns and purchase local products. Knitting and crochet, pottery and woodwork and things like that once we get settled. What do you think, girls?'

Gemma nodded. 'Yeah, that would be good, but I'm going to be busy setting up my salon. I've got no idea how many clients I'll have because the town doesn't look anywhere near as big as I was expecting. I hope we haven't made a mistake.'

'Gemma, it'll be fine. As well as all the outlying properties, apparently there are a lot of new people moving into town. I was talking to a local lady and her nephew a short while ago, and she was telling me there are so many people coming into town that they sometimes have welcome functions at the park.'

'We could do something social in the back of the second shed. You haven't looked at it yet?' Greg asked.

'I can't wait.' Chloe said. 'Let's go and have a look.'

Chapter 8

Callie was staying back at school late this afternoon as the new teacher who had moved out from Brisbane was meeting her to look at the special education classroom. So it was Braden's job to pick up the boys, give them afternoon tea in town, and then pick up Callie at five o'clock.

'I'm so excited that we've got a specialist special education teacher,' Callie had said that morning as he dropped her and the two boys at school before he dropped Petie off to Prep at ten o'clock. They'd dropped the twins to Ruth on the way into town. 'Her qualifications are fabulous, and I can't wait to meet her.'

'What does her husband do? Will he be looking for work?' Braden asked.

'When I was talking to Leah on the phone, she said that her husband got a transfer out here, but I'm not sure what he does. Out here in Augathella, there isn't much to transfer to, apart from the hospital, the police station, or the school.'

Braden nodded slowly. 'Yeah, Sergeant Mitcham said he was looking at retiring shortly. Maybe he's done it on the quiet, and a new policeman is coming to town. It'll be good to have more new people in town, too.'

'Yes,' Callie agreed. 'We've got so many in the agricultural sector and some new people at that function in the park the afternoon I had the twins. It's so exciting to see the town growing.'

'We might have to hold another welcome function,' Braden said.

'Sounds like a plan, with whatever's happening with those sheds and the new houses down in Hill Street. I'll ask Leah where her husband works when I'm talking to her this afternoon.'

'Well, it's certainly not them building the new sheds, if

they've both got transfers to town,' Braden commented.

Callie leaned over and kissed him. 'Come on, boys, we don't want to be late.' Rory and Nigel jumped out of each side of the car.

Braden chided Nigel. 'How many times have I told you not to get out on the roadside?'

'Sorry, Dad, I forgot. I couldn't get past Petie. He's got his leg stuck up. On purpose,' Nigel snarled. 'I looked first to see if any cars were coming.'

'Well, don't do it again; it's dangerous.'

Peter stuck out his tongue. 'I did not.'

'You did so. I was watching. You put your legs up,' Nigel yelled.

Callie rolled her eyes. 'Come on, you pair. Nigel, lose that temper before you go into class. I don't want you hassling Miss Emily. I'll see you about five, Bray.'

'Love you, Callie.'

'Love you too,' Callie said as she climbed out of the car.

Braden headed down the street towards the park. They had an hour to fill in before Perie started prep.

Petie pointed out the window. 'Dad, have you seen that truck? The one I told you about, the purple swirly one. Go up past Meat Ant Park, and you'll see them.'

Braden glanced at his watch; he had plenty of time before he had to be at Craig Wilson's property. He was looking at some cattle there today and meeting Jon Ingram out there as well.

'Mate, I've got time.' He put the indicator on and waited for some children to cross at the crossing before turning down Main Street.

'Look, it's still there' Petie said. 'And there's more! There's three of those flash trucks now.'

Braden parked a little way down from the butcher shop that had newspapers covering the front windows.

'I wonder what's happening?'

'Aunty Laura asked that the other day too. I've heard her

talking to Emily about it, and there's gonna be a new butcher shop too.'

'Wow, things are changing,' Braden said.

'I like it, Dad. I think these trucks are doing special things in our town. I liked the lady.'

'I don't think they've got anything to do with the butcher, mate.'

'I bet they have. That lady was really nice.'

'Which lady was that?'

'The lady who got out of the truck. She talked to us for a long time. If the trucks are there, she might still be there,' Petie said. 'Can we go and see?'

Braden parked the Landcruiser down from the park. 'Come on, jump out, and we'll go for a stroll.'

'Can I have a swing at the park too?'

'I suppose you can. I've got a while before I have to meet Jon. But you don't want to be late for school.'

'I hate prep with the little kids. I want to go to big school.'

Braden rolled his eyes. His sweet little Petie was turning into another Nigel. 'Next year, mate. Not long. We don't want you to grow up too quick.'

'Why not? We've got the twins now.' Petie yelled back as he raced over to the swings in the park. 'Do you want to come push me, Dad?'

'Sure.' Brayden walked over and gave the swing a solid push. 'I'm just going to suss out these trucks, mate.'

'I wonder what's inside them? Do you think there's something special in there, or do you think it's just boring stuff?' Petie asked as he made the swing go higher. 'Maybe it's a circus.'

Ever since the circus had come to town when Petie was three, he talked about it incessantly. Maybe one day it would come back, but Braden doubted very much this was a circus. He walked along the road, keeping one eye on Petie as he swung himself on the swing.

He looked at the logo on the trucks wondering if it was the name of a company or whether it was the name of some sort of church.

There was activity at the back of both sheds, so he yelled at Petie, 'Come on, mate. I'm going down to have a look, hop off and catch me up.'

Petie soon caught up to Braden, with his eyes wide as he looked at the three trucks. 'They're much bigger than your cattle truck, Dad.'

'Sure are, mate.'

'Maybe we can go and ask them what's inside,' he said.

'I'm sure we'll find out. Come on.' Braden looked down with a smile as Petie slipped his little hand into his.

Contentment filled him as he walked along with Petie swinging their arms. Life was good, even though he and Callie might both be a bit tired with the twins.

'Good morning,' he said, as a guy walked around the side of the first shed.

'Hey there.' The man was tall with broad shoulders and a wide smile, dressed in a pair of khaki pants and a long-sleeved shirt. Braden walked over and held out his hand. 'Braden Cartwright.'

'I'm Lex Renouf. You live in town, Braden?'

'Sort of, I'm a local from birth. I've got a cattle property about thirty ks out on the old Charleville Road.'

The guy's eyes brightened. 'I might be in touch with you, mate. I'm starting a little property close to town, but I'm a city slicker and I've got no idea what I'm doing.'

'Great to make a change. I'm happy to help. We'll have a chat when you get organised,' Braden said. He gestured with his head to the trucks. 'These your trucks?'

Lex nodded. 'Yes, there's a few of us moving to town.'

'The town's a little bit intrigued by what's happening,' Braden replied. 'Are these sheds yours? Or are you working here?'

'They're ours,' Lex said. 'Come round the back and meet

the others, and I'll show you what we're doing.'

Petie's eyes were wide as they walked around, Braden still holding his hand. There was a small area behind the first and largest building—they were more than the sheds he'd thought—with some tables and chairs and an outdoor kitchen. At the back of the smaller building, was a huge outdoor entertainment area with a wood fire, a barbecue, and a lot of furniture that was waiting to be arranged.

'Looks interesting,' Braden commented.

'Yes, we're hoping it'll all work out for us. Augathella's a little bit smaller than we thought, but it was the town we chose to move to. Come and I'll introduce you to the others. Would you like a cup of tea? We were about to take a break. We've been unloading the trucks since we arrived.' The English accent was very pronounced and Braden wondered if they'd emigrated from the UK to Augathella. He glanced at his watch. 'Won't say no to that. I just have to drop my boy at school before ten.'

As he spoke, a woman came out of the second shed, carrying a small box.

She smiled as she spotted them. 'Hello, Petie.'

'Hello, Rosie,' Petie said.

'Hi, I met your son yesterday. I'm Rosie, Lex's wife. I see you've already met him.' Three other couples walked out of the shed carrying empty boxes, and Braden wondered what was going on as they flattened them and added them to a pile of cardboard.

'Guys, come and meet Braden,' Lex said. 'He's a local cattle farmer. I'll be picking his brains, I'm sure.'

Braden was introduced to Leah and Mick first. He held out his hand and Mick's grip was firm.

'Good to meet you, Braden,' Mick said. 'I've been transferred here as the new police sergeant.'

'Congratulations. I heard old Sarge was thinking of retiring.' He turned back to Leah. 'Are you the new teacher at the school?'

'I am,' she said. 'I've got a meeting there this afternoon.'

Braden smiled. 'I know. With Callie Cartwright, my wife. She's looking forward to meeting you.'

'Oh, that's wonderful. And this is Petie. Do you have any brothers and sisters, Petie?' Leah crouched down and spoke to him face-to-face.

'I have two big brothers, Rory and Nigel, and a little brother and a little sister. They're twins, and they're babies, and really noisy, and Mum and Dad are always complaining that they don't get enough sleep.'

Braden chuckled. 'Yes, we're in that first six months stage when sleep is very precious when it does happen.'

'Something to look forward to when we start a family.' Mick grinned and gestured to the two couples who joined them, but before he could introduce them, Petie tugged on Braden's arm.

'Excuse me, Dad? Can I go and play outside?' He pulled his favourite metal car out of his pocket.

'As long as you don't go out the front. And watch out for snakes.'

'Okay, I will.' Petie headed off to a pile of dirt near the side fence.

'Lovely manners,' Leah commented.

'Most of the time. We've got good kids.'

Leah smiled. 'This is Gemma and Peter, and Chloe and Greg.

'Welcome to town,' Braden said as he shook hands with both men and smiled at the women.

'Peter's managing the store,' Mick added.

'The store?'

'We haven't put the sign up yet, but we're opening a department store in the other building,' Peter replied.

Braden whistled. 'Holy heck, that's a big step for all you guys. But great for our town.'

'Yes, we're a bit worried that maybe we've overcapitalised considering the size of the town, but nothing ventured, nothing gained, is our motto.'

'Don't worry, there's a fair-sized population on the outlying properties, and I know they'll be grateful not to have to drive to Charleville.' Braden chuckled. 'When I saw "New Life" on your truck, I thought you might've been setting up a church here.'

'Oh gosh, no,' Chloe said. 'We've come here to start our new life in the country.'

'You'll certainly make an impact on the town with the new store. What's this building for?'

'It's a storage shed, and at the back, we're opening an indoor and outdoor entertainment and function centre. If a band comes to town or if someone wants to get married or hold a party, we figured the town could use a venue,' Greg said. 'We did some research on the climate when we chose Augathella, and realised the heat would restrict a lot of outdoor functions.'

'We do have the pub, but even though it's a bit small, it's always busy. It's closed for renovations at the moment.'

Greg nodded and glanced at the others. 'Yes, we've bought the pub too. We're refurbishing that, and we're hoping to get it open in the next month or so.'

'You bought the pub too,' Braden exclaimed, his eyes wide. Who were these people—a fleet of trucks, two big sheds, and they'd bought the pub as well? 'Wow, what made you choose our town? Do you have connections here?'

'No, we don't.' Chloe looked sheepish. 'Well, when we all decided to move west, we pulled out a map and all put our fingers on it, and Augathella was the place we picked.'

'I'm pleased you chose us. So, hang on, are you building those new houses in Hill Street too?' he asked.

Chloe nodded. 'Yes, we bought up half a dozen empty houses. We made sure no one was planning on moving into them, and that they didn't belong to any families. We would hate to upset the town, and we've merged each of the two blocks into one. Leah and Mick, and Gemma and Peter, and

Greg and I, are moving down there when they're finished. Until then, we're going to bunk in the second shed.'

'We slept in there, last night,' Rosie said. 'It's pretty comfortable, and the guest amenities are certainly big enough for the eight of us to share for a while. Shouldn't be too long though till our farm homestead is ready.'

'Well, you're certainly busy.' Another thought struck him. 'Tell me, what about the butcher shop?'

Rosie nodded. 'Yes, we bought that too. After we chose Augathella, our partner in Brisbane had a look at what was for sale in town, and here we are. It was all Chloe's doing.'

'Well, Chloe, you're certainly the entrepreneur,' Braden said, blown away by this group of people. 'I don't think the town is going to know what's hit it. Crumbs, between the lot of you, you own more of the town than anyone. You'll be made very much welcome,' he said, smiling. 'Anyway, it's been great to meet you all and welcome again. Leah, I'll give Callie a call and organise a time for all of you to come out and visit us at *Kilcoy Station.* How would you like that?'

The girls beamed, and the guys nodded. 'That sounds fabulous. A great welcome to the community.'

***

Callie turned to her handbag as her phone beeped as she prepared the classroom for the first session of the day. The message was from Braden. '**Are you in class yet?**'

She hit speed dial and called him and he picked up straight away.

'Hi sweetie, what's up? Everything okay?'

'Yeah, everything's fine. Petie and I went to the park, and we met the people he was talking about with the "swirly" truck. There's quite a big concern happening in town. There are four couples in their group and they seem like good people. Leah, your teacher, is one of them, and her husband is the new sergeant. I mentioned that I'd speak to you and suggested that we have them all out for a barbeque on the weekend. I hope that's okay.'

'No, that's fine, as long as the twins get some sleep.'

'What about we invite Sophie and Kent, and Fallon and Jon too?'

'You must have been impressed to invite them out so soon.'

'Yeah, one of the guys is starting a small property, and he's a bit of a greenhorn. I think he'd appreciate having a couple of us to talk to.'

'Sounds good.'

'What about the others? What are they doing?'

'Lots of stories there; I'll tell you when I pick you up this afternoon. But it involves a new department store in town, the butcher shop, and would you believe they've bought the pub as well? And they're building all those houses in Hill Street.'

'Oh, my goodness, there will be some change in town. Anyway, I have to go, love; the bell's about to ring. I'll look forward to meeting them, and I'll see you this afternoon, sweetheart. Have a good day and drive safe. Bye.'

Chapter 9

'Another lovely welcome to town,' Rosie said to Chloe as she stocked the small kitchen in the back of the first shed. Braden had stayed for a cup of tea, and Rosie had made Petie a small milkshake. They had a great chat, found out a lot about the town, and added to their certainty that they had done the right thing.

'You're quiet today, Chloe. Are you okay?' Rosie asked.

Chloe smiled. She had something on her mind, and she was pretty sure that she was right. However, she was not going to breathe a word of it to anybody until she was certain or before she told Greg.

'Yeah, I'm fine, just a bit tired from that trip. I'm gonna go for a wander around the street later. Do you want to come for a walk, Rosie?'

'I promised Lex we'd go out and check out our farm and see how close the house is to moving in.'

'I keep forgetting that you've got the farm out there, and we're all in town,' Chloe said. 'Okay.' She reached over and hugged her friend. 'I'm going to go for a bit of a wander now. I'll see you when you get back from your farm.'

'Who'd a thought it?' Rosie grinned, and her cockney accent was strong.

'Meant to be, Rosie dear.' Chloe picked up her purse and walked out to the truck where Greg, Lex, Mick, and Peter were wrangling some extra heavy boxes to bring in. They had brought quite a bit of stock for the store in two of the trucks, and the other trucks held their furniture and personal possessions.

'I'm just going for a stroll down the street,' Chloe said.

'Okay, babe, catch you when you get back. Have fun.' Greg leaned over and kissed her.

'Don't overdo it,' she said. 'We don't have to rush to

unpack.' The four men had perspiration running down their faces, and their shirts were soaked.

'We won't,' Peter said.

Chloe didn't look at the Google map on her phone as she walked. As it was such a small town, if she got lost, it didn't matter. She knew the general direction of where their houses were, but she wouldn't go down and look at them until Greg was with her.

She walked down the main street and saw the hotel on the corner with several builders' utes parked outside. The butcher shop had newspapers over the front windows.

Chloe walked past one intersection and then saw the sign for the hospital. She smiled and then turned left into the street.

***

Laura had come into the hospital to do a couple of hours over the lunch break. Harry was in Charleville at yet another meeting, and she had antenatal checks for two pregnant women who had come in at lunchtime.

She'd just finished when Helen, the receptionist from the front counter, came in. 'Are you still here, Laura?

'I am. Just finished.'

'Great, there's a young woman at the front who was hoping to visit the clinic, and I said I wasn't sure if you were here. Are you happy to see another patient?'

'Of course, not a problem. What's her name?'

'Her name is Chloe Redman.'

'Sure, just ask her to take a seat in the waiting room, and I'll be out in a moment.'

'I'll give her a patient form to fill in,' Helen said.'

'Thank you.' Laura quickly tidied up the room. After having a wash, she made her way out to the waiting room.

'Chloe?' she said to the young woman sitting in the chair.

'Yes, I'm Chloe, thank you for seeing me.'

'Hello, I'm Sister Adnum, but please call me Laura. Come on in.'

Chloe was a stunningly beautiful young woman with black curls pulled back from her face, and her cheeks held a pretty pink flush. As she handed over the patient information form, big brown eyes looked directly at Laura as though she could see into her thoughts. A ripple of goosebumps ran down Laura's back.

'So, come on in, Chloe. Have a seat. What can I do for you?' She glanced down at the form.

'Well,' Chloe said, 'we've just moved to town.'

'Ah, I see you live in Hill Street.'

'Yes, we will be living there. We're waiting for our house to be finished. We're camping out at the sheds we've built near the park while we wait.'

'Oh, are you with Rosie? I met her there yesterday.'

'Yes, that's me, that's us. The rest of us arrived this morning.'

'Welcome to town. Now, what can I do for you?'

'I'm pregnant,' Chloe said, and a happy smile tilted her lips.

'You're sure you're pregnant? Have you done a pregnancy test?' Laura asked.

She shook her head. 'No, I haven't, but I know I'm pregnant.'

'So, let's do a pregnancy test. I can draw blood, and it will take a couple of days to come back, or if you are further along, a urine test will confirm your pregnancy today.'

'A urine test will be fine,' Chloe said calmly. 'It's just a confirmation for me so I can be sure when my husband asks for the proof.' She chuckled.

Fifteen minutes later, they were sitting back at Laura's desk.

'Well, Chloe, you were right. The urine test has confirmed your assumption.'

Laura was taken aback by the sudden tears rolling down her patient's face. 'So, were you trying to fall pregnant, or is it a surprise to you?'

The young woman dabbed at her tears, and her smile widened if that was possible. 'Greg, my husband, and I have been through three rounds of IVF, and we weren't successful. I knew I had to have faith, and I was right. This is a natural pregnancy.'

'Well, we'll have to take extra special care of you, won't we?'

Chloe nodded and smiled, and her eyes held Laura's intently.

'When are you due, Laura?'

'I'm sorry? You mean, when are you due?'

Chloe shook her head. 'No, I know the day I fell pregnant. It was two months ago, so I'm due at the end of September. I thought you were pregnant?'

'No, of course I'm not.' She frowned as Chloe's gaze ran down her front, and she placed a hand on her flat stomach.

'I'm sorry, Laura. I shouldn't have said anything. I'm sure you'll hear about me when you get to know the girls, but my intuition is nothing sinister. I just have this skill—I suppose you should call it—where I seem to know things. I'm sorry I blurted that out. I just got a very strong sense that you were carrying a baby.'

What a strange young woman. Perhaps she picked up the very strong sense that she would love to have a baby. Was her yearning so obvious?

'You take care of yourself, Chloe, and I'll get you to come and see Dr Higgins in the next week or so, and then I'm sure I'll see you at our clinic again in the next few weeks. Welcome to Augathella.'

Chapter 10

When Laura left the hospital, she called in at the small supermarket.

Harry would be tired after his meeting and the drive home, and she decided to prepare his favourite dinner. With the butcher being shut, she went straight to the back of the store and picked a small leg of lamb from the meat cabinet.

She knew Harry wouldn't be home for ages. So, she wandered along the aisles, taking more time than she usually did on her rushed weekly shopping trip. Her thoughts were churning, with that inappropriate comment that Chloe had made; there was no way she could be pregnant.

Laura found rosemary and quince gourmet gravy and added it to her basket. Then she walked down the confectionery aisle, added a small box of chocolates, and headed back to the cold section to pick out a frozen cheesecake. Loving cooking, she didn't often buy pre-packaged food, but tonight, the thought of cooking made her feel even more tired. It wouldn't hurt them to have a Sara-Lee cheesecake and packet gravy. It would give her time to sit down and put her feet up when she got home. She was back at work tomorrow, so an easy night watching a movie with Harry would be nice.

Debbie Allen, one of the regular cashiers at the supermarket, smiled at her as she unloaded her basket onto the counter.

'Hi Laura, how are you. Day off?'

'Hello, Debbie. Sort of. I've had a couple of days off, but I had to go into the clinic for a couple of hours this morning.'

'I saw you walk past across the road to the park with young Petie yesterday. Is he okay? He's not had a relapse, has he?' The whole town had pulled together last year when Petie had had a serious head injury.

'He's fine. He had a bit of an upset tummy, so I offered to look after him for Callie. We had a lovely day.'

'He's a sweet child, that miracle boy. Some of the things that he and those boys get up to and some of the things Peter comes out with, I laugh every time Callie brings him in here. I hope the twins are a bit quieter. You're their aunt, aren't you?' Debbie asked with a frown.

'Yes, I am. I don't know if you knew Julia, Braden's first wife and their mum. She was my sister.'

'I did. She was a beautiful girl.'

'Thank you. Anyway, I better get home and get this leg of lamb in the oven.'

'Looks like a special tea tonight. Birthday?'

'No, just a roast dinner.'

'I'll see you next time. Laura, don't work too hard.'

Laura breathed deeply as she walked home. The weather was still warm, and the air was dry, but despite the climate being so different to what she was used to, she still loved living here. She pushed aside her worries about Harry, but she would sit down and have a chat with him tonight.

And Chloe's strange words wouldn't leave her.

Chapter 11
Later that day

Rosie's excitement was bubbling over so much she didn't know if she could handle it as she stood in the middle of the huge storage shed and twirled around, looking at the hundreds and hundreds and hundreds of unopened boxes that still filled the space. They had done it—the first part of the dream was happening.

Chloe wandered over with Gemma. 'Are you all right there, Rosie? You look like you're going to burst.'

Rosie grabbed Chloe's shoulders and hugged her, then turned to Gemma and hugged her as well. 'I am just so happy.'

She knew when she got excited, her Cockney accent became more pronounced, and Chloe and Gemma smiled.

'Slow down, you're hard to understand sometimes, girlfriend.'

'I'm so excited. I can't believe we've done this. We're in a new town. The first stock has been unpacked. And while we've got to unpack the rest, I think we need to get onto the community Facebook page and start advertising for some young people to come and help us. What do you think, Chloe?'

'I think that's a great idea, but we have to wait until the rest of the shelves come down from Longreach tomorrow. The shop fitter is coming back to put the shelves for the goods in the storage area, and then we can get it all unpacked. He's going to do the shelves in the aisles of this front part for us first. It will give us a lot more room while we're camping here.'

'What about the third other shed they're planning to

build?' Gemma asked. 'We still haven't completely decided what to do with that one.'

'I think the boys are still talking about it, but I'm pretty sure they're going to turn it into a car showroom, and Mick says boats are a must.'

'Why on earth would anyone need a boat out here?' Leah asked.

Chloe laughed. 'You're such a coastie, Leah. There *is* a river and there are lots of big dams around. We'll have to take you yabby fishing.'

'Good, I love fishing.'

'Maybe we need to give that shed a bit more thought,' Rosie said. 'We've got enough work to keep us going for a while. How are the guys going with the pub?'

'They've got onto this great builder from Tambo,' Chloe said.

'Tambo, that's a funny name,' Rosie commented.

'Yeah, it's a cute little town just up the way, and it's really progressive. There's an art gallery there and a couple of smaller galleries plus a community centre and three or four pubs. It's only a small town. I don't think it's as big as our town.'

'I like the sound of that, *our* town.' Rosie smiled.

'Anyway, the pub is going well. He reckons he can have it open again in three weeks. I guess the community hasn't been happy with losing their watering hole,' Chloe said.

'How about,' Rosie put her head on the side, 'while the pub is being refurbished, how hard would it be to move the pub to the shed next door while we work on this one?'

'But we wouldn't have a license to sell alcohol.'

'We could use the licence for the pub; we own the pub and the licence. We could just move the premises while it's being refurbished. I can't see a problem with that. I'll run it by the guys later and make some inquiries. I'll ring the council and everything or whoever I have to ring—maybe a liquor board.'

'Sounds good to me. Robert, the butcher who the guys hired to run the shop, has had a good look around, and there's hardly anything that needs doing down there. We're just going to order some gourmet products from Brisbane and get it flown out so we've got some different stuff to the normal cuts of beef and lamb and chicken.'

'And the new houses are going well,' Leah said. 'They've found another six that they're going to refurbish.'

'Do we really have enough time to do all this?' Chloe said.

'Don't you start doubting now; this was all your idea, and it was the most wonderful idea.'

'I still can't believe we pulled it off in just a few short months.' Gemma's eyes were wide as she shook her head. 'It's incredible how everything is going to plan.'

'And Rob was a great help. And yes, the universe is looking out for us. I always knew it would,' Chloe said. 'I had no doubt, and I think if we stay positive and keep in mind our reasons for what we're doing, it's going to be absolutely wonderful. Give it six months, and then we'll see what the town looks like.'

'The only thing I'm worried about,' Rosie said with a frown, 'is that the locals might see us as interlopers. I mean, I imagine a lot of people would've lived here most of their lives, and here comes the eight of us bowling into town, buying the pub, buying the butcher shop, and changing things that they've always had.'

'But look what we're doing,' Leah said. 'We're starting new facilities, and we're offering more in the existing businesses. And we'll create jobs for the locals, too.'

'It's hard with the pub being renovated, we sort of can't go anywhere and meet anyone,' Gemma said.

Rosie answered quickly. 'Lex is organising that with Braden Cartwright. He was going to talk to the guys about it this afternoon. Have some sort of function here. But I guess if we go with the idea of having a temporary pub, we can have the complimentary welcome do to start with and invite the town, and then have the pub open here for the next two or three weeks. We'd get to know a lot of people that way.'

'See, we're not just coming in and taking over the town; we're coming in and providing lots of services.'

'Well, let's just take it easy and wait and see that we don't put a step wrong.' Chloe's eyes were bright, and her voice was full of confidence. 'I think it's time we grabbed our men and went down and had a look at our new houses.'

Chapter 12

Laura was sitting on the back patio with a drink when she heard the front door open. She'd put a wine glass out for Harry, too, and had a bottle cooling in an ice cooler on the table, along with a small tray of nibbles. She stood and went to the sliding door and called out, 'I'm out the back, Harry. I've got a wine ready for you.'

'Thanks, love. I'll be a minute. I want to take a quick shower. I feel like I've got the whole of Charleville Hospital on me today; it's been a busy couple of days.'

'I missed you,' she said. Harry simply smiled as he headed for the bathroom.

Laura sat out there for ten minutes and waited, and eventually, Harry came out, his damp hair slicked back, looking casual in a pair of shorts and a short-sleeved T-shirt. He reached over and kissed her cheek.

'You look refreshed and rested,' he said.

'I am, even though Petie nearly wore me out yesterday. And then Deb called me into the hospital today for a couple of hours.'

Harry chuckled. 'How is the little monkey?'

'He's a beautiful boy.'

'I think you have a soft spot for your almost youngest nephew, not forgetting Munro.'

'I didn't see the twins. They were already at Ruth's when I met Callie and Petie yesterday morning. But I did see Rory and Nigel in the afternoon. They were full of beans as usual, too.'

Harry sat back and closed his eyes as Laura poured his glass of wine. She put it on the coaster in front of him and sat back, letting him rest.

A lazy late summer afternoon with only the soothing drone of a mower two or three doors and the occasional bird squawking down the back in the thicket of bush broke the comfortable silence.

Eventually, Harry stretched and reached for his wine. 'Thank you. This will go down well.'

'A busy couple of days?'

'Not so much bad as busy. The meeting with the remote specialists yesterday was good, but the meeting with the hospital board at Charleville today was stressful. I managed to have about three wins.'

'That's good.' Laura looked at him intently. 'No more news about our maternity ward closing again?'

'No, we managed to come to an agreement, and we've been given a three-month reprieve. But we need to have more women coming through for their antenatal check-ups to make them realise it's a viable service.'

Laura sighed. 'I know they think about the money. We've got the staffing and the board, and we have a small community who would like to see their local hospital retain its services.'

'If the board down in Charleville gets their way, the whole hospital will become an aged-care facility. I could see the town in a few years, not even having a doctor in it, to be truthful.'

'But you can't expect people to travel eighty kilometres for medical help.'

Harry shrugged. 'It's the way things are going. They can't get enough staff out here; they can't get doctors.'

'Okay, let's talk about something nice. You've been doing this stuff all day. You don't want to spend the evening talking about politics and hospitals and medical services.'

'True. I've been thinking, Laura. Maybe we should go away for a week or even a couple of days next time we both have time off at the same time.'

'That would be nice. Where would we go? Maybe we could fly somewhere from Charleville. Do something really exciting.'

'Do you think we're in a bit of a rut?' Harry's tone was serious, and a quiver of uncertainty ran through Laura.

'Oh no, I didn't mean that,' she said. 'I didn't think we were in a rut at all. Do you?' she asked carefully.

Harry was silent for a moment, but he held her gaze. Eventually, he shook his head. 'No, of course I don't.' As soon as he spoke, he stood up and finished the wine that was in his glass. 'I'm going to go and put the news on. Are you going to come inside shortly?'

'Yes, I have to come in and turn the vegetables over.'

'Smells good, love,' he said. 'I'll see you inside.'

Laura sat out there for a moment and couldn't help the tears prickling in her eyes. Somehow, their closeness seemed to have lessened over the past few months. She hadn't noticed it at first; they were only little things. But now, Harry didn't seem as invested in their relationship as he had been twelve months ago.

She took a deep breath and stood up. She was strong; she had been through the loss of a relationship before, and at that time, it had been exacerbated by the loss of their child, their stillborn baby. She closed her eyes to stop tears from forming, realising she had to pull herself together. She had a lot to be thankful for. She couldn't expect Harry to be Romeo; for goodness' sake, he was not far off fifty. He'd had a long and happy first marriage, and they had been together for only a little while. They had settled into a relationship like a comfortable pair of shoes, and that's what she had to be happy with.

'Thank you,' Harry said as he picked up the napkin that Laura had placed in the centre of the table and dabbed his mouth. 'That was beautiful. Thank you, Laura. It's exactly what I needed.' As well as eating the roast lamb, baked vegetables, and a healthy-sized piece of cheesecake, Harry drank half the bottle of wine.

She smiled as some of the tension that had built over the past two days left her as he held her gaze, her limbs loose and her confidence building. That silly young woman at the hospital had really unsettled her for a while. 'Harry, can I ask you something?'

'Of course, you can.' He stood and turned to the small living room adjacent to the kitchen. 'Come and sit with me.'

'Doesn't matter.'

'Come on. What did you want to ask me?'

Laura's confidence fled. She didn't want to ask Harry outright whether he was a little bit over having her as a new partner because she knew he was honest and would tell the truth, and she didn't want to hear it.

'Okay, I've heard about this fantastic new series on Netflix, and I was hoping you'd watch it with me tonight. Maybe the first or second episodes. We could snuggle up on the couch,' she suggested. 'I'll leave the dishes till the morning. It's my last day off.'

Harry shook his head. 'I'm sorry, love. I'm too tired to watch a series. I'm going to go to bed as soon as I help you clear the kitchen, but you stay up and watch your show. I'll just go to bed and get some sleep.'

##

Laura yawned as she switched the television off. She had enjoyed the first two episodes of the new series and had smiled a couple of times when she heard Harry's gentle snores coming from their bedroom.

The series episodes had been a little bit sad, and she wiped away a couple of tears. However, the end of the second episode left her with a smile on her face, and she was heading off to bed feeling a little bit happier.

Even though Harry hadn't watched the movie with her, they'd had a lovely evening before he went to bed.

She reached over and picked up the cushion, holding it against her as she walked to the end of the lounge to reposition them. Even though it was a little rented cottage, Laura had added lots of homely touches. She had done an interior design course when she had been in New Zealand and enjoyed having a nice space to live in. She frowned as the cushion moved; her breast was tender. She placed the cushion carefully on the end of the three-seater sofa, moved her fingers along the soft tissue and felt around. There was no doubt about it. Her right breast was tender. Her mouth dried. Her aunt had breast cancer when she was in her forties, but Laura had taken the test and wasn't carrying the gene.

Still, it would be worth going to Charleville and having a mammogram. She moved her fingers gently and slowly over to her left breast and frowned when it was tender too. It was the sort of tenderness that she used to have when she was in her teens when her period was due.

She sat on the lounge and thought for a moment, and suddenly a cold feeling ran through her as Chloe's question came back to her, quickly followed by a gush of joy.

Surely she couldn't be pregnant. They used contraception. No, she couldn't be.

There was only one way to check.

But there was no way she was going to do a pregnancy test at the hospital on her day off or buy one from the local pharmacy, so she would go down to Charleville and do it.

Her thoughts went rapidly around her head as she walked down the hallway to the bedroom. Harry's gentle snores were still puffing away. She climbed into bed and lay beside him with her eyes wide open. There was a tight muscle twinge down in her lower belly like she'd had early in her first pregnancy. Laura moved her hand down gently on her nightie, feeling the firmness at the base of her stomach.

Surely not? Oh, my God, what was Harry going to say just when she was wondering whether he was ready to end their relationship?

She *could* be pregnant, but the worry was superseded by the happiness that flooded through her. She knew Harry would do the right thing by her, even if they weren't a couple anymore. And if she was pregnant, it would mean that she'd have the baby she'd always wanted.

Laura's eyes closed, and she went to sleep with a smile on her face.

Chapter 13

Laura sat in the new coffee shop near the central intersection of the main street in Charleville as she worked up her courage. Her trip to Charleville had been timely as Harry had a delivery to pick up from the hospital there, and she offered to get it while she was in town.

'Not like you to go to Charleville, Laura,' he asked with a smile. 'What are you up to down there?'

'I just thought I'd like to get a couple of new things for the house. I need a vase for the kitchen. Jenny gives me so many flowers; I'd like to have a bigger vase to put on the kitchen table.'

Harry nodded. 'Well, you have a lovely day.' He gave her an absent-minded kiss on the cheek and headed out to the car to go to work at the hospital. He was certainly preoccupied, and she tried not to put too much emphasis on the cause of his preoccupation being their relationship.

He was very professional and rarely talked about any of the issues he faced at the hospital, but she knew it was a difficult job.

She went to one of the chemists in town and lingered outside until it was almost empty. She walked in, and unfortunately, when she picked up the pregnancy kit at the front counter, the woman looked at her.

'Oh, you're the midwife at the hospital at Augathella. I suppose you need this for some of the young women up there.'

Laura looked at her and nodded. She didn't want to get into a conversation about what she was buying. She paid for it and quickly added a few other things to her purchase so it didn't look too obvious that's what she came in for.

She made her way to the coffee shop, and now she was

sitting there with a latte and a slice of cake that tasted like straw.

Would she do it here or would she do it at home?

No, she would do it here. Finishing off her coffee and pushing the half-eaten cake away, Laura stood and made her way out to the street.

There was a block of public amenities at the back of the park, and she knew that they were clean. Taking a deep breath, she picked her bag up and headed down the street.

***

Harry had a quiet day at the hospital. He'd seen a couple of patients from the aged-care wing, and there had been a student from the primary school with a sprained ankle. Callie had brought the young boy in before his parents arrived, and Harry had him X-rayed, bandaged, and in the waiting room before they arrived; they had given their permission over the phone as they lived on a property an hour out of town.

'How are you, Callie?' he asked. 'How are you going with those twins of yours? Laura keeps me in the loop. She says they're growing fast.'

'Yes, they are.'

'We must get together,' Harry said.

'Braden and I are thinking about having a barbecue at our place to welcome some of the new people in town. You and Laura would be most welcome to come out.'

'Sounds good.'

'I'll keep in touch.'

'I did wonder what was going on in town,' he said. 'Laura mentioned this morning that she met a couple while I was away. So, you're back at work, Callie? How are you coping? Not too tired? You've got a big load.'

'I have, but Braden is wonderful, so I'm very good. How about you, Harry?' she said. 'I'm not asking as a doctor; I'm asking as a friend.'

He chuckled. 'I'm good. Just a bit preoccupied.'

'Everything okay?'

'Everything is really okay; I've just got a bit on my mind,' he said.

'Well, if you ever need anyone to chat to, I'm sure Laura is there for you. But if you need to talk about anything else, I think we're close enough friends, and you and Braden are good mates. Anyway, I'd better get back to school. I'll get Braden to give you a call once this barbeque is organised.'

'Thanks, Callie, you're a good friend.'

Harry glanced at his watch; Laura should be home by now. He might go home and have lunch with her. It was so quiet here. He knew he'd been a little bit distant lately, but the decision he had to make was a big one, and he wanted to give it lots of thought; he didn't want to pressure her into anything that she didn't want to do.

He decided to walk home to get a bit of exercise and was pleased as he turned into their street and saw Laura's car in the driveway.

He tapped lightly on the door before he pushed it open. 'Laura, it's only me. I've come home for lunch.'

All was quiet. He walked through the house, but there was no sign of her, apart from some parcels on the kitchen table, and it didn't look like any of them would hold a very big vase.

He walked through the laundry and closed his eyes at the familiar smell. The old-fashioned laundry had a concrete floor and a concrete tub that reminded him of his childhood when they had a similar set-up in Maryborough. The same damp concrete smell brought back some nostalgic feelings. He missed his family; his parents had long passed away, and he had been an only child. Over the past few years, his aunt and uncles had all gone as well. Now, he was pretty much the only Higgins left.

He went down the three steps that led to the back door and pushed it open. There she was, sitting on the back porch.

Laura jumped and put a hand to her chest. 'Oh, Harry, you gave me a fright.'

'I came home to have lunch with you. What are you doing out here?'

Laura's eyes were full of tears, and he hurried over and sat beside her, picking up both of her hands and holding them tightly.

'Sweetheart, what's wrong? Are you all right? You're not sick, are you? Nothing's happened, has it? Did you get some bad news from New Zealand?'

'I'm fine; it's just a few things I want to talk to you about. But first of all, I want to ask you one thing.' Her eyes were wide as she held his.

'Ask away, sweetheart.'

Her eyes brightened at the endearment, and she squeezed his hands back. 'Just one question, Harry. I just want to ask you one thing.'

He was quiet as he looked at her, and her eyes held his as she asked, 'Do you still love me?' Tears hovered on her lower lashes.

Harry's eyes widened and distress crossed his face. 'Sweetheart, I'm so sorry I've been preoccupied lately, and I feel terrible you have to ask that. The answer is a simple yes. Of course, I love you; I couldn't imagine life without you, Laura. I adore you; you've pre-empted me. There's something I've been working up to asking you, but I've been giving it a lot of thought first. That's why I've been quiet. I didn't want to pressure you.'

'I thought you were wanting to break up with me,' she said. 'You've been so quiet.'

'Love, I'm so sorry. Come here.' Harry stood and lifted Laura to her feet, and then he sat down and gestured for her to sit on his knee.

He wrapped his arms around her waist and rested his cheek against hers.

'Laura Adnum, you have no idea how much I love you. I thought love had gone forever for me when Jenny died, but then I met you. I was going to take you away and find a beautiful place. I was going to ask you to marry me.'

She drew a short breath, and her eyes widened. 'You . . . you want to marry me?'

'Of course I want to marry you. With all my heart. Laura, my dear love, will you do me the honour of becoming Mrs Higgins?'

Laura's arms went around his neck as he held her. 'Harry . . . oh, Harry, I love you so much. Of course, I'll marry you, but you might not want to marry me when I tell you my news.'

'Why? What's wrong? Why were you sitting out here crying?'

As he watched her, her lower lip trembled. 'Come on, sweetheart. Tell me what's wrong.'

'Harry? I'm pregnant; you're going to be a dad.'

Chapter 14

The three boys ran ahead as Callie and Braden put the twins into the double stroller When Braden had called into the shed earlier in the week to invite them out to the station the new owners had asked if he would mind having a function at the shed on Saturday night instead of coming out to *Kilcoy Station.*

'But we'd love to come out there soon,' Greg had assured him.

'Not a problem at all, mate,' he replied. 'This way, you can get to know more of the townsfolk in one go.'

'We've had a lot of people calling in. There's been interest in the place and lots of questions. So, we figured that if we have everyone here on Saturday night, we can get the usual pub crowd and have a bit of a talk about what we're doing in town.'

'Sounds good to me,' Braden had said.

Callie and Braden were surprised to see how many cars had pulled up on the road between the park and the two new buildings. Most of the townspeople would've walked there tonight, so it appeared there was a lot of interest from people living on outlying properties. Craig Wilson and Quinn Calthorpe had told him they wouldn't miss it. Jon and Fallon were coming, and Ruth said she was keen to see it too.

Sophie and Kent were already here; he'd noticed their car parked at the end of the road near the church. Harry and Laura had said that they'd be here too. Braden bumped into them at the supermarket, and from their purchases, it was apparent they were having some sort of celebratory meal.

'That's good because Laura looked a bit off the other day, and Harry looked tired when I saw him at the hospital. Whatever was bothering him, he must've got it sorted,' Callie said when he told her that he'd seen them.

'I'm sure we'll find out if there's any news,' Braden said.

'What sort of news do you mean?' Callie asked with a frown. 'They're not moving away, are they?'

Braden tried to look innocent and shrugged. He hadn't told Callie he'd noticed the ring on Laura's finger. It was up to Laura and Harry to share their news, and there was a chance he might have misunderstood. It could be a ring from her previous marriage.

Callie drew a sharp breath as they pushed the pram around the back of the first building and looked up at Braden. Her eyes were wide.

'It's pretty incredible, isn't it?' he said.

'How can somebody do something with the previously dry grass, and now it looks like a fairy garden?' she said.

Braden looked around. 'They must have used some damn good fertiliser when they put the turf down.'

He knew they'd had landscapers up from Charleville, and they'd done a mighty fine job of getting a beautiful lawn from the back of the big paved area that came off the edge of the shed. There were dozens of tables with wine glasses and tea lights and fairy lights hanging above them from the pergola that somehow already had standard roses growing through the slats.

It looked like a wedding venue, and from all accounts, the group were planning on having functions like that at the back of the shed.

Sophie and Kent were standing at the edge of the lawn, Kent nursing Ruby as they chatted with Emily and Luke.

Sophie's eyes were wide, and she was saying, 'You pair, I do not believe it.'

Jenna and Josh walked over and joined them as Braden and Callie approached.

'I know,' Jenna said. 'I was lucky enough to be—well you could call me the bridesmaid but I suppose I was the witness.'

Callie looked curiously at Emily, and Emily held up her

left hand, and then Luke held up his too. Shiny gold wedding rings were on their ring fingers.

'Go on, get out of it. Don't tell me you two snuck off and got married?'

'Yes, we did. Last Saturday. We couldn't wait for the pub to reopen to have our reception, so we decided we wanted to get married straight away.'

'Congratulations!' There were hugs and kisses all around as people came up and congratulated Luke and Emily. Ophelia put her cheek up, insisting on a kiss each time someone kissed Emily's cheek. 'Kiss me, kiss me too,' she said.

'Anyway,' Emily looked up at Luke, 'Tell them what you've just decided and organised, love.'

'We are going to be the first wedding function here at "The Shed" in a couple of weeks,' he said.

'Greg was saying that they've got a liquor license, and they're refurbishing the pub, the downstairs bars, the restaurant and the bistro, and the upstairs rooms, and it's going to take a little bit longer than they thought, so they're going to get this one off the ground. It's sort of going to be like a semi-pub with drinks every afternoon, and they've got Sean over from the pub to cook meals in the shed until the pub is ready.'

'Cook, where can he cook?' Braden asked. 'Do they know how fussy Sean is?'

Sophie looked at Braden. 'Go in there, bro, and have a look. There's a whole commercial kitchen in the back of that second shed. It's supposed to be storage for the stuff they're putting in the shop shed.' As she was speaking, Greg and Chloe walked over.

'Hi, everyone, welcome to "The Shed".'

Chloe looked up at her husband with a smile. 'Everyone in town had been referring to it as "the shed". We've decided that we're going to call our new department store and function venue "The Shed". What do you think about that?'

Braden grinned. 'Works for me. Just what the town needs.'

'Anyway, guys, come and sit down, grab a drink. I hope you didn't bring anything because it's all on us tonight.'

Greg walked away and greeted the next group of people. Sophie leaned over to Braden. 'How can they afford all this? My goodness, they've bought at least six houses in town. Lex and Rosie, who I met earlier, have got a little property out on the river. They built these two sheds. They're refurbishing the pub, which they bought, and they've bought the butcher shop. That's all that we know about.'

'None of our business, Sophie. Maybe they've come into an inheritance or something. Anyway, they all seem like really good people, and I think it's great that they've come to town and given Augathella a big injection of enthusiasm and rebuilding.'

'Oh, I'm not criticising,' she said. 'I think it's wonderful. But look, they're feeding a third of the district tonight, and Sean is in there in his absolute element.'

'Let's just enjoy ourselves.' Braden hugged his sister. 'Anyway, sis, you're looking well. Getting a bit more sleep than we are, I guess.'

'She's a little beauty, just like her mum. Very well-behaved, very serene, very quiet.'

Braden laughed so loudly that Callie turned around. 'What are you two fighting about now?'

It was a wonderful evening with two stand-out moments.

The first one was when Greg and the rest of the group who had come to town stood up and told the townsfolk what their plans were. After outlining everything they were doing, there was a huge round of applause, and Braden was pleased to see how happy they all looked.

The second highlight of the night was the one that he had suspected, and he kept his face bland. When Dr Harry took the microphone after Greg finished speaking, he announced that Laura had agreed to marry him.

Again, there was a standing ovation. Dr Harry had come to town a year ago and met Braden's sister-in-law, and they had fallen in love.

'Soph, can you keep an eye on the twins for us?' Braden tugged at Callie's hand. 'Come on, we're going to be the first to congratulate them.'

He walked over and held out his arms to Laura. 'Congratulations, sis. I'm pleased. You couldn't have picked a nicer guy.' He turned around and shook Harry's hand. 'You look after my sister-in-law, won't you, Dr Harry?'

'I certainly will.'

The night was full of joy as the children ran around the paddocks until well after dark.

Braden smiled at Callie as the three boys and the twins all fell asleep as soon as the car started.

Chapter 15
The wedding

Braden had been chuffed when Laura had asked him to give her away at the wedding. And Callie blinked back tears when Laura had asked her to be her bridesmaid along with Jenny Riley.

Jenny had harrumphed a few times. 'I'm too old to be a bridesmaid.'

'Well, you're my matron of honour if you don't want to be bridesmaid,' Laura said. 'I'm so grateful for your friendship over the past few months, Jenny.'

Emily and Luke's wedding breakfast at "The Shed" had been a huge success the weekend following the welcome dinner. The pub was open again and doing a roaring trade.

Now, on this last weekend in March, Laura, Callie, and Jenny were at the Higgins house getting ready to go to "The Shed" for the ceremony and reception.

Harry stayed overnight at Riley's house with Tom, who was his best man.

'I'm so sorry that Ben and Amelia have gone away,' Jenny said as they were waiting to be picked up by Kent in a vintage car loaned by Craig Wilson's father. They would've so enjoyed these last few weeks in town.' Amelia and Ben had taken the baby up to the Foley property in the Gulf country to spend some time with her parents

'Oh my God, Laura, you look absolutely beautiful,' Jenny said.

Laura's dress was off the shoulder with lace cap sleeves. The dress was slim-fitting and had a short train sweeping from the back.

'You're glowing.' Callie held her breath as Laura put her hand on her flat stomach and smiled.

A secret smile.

'There's a reason for that,' she said, 'but we're not making it public yet.'

'Oh Laura, you're having a baby!' Jenny said.

Laura nodded. 'We are, but it's just between the three of us for the time being. We're waiting to tell everyone until I get to the three-month mark.'

'Here's the car now,' Callie said as she heard a car door close in the driveway. Her heart filled with love as Braden came to the door looking handsome in his good suit.

'Ready, Laura?' he asked.

'I am. More than ready.' Laura was cool and calm as she took the hand that Braden held out to her.

It only took a few minutes to drive to "The Shed".

Callie was taken aback by the number of locals standing on the side of the footpath as the vintage car made its way slowly down the streets. Cheers and waves came from all ages, from school children to the folk from the aged-care facility; Harry and Laura were well-loved by the community, even after only a year in town. And once again Callie's heart filled as she felt proud to be a member of this community.

Tears pricked her eyes as she spotted Rory, Nigel, and Petie standing on the footpath near the park in the suits they'd hired for them in Charleville.

They all looked so grown up, and Rory was the image of Braden. She grinned as she noticed Nigel pulling at the neck of his shirt.

Dear Nigel, he was their character, that's for sure.

Braden helped Laura from the front of the car and waited while Jenny and Callie climbed out of the back seat. They were both dressed in matching soft peach dresses.

The boys walked ahead, and soon, the strands of the Wedding March drifted from inside the building.

Laura was serene as Braden waited with her beside the flower-decked arch at the door. Nigel and Rory followed Petie and led Jenny and Callie down the aisle to the front of the room, where the celebrant waited with Harry and Tom Riley.

The music swelled, and Callie's eyes filled with tears as Braden escorted his sister-in-law down the aisle, and Harry took her hand, love shining from his face.

***

Rosie stood with Chloe at the edge of the lawn. 'We've done good,' she said softly.

'Yes, it was a lovely wedding,' Chloe said. They watched as Harry swept Laura around the dance floor.

Rosie shook her head. 'Yes, the wedding was lovely, but I mean, we've made a good choice. I think we're all going to be very happy in this town.'

'We are. Very happy. We'll raise our families here, and we'll leave part of ourselves in this town when we move on,' Chloe said. Her eyes held that faraway look. 'Augathella is a very special place,' she said softly.

An Augathella Easter

ANNIE SEATON

Augathella Short and Sweet: 6

Chapter 1
Spring - Eight months after Dr Harry and Laura's wedding

The minute Bec Hunter met Chloe and Rosie, newcomers to town and proprietors of the New Life store and several other businesses, she knew instantly they were good people. It didn't take her long to get to know the girls: a couple of coffee dates at Jenna's Vintage Tea Room and one hilarious trivia night at the renovated pub with her partner, Matt and the girls' partners, Greg and Lex, saw a budding friendship firm up.

When the four new couples arrived in town back in March last year, Matt and Bec had been away. Bec was attending an intensive training course for her new job as a community youth worker at the Choice for Youth Centre in Charleville, and Matt had been catching up with some friends in Brisbane.

When they returned to Augathella after three months away, they were stunned by the changes that had taken place in town in that time.

Not only had they missed the arrival of the four new couples, the establishment of the new store, the pub renovations, and the new houses being built, but they'd also missed Harry and Laura's wedding.

'That'll teach us to stay put,' Matt said. He'd arrived in town with the nickname of the drifter, but since he and Bec had got together, Matt had taken to small-town life like a duck to water.

Bec grinned on the way home from Brisbane when he recounted the reaction of his city friends to the news that he had settled happily in the small town out west. 'They're running bets on how long I'll last,' he said, shaking his head.

'But I'm not going anywhere.'

'You'd better not be,' Bec said, squeezing his arm.

Life was good.

Bec and Matt had settled into a happy and contented relationship; he'd stayed at her house—and insisted on taking over the mortgage payments—and now she'd started her new job as a leader of the youth workers at the new community youth centre.

As the months passed and the four new couples settled into town, their friendship grew even more. They had a lot in common, and Matt loved playing with Travis, Chloe and Greg's little boy.

'I had the best night tonight,' Matt said as they walked home from the pub after collecting their prize for winning the trivia night. 'How amazing are those guys? So much energy.'

Bec slipped her arm through his.

'How amazing are you?' she said, leaning into Matt. 'You have an excellent knowledge of history. I thought you'd know all the song questions, but you blitzed the history ones, too.'

'I was a model student at school,' Matt said, grinning down at her.

'That's not what you've told me before. Or what your mates said when they visited at Christmas.'

'Well, I enjoyed learning about the outback and the explorers. I fluked most of those answers tonight. But hey, I really enjoy spending time with those guys. They're fun. And Chloe has a wicked sense of humour.'

'She sure does.'

'I thought Gladys Tingle was going to come over and chip her for laughing so loudly. If looks could kill . . .'

'I saw that. Poor Gladys. She does like to be around everyone, but then she always looks so sour and disapproving.' Bec smiled up at Matt. 'You were kind to her tonight.'

'I think she's lonely. I did have a bit of a chat with her.

So did Chloe.'

'I didn't see that,' Bec said.

'You were talking to the Cartwrights. And how cute are those kids?'

Matt loved kids, no matter their age, but Bec had never had much to do with them. She had no family close by, and working in the aged care unit had made her wary of spending time with little ones. She had no idea what to do.

'Chloe's a good person. She brings happiness wherever she goes,' she agreed. 'I've had a lot to do with her and Rosie lately. Not so much with Leah and Gemma, but they seem nice too,' Bec said. 'The things they've done in town since they arrived here are almost unbelievable.'

'A breath of fresh air. And *young* fresh air,' Matt agreed. 'It's certainly given our town a lift.'

Our town.

Bec smiled. Matt had really settled into Augathella since he'd drifted in last year in his old van. And she had to admit that in the five years she'd lived here, she had settled too.

But he was right. The residents of the town had taken the enthusiasm of the new arrivals on board; houses were painted, extensions completed, gardens tidied up, and fences replaced. A new broom had certainly come to Augathella.

'And the population's growing too,' Matt continued. 'How cute is Chloe and Greg's little fella?'

Bec knew that Matt was looking at her, but she pretended to look at the seedlings that Gladys Tingle had planted along the footpath at the front of her house.

'Wow, look how many seedlings Gladys has planted out,' she said, pointing to the array of seedlings planted out in neat lines.

That was the one sticking point in their relationship, and it was the reason Bec kept saying no every time Matt mentioned marriage. He wanted kids soon; Bec wanted a career, and even though her new job was a total change of direction from nursing and studying for her Masters degree in dementia, she loved it. Working with young people—even though many were troubled—was refreshing.

'Hmm,' he said, putting his arm around her shoulder as they turned the corner to their house.

Bec took a deep breath; they'd had such a fun night, and she didn't want to get into a discussion now. When Matt had moved in with her while his arm healed after the accident when he'd saved Petie Cartwright at Sophie and Kent's wedding, Bec had no idea that he would end up moving in permanently. She'd had plans to finish her degree and move to Cairns, and then she'd gone and fallen in love with Matt Randall. She'd learned about his sad past, losing his girlfriend, Marianne, in a car accident that he'd been blamed for, and their love had grown.

And she loved him more every day; she just wasn't ready to have kids yet.

One day, she was sure she'd be ready.

Bec stopped at the fence on the far side of Gladys' property and looked up at Matt. His eyes were shadowed, and she knew she'd put the shadows there.

'I'm sorry, love. You know I'm not ready.' She tried to lighten her words. 'Anyway, with Laura and Harry's new little Henry and Chloe and Greg's Travis, there's no room for more babies in town. Not this year anyway.'

'You'd better tell Sophie and Kent that.' Matt smiled down at her, but she knew him well enough to know his smile was forced.

'Sophie's pregnant again?'

'Yes, Kent told me when I saw him at the pub the other night. I didn't tell you because I didn't want you to think I was pressuring you.' Matt reached down and lifted a stray lock of hair from her cheek. 'And I'm not, love. I just wish you'd agree to marry me.'

'Maybe Gladys' garden isn't the right place to be having this conversation.' Bec reached up and kissed his cheek.

'Let's go home, and we'll talk about it,' Matt said

hopefully.

Chapter 2
Bec – mid-summer

New gardens had been planted in every street in town, and blossoms began to appear on trees and shrubs.

January was quiet, with a few changes in town. The newcomers who had given a lift to an already lovely town relaxed and settled into their jobs.

Bec smiled as Matt backed the van out of the driveway one night in early February. At home, after the trivia night, Matt had agreed he was happy to wait until Bec had settled into her new career.

'Ask me at Easter,' she said. 'A proper proposal. And until then, just know how much I love you. Okay?'

'I can do that.' His smile was wide. 'I love you too, Bec. And if you don't want to get married, that's okay.'

'Easter,' she said as he bent to kiss her.

Tonight, Matt was singing at the Tambo pub, and Chloe, Greg, Rosie, and Lex were travelling up in Matt's van with them. Ruth Mason had offered to mind Travis. There was plenty of room for all of them, as well as Matt's sound gear.

'Thanks for taking us, mate,' Lex said as he climbed in after Rosie.

'You might as well have me as driver, and then, if you want, you can have a drink or two.' One thing Matt never did was have even one beer when he was driving. Bec knew that he still carried emotional scars from the tragedy that had led to him leaving his life and career in Cairns four years ago.

Bec was pleased that Matt got along so well with their new friends. The guys had been off on a couple of camping weekends together—male bonding, Matt called it—and their social life had gotten even busier. Her new job took up a lot of her free time, but she loved what she did.

The evening was so still and warm that Matt had set up to play outside. The evening sky was a soft apricot, and a gentle breeze took away the lingering heat of the summer's day as they sat at the edge of the lawn in front of the outside bar.

The crowd was quickly building; Matt's reputation had spread. His gigs at small local pubs each weekend were attracting sizable crowds.

As he set up, the others chatted, and Bec's thoughts drifted to the issue that had been nagging at her for the last week. She sighed and looked over the paddock behind the pub.

'That was a big sigh. You sound like you've got the weight of the world on your shoulders. What's wrong?' Chloe asked as she passed over the wine that Greg had bought for Bec at the bar.

'Thanks. I'm just trying to nut out the Easter camp. We've got some funding, and I've got enough to hire two new youth workers, but that doesn't leave enough to run a camp for the ages I want to include.'

'There's a lot of interest already,' Chloe said as she sipped her soft drink. 'We were out at the Cartwrights last weekend, and Nigel and Rory were telling us about it. It's for all ages, is it?'

'We're hoping for ten and up. Since the national fitness camps have ended, there's nothing for the upper primary school kids. They have their end of Year Six school camp, but there's a need for more.' Bec held her hands up and shook her head at Chloe. 'And please don't think I'm asking you for money. I'll get a grant.'

'I wouldn't ever think that, sweetie. I simply asked why you sighed.' Chloe's eyes were wide and innocent.

Bec rolled her eyes when Rosie and Chloe exchanged a significant glance.

'No, you're not giving me money for what I need. I'm in the middle of applying for funds and grants, and I'll get enough.'

'Tell us more about this Easter camp. Can we help? Can we come and volunteer? Can we cook or something?'

'Volunteers would be awesome,' Bec said. 'But you have to have your working with children checks and all the paperwork filled out, and I need to do risk assessments for all activities.'

'Sounds like you'll be busy,' Rosie said.

'I will be, but I love every minute of it,' Bec said with a smile.

'Where's it being held?'

'I think I've found a venue. It's far enough away from Augathella, so it will be new to the kids. There's this lake no one seems to have heard of. It's at the back of Quinn Calthorpe's property, about fifty ks out of town. We were visiting Quinn and Kimberley one weekend, and Matt decided to take a back road home.' Bec's voice filled with enthusiasm. 'You should see it. Two thick groves of trees that provide shade and a lake—not a dam—clear enough to swim in. There's even a sort of sandy beach on one side.'

'Who owns it? Quinn?'

'Yes, I rang him when I got home. It's on his property, and with the right paperwork filled out and approval of the relevant bodies, he's happy for the camp to be held there. I can get the buses to transport the kids up there without a problem. The council can get them as part of the contract with the local bus company, and I've had some good applicants for the youth worker position. It's mainly accommodation that's the problem. A lot of funding bodies aren't keen on providing grants for things that are ephemeral, like tents and barbecues and things like that. They want to see permanent structures before they approve the grants. Apparently, a lot of organisers keep the gear after it's purchased, and the benefactors are tightening up.'

Chloe and Rosie exchanged another glance. Bec shook her head. 'Like I said, don't even think about it, you pair.'

'Well, I'm not thinking about it for your camp specifically, but I think it would be a good idea for us to set up a retreat like that somewhere,' Chloe said. 'Then your community group and schools could use it for camps too.'

Bec sighed again. 'You guys are absolutely amazing. You have breathed so much life into our town and the district that you'll spread yourselves too thin. And Chloe, now that you've got Travis, you can't take on any more projects.'

Chloe grinned at her. 'Would you believe we're getting a bit bored? You know the department store is running really well. The pub's really busy; we've just put on a third chef, and the butcher shop is gaining a really good reputation. We even had some customers come up from Charleville the other day.'

'It's all those gourmet cuts you've got in there. Matt reckons he's never eaten so well. So, Chloe, you all need to take a bow and have a break, not take on another project!'

They all turned as Matt's voice came over the microphone.

'I'm taking requests, ladies and gents. Hit me with your favourite songs.' He looked over at Bec and smiled. 'And I've got a special one to sing to my lady tonight.'

'Aw, Matt's so sweet,' Chloe said. 'Now let's enjoy the music. You can tell us more about your camp later on.'

Bec nodded, but her thoughts were still on her funding issue as Matt's voice filled the air.

Chapter 3
Jenna's Vintage Tearoom - Bec

Two weeks passed before the girls caught up again. On Saturday morning, they met for coffee at Jenna's tearoom.

Bec was running late. Matt had gone over to help Ben Riley build a shed at his parents' house, and Bec had started weeding the veggie patch. Time had gotten away from her as she mulled over funding grants while she trimmed the tomato bushes. Matt had a green thumb, and an excellent crop of tomatoes, lettuce, beetroot, and spring onions had complemented the meat from the new butcher shop each night.

She took a quick shower, pulled a clean dress over her head and slipped on a pair of sandals before jumping into her car and driving the short distance to the tearoom that her friend, Jenna, had established on the highway. Even though it was late summer, the car park already held several caravans and motorhomes. Jenna said the grey nomies were getting earlier each year.

As Bec hurried up the steps, Chloe and Rose waved to her from a table on the veranda.

'Hi, girls, sorry I'm a bit late. I was weeding Matt's garden and lost track of the time.'

'No problem. We thought you might have been working,' Rosie said. 'We were just about to order.' She waved to Jenna, who immediately came over to the table with an order pad.

'Good morning, girls. Good to see you all out and about on this lovely Saturday morning,' she said.

'Hi, Jenna, how are you?' Bec said.

'Absolutely flat chat,' Jenna said. 'We've been so busy. We did so many hot breakfasts this morning poor Ellie is just about run off her feet. What can I get you today?'

'The usual coffees, please,' the three girls replied.

'And may I tempt you with Ellie's new specialty?'

'I saw some interesting cakes in the cabinet as we walked in,' Chloe said. 'What's the specialty today?'

'Tiramisu slice.'

'Yum, yes, please.'

Jenna quickly wrote the orders and walked away.

'Where's Travis?' Bec asked as she looked around for the pram that Chloe seemed to have with her all the time.

'I asked Greg to mind him because we wanted to have a chat with you.'

Bec frowned. 'A chat with me? Sounds like I'm in trouble.'

Chloe chuckled. 'No, of course not. I wanted to talk to you about your Easter camp. I loved going to camps when I was a kid *and* into my teens. I have fond memories of romance back in those days.'

'Romance? What sort of camp was it?' Bec asked. 'One of those fitness camp ones that we went to at high school?'

'No, it was a youth camp. I had a friend whose dad was a minister, and she used to drag me along there to Sunday school sometimes. I found that a bit boring as I got into my teens, but I loved the youth fellowship on Friday nights. We used to go sand surfing on the dunes at the back of Anna Bay sometimes. We had so much fun.'

'Anna Bay? Where's that?' Bec asked.

'North of Newcastle, before you get to Port Stephens. I spent some of my childhood in Newcastle, and I learned a lot about the region and various sites on those Friday nights. I made new friends, and that year, we went off to a couple of camps.' Chloe chuckled. 'I saw a different side to some of those kids. They ran wild while the poor youth workers were running around all night with torches, trying to find them all around the side of the lake.'

'Don't tell me that. I'll have to add torches to my list for our camp,' Bec said.

'I was fifteen.' Chloe's cheeks went pink with a pretty blush. 'The camp was at Lake Macquarie and that's where I had my first kiss. I always thought of it when Mum and Dad drove past it up the motorway before we moved to Brisbane. I learned a lot about the area when we lived down there. We went to lots of different places every Friday night.'

'Sounds like a lot of fun. That's what I want to make our camp for the local kids. Fun that leaves lifelong memories.' Bec turned to Rosie. 'Where did you have your first kiss?'

Rose giggled. 'Makes me sound like a bit of a tart. Would you believe in the back seat of the bus on the way home from school?'

Bec laughed. 'How old were you?'

'I was only fourteen,' Rosie admitted. 'Now, Bec. Your turn. What about you?'

'Well, it's pretty embarrassing after listening to you, but at fourteen and fifteen, my life was pretty sheltered.'

'Come on, tell us. First kiss. How old were you?'

'Would you believe seventeen and a half, my last year of high school? At the year twelve farewell.'

'Was he your boyfriend?'

'He was, and he was a lovely guy. We actually did go out on a few dates for a couple of months until I headed off to uni to do my nursing, and then he headed off somewhere. We lost touch. But those memories are sweet.'

'It was a special time, wasn't it?'

'It was. So what have you girls been up to the last couple of weeks while I've been ploughing through grant applications?' Bec asked.

Chloe and Rosie exchanged a glance. 'Well, as much as it's been nice sharing memories, we do actually have an ulterior motive. We wanted to speak to you, Bec.'

'Okay, what about?'

'Well, we went for a drive last weekend, and we just happened to stumble upon your lake.'

'Oh?' Bec said suspiciously. 'You just happened to stumble upon *my* lake? I don't own a lake.'

'Quinn's lake.'

'That's a long way to go for a drive.'

Chloe's eyes were wide with innocence. 'It was. And we just happened to bump into Quinn and Kimberley while we were out there.'

'Wow,' said Bec. 'They just happened to be down at the back of their property on the lake. Come clean, you guys. What were you doing out there?'

Chloe's smile was wide and still innocent. 'Well, we knew that you were after the grants, and we know that you're having problems because it was tent accommodation and not permanent dwellings, so we got to thinking.'

'Okay, tell me about thinking.' Bec narrowed her eyes.

'Quinn and the rest of us have come to an agreement.' Rosie said with a nod.

'We've bought some land off him,' Chloe added.

'You've bought some land?' Bec widened her eyes. 'Just like that?'

'Don't be cross. It's not just because you're having a camp. We're not stepping on your toes, Bec.' Rosie looked worried.

'I'm not cross. I am filled with awe at what you guys can achieve with very little effort.'

'It's sad that it boils down to money,' Chloe said. 'But being in the position that we're in since we had that win means we can create change more quickly. We can see where it's needed, and we can try to contribute.'

Bec shook her head. 'You guys deserve an award—citizens of the century. The difference you have made to this town has been amazing. And not just cosmetic changes; you've made a difference to many lives already.'

Chloe's smile was gentle. 'You know the most wonderful

thing about our situation? If we get an idea, we don't have to worry about how we can implement it. We can just go ahead and do it. We've been blessed, and it is up to us to share our good fortune and make a difference where we can.'

'Tell me more,' Bec said.

'We thought about it the weekend after Matt sang up at Tambo,' Chloe said. 'There was an obvious need for a venue for all sorts of things.'

Rosie interrupted. 'Like yoga retreats, women's weekends, men's camps, all sorts of things that can contribute to the mental health of our community. And you're doing the same in your job with the youth in the district, so if—'

Bec leaned back and folded her arms. 'Hang on, here comes Jenna with our coffee.'

Jenna placed three cups of coffee on the table. 'I'll be back with your slices shortly,' she said.

'Okay, Chloe, keep going,' Bec said once Jenna had gone back to the kitchen.

'Quinn sold us just a little strip of land along one side of the lake. We didn't want to interfere with his property, and we didn't want to take his lake away from him, but he was more than happy to sell us that strip of land.'

'He's also agreed to put in a new road from the highway, but it will be gated, so not just anyone can drive out to the lake. He's happy for us to build some permanent structures there too,' Rosie added.

Bec kept her arms folded and shook her head as Chloe and Rosie picked up their cups and sipped their coffee. 'Really,' she said slowly. 'You've achieved that much in only two weeks?'

'What it means now is that you can concentrate on your funding grants for staff and food and stuff like that, but if you want, we'd love you to have your Easter camp on the land we've bought from Quinn.'

'I'd love to, but our camp's only eight weeks away. It won't be ready in time.' Bec reached for her coffee as Jenna appeared with their food. 'Yum, that looks divine.'

Chloe reached out and put her hand on Bec's arm. 'No, it will be ready. Our builder, who did the renovations for the pub, was happy to slip the building of the cabins in between other commitments. Ben helped us fast-track the plans through council, and as a favour, Greg and Lex are helping him do some work at his parents' house this morning.'

'Matt's there too,' Bec said. 'What about Travis? I thought Greg was minding him.'

'Jenny said she'd keep an eye out when he had a sleep, and I'm picking him up after we're done here.'

'You girls have got it all organised, haven't you?' Bec said. She'd always been a bit of a loner, but Chloe and Rosie had become close friends over the past months. But what they had done now filled her with appreciation for what special people they were. She blinked back tears.

'I hope you don't mind, Bec. It's not like we've taken over your initiative. If you still want to get tents and swags and things like that for a real camp, we'll just keep building our retreat on the other side of the lake. We don't expect you to come if you'd prefer the other way.'

'No, of course not. We'll be there with bells on. I think you're absolutely wonderful. It means now that I can advertise for the youth workers. Now that I don't have to worry about tents and swags and figure out how to overcome that hurdle, I can definitely hire two, maybe three. If we have three, we can have the two age groups there. So, tell me about these buildings that are getting built.'

Chloe was full of enthusiasm as she described their plans, and Bec's thoughts churned wildly as she heard her describe four separate dormitories, two ablution blocks, a cookhouse, and a big open-air fire pit for the winter camps.

Bec's hand shook as she held her cup. She put her cup in the saucer and lifted her hand to wipe the tears from her eyes.

Chloe looked at her and shook her head. 'Don't go crying, Bec. What's the matter?'

'Do you know how many people would've won a fortune like you guys? Would've bought flash houses for themselves and fancy boats and overseas trips, or wasted it? You guys are making a difference. And you keep it so quiet. It's an absolute credit to you, what you're doing. I'm simply overwhelmed,' Bec said. 'Thank you so much.'

Chloe and Rosie both looked embarrassed. 'We love doing what we're doing.'

Chapter 4
Bec - February

Bec stood at the door of the CFY office at the back of the Charleville shire chambers. Rivers of water covered the green grass in the flat back area, and the barbeque table, where they often sat and had meetings or morning tea and lunch, was almost underwater in the far corner.

She turned to Alice, her offsider. 'It doesn't bode well for our Easter camp, does it, Alice?'

'It will be fine. I think this is just localised rain. I had a look at the BOM site before, and we're copping it about ten kilometres around Charleville. I reckon you'll go home tonight, and Augathella will still be as dry as a bone. And remember, the lake is another fifty ks northwest from there too. I'm sure it'll be fine. And if it is raining a bit there, it'll mean more water in the lake. And green grass.'

'I love your confidence. Well, I'm going to cross my fingers and toes, and I'll be looking at that weather site for the next four weeks.'

'It's only a localised storm, late summer rain,' Alice said.

'I don't know, my first year at Augathella, they kept saying it was going to be dry, and we had the wettest winter on record. We've put so much work into organising this camp and getting the funding for it. I'll be so disappointed if it has to be cancelled due to the weather.'

Alice, ever the optimist, shook her head. 'Bec, if it's cancelled—and it won't be—we'll reschedule. We'll have some disappointed kids, and it won't be an Easter camp. We won't be having the Easter activities, but we can do other things at another time. Maybe the next school holidays long weekend.'

'I guess you're right.' Bec stared at the fat raindrops still splashing in the puddles. 'Matt says I'm a worrier. He's always telling me to chill.' She chuckled. 'I just don't want to chill as much as he does.'

'Has he been enjoying working as an accountant again?'

'He has, but between you and me, I think he enjoys his singing nights more.'

They both turned and headed back inside, closing the door behind them.

'I've been going through the applications for the youth workers.'

'Got many good ones?'

'Yes, interviews are on Friday. I think it's going to be hard to choose. I'm going to read through them all again tonight.'

'Many applications?'

'Twelve. I'll hand them over to you when I finish.' Alice was on the panel as well.

'Don't you work too hard.'

'It's fine. I work at home when Matt works. The word is spreading about how good he is, and he's picked up a heap of new clients, not only in Augathella but also in Charleville and Tambo. He doesn't know if he's Arthur or Martha at the moment. I think he spends more time on the road than I do. It's not at all what he imagined when he set up his home office. I think he had visions of working a few hours a day at home, and that was it.'

'But is he enjoying it?'

'He loves it. He whinges, but I can tell he enjoys what he's doing. He's making a difference.'

'What about his singing? He's fabulous,' Alice said. 'We heard him at the club on Saturday.'

'Well, he's got a regular gig at the Tambo pub, and he's had a few offers from Blackall, but he's saying no for the time being. It's a bit far to drive home after a show.'

Alice's look was coy. 'And you two still getting on as well as you always did?'

'Of course, we are,' Bec said. 'I adore the man.'

Alice pulled a mock face. 'Well, a girl can only hope. I grew up in Augathella, and all the good catches left town after high school. That's why I moved to Charleville. I think I'm destined to never find love.' Alice put a hand on her chest and sighed. 'Hire a good-looking youth worker around twenty-five. That would suit me.'

Bec smiled. 'You'll meet someone one day. Matt was the last person I imagined would come into my life.'

'But he worked hard at it, didn't he?'

'He surely did, but I knew pretty much from the beginning that he was the one.'

'You dark horse, you never let on.'

'I was too busy then, working at the hospital. By the time Matt and I got together, I was pretty much burned out.'

'And you've got no regrets doing youth work now?' Alice asked.

'I said I'd give it a try and see how I went. I only took leave from the hospital, but I've loved every minute of it. I actually put in my notice at the hospital a couple of weeks ago, so I hope the funding stays up for our centre.'

'I'd love to know who funded it,' Alice said. 'Apparently, it's hush-hush, and no one is letting on where it came from. That worries me a bit in case it does go.'

'It's certainly been generous. I mean, look at the new office.' Bec changed the subject as she gestured around to the freshly painted walls, the brand-new furniture and the two new computers. Even the little kitchenette had been refurbished with a new benchtop. It had previously been a room that the museum had used to store things, and now it was a lovely workplace.

When it wasn't raining, that was.

She had her suspicions as to the funding source, but Chloe and Rosie had never said anything, and it wasn't her place to ask. She knew that they had built the retreat as the venue for the camp, and that was all she needed to know.

'Okay, I've got a couple more submissions to do,' Bec said, 'and then I'm going to call it a day and drive home. I hope it's not raining all the way to Augathella.'

'Which road do you take?' Alice asked.

'I think I'll go the main highway today; there's more chance of water not lying there than there is on the back one. There are a few hollows along that way; I'd hate to get stranded.'

'I'm going to leave now. I'm going to visit my gran.'

'How's she going?'

'Well, it took six months to persuade her to go into the aged care facility, but you know what? She's loving every minute. The day she arrived, the residents had made a huge fresh floral bouquet to welcome her, and she hasn't had one regret since she arrived. I've never seen her so happy. She's joined every club that's going and watched more movies than she ever watched at home, and she's put on about three kilograms, so that proves to us that she wasn't eating properly when she was looking after herself.'

'And you're still living in her house?' Bec asked.

'Yeah, Gran doesn't want to sell it, so while she was able to afford the fees for the aged care facility, I still insist on paying rent, and she reckons she's just putting it away for me to get when she carks it! Her words!'

'I love your grandmother,' Bec said. 'I met her a couple of times when I used to come down to the hospital from Augathella when she was in with her broken hip.'

'She's a sweet thing, isn't she?' Alice said.

Bec reached over and hugged Alice. 'Just like her granddaughter. I love working with you too, Alice. Okay, I'm going to hit the road; I'll see you later.'

'Remember, Bec?' Alice called after her as Bec reached the door.

She turned with a frown. 'Remember what?

'Twenty-five and good-looking.'

Bec was still smiling when she got in her car.

186

Chapter 5

Bec's smile was still there as she turned off the highway. For a moment, she had considered pulling up at Jenna's tearoom, but she thought Jenna had probably turned off the machine for the day. Besides, she had a perfectly good coffee machine at home; she could make a coffee there when she arrived home.

Alice had been right; the rain stopped exactly ten kilometres north of Charleville, and Bec had driven into afternoon sunshine. The weather out west never ceased to amaze her, and it was hard to predict what it was going to do. Everyone thought it was dry and hot out here all the time, but she'd been pleasantly surprised in the years since she'd moved to the district. It was a beautiful climate, and the countryside was as pretty as anything she'd seen on the coast.

Matt's car wasn't in the driveway, and she pulled a face. She had been hoping to sit and relax and have a coffee with him. She picked up her briefcase, locked her car, and climbed up the front steps. Putting a key in the lock, she called out anyway, just in case he was parked around the back. 'You home, Matt?'

She was met by silence, and when she got into the kitchen, there was a handwritten note on the kitchen bench: 'Hi sweets, I had to go out to Braden's place, so I'll probably be late. I made a booking at the pub. I'll meet you there for dinner at seven.'

'Oh, good.' Since the newcomers had refurbished the pub and taken it over, it had been an extremely popular place in town. Not that it hadn't been before, but these days it was essential to book, no matter which night of the week you went for dinner. Sean had taken over the management of the whole business and was still cooking occasionally when needed, but there was a new chef from the Sunshine Coast, and the pub was starting to get excellent reviews in the city. Sean said he preferred being out in the bar to keep up with the locals.

Bec had noticed the few times they'd been there and sometimes on the weekend when they drove past that there were some luxurious cars and sports cars parked there on a Saturday night.

The rooms upstairs had also been refurbished, and the Augathella pub was now rated a five-star establishment.

She took a quick shower and went to the wardrobe, looking for something pretty to wear out. If the pub had been done up, she could make an effort too. She knew Matt would be late. She grinned. He always was, so there was no rush to get ready.

Maybe she could make a couple of referee calls.

Kimberley Calthorpe had been named as a referee on two of the applications, and Bec guessed that the applicants were either locals or had been at some point.

As she dried her hair and pulled it up into a clip, the early evening was still warm, even though Easter was approaching quickly. She thought about the benefactor who supported everything they were doing for the district's youth. The only prerequisite for the funding was that they use the name "Choice for Youth," and Alice, Bec and the members of the shire council who accepted the funding were certainly happy to go along with that.

Bec had been writing submissions for government grants and funding towards other initiatives. Even though the funding was good and they now had a venue for the camp, she still had some other ideas that would need funding. If there's one thing Bec had, it was grand plans and big ideas because she thought if no one had them and no one tried for them, it would never happen.

Ideas were forming as she sat down at her laptop and pulled up the applications on the screen.

She had chosen five to interview. one females and four males had fulfilled all the criteria and had listed referees.

She scanned through the applications of those she had chosen to interview and who had been approved by the human resources officer at the council: Matilda Tingle, a part-time youth worker from Brisbane—Bec had wondered if she was related to Gladys. Tingle was an unusual name. Jeremy Johnson, currently working as a nurse in St George; Rory McArthur, a mine worker; Brian Harris, a children's librarian at Charleville; and Neil Evans, who had listed himself as currently a full-time father but had extensive experience in the youth work sector.

Bec glanced at her watch; it was six forty-five. If she left for the pub a bit after seven, she could guarantee she'd still beat Matt. She'd call Kimberley and ask her for a reference for the two who had listed her as their first referee: Matilda Tingle and Jeremy Johnson.

Kimberley would be home from school by now, and Bec hoped she didn't interrupt their dinner. She dialled the number and waited, but the call eventually went to voicemail.

'Hello, you've reached Kimberley Calthorpe. Please leave a message, and I'll get back to you.'

'Bec Hunter, Kimberley. No need to call back, I'm going out, so I'll catch you tomorrow.'

With a last swipe of lipstick over her mouth, Bec picked up her purse and keys, and locked the front door behind her. The twilight bathed their small house in soft light, and she smiled as she noticed Matt had mowed the footpath and weeded the front gardens, in between the many jobs that she knew he had on today. He must have had a call from Braden Cartwright, as he hadn't mentioned going out there when they'd had breakfast together this morning.

Every morning, Matt listed for her what jobs he had on that day. She suspected he was trying to justify working from home, so she broached the subject one morning last week.

'Sweetie, you don't have to tell me what you're doing. I

know you work hard, and even if you just wanted to sing at the pubs, I'd be happy with whatever you chose to do.'

Matt walked over when she picked up her keys, put his arms around her, and kissed her cheek. 'Do you know how much I love you, Bec Hunter?'

'As much as I love you, I hope,' she said. His lips moved to hers, and Bec was quite late for work that morning.

So he'd mowed the lawn, weeded the gardens, and headed out to Braden's today. Sometimes, she wondered if he spent so much time out there because he enjoyed playing with the kids. He and Petie had a special bond from the night that Matt had saved him from more serious injury at Sophie and Kent's wedding, and they got on like a house on fire.

She also noticed when he was nursing Braden and Callie's twins, Meggie and Munro, how much he enjoyed playing with the babies now. They were sitting up and taking notice and babbling back to him. One day he would make a great father.

One day, when she was ready.

Guilt trickled through Bec. Maybe she needed to look at her priorities.

She wasn't quite ready yet, but she would like to have children before she was thirty, but that was a couple of years away. She just hoped that Matt could wait and it didn't cause any friction between them.

Chapter 6
The Cartwrights and the Rileys

'Are you nearly ready, Brae?' Callie called out as the six o'clock news blared from the television in the kitchen where Meggie and Munro were sitting in their high chairs having dinner. 'We can't be late; Matt was most particular that we had to be there before seven o'clock. That's the time he told Bec to be there.'

'Yeah, darling, thank you. Don't get your knickers in a twist. I've just got to find a clean shirt,' he called from up the hall.

'Braden Cartwright, there are plenty of clean shirts hanging up in our wardrobe.'

He came into the kitchen with a wide grin, dressed in his good trousers and favourite shirt, with his damp hair slicked back. 'Yep, I was just winding you up.'

Callie pulled a face at him. 'What about the boys?'

'Dressed, clean faces and boots on, watching TV in the family room.'

'Right,' she said. 'You finish feeding this pair and make sure you keep them clean while I go and get changed. I had my shower when they were napping. When they're done, just wipe their faces and hands. They're ready to go into the car seats.'

'You're an amazing woman, Callie,' he said, dropping a kiss on her cheek.

'I am. I'm clever. I married you. Come on, Braden, we have to be on time.'

***

Jenny Riley stood at the doorway of the living room and frowned at her husband, Tom. 'Are you ready to go yet?'

'Go? Go where?' he asked as he picked up the remote and turned the news down. 'Where are we going?'

'I told you this afternoon we were going to Bec Hunter's surprise birthday party at the pub. Matt booked the whole dining room out about three months ago.'

'You didn't tell me.' Tom threw the remote into the basket and stood there looking at her.

'Yes, we talked about it this afternoon, sweetheart.' A trickle of worry went through Jenny. 'Don't you remember us talking about it over a coffee?'

Tom looked at her and shook his head. 'I'm sure we didn't.'

Jenny frowned. It was about the third time in the last couple of weeks that Tom had been forgetful, and she was getting a little bit concerned. It was time for him to see Dr. Harry and have a check-up. He was almost seventy, and she was worried. Hopefully, it was just his usual vagueness.

'Go and have a quick shower, and I'll put some clothes out on the bed for you. Ben and Amelia are picking us up in about fifteen minutes.'

'I'm coming, I'm coming,' he said. 'Can I just watch this item?'

'No, Tom, go and get ready now.'

'Yes, dear.' He threw her a grin and disappeared down the hall; maybe it was just his usual absentmindedness that had kicked in this afternoon. She really hoped it was since she wasn't going to say anything to Ben because she didn't want to worry him.

'Hi, sweetheart,' she said five minutes later as Ben stepped through the front door.

'Where's Amelia?'

'They're waiting in the car; we thought we'd drive you and Dad down to the pub a bit early. If you're ready . . .'

'I'm ready, but your father forgot we were going.'

Ben looked concerned, and Jenny looked at her son, wondering why he was frowning. 'What's wrong, love?'

'Mum, have you noticed anything a bit strange with Dad lately?'

An ice-cold knife seemed to plunge into Jenny's chest. She put her hand there and rubbed. 'Why, what's wrong? Why do you ask, Ben?'

'I don't want to worry you, but just a couple of times in the last month or so, Dad's totally forgotten things I've already told him. And he asked me one day last week when the NRL grand final was.'

Jenny sighed. 'Would you believe I was just thinking the same thing, and I decided not to mention it to you? I didn't want to worry you.'

'Perhaps a visit to Harry?' Ben suggested.

'I think so, but trying to get your father to go to the doctor is like trying to pull teeth,' she said.

'Do you want me to talk to him about it, or do you want me to come over, and we'll both talk to him together?'

'No, I think if both of us talk to him and make it into a really big deal he'll be a bit upset, and feel that we've been talking about him behind his back. Leave it with me, Ben, I'll sort it.'

'Sort what?'

They both jumped and turned around as Tom walked into the living room.

'Didn't you have a shower?' Jenny said.

'Just a spray of deodorant.' Tom grinned. 'I heard Ben arrive, so I thought I'd be quick.'

'What about the shirt I put out for you?'

'What shirt?' Tom said, looking down 'Nothing wrong with this one. It's comfortable.'

Jenny reached out and took his hand. 'Okay, you look fine.'

'Gidday, son.' Tom went over and hugged Ben. 'Good to see you. It's been a while.'

Ben's eyes widened as he held Jenny's gaze for a few seconds. 'Yeah,' he said.

Jenny pushed away the worry that gripped her. Ben had been over for dinner last night with Sebastian while Amelia went to a planning meeting for the ball they were organising later in the year.

***

Bec

Bec chose to walk down to the pub because it was such a lovely evening. It was hard to believe that so much water had been running in the yard at Charleville, and here, it was dry as Alice said it would be.

Alice had grown up in the district, and Bec appreciated her passion for doing the right thing for the district's youth. However, Alice had much more local knowledge, and when Bec applied for grants and funding, Alice suggested different places that she could use as examples and different funding sources. Alice Templeton was a mine of information.

As Bec crossed the road, turned onto Main Street, and approached the pub, she smiled as Sophie and Kent Mason got out of their four-wheel-drive. Her smile widened as Fallon and Jon parked behind them and lifted out little Ryan, who was now toddling around.

'Hey, guys, are you having dinner here tonight?' she said.

'Hi Bec,' Sophie said, reaching over and kissing her cheek. 'I haven't seen you for ages.'

'Now that I'm working down in Charleville, I don't see people nearly as much,' she said.

'How's the new job going?' Fallon asked.

'I love it,' Bec said.

'You look a lot more relaxed. I suppose it's the pretty dress, not in the hospital uniform, that makes you look different.'

'And no stress,' Fallon said. 'You look lovely, Bec.'

'Thank you.' Heat ran up her neck; she hated people commenting on her appearance. Bec had always felt as though she didn't have much fashion sense, and most of the

194

time, it didn't bother her. 'I figured I'd better get dressed up. It's pretty swish in there now. Are you guys staying for dinner?'

'Yeah, we are. Have you guys booked?' Sophie glanced at Fallon.

'Yes, we have.'

'I'm not sure whether Matt's booked just for the two of us or not. I don't know what else he's planned.'

Sophie and Fallon exchanged another glance, and Bec was disappointed when they didn't suggest that perhaps she and Matt could join them anyway. They probably wanted to have a chat together; Sophie and Fallon were friends.

'Okay, we might see you in there. I'm going to go to the front bar and get a drink while I wait for Matt,' she said.

***

'You were running late too?' Sophie asked Fallon quietly as Bec went through the side entrance of the pub.

'Yes, Ruby was fussing,' Sophie said. 'How mean did I feel not asking Bec to join us?'

'Matt is a great guy, but I don't think he thought this through very well.'

'When's Bec's birthday? Do you think she suspects?'

'I don't think she's got any idea at all. Her birthday is next Saturday, but Matt said he was singing up at Tambo, and he felt bad that he hadn't realised the date before he accepted the gig. That's why he's organised the surprise party for tonight.'

'Well, Bec's certainly going to get a surprise. I'm so pleased she got dressed up. She would've killed him if she'd turned up in jeans and a T-shirt.'

'She looked lovely, didn't she?'

'She did. She's obviously loving her new job.'

'From what I've read in the paper, they're doing a great job. Alice Templeton is a lovely girl, too.'

'The youth of Charleville and Augie are very lucky, and from what I hear, Tambo and Cunnamulla too,' Fallon added.

'It's certainly made a difference to our district.'

'Not to mention what our new friends in town are doing. Did you hear that they're building a retreat out near Quinn Calthorpe's place now?' Fallon handed Ryan over to Jon as he stood beside Kent, who was nursing Ruby Rose.

Sophie and Fallon chatted as they walked in together, behind Jon and Kent, and chose a table close to the entrance.

'Easier to get out in the event of a crying baby,' Fallon said.

Sophie grinned. 'I hear you.'

Chapter 7
Kimberley

'Excuse me for a moment, Callie. I need to take this call. I think it's Lindy. I probably need to find a substitute for her class for next week.'

Callie smiled and took Megan back from Kimberley as she reached for her phone on the table.

'I'll be back in a moment,' she said to Quinn on her way out to the side entrance. As soon as she was through the door, she pressed the answer icon. 'Kimberley Calthorpe.'

As she put the phone on speaker, Kimberley glanced at the number. It wasn't the one she'd been expecting. Lindy's husband had been ill for a couple of weeks, and they were going to Brisbane for him to have some tests. She'd expected that call, but it looked like it was someone else calling.

Please, no one else be sick for school next week. Substitute teachers were short.

'Hello, Kimberley,' said an unfamiliar voice. 'I don't know whether you remember me or not. It's Matilda Tingle. You might remember me as Tilly.'

'Tilly, of course I do,' Kimberley said. 'How are you? I haven't seen you for years.'

'It's been a long time. I haven't been back to Augathella since I left high school,' Tilly replied.

'Well, it's good to hear from you now. What can I do for you?'

Kimberley and Tilly had been great mates for the last two years of high school, but as always happens when everyone finishes that final year, they'd headed off in different directions. Kimberley had headed off to Brisbane to do her teaching degree, and she wasn't sure where Matilda had gone.

The phone was silent. 'It's so good to hear from you,' Kimberley repeated.

'Sorry, I was just distracted here. I'm waiting for a ferry, but it was the wrong one.'

'Ferry? Where are you?'

'I'm in Brisbane. I've got a big favour to ask, Kimberley. I know you haven't seen me for ages, but I was hoping that someone from Augathella might be able to help me a little bit.'

'Why's that? What's happened?'

'Well, I'd like to come back to town. My grandma's getting on, and I suspect she needs me. I don't know if you remember Gladys Tingle or not.'

Kimberley smiled. 'Not only do I remember her, we're at the pub for a birthday party tonight, and your grandmother is here too.'

'Oh, that's good to hear. How does she look?' Tilly asked.

Kimberley answered carefully because Gladys wasn't a popular person in town at the best of times. Every town had a busybody, and Gladys was Augathella's finest. The sad part was she was often negative.

'She looks fine. Actually, very well. We've had a lot of new people in town who've started new businesses, built new homes and refurbished some of the older houses. Your gran has joined in and tidied up her front garden. It's one of the prettiest in town this summer.' Kimberley pulled a face. It was hard to think of something nice to say about Gladys.

'That's good to hear, but I think it's hard for her by herself since my dad left to work in the mines a couple of years back. I figured I might come home for a while and help her out.'

'It would be lovely to see you,' Kimberley said. 'But how can I help you?'

'Well, I've applied for a job at the youth centre in

Charleville, and I was hoping it's okay that I've put your name down as a referee. I meant to ring you earlier in the week, but I worked double shifts all week, and I didn't get a chance. So, I really hope you don't mind because I put it in before I asked you. If it's a problem, tell me, and I'll contact the convener and ask them to take your name off the list.'

'Tilly, no problem at all, that's fine. I'm happy to give you a character reference. We were such great mates back then, weren't we? It's such a shame we lost touch.'

'Yes, it is.'

'Which centre have you applied to, so I know who to expect to call?'

'The name of the person I've been dealing with is Rebecca Hunter.'

Kimberley nodded. 'I know Bec well. She's a good person, and I'll have no hesitation in giving you a reference. Actually, tonight is a surprise party for her birthday.'

'So you know her?'

Kimberley could hear the relief in Tilly's voice.

'I do.'

'Thank you so much, Kimberley. I truly appreciate it. It'll be great to catch up. Fingers crossed, I can get out there, at least for an interview.'

'Well, I'll look forward to seeing you. If you do come to town for an interview, please make sure we catch up.' Kimberley frowned. 'How did you get my mobile? Not that I mind. Just curious.'

'It was a long shot. I asked Nana Tingle if you were back in town, and she said she had your number from some committee you were on together. Congratulations, by the way. I hear you're married to Quinn now..'

'I am. What about you? Married? Kids? Significant other?'

There was a bit of a quiet sigh at the end of the phone. 'Yep, life happens and often not the way we hoped. And no, I'm not married. Living the single life. No ties, so I can come home. I think it's time.'

'We'll certainly catch up. You won't know the town.'

'Kimberley? I just want to ask you one more thing. You might think I'm silly, but is Jeremy Johnson still in town?'

'Not that I know of, Tilly, and I'm sure I would've heard if he was. I actually haven't seen him since the end of high school, either. Last I heard, he was working as a nurse at St George. I remember Jacinta Mason mentioning that before she left town. Sophie was friends with him too.'

'It's great to hear all these familiar names. Did Sophie Cartwright marry Kent Mason?'

'She did.'

'That's not a surprise,' Tilly said. 'The "couple most likely".'

Kimberley could hear the sadness in her voice. 'They were, but they've only married recently. Sophie was away for a while. And I don't know if you heard, but sadly, Julia Cartwright, Braden's wife, died in an accident a few years back, and Braden's now remarried. A lovely girl from Brisbane who came out to be the boys' nanny.'

'Braden and Julia had children?'

'Yes, I keep forgetting how long you've been gone. Three energetic boys. And Braden and Callie are here tonight too; they've got the most gorgeous almost one-year-old twins. There's been a lot of new people coming to town. It's a different place than what it was when we were at school, Tilly. It's a great place to live now. I do hope you get the job.'

'Me too. The Choice for Youth centre sounds like a good initiative from what Rebecca told me when I called to get the information pack. I like their philosophy statement.'

'There's a branch in Augathella and the centre is reaching out to other towns from what I've gathered since Bec's been involved. If I get a referee call or if Bec comes to see me, I'll talk you up. You were always good with the problem kids, even at school. Please stay in touch. I'll save your number in my contacts.'

'I will. Thank you so much, Kimberley. It *will* be good to see you again.'

'Bye for now.' Kimberley put her phone in her pocket and walked back to the dining room. She smiled at Gladys as she looked up at Kimberley curiously.

'I thought you were leaving already.' Gladys frowned. 'Seemed a bit rude.'

'No. I just had to take a phone call. How are you, Mrs Tingle?' she asked, not mentioning that she had just been speaking to her granddaughter.

'I'm well, thank you, Kimberley.'

'Hello, Beryl,' Kimberley smiled at the other woman sitting beside Gladys. Beryl was Gladys' constant companion around town.

Gladys frowned and looked at the old-fashioned watch on her wrist. 'How long before Rebecca gets here?' she said.

'I'm sure it won't be much longer. I think just about everyone is here.'

'It's way past my dinner time.'

Kimberley smiled. 'But think how good it will be to have a meal cooked for you and no washing up afterwards.' She could be diplomatic when she had to.

'I suppose. It's quite a big party. Is she turning forty?' Gladys asked.

'Don't be ridiculous, Gladys. Bec's not even thirty,' Beryl snapped. 'Not until in a few days anyway.'

Kimberley straightened as the conversations in the room quietened. Matt moved away from the door with his finger to his lips. He'd asked everyone to try to keep the noise down so that when Bec arrived and was seated outside in the bistro by Sean—Matt had asked him to tell Bec he was running late and to put her at a table in there so she wouldn't get suspicious—she wouldn't hear familiar voices. He'd organised for one of the barmen to come in and take the drink orders and the door between the bistro and dining room was locked.

Kimberley smiled. Matt and Bec were so happy together; she wouldn't be surprised to see another Augathella wedding this year.

The town was growing, and she really hoped Tilly would come back, although putting up with Gladys might be a bit hard if she moved in with her. But Tilly had always been kind and had seen the best in everyone. Kimberley had been sincere when she'd said that she would be happy to give her a reference. Tilly was one of the most genuine women she'd ever known.

It would be good to see her again. Tilly had been a pretty eighteen-year-old, and like Sophie and Kent, she and Jeremy Johnson had been voted a "couple most likely" at the Year 12 formal, the year they had all finished school.

They'd both left town at the same time, and Kimberley hadn't seen either of them since. She'd been disappointed that they hadn't said goodbye, but at the end of the school year, everyone had been busy getting their plans in place. She'd often wondered if Tilly and Jeremy had stayed together, and she guessed she had her answer now.

Chapter 8

Matt was talking to Quinn at their table at their table when Kimberley made her way back. She shot him an apologetic smile. 'Sorry, Matt. I hope you weren't waiting for me. I just had a call come in. I thought it was work, but it wasn't.'

'No, we're waiting for Ben and Amelia to come back. Apparently, there was some drama in the car with Sebastian, and they had to go home and get a change of clothes.'

Callie smiled across the table. 'I can understand that. I believe Jenny had Sebastian at her place this morning, and she fed him pureed prunes for his dessert after his lunch and then sent him home. Apparently, the nappy he filled in the car on the way over was pretty spectacular.'

Kimberley pulled a face. 'Too much information. I don't think I could cope with that. Give me kindergarten kids over babies any day.'

'You'll change your mind when you've got your own,' Callie said with a smile as she looked at Megan and Munro in their high chairs at the end of the table.

Matt waited until they finished speaking. 'Still be about ten minutes,' he said. 'So not a problem at all. Sean came in and told me that Bec is sitting quietly, having a drink, waiting for me to arrive. He told her that there's a function in here tonight and that I booked the table outside so we could be private.'

'As long as she doesn't get curious and comes to the door to see who's in here,' Callie said.

'No, Sean's locked the door to the bar. And we've all been pretty quiet. I must thank everyone when I can get on the microphone later.'

Kimberley's phone chimed again in her pocket, and she rolled her eyes. 'I'm sorry, this must be the call I'm waiting for. I'll be quick, and if I see Ben and Amelia arrive, I'll come back in with them,' she said to Matt with an apologetic smile before she hurried over to the side door and went out to the beer garden. 'Hello, Kimberley Calthorpe,' she said for the second time this afternoon.

'Hello, Kimberley.' This time, an unfamiliar male voice greeted her.

'Yes, who's speaking, please?' Kimberley asked.

'I wonder if you remember me from high school. My name is Jeremy Johnson.'

Kimberley's eyes widened. 'Yes, Jeremy, of course I do. What can I do for you?'

Perhaps he knew that Tilly had called, but it seemed strange that she had asked after him.

'I was wondering if I could ask you a favour. I'm coming back to live in Augathella. Or at least that's my plan.'

Kimberley listened carefully as he continued.

'I've applied for a job in Charleville. We were mates growing up. I was hoping I could ask you for a character reference.'

Kimberley nodded slowly. Until Tilly had moved to town in Year Ten, she and Jeremy had been very good mates, but they'd drifted apart as the romance between Tilly and Jeremy started. She and Tilly had spent a lot of time together in Years 11 and 12 when they'd chosen the same subjects. Many afternoons had been spent at Tilly's house when they planned to study, but usually ended up talking about fashion and bands.

'You're nursing, aren't you, Jeremy? Jacinta kept me up to date. Is the job at Charleville Hospital?'

'No. I'm leaving nursing. I took one break and worked in Melbourne for a few years, but I went back to St George and did my paediatric nursing pracs. I've decided to come back home for a while. My granddad is getting on, and he needs a bit of a hand on the farm, so I thought I'd see if I like living out there again and pick up a job at the same time.'

'So, what sort of job are you applying for?' Kimberley asked slowly. *Surely not,* it would be too much of a coincidence, she thought.

'Apparently, the community centre down at Charleville, Choice for Youth, is looking for a couple of new youth workers. I saw it in our public service gazette, applied, and I've got my work referees from Melbourne, but I was hoping that someone with a bit of knowledge of me as a local might put in a good word for me. I thought of you straightaway, Kim. Even though it's been a long time since I left town.'

'Of course, Jeremy. I don't know anything about your work since you left, but I'd be more than happy to give you a character reference. You mentioned a couple of youth workers. Is there more than one position coming up?' she asked.

'I believe they're looking for a number of new youth workers. The convenor told me about some funding grant when I called to enquire about the job. So I'd like to throw my hat in the ring and hope I've got a chance of coming home.'

'Ten years, a long time to still consider it home.'

'Yes, but I think where you're born and spend your school years is always home, no matter how long you're gone, don't you? What about you, Kimberley? What are you doing these days?'

'I'm the assistant principal at our primary school,' Kimberley said.

'Married?'

'Yes.'

'Kids?'

'No kids. What about you, Jeremy?' Maybe she could get to the bottom of why Tilly was asking if he was still in town. Was it a conflict of interest to give a reference for two people applying for the same job? She'd have to ask Bec. But not tonight.

'No, single. Free as a bird. Hope you don't mind me asking all the personal questions. We always got on well, didn't we?'

'We did. From our first day of kindergarten.'

'I've never been ready to settle down, much to the disappointment of several women.' His chuckle came across the phone, and Kimberley remembered it well. Jeremy had always been a smiler. He had always been the happy one in the group and was always able to lift anyone who was a bit down. 'Do I sound big-headed saying that?'

'Not at all. I know you well enough.' Kimberley swallowed. Even though it had been a long time, she felt she knew Jeremy well enough to ask. 'Do you mind me asking about Tilly? I thought you were heading off to get married?'

There was quiet for a while, and she wondered if she had overstepped.

'A long story there, Kimberley. And not a pretty one. One for a night over a good bottle of red. Do you know where Tilly is these days? I hope she's happy. She deserves to be.'

Kimberley swallowed again as she thought quickly. She was damned if she did and damned if she didn't.

'Last I heard, she was in Brisbane. Anyway, look, I have to go, Jeremy, and yes, I'm more than happy to be your referee. When or if I get the call, I'll let you know. Got your number in my phone now.'

'Thanks, Kim. I knew I could depend on you. Hopefully, we'll catch up soon.'

Kimberley walked across the beer garden, thoughtful again. Should she ring Tilly and let her know that Jeremy applied for the job, too, or should she just let things take their natural course?

Never one to interfere, she realised it wasn't up to her to decide. She'd be breaching confidentiality if she did.

If Bec asked her to be a referee for both of them, she would, and she'd think carefully about what to say.

It had turned into an interesting night. Ben and Amelia pulled up as she was about to go inside, and she waited for them by the door.

'Bit of a nappy drama, I hear,' she said with a grin.

Ben was actually a bit pale. 'Oh my God, don't even talk about it. I'm going to have a word with my mother about feeding Sebastian prunes. Never again! It was right up into his—'

Kimberley put a hand up. 'Too much information, you guys. I don't need to know.'

But Amelia finished Ben's sentence for him. 'The contents of his nappy had gone right up to the back of his neck and into his hair.' She smiled down at her now-clean baby. 'We had to give him a bath.'

'Oh yuk, gross. I won't be able to eat now,' Kimberley said.

'Not prunes for dessert, anyway.' Ben laughed at the look on Kimberley's face as they followed her in.

'You'll keep, Ben Riley,' she said.

Matt was standing by the other door and gave them a thumbs-up as they walked in. Kimberley went over and sat with Quinn. Matt spoke quietly as everyone stopped talking.

'Everyone ready?' he asked.

The room was quiet as everyone smiled and nodded. Pointing to the side door, Matt indicated he was going that way.

That way, Bec wouldn't wonder why he was coming out of the private function room, Kimberley thought.

'Be back with her in five. Lights out when Sean gives you the nod from the bar?' he said.

Kimberley stood by the light switch and nodded as conversations resumed quietly. She couldn't wait to see the look on Bec's face. It was going to be a good night. Chloe caught her eye from two tables away, smiling with anticipation.

Kimberley scanned the room. All of Bec's friends were

here tonight, including the four new couples in town: the Cartwrights, with their five children; Dr Harry and Laura, heads close together, looking like two lovebirds; Sophie and Kent; Fallon and Jon, and their respective children. Jenna and Josh Foley were at the table with Chloe and her friends, and most of the teachers from the primary school and the staff from the hospital filled two long tables at the back of the room. The only close friends missing were Jacinta and Ryan Francesco, who had moved to Brisbane.

Sean gave her a nod, and Kimberley flicked the light switch.

Chapter 9
Tilly Tingle - Brisbane

Tilly sat on the bench of the sheltered area as she waited for the next river cat to arrive and give her a ride back to her apartment. It had been a good conversation with Kimberley, and she was relieved to hear that Jeremy had left Augathella. She didn't want to ask too many questions in case Kimberley wondered why she was so curious.

She wondered if Jeremy's family had also left town, but she quickly pushed that thought out of her mind. All she could do was hope.

In any case, Tilly had left town and hadn't been back since. If it weren't for Nana needing her, she would never have considered going back. The memories associated with Augathella were difficult to face. Six months ago, Nana had surprised her with a phone call asking her to come home. She'd finished her studies in the months since Nana had called and worked on building her courage.

Tilly and Nana had always had a close relationship despite Nana's occasionally abrasive demeanour. Tilly knew Nana had her reasons for being that way; she hadn't had an easy life, especially after losing Pop when Tilly was just a baby. Tilly only hoped she wouldn't become bitter like Nana.

All Tilly wanted in life was a happy relationship and someone to love—just as she had back in high school. It seemed she was bad at forming relationships. Every relationship she'd had since Jeremy had ended in failure, and she knew most of the time, it had been her fault. No one ever measured up to him.

Or measured up to the Jeremy that she had known until

he had let her down.

So when Nana asked for help, she was more than happy to provide it, even though it had taken her a while to organise herself.

Tilly knew the thought of the Johnsons still being in Augathella had stopped her from moving back for the past six months, but she'd finally convinced herself that if they were there, she would deal with it.

At least she knew now that Jeremy wasn't there; it would make the move a lot easier. All she had to do was get a job.

She'd wondered about him over the years as she moved from job to job and city to city, never being able to settle. She knew she'd suffered emotionally dealing with the situation when she left, but she didn't imagine that ten years later, it would still be impacting her decision-making.

Tilly had actually felt sick at the thought of moving when Nana had first asked her, but her grandmother's plea had finally won her over, and she'd put in her notice at her most recent casual job in the bar in the Valley.

Nana was always interested in what she was doing when they had their fortnightly call and where Tilly was working. Her grandmother told Tilly she was living an adventurous life. Maybe working on a cruise boat in Cairns, working in a bar in the city, and, in between jobs when she saved up enough, travelling overseas to what Nana always said were exotic locations had sounded adventurous.

But Nana always ended the conversation with, 'Don't you think it's time to get a real job and settle down, Matilda?'

Tilly's preferred destinations had been third-world countries. She had been taken aback by the poverty and the children begging in many of the places she'd visited, and the experiences had awakened a need in her.

She wanted to help. If she couldn't be happy, maybe she could get a job where she was helping others. Two years ago, when she had been working at the bar in the Valley, she picked up a casual position at a community centre working with troubled young adults. She worked there for a few weeks as a volunteer, and she'd fitted in so well that Chris, her boss, had asked her to come and work in a paid position at the drop-in centre two nights a week. Her Friday and Saturday nights for the last two years had been spent there. It wasn't pretty; she encountered many kids with drug and alcohol addiction and some who had been sexually assaulted, but Tilly loved her work. She finally felt she was making a difference and was doing something worthwhile. So Chris had recommended the course for her to enrol in, and she'd graduated with flying colours about three weeks ago.

Seeing the job in the Charleville paper last week was a sign for her. She could go and live with Nana Tingle and continue the work she loved.

If she got the job.

If she was going to live with Nana, there was no way she could stay home with her all day. She had a car, so if she was successful, it wouldn't be a problem to travel down to Charleville for however many days she had to work.

Tilly doubted herself, but she knew she had a good chance of success, based on the brilliant reference Chris had given her for her work, her outstanding results in her Certificate IV in Youth Work course, and hopefully, with a bit of a local push from Kimberley. She just had to get her head together, forget about her Augathella history, and try to present her best side if she got to interview.

The river cat appeared around the bend of the river, and Tilly stood up. If she didn't get the position, she'd make the best of it. She was sure she could find a job in Augathella or Charleville, but working as a youth worker where she grew up would be a way to redeem herself.

Be positive, she told herself.

Chapter 10
Bec - 29th February

Bec smiled at Sean as he came into the bar and went to the wine fridge at the far end. He lifted out three bottles of champagne and hurried back out of sight. Bec wondered what the function was in the dining room tonight; she hadn't heard of anything in town. Maybe it was a work do, or maybe it was a group of tourists. She noticed quite a few vans parked down at the recreation centre at the free camp a couple of days ago. She was surprised at how quiet the rest of the pub was tonight. None of the usual locals were there, even though she did realise it was past drinks time and all of the road workers, mine workers, and station workers that often called in for a beer on their way home would've been gone by now. The only person in the bar was an elderly lady sitting by the door, reading a magazine, someone she didn't recognise.

The pub was barely recognisable these days compared to what it had been this time last year. The old timber wall in the bistro had been relined with plaster and painted a warm copper colour. Chloe and Rosie had found pieces of old farm equipment and implements, and they hung from the ceiling in various places and were on the top of the new corner cupboards that were in each corner of the bar. The old chipped wooden tables and chairs had gone, and there was modern furniture in the bistro. They'd managed to source some old-fashioned bar stools, and there were a dozen or so along the length of the bar that really fit in with the old-world look. The original bar had been sanded back and polished to a deep shine. She recalled a conversation with Reg, the town icon who had sadly passed away last year. He told her the history of the pub and how the timber in the bar had come from a local property back in the early 1900s; she was pleased to see that there was still a chair out the front with a little black plaque in remembrance of Reg.

She was disappointed that she couldn't peek in the dining room; she was keen to see what had been done there, too.

Bec glanced at her watch. It was only a couple of minutes past seven, so with Matt's usual tardiness, he could still be a while. She waited till Sean came back into the bar, and she walked over with her empty glass. 'Would you like another drink, Bec?'

'Maybe a soft drink?' she said, and then she reconsidered. 'Yes, why not? It's my birthday week. I'll have another wine, thanks, Sean, but I'll sit on it over dinner too. What are the specials on the menu tonight?'

Sean shook his head. 'I'm not sure if the new chef's got any specials on tonight, just the usual weeknight menu. I think chicken pie's in the—'

'Okay, the usual is good. Whatever it is.'

Sean poured her wine. 'Just a small one,' she said, and he filled it to the line that came halfway up the glass. 'Thank you, Sean. Looks like you're busy tonight. Matt shouldn't be long. We'll order quickly and won't stay late.'

'Yes, big crowd. I'd better get back in there.' He kept glancing nervously at the closed door at the end of the bar.

'Thank you.' Bec made her way back to the table and sat. It was lovely to sit down and have some headspace; she forced herself to stop worrying about the rain. It was beautiful here tonight. She had good applications for the youth worker's position, and she should hear back about her grant any day now.

When she bumped into them in IGA yesterday, Chloe and Rosie told her that the building work was going really well, and she had organised to go out there for a look in the next week or so.

Her main worry now was that Easter was early this year,

and today was the twenty-ninth; she had four weeks and two days to get everything sorted. She drew a deep breath and tried to relax as a bit of tension started to filter in. 'It will be fine,' she told herself.

The main door pushed open, and her smile widened as Matt stepped into the bistro. Her breath caught; she would never get tired of looking at him, and tonight, he'd made a special effort. If she didn't know better, she'd say he had new clothes on. She hadn't recalled seeing those before or in their wardrobe; his jeans were black, with a shiny belt and a pale blue shirt. As he walked over, she noticed the glossy shine on his boots.

Matt paused beside an elderly woman who was sitting alone. He leaned down, put his hand on her shoulder, and spoke to her. She looked up at him, smiled, and nodded. He stepped back as she rose, took the woman's hand, and led her out the door.

Bec frowned. What on earth was he doing? Perhaps she'd broken down and had been waiting for a lift, and Matt had offered to help. Perhaps not.

He was back within a minute or so, and warmth curled in her stomach as he met her gaze. Matt was in need of a haircut, but the longer curls touching the back of his neck suited him. His smile was just for her. His beautiful eyes lit up, and a wave of love warmed Bec. She loved this man more than she'd ever thought was possible.

Matt didn't sit down. His hand cupped the back of her neck as he leaned down, and his lips took hers in a slow, tender kiss. 'You look absolutely beautiful, sweetheart.'

'You look good, too. I'm so pleased you got dressed up for me. New clothes?'

'It's a special night, babe, not often a young lady turns thirty. I'm sorry we couldn't do it on Saturday night, on your birthday.'

'You know, I think this is nicer. It's not crowded here tonight, and it's just you and me. That makes it special.'

Matt kept standing beside her, his smile wide.

'Are you going to sit down?' she asked. 'Sean should be back in a moment to get you a drink. I didn't order you one because I thought you'd be a lot later.'

'You know me well, don't you?'

'I do.' She reached up and squeezed his hand. 'Who was the lady at the door?' she asked curiously.

'She used to work at IGA.'

Bec raised her eyebrows; that didn't tell her much. She shrugged. Matt seemed preoccupied.

'Sit down,' she said.

'Do you want another drink, or do you want to eat first? I thought we might go in and order now.'

'Go in?' Bec frowned, 'I thought we were eating out here. There's a private function in the dining room. Sean's been run off his feet.'

'There's room for us. I made sure.'

Her physical attraction to Matt was overwhelming. Even though they'd been together for over a year, that lazy smile always sent her heart racing. Bec made an instant decision; she'd put it off too long. She'd let life get in the way, and it was time she got her priorities right. She reached up and grabbed his hand.

'Matt, sit down for a minute. I want to ask you something.'

'Okay, you're not too hungry?'

'I am, but not for food. I want to tell you how much I love you.'

'That goes without saying.' His fingers curled around hers. 'I love you too, Bec Hunter.'

'Sit down, Matt.'

'Yes, ma'am.' He obliged, still holding her hand.

'Do you know what date it is?'

'Nope,' he said with a grin. Despite being an accountant and focusing on figures and numbers all day long, Matt rarely knew what day of the week it was. 'I do know it's your birthday in a couple of days, so let me work it out. Your birthday's the third of March.' Bec grinned as he counted back on his fingers. 'So that makes today the twenty-eighth of February.'

She shook her head. 'No, it's the twenty-ninth of February today.'

'Oh, I forgot it was a leap year.' He squeezed her fingers.

'Matt, do you know what that means?'

'It means that I haven't done my spreadsheets properly for my clients. What did you want to ask me? We probably need to go to our table.'

She laughed. 'In a minute. No, Matt, do you know what can happen on the twenty-ninth of February?'

He shook his head, looking confused.

Bec took a deep breath and put her other hand on his. They were the only ones in the room and all was quiet. Sean wasn't behind the bar, and the refrigerator filled the silence. A murmur of conversation came in from the dining room occasionally, but they were in their own world.

'It's a month until Easter,' she said, 'but I don't want to wait that long.'

Confusion crossed his face. 'For your camp?'

'No, for what we talked about. What I was waiting for.'

Matt nodded slowly as he realised what she meant.

'Hang on,' she said before he could say anything. 'Matt Randall, I love you to the moon and back, and I want to spend the rest of my life with you.' A smile crept across her face as she held his eyes. 'Will you marry me, Matt?' she said.

His mouth dropped open and widened. Matt dropped her hands and jumped to his feet. He reached out and took Bec's hands again and pulled her up beside him. His arms went around her, and he rested his cheek against hers.

'Did you just propose to me, Bec?'

'I did. I took advantage of it being the one day of the year when a woman can propose to their man. Are you going to answer me?' she said.

'It would give me the greatest pleasure to accept your proposal.' His fingers lifted her chin, and his lips took her in a tender kiss.

'I pre-empted you,' she murmured against his mouth.

Matt leaned back, and his eyes held hers. 'Yes, I was intending to ask you again on your birthday, even though you told me to wait until Easter. I didn't think it was the sort of thing we could put a date on. And for me, tonight we are celebrating your birthday, so I came prepared. But, Bec?' His voice shook with emotion. 'You asking me has just filled me with more happiness than I ever thought I could feel.'

Matt moved away, reached into his shirt pocket, and pulled out a small royal blue box. Bec looked at him as he flipped open the box, and the brilliant shine of a single diamond caught the light from above.

'I intended getting down on one knee after dinner tonight, but you've beaten me, so I guess I don't have to ask before I put my ring on your finger,' he said, his eyes filled with love.

Bec held out her left hand, her eyes filling with tears as Matt slid the perfectly fitting ring onto her ring finger.

'I guess we're formally engaged now,' he said, his beautiful smile as wide as she'd ever seen it. His arms went around her again, and it was just as well they were alone in the bar. There was no sign of Sean yet.

'Now that was going to be for later,' he said, 'but I'm so happy that we sorted that now. I've got a surprise for you, too,' he said.

'Have you bought me a birthday cake?' she replied with a grin.

The door opened, and Sean reappeared behind the bar.

'Table set in there for us?' Matt asked.

'There is, Matt. I'll just open the door for you,' he said.

Matt took Bec's hand and held it tightly, but she kept lifting her left hand and looking at the ring. She'd never forget the look in his eyes when she proposed to him.

'You like it?' he said.

'I love it. When did you get it?'

'I've had it for about three months. I got it when we went to Brisbane before Christmas.'

'You're good at keeping secrets,' she said. Matt put his hand on her back and showed her through the door that Sean had opened ahead of him.

The room was quiet now and in darkness as Bec turned to Matt in confusion. 'Are you sure the dining room's open?'

'I am.' Suddenly, the lights came on, and cries of surprise filled the room. Bec looked around, the room was full. It didn't register for a moment that they were all people she knew. Matt nudged her and pointed to the right of the room, and her mouth dropped open as she saw the huge 'Happy Birthday, Bec' banner strung along the sidewall.

'Happy birthday, my love,' he said.

She put a hand to her mouth. 'Oh my God, Matt, you, you—what, I don't know—oh, thank you. I had no idea.'

'I did pretty good, I think. But the surprise you've given me tonight beats this.' Matt put his arm around her as the room quieted. 'Hey everyone, I have to tell you what's just happened. It's a pretty special night for us. Not only is it Bec's birthday, and we're all celebrating with her tonight.' He looked down at her, and his eyes were filled with love. 'But this beautiful woman just proposed to me.' He held up her left hand and smiled around the room. 'And I accepted. So, as well as being a birthday party, let's turn tonight into an engagement party!'

Everyone stood and clapped, and Bec realised how much she loved living in this community. Chloe and Rosie were the first to hug them both.

'Congratulations, you guys! What a fabulous surprise.'

The Ingrams and the Masons weren't far behind. Jon and then Kent shook Matt's hand and reached over to kiss Bec's cheek.

'Congratulations,' they said as Sophie stepped closer and hugged her tightly.

'So happy for you, Bec. You couldn't have picked a better man.' Sophie chuckled. 'And I *love* that you proposed to him.'

'I think champagne is in order,' Braden Cartwright's voice came from behind them. 'My shout, Matt. A bottle for every table.'

'Braden, you don't have to do that,' Matt said.

'Oh yes, I do, mate. I know exactly how you're feeling.' He put his arm around Callie, who stood behind him. 'I think this will be one of the happiest nights of your life. I wish you both a happy life.'

Bec's eyes filled with tears as she saw the look on Callie's face as she looked up at her husband. She knew they'd had some tough times, but if it hadn't been for little Petie Cartwright, Bec knew she probably wouldn't be standing here engaged to the man that she loved. She reached up and kissed Braden's cheek. 'Thank you, Braden. That's very generous of you.'

Callie squeezed her hands. 'I am so happy for you. What a night! Whoever would've thought that a Thursday night in Augathella could be filled with so much joy?'

She looked down as Petie pushed his way between Matt and Bec. He held out his hand to Matt and shook his hand.

'Congratulations, Matt,' he said. Callie's eyes met Bec's, and Callie ruffled Petie's hair. 'That was lovely of you, Petie. Very grown-up, my little man.'

Petie turned to Bec and said, 'You'll have to bend down so I can kiss your cheek, Bec.'

Bending down, Pete whispered in her ear, 'He's a very good man, Matt Randall is, so you take care of him, won't you, Bec?'

Bec put her arms around Petie and squeezed him. 'He thinks you're pretty special too, Petie, and yes, I will look after him very well.'

'When will you have kids?' the little boy asked. 'That usually happens after people get married?'

Bec chuckled. 'Yes, but maybe not straight away.'

'Well, Matt's been sort of like a bit of a special person to me, so when you do have kids, I'll be good friends with them,' Petey said. 'They'll sort of be like half-brothers to me, I think.'

'I think you're getting ahead of yourself there, mate,' Braden said.

'But what a lovely sentiment,' Matt said. 'Thank you, Petie. You're pretty special to me too, mate. Forget this handshaking.' He reached down and lifted Petie up and gave him a massive hug.

A stream of well-wishers surrounded them, and congratulations went on for about fifteen minutes. Bec felt totally surrounded by love. Even Gladys Tingle came up and hugged her.

Finally, Sean came out and said to Matt, 'The chef's getting anxious in there. He's got a few special sauces and things simmering on the stove, and he's wondering when everyone's ready to eat.'

Matt grinned. 'There's a very special menu tonight, Bec. No chicken Parmis for you. I hope you weren't depending on one for your dinner.'

Matt led Bec to the table near the bar, and she smiled as she saw how beautifully the table was set. Sean had somehow managed to find a plastic bride and groom, which now took pride of place in the middle of the table.

'Thank you, Sean. Where on earth did you find that?'

'You'd be surprised what we've got out in the back room,' Sean said. 'Now, would you like chicken or beef, guys?'

The evening was full of happiness and hilarity. Bec was overwhelmed again when, after dinner, Sean lifted a cloth off a table in the corner of the room that was filled with presents.

'Oh, you guys—you're so naughty! You didn't need to buy me birthday presents.'

'Now we have to get you engagement presents too,' Ben

Riley called out.

'No, you won't. Don't be silly. Leave it for the wedding,' she said.

'When is the wedding?' Ben called out. 'You're not going to elope, are you? It's about time we had a wedding in town again.'

Kimberley and Quinn Calthorpe looked at each other and smiled. They'd surprised everybody by eloping.

Bec leaned over and kissed Matt as they took their seats.

'Thank you. This is a lovely surprise. Everyone I care about is here.' She grinned at him and nodded to a table a couple of rows away where the woman Matt had spoken to at the door was sitting beside Gladys Tingle and Beryl. 'Even some I don't know.'

'She looked lonely,' he said.

'You're a good man, Matt Randall, and I love you.' Bec held her hand out and gazed at her engagement ring.

Chapter 11
Tilly

Tilly smoothed her hands down the front of her dress as she made her way to the chair in the waiting room of the Shire Council chambers at Charleville. She wasn't usually one to dress up, preferring to spend her time in jeans and T-shirts, but to look professional, she'd bought a navy dress before she left Brisbane and pressed it in the motel room this morning. She hadn't expected to feel so nervous, and it made her realise how much she wanted this job. She deliberately hadn't been to see her grandmother yet because she didn't want to get her hopes up. She would wait and see how long it would be after the interview before she knew if she was successful or not. Depending on that answer, she might go up to Augathella in the next day or two. In the meantime, she was going to play tourist. She was fascinated by the World War II exhibition that she'd read about and also by the star viewing at the Cosmos Centre. She'd have no trouble filling in a few days, and then she'd go up and see Nana Tingle.

She was the only one in the waiting room, and she wondered how many applicants there were. She imagined they would be spaced half an hour apart so they wouldn't see each other in the waiting room. There would be nothing more embarrassing than talking to someone else who was going for the same job as you before you went in for your interview.

The door opened, and she looked up as a dark-haired woman walked into the waiting room.

'Hello, I'm assuming you're Tilly Tingle,' she said.

'Yes,' Tilly confirmed. 'I am.'

'Welcome, Tilly. I'm Bec Hunter. Come on through.'

Another woman stood from the table where she was sitting as Tilly and Bec walked into the room. 'Tilly, this is my assistant, Alice Templeton.'

'Please sit down,' Alice said. 'Would you like a glass of water?'

'Yes, please. My throat is a bit dry from nerves,' Tilly said.

'Don't be nervous. We've read your application, and we've seen the results of your course. You've done very well, and your two referees spoke very highly of you, too.'

'And being an Augathella local means that you know the district,' Alice added.

'Yes, I understand how these positions work. I hope I have met all the criteria,' Tilly said.

By the time the interview was over, her nerves had completely gone; she'd settled into more of a conversation than an interview. Bec and Alice were professional and easy to talk to.

'Thanks so much for coming in today. Are you staying in town very long? I see that you have a Brisbane address,' Bec noted.

'I did have a Brisbane address, but I've actually left there. I really have no fixed address at the moment,' Tilly chuckled. 'I'm going up to Augathella later in the week, and I'll stay with my grandmother. But in the interim, if you need to contact me, just call my mobile.'

'Do you have any questions?' Bec asked.

'Just the usual one that I'm sure you're used to getting in interviews,' Tilly said. 'I'm just wondering how long it would be before you make a decision.'

'Well, we've already read all of the applications and called all the referees, so once we finish interviewing today, we're hoping that we come to a decision this afternoon or first thing in the morning. So, you'll get a call either way, say, by lunchtime tomorrow. Does that suit you, Tilly?'

'That's really good, thank you,' Tilly said, feeling

relieved.

'I can't promise anything. And we're very appreciative that you've come from Brisbane to be interviewed.' Bec nodded and smiled.

'We are,' Alice agreed.

Tilly stood and shook both their hands, feeling good. Even if she didn't get the job, she'd given it her best shot.

***

Jeremy Johnson glanced at his phone to check the time as he locked the car door. He stifled a yawn and hoped being tired wouldn't impact his performance at the interview today. He'd worked the night shift at the hospital in St. George last night and grabbed about four hours of sleep before leaving early to drive up to Charleville.

He checked into a motel room on arrival and got a curious look from the receptionist. 'Are you going to stay the night too, or just use the room for the day?'

He grinned to himself; he knew what she was thinking. Singe bloke, early daytime only booking at a motel.

'It depends,' he said. 'I've got a job interview today. I've just driven up a long way for it.'

Her cheeks flushed, and he grinned again. 'I will probably come back here afterwards and have a sleep, and then I'll see whether I'll be driving back tonight or not or whether I'll stay.'

'Thank you, Mr Johnson.' She handed over the room key. 'Room 17, up the steps and along to the right. Thank you.'

Jeremy was aware of the interest in her eyes, and he thought what a pretty girl she was, but his focus was on the upcoming interview.

He put the car keys in his pocket after locking his car and crossed the road, heading towards the council chambers where the interview was being held. As he passed the museum, three doors away from the building, a young woman walked down the steps of the council building, turned onto the street and walked away from him.

It was Tilly.

The minute Jeremy saw her step out of the door, he stopped. She must have moved back to the district. The last thing he needed was to see Tilly Tingle this morning. He couldn't afford to let his emotions get tangled. He really wanted this job in Charleville, but he also would appreciate the chance to finally talk to Tilly. There was so much unresolved between them. Jeremy hesitated and then made up his mind. He broke into a light jog and ran past the steps and in her direction.

'Tilly!' he called out as he was close behind her. Her shoulders tensed, and she walked faster without turning. It was clear she recognised his voice.

'Tilly!' he called a second time.

She stopped and turned slowly. Tilly Tingle, the girl he had fallen in love with at seventeen, looked no different to than she had ten years ago. The same as she looked in the dreams he still had about her, and the same as she did in the photo that was still in his wallet, the photo that had caused comments with the couple of women he had attempted to have a relationship with.

'Jeremy.' Her voice caught as she looked at him, her beautiful hazel eyes wide.

'Hello, Tilly. It's been a long time.'

Her throat worked as she swallowed, and she struggled to answer him.

'It has. What are you doing in Charleville?'

'I've got an appointment,' he replied.

'Oh. I won't hold you up then.' She began to move away from him; it was clear she didn't want to speak to him.

'No. Wait. I've got a few minutes to spare. I'd really like to speak to you. Could you meet me in a little while?'

She hesitated, then sighed. 'I suppose I could wait.'

'Good. Where can we meet?'

'There's a coffee shop in the next block, on the other side of the road. I'll meet you there at 11.15.' She glanced down at the gold watch on her left wrist. 'I haven't got much time. If you're not there by 11:30, I'll be gone.'

'I'll be there,' he said. 'Thank you, Tilly.'

He resisted watching her as she walked away, and he realised that no matter how long it had been, she was still a part of him. She always had been, and Jeremy knew she always would be. Even if it had only been a teenage romance—and he knew it had been more than that—Tilly would always be a part of him.

He walked up the steps of the council chambers and into the front foyer, trying to get Tilly out of his mind and focus on the interview ahead. The receptionist at the counter looked at him with a smile. 'May I help you?'

'Yes, I have an appointment with Bec Hunter at 10:30,' he said.

'Take a seat,' she said. 'I'll let Bec know you're here.'

Despite not being one hundred percent focused on the interview, Jeremy thought he had done okay. He probably could've done better, but he answered all the questions, and Bec and Alice, the interviewers, commented on his excellent references. He stood as the interview finished and shook both their hands.

'Are you heading back to St. George today?' Bec asked.

'I'm not sure yet. I don't have to go back to work at the hospital for a couple of days, so I might hang around town for a while. I've booked into a motel,' he said.

'That sounds good. We'll be giving you a call tomorrow by lunchtime at the latest, Jeremy,' Alice said with a smile.

'Thank you. I'll look forward to it.'

He pulled out his phone and glanced at the clock on the wall again as he left. He hoped he hadn't been too obvious; his eyes had flicked to the clock on the wall of the interview room a number of times during the interview. He'd tried to focus on the questions, but in the back of his mind the whole time, was Tilly Tingle waiting for him at the coffee shop.

The door closed behind him, and he picked up his pace as

he crossed the foyer, went through the door, and hurried down the steps. He turned right and headed up the street before crossing at the pedestrian crossing and then crossing the main highway. He spotted the coffee shop that Tilly had mentioned; it was 11:10. He'd been gone for just under forty-five minutes, so hopefully, she was still there, and she hadn't had second thoughts.

It was past the morning coffee time and not yet time for the lunch trade, so the coffee shop was quite empty. A mother with a pram sat at the corner table reading a book as her child slept. Tilly was sitting facing the door on the other side of the coffee shop, a cup in front of her.

Jeremy walked over. 'Thanks for meeting me, Tilly. I appreciate it. Would you like another drink? I'm going to get a coffee.' He needed the caffeine to concentrate when he spoke to her.

'Yes, thanks. A chai tea would be good.' Her face was expressionless, and her tone flat, and Jeremy wondered what the hell he was going to say. There was so much he needed to say, so much he wanted to tell her, but he didn't want to blow it by rushing in. First, he wanted to find out where she lived and what she was doing.

No matter how hard he'd tried to find her on social media or asking friends over the years, Tilly had disappeared into thin air when she'd left him ten years ago.

Overnight.

When Jeremy discovered why she'd left town, guilt and regret had filled him. He should have stood up to his parents, but at nineteen, it had been hard to buck the rigid environment he had grown up in.

That day had been the beginning of the end of his relationship with his parents. He'd never forgiven them for what they'd done, but his greatest regret was that he hadn't gone to see Tilly as soon as he'd heard what had happened that night. Dad had forbidden him to leave the house, and foolishly, Jeremy had obeyed. By the time he'd gone to see her the next morning, she'd already left, and he hadn't been able to find her. Her parents wouldn't tell him where she'd gone; they would barely speak to him. He'd obviously been lumped in the same basket as his parents.

Even though he had only been nineteen, he'd known Tilly was the woman for him. Age had nothing to do with it; he'd known she'd felt the same. Tilly had set the bar so high no other woman had ever measured up, no matter how hard he'd tried to forget her. He had to talk to her, ask her to forgive him, make sure she was happy, and he would be able to get on with his life.

Now, here she was, sitting in front of him, as pretty as ever, and Jeremy was tongue-tied.

More than pretty, she had grown into a beautiful woman. During the interview, all he could think of was Tilly standing on the footpath in her navy blue dress, looking at him as though he'd crawled out from under a stone.

Well, he had half an hour or so to sort it out and seek forgiveness from the woman he'd loved.

***

Jeremy was directly in Tilly's line of sight as he stood at the counter ordering the two hot drinks. Even though she was sure the waitress would bring them over, Jeremy waited until they were made and then carried them over himself.

That pause gave Tilly a little time to compose herself; seeing Jeremy again, looking into his eyes, and hearing his voice had thrown her into a spin. Her usual serenity was long gone.

She tried to bring back those feelings of anger she had carried for so long before she finally pushed them away a few years later.

The problem was even though she had been angry, losing Jeremy from her life had left her empty. She'd tried to fill it with work and travel, and it had taken a long time before her heartache had eased.

She knew what carrying anger had done to her mother,

228

even though Dad had tried to tell her that the cancer that took her mother at a far too young age had been there before the incident with the Johnsons. Tilly had always blamed his parents, and to a certain extent, she blamed Jeremy himself. He hadn't done anything to stop what was said, the rumours that circulated. She would never forgive him for that. All she'd wanted to do was forget about it and move on with her life.

His hands shook as he put her tea in front of her and then walked around the table to sit opposite her. He reached for the spoon, his eyes on his cup, before eventually lifting his head to hold her gaze.

'It's good to see you, Tilly. It's been a very long time,' he said.

'It has,' she replied, keeping her voice expressionless.

'I tried to find you, you know, but you were gone, and no one would tell me where you were.'

She shrugged. 'I moved away. It was necessary. I had no choice.'

'I know, but I should've done something. I should've looked harder for you. But more than anything, I should have come over that night.'

'Jeremy, can I just ask you one thing?'

'Yes, of course,' he said slowly.

'It's all in the past; it's been ten years. We've moved on. We're different people now, and we don't see each other, so I can't see any point in discussing what happened. It's all water under the bridge. It's nice to see you and say hello, but let's leave it at that, shall we?'

He held her gaze for a few seconds before nodding slowly. 'Well, if that's what you need, I guess all I can do is tell you I'm sorry, give you my apology, and hope that you'll accept it.'

'I accept your apology, okay? I have to go now.'

'Wait, you haven't drunk your tea, and I want to know a little bit about you. I want to know that you're happy, Tilly.'

She picked up her tea; it was so hot she burnt her tongue, trying to drink it too fast. She picked up the napkin from the saucer and dabbed her lips.

'I'm happy,' she said, hoping he couldn't hear the untruth in her expression. Happy? She'd forgotten what that felt like when he had let her down.

'I'm pleased. Where do you live these days?' he asked.

'I live in Brisbane,' she said, deciding not to tell him she had moved back to the Murweh district in case he was still around. God, she hoped he wasn't. That was the last thing she needed—Jeremy Johnson in town. If that was the case, she wouldn't be accepting the job if it was offered.

She pushed that thought away. As soon as she said she had forgiven him, maybe she could move on. 'What about you? Where do you live?'

'I live down in St. George,' he said. 'Just had to come up here for the day. I'm a nurse. I went to uni in Brisbane. Shame we didn't run into each other there a little bit sooner.'

'I haven't always lived there. I've been around,' she said.

'What sort of work do you do?' he asked. 'Did you do the teaching degree you'd applied for?'

'No.' Her voice was clipped. 'A bit of uni, waitressing, some travelling.'

'I—'

Tilly cut him off. 'I have to go now.'

She was sure he could see the lack of interest she forced into her expression. It was as though they had never been more than casual acquaintances. She blew on her tea before drinking it quickly and setting the cup down.

'Well, it has been nice to see you,' she tried to be as polite as she could. 'Maybe we'll run into each other again one day.'

'I hope so, Tilly. It's been good to see you, and thank you for letting me apologise to you.'

She shrugged again and stood, smoothing down the fabric of her dress. She picked up her bag. 'Thanks for the tea. See you around. Bye.'

As she walked to the door, she knew his eyes were on her.

Chapter 12
Bec

Bec sat down, staring at the diamond ring on her finger, still unable to believe that she had proposed to Matt last night. Even though she had known it was February twenty-nine, she'd had no intention of doing so. When he walked in with that gorgeous, sexy smile, the idea had come rocketing in. Now, she couldn't help but smile every time she looked at the glinting stone on her left hand.

'Stop looking at that ring,' Alice said with a grin. 'Although I couldn't be happier for you, Bec, I can't believe you proposed. When you and Matt walked into the dining room last night, I knew something had happened. You were both glowing.'

'Neither can I, but it was the right time. Anyway,' Bec said briskly, pulling some papers on the desk towards her, 'we've got a decision to make. So tell me what you think, okay? I've decided which two of the five I would like to select,' Bec said.

'There were two standout candidates for me too. Let's see if our decisions correspond,' Alice commented. 'Who did you choose?'

'Well, Tilly Tingle and Jeremy Johnson were the top two candidates for me. As well as having local backgrounds, they were outstanding. Nothing to do with being from the local area, but the way they answered the questions and the fact that their philosophies are all in line with what I'd like to see in a youth worker on our team. What about you, Alice?'

'I'm with you. They were the two standouts for me. The others were okay, but I didn't feel as connected with the three of them as much. Tilly and Jeremy were spot on.'

'Great.' Bec smiled.

'What do we do now?' Alice asked. 'This is my first interview panel.'

'Well, we've both made a decision. We won't offer the job until we call the third referee for both of them and then it has to go through human resources for a final check. If everything is in order, we should be able to make an offer to both of them tomorrow.'

'Fabulous. So, apart from our two new staff members, how's everything else going? With the camp, I mean.'

'In all the excitement last night, I had a brief talk with Chloe and Rosie after dinner. They didn't want to talk to me about it, but I asked how the buildings were going, and apparently, the bunkhouses are finished. The amenities block has to be tiled, but all the fittings are installed, and it's pretty much ready to go. So, we've still got a month up our sleeves, so we're good. I just have to wait for the funds to arrive and we can get the furniture sorted for the kitchen area, and we'll be ready. Building-wise anyway.'

'It's come together so quickly; I can't believe it.'

'Yes, it's been a pretty easy ride, this one. I'm looking forward to the camp. How many applicants for the camp do we have so far?' Bec asked.

'Well, now that we've reduced the age to ten, we've got quite a few from the primary schools in Augathella and Charleville, and the Catholic school as well. So, I think about fifteen applications for the juniors and from the high schools, I think we're up to about thirty. So, that'll give us forty-five, which I worry is too many.'

'Maybe, maybe not. We'll have to wait until we go out and have a look at the camp later in the week. If Jeremy and Tilly are successful, get through the rest of the process, and accept the positions, I'll leave it for a couple of days. I'd like to take them out and show them what we've done.'

'Sounds good to me.'

Chapter 13
Tilly

After meeting with Jeremy, Tilly tried to fill her afternoon and not focus on her churning emotions. She should have been on top of the world after the interview because she knew it had gone really well.

She didn't imagine many applicants would be prepared to travel west for a job that didn't pay terribly well, but it suited her.

She went to the World War II Centre, and as she walked around looking at the visual displays, she consciously pushed the thoughts of the conversation with Jeremy out of her mind. She couldn't cope with it this afternoon. Then, later in the evening, after a solitary dinner at the hotel on the corner near the coffee shop, she went to the Cosmos Centre and tried to focus on the stars. Accompanied by an interesting talk, what she saw through the telescopes was beyond all expectations, but she still couldn't get Jeremy Johnson out of her mind.

As soon as she saw him, all her feelings from ten years ago came flooding back. She couldn't believe it. She was a grown woman of almost thirty now. How could she still consider herself in love with someone she knew in her teens?

She lay back on the bed in the bland motel room and picked up her phone. It was eleven o'clock, and she'd been up since dawn. She was hoping she'd get a call from Bec Hunter soon, one way or the other. If she was successful, she'd accept.

Jeremy had said he was going back to St. George, so she wouldn't have to worry about him being around. If she was unsuccessful, she'd drive up and see Nana, then head back to Brisbane and look for a job. There was always plenty of bar and waitressing work, and hopefully, Chris would keep giving her a couple of days a week at the centre in the Valley.

Tilly hated not having a plan. Ever since she fled from Augathella, even though she'd had itinerant work and travelled to many destinations, she always had a plan ahead. Something to focus on, something to keep her thoughts in order.

Closing her eyes, she focused on her breathing and staying calm, putting into action some meditation techniques she'd learned over the years when she'd been feeling unhappy. She just got as far as relaxing her ankles, feet, toes, and up to her knees when her phone rang beside her. She grabbed it and pressed answer. 'Hello, Tilly Tingle speaking.'

'Hello Tilly, it's Bec Hunter here. How are you this morning?'

'I'm fine, thanks. How are you?'

'I'm really good. I'll get straight to it. It gives me great pleasure to offer you the position of youth worker for our community organisation, Choice For Youth.'

'Wow!' Tilly put a hand to her chest. 'That's wonderful, thank you so much.'

'Would you like a couple of hours to think about the offer after I outline the salary and the conditions attached to the full-time job?'

But Tilly shook her head, forgetting that Bec couldn't see her. 'No, no, no, that's fine, thank you. It also gives me great pleasure to say yes, I accept it.'

'That's fabulous,' Bec said. 'If you'd like to come into the office this afternoon, there are a few papers to sign. When you were here, you said you didn't have an address in Brisbane, but do you still have a job that you have to go back to?'

'No,' Tilly said. 'My casual work has ended, and I'm a free agent at the moment. So, whatever day suits you.'

'How about this afternoon?' Bec said.

'Could we make it tomorrow? Oh, hang on. No, this

afternoon will be fine,' Tilly said quickly; she could drive up to Augathella tomorrow and see Nana.

'Are you sure?' Bec said.

'Yes, I was going to visit my grandmother in Augathella—not that you need to know all my personal stuff—to let her know that I was moving back to the district. I'm even hoping that I might live with her.'

'Who is your grandmother?' Bec asked curiously.

'Gladys Tingle.'

'Of course,' Bec said. 'It's an unusual name. I wondered if there was a relationship when we interviewed you.'

'Yes, I spent some of my childhood in Augathella, but I haven't seen much of Nana since then, so I'm not sure whether she'll be in a position for me to move in with her. If not, I'll find somewhere else to live.'

'Well, if you need a hand with any of that, yell out and I'm happy to help.'

'Thank you. What time would you like me to come into the office? I can come in straight away if you like and then head off to Augathella.'

'That suits me perfectly. We can do it before I go to lunch,' Bec said.

'Thank you, Bec. Thank you so much. I'll see you soon.'

***

Bec

Bec had spoken to the referees for both of their chosen candidates. Both referees confirmed what Alice and Bec had picked up from interviews and resumes. Tilly Tingle had accepted the position and was coming in shortly. Bec just had time to call Jeremy Johnson and offer him the other position. She dialled his number, and he picked up as quickly as Tilly had.

'Good morning, Jeremy, it's Bec Hunter here.'

'Good morning, Bec, good to hear from you.'

'Jeremy, we were very impressed yesterday, and we'd like to offer you the position as one of the youth workers at

Choice for Youth in Charleville.'

'That's fabulous news, thank you so much.'

'Do you have any questions for me before you consider the position?'

'Just the hours and starting date, things like that.'

Bec quickly repeated what she told Tilly, offered the salary package and waited for Jeremy's reply.

'Would you like time to think about it?' she said, 'Or can you give me a decision now? Not that I'm putting pressure on, but I've got a few other candidates I have to call.'

'Thanks so much for your call. I'm very happy to accept your offer. When would you like me to start?'

'What's your position? You still have a - you're still working at St. George Hospital?'

'But I'm only day-to-day casual. If you can just give me a couple of days to go back and sort out my stuff, I could start next week if that suits you.'

'That'll be great,' Bec said. 'Are you able to come in and sign some paperwork before you head back this afternoon?'

'I am. What time would you like me in?'

'Well, I have an appointment now, and then I'll take my lunch break. I hope it doesn't hold you up too much if I say about 1:30?'

'That's fine. I'll see you then, and thank you, Bec. Great news. It will be good to be home.'

When the call ended, Bec quickly called the other three applicants, informing them that they were now on an eligibility list for any future positions because even if they weren't as good as the first two, they were excellent candidates.

Fifteen minutes later, she opened her email to find an acceptance of her funding grant and some paperwork to be filled out for the funding to go in. Bec sat back with her arms folded, satisfied that everything had gone so well. Life was pretty damn good.

Chapter 14
Tilly

Tilly stood at the door of her grandmother's house and knocked for the third time. Both the front and back doors were shut and locked, and all the windows were closed. She began to wonder if she'd gone away. Just as she was about to give up, the front gate creaked.

'Matilda! What are you doing here?' her grandmother asked with a stern face.

Tilly turned and smiled at her. 'Hello, Nana. I've come for a visit and a chat.'

'Well, you'd better come inside then. Just as well I baked yesterday.'

As usual, Nana was gruff, but the hug that she gave Tilly and the familiar smell of violet perfume made her feel welcome.

'It's so good to see you, Nana.' She hugged her back as they stood on the front porch. 'I've got a job locally, and I'm moving back to town.'

'Yes, but some might think you could've come back a little bit sooner than ten years, girl.'

Tilly nodded as guilt flooded through her. 'Yes, but I'm here now. Since you rang me about coming to stay a few months ago, I've given it a lot of thought, and well, here I am.'

Nana looked at her with a frown. 'Have you heard from your father lately?'

'Yes, he called me a couple of weeks ago. He's still at the Mt Isa mine.'

Tilly's mum passed away a couple of years after all the drama, and Tilly blamed the stress that her mother had endured for the fast onset of her illness. She would never forgive Jeremy's parents for that.

Mum's funeral had been in Dalby where she and Dad had spent most of their early married life, and where Tilly had attended primary school before the move to Augathella. Tilly had travelled from Brisbane to attend the funeral. Nana hadn't bothered coming; she'd never liked her daughter-in-law; that was the reason that Mum and Dad had moved to Dalby. After Mum's funeral, Dad based himself at Augathella as he took up fly-in fly-out work at various mines, and then a couple of years ago, he'd moved to Mt Isa, where he'd started a new relationship.

He hadn't been home to check on Nana since then, and it was Tilly's guilt that had brought her home.

'Barely rings me these days,' Nana complained. 'I might as well not have a son. Or a granddaughter.' She flicked a look at Tilly as she put the key in the front door.

'Well, the good news is, Nana, I've got a job in Charleville, and I was wondering whether you'd like me to come and live here with you.'

'Of course you can't. I won't be here much longer.'

'Oh, Nana!' Tilly panicked and grabbed her hand. 'Are you sick?'

'No, you silly girl, I've booked myself into the aged care facility. Got sick of caring for myself and cleaning a house. And waiting for you or your father to turn up.'

'Oh,' Tilly said slowly. 'I guess that's good news then. If you're happy about it.'

'Why wouldn't I be happy about it?' said Nana. 'All my friends are there, and Beryl's just moved in, so I'll have company instead of sitting here all day long waiting for my family to call me.'

'Well, I can come and visit you because I'll be living locally once I find somewhere to live.

'Don't think you're going to be staying here. I'm selling the house.'

'No. No, of course not. I'll find somewhere to live. It would be easier for me to work and live in Charleville anyway because that's where I'll be working.'

'What's this job you've got?'

'I'm working with a youth centre in Charleville. It's called Choice For Youth.'

'Is that the one where Bec Hunter works?'

'Yes, it is.'

'She's a lovely girl. She looked after me when I was in hospital last year. I was at her engagement party last night.'

Tilly was surprised. 'Her engagement party? She didn't mention it. I did notice a pretty ring on her finger, but I didn't realise it was new.'

'Yes, now there's a spirited girl for you; it was actually a surprise birthday party for her, and she proposed to her partner. He's a lovely young man, and they had a combined engagement party. Matt even asked me to dance.'

'She was very professional and kind,' Tilly said.

'Rebecca was working at the hospital in the dementia ward for a while—but don't you go thinking that's why I was in there—and she had a bit to do with the aged care facility, too. Rebecca told me that it would be worth my while going to the facility and having some company instead of wasting away lonely in this house.'

Tilly stifled a grin. If there was one thing that Nana wasn't in danger of, it was wasting away. Tilly had inherited her fine frame from her mother's side. The Tingles were all big-boned and broad-shouldered.

'That was kind of her to advise you. Are you sure you won't mind leaving your house?' Tilly asked as she followed Nana down the hall. The overpowering smell of mothballs that she always remembered surrounded her.

'Not one bit. I won't be locked up, though. I'm still free. I can come and go as I please. I can still do my committees and do the things around town where I'm very much needed.'

'I'm sure you are, Nana.'

'So where are you going to live, girl?'

'Don't worry. I'll rent in Charleville. Less driving.'

'Do you have enough money?'

'I have, Nana,' Tilly said with a smile.

'Good. And when are you starting work?'

'I'm not going back to Brisbane. I'm starting work tomorrow.'

'Well, you'd better find yourself somewhere to live.' A smile finally tilted Nana's lips. 'If you need to stay here, I can put you up for a couple of nights.'

'It's okay, Nana. I'll head back to Charleville soon and see what I can find. I'll come back and see you in a couple of days, though. Will you be here? When are you moving?'

'Not for a week or so. Now, would you like a cup of tea? I guess you're a bit grown up for the lemon syrup and fairy cakes you used to love.'

Nostalgia gripped Tilly. She and Dad used to come over to Nana's every Sunday when Mum was at church. She remembered the taste of the homemade lemon syrup cordial and fairy cakes well.

'Just a little bit grown up these days. And yes, a cup of tea would be good, thank you.' Tilly reached over and hugged Nana and was pleased when her grandmother clung to her for a few seconds.

Nana stepped back; her eyes were a bit misty. 'It is good to see you, Tilly.'

'It's good to be here with you too. I'm sorry it's been so long.' Tilly smiled, feeling the warmth come back to their relationship.

Nana relaxed, and they chatted happily until Tilly left to return to Charleville. Now, she had to find somewhere to live.

Chapter 15

Tilly checked into the Corones Hotel on her return to Charleville. She had decided to indulge herself with a nice room, a celebratory dinner, and a glass of wine. Her evening alone was pleasant, but as she sat in the outdoor area next to the restaurant, her thoughts inevitably turned to the days when she lived in Augathella, when she was still innocent, trusting, and happy.

The one thing Tilly could never move on from was her disappointment in Jeremy and how easily he had taken his parents' side. After the incident, he hadn't come to see her, and she left town the next day, much to her mother's distress.

It wasn't so much the accusation itself that made it difficult for Tilly to stay in town; it was primarily because Jeremy immediately believed the worst of her.

Over the past ten years, she had travelled the world, met countless people, and now realised that the incident in Augathella ten years ago wasn't as significant as she once thought. With maturity, she had gained perspective, but the disappointment in the young man she believed to be her soulmate always lingered.

When she saw Jeremy on the day of the interview, everything came rushing back. She managed to keep her composure, but she was overwhelmed by a surge of past emotions.

Some people believe in the concept of having a lifelong soulmate, the one you just know is the person for you when you first meet. Tilly might have been young, but she had believed Jeremy was her soulmate. They had been so close and made plans for the future together as they completed their final year of high school. Tilly was going to university to become a social worker, and Jeremy had applied for medical school. They had both chosen the same university in Brisbane and had spent many happy afternoons daydreaming about where they would live and the new life they would build together in the city.

But everything changed on that fateful afternoon. The afternoon, she learned you couldn't trust anyone.

##

Tilly arrived at the youth centre on Thursday morning, excited to start work. Alice greeted her and immediately apologised. She was ill, and Bec was out of town for a conference.

'I'm so sorry, Tilly. I'm not feeling well, so I'm going to take the next two days off. Maybe you could start on Monday instead?'

Tilly was disappointed. 'I'm happy to manage the office today. I can take messages, do filing, or do anything you can give me. If that suits you and Bec, of course.'

'That would be awesome. Bec asked me to apologise for her having to go away at short notice. I haven't been able to reach her this morning to let her know I'm not well. If you're fine with doing some data entry, organising files, and reading our policy documents, that would be great. The only thing is you'll be in the office by yourself.'

'That's not a problem,' Tilly replied.

Alice covered her mouth with her forearm and coughed. 'It's not COVID. I did a test this morning. I just have a head cold from getting wet in the rain last week,' Alice explained as she led Tilly into the office.

Tilly had been in the reception area during her interview and was pleasantly surprised as she looked around the airy office space. A large window overlooked a flat grass area with a barbeque table and outdoor seating.

'That's the outdoor area.' Alice gestured to the window. 'We hold a lot of youth meetings and functions outside. The council provided the barbeque and outdoor furniture. It's a popular area with the kids—a few of them don't like being confined—and we also have our breaks out there. That's Bec's desk over there. She has the humongous screen, but if you'd like to use it today, feel free. My desk is over in the corner, and there are three other workstations with computers, so pick whichever one you like, make it yours and settle in. Again, I'm sorry that you're going to be here alone today.'

'No problem at all. Just show me quickly what I need to do, and I'll settle in.'

Alice walked over to a bank of filing cabinets adjacent to the entrance and pointed to the one on the left. 'In the top drawer here, you'll see policy documents. They're all clearly marked. Pull out the ones on our mission statement and the philosophy of the centre, and read about what Choice for Youth is about. It's a great initiative, and we've been fortunate that Bec is an excellent grants person. She knows how to secure funding. She was really happy yesterday when we received confirmation that the grant she applied for—for the Easter camp—at the lake came through.' Alice pointed to a pile of folders on the last desk. 'The applications for the camp need to be sorted too, by age groups and gender. As soon as we're back in the office on Monday and the other new youth worker arrives, we'll really get into organising the camp. I know Bec wants us all to go out and look at the site.'

'It sounds great. I'm so happy to be here,' Tilly said.

'And we're happy to have you. I think you'll fit in really well.' Alice turned away and held her breath, then let out a loud sneeze. 'I'm so sorry, I'm going to have to get out of here. I'll leave you my mobile number in case you have any questions. You probably have Bec's number on your phone, but don't call her today because she's on a course over in Roma.'

'That's a fair drive, isn't it?'

'Yeah, she left early this morning, and she'll be back late tomorrow night, so we'll both see you on Monday morning. If you're able to come in a little bit early, maybe an eight o'clock start instead of nine like today, that would be good.

We're pretty flexible with hours, but the system is fair.'

'Sounds good to me,' Tilly said.

'Thank you so much.'

When Alice left, Tilly locked the main door and settled into the tasks that Alice had given her.

The first two days in the office gave Tilly an opportunity to learn what they were doing, and she was really impressed. She was also excited to be a part of the team, and as Alice had said, it seemed that Bec was a whiz at getting funding. She read the write-up on the Easter camp, and it sounded really good. It was being held at the property near the Calthorpe's place, and when Tilly recognised Kimberley's married name, she realised Kimberley must live out that way now. If she got a chance over the weekend, she would give her a call and organise a catchup.

According to Nana, a few people she went to school with still lived in Augathella. Excluding Jeremy, of course, she preferred not to think about him at the moment.

Tilly spent her second day in the office looking at the camp applications. Some of the names from all those years ago were familiar: Cartwright, Mason, Wilson—all names she knew from high school. She wondered how much the rumour had spread through town ten years ago and whether her reputation had been tainted by lies.

For the second time since she arrived, her thoughts took her back to that day.

Mum had begged her to stay as Tilly packed her bags. 'Sweetheart, people who knew you won't believe the Johnsons.'

Anyway, that was water under the bridge now, and yes, Mum had probably been right. In hindsight, she knew her friends wouldn't have judged her on what had happened, or more to the point, what had been said, but at the time, all she wanted to do was get away.

As her mother had said to her at the time: 'Those who

know you and love you know that it's a lie. And anyone else who thinks the worst of you, that's their problem.'

It had taken Tilly quite a few years to accept that, but she had moved on now. Now she was back in town, and she was here to stay as long as the job lasted. When she caught up with Kimberley she would tell her why she'd left so suddenly.

Tilly finished all the tasks Alice had given her on Friday afternoon around three o'clock and locked the door with a smile as she left the youth centre. She had made the right decision; the work here was going to be fulfilling.

She had always wanted to continue her education, and now that she had her Certificate in Youth Work, she was motivated to research a university course. She had the time to study now and a job where she could put the theory into practice. Things had certainly taken a turn for the better. It might have taken ten years, but Tilly had finally settled somewhere. She had come full circle, back to the area where she had spent her happiest years.

Chapter 16
Kimberley

When her phone rang after dinner on Friday night, Kimberley was pleased to hear Tilly's voice and even happier when she heard her good news.

'I got the job, Kim. I've already started work, and I love it,' Tilly said. 'Thanks so much for your reference supporting me.'

'My pleasure, Tilly, but your qualifications and experience would have held equal weight.'

'Now that I'm back to stay let's catch up.'

Kimberley smiled at the happiness in Tilly's voice. 'I'd love to. It's fabulous that you're back home. When are you free?'

'Whenever it suits you. I can come up to Augathella any time.'

'How about tomorrow morning? I've got a meeting at Jenna's Tearoom at lunchtime, but I could get there earlier. Are you sure you're happy to drive up?'

'Yes, I'll take the opportunity to see Nana too. You give me a time, and I'll be there. That's the tearoom on the highway, isn't it?'

'That's right. Is ten o'clock too early for you?'

'That's fine. I'll see you then. And Kim?'

'Yes?'

'I've got a lot to tell you. About why I left and everything.'

'It will be good to catch up. I'll see you tomorrow.'

Kimberley was thoughtful as she hung up. Quinn was engrossed in the football on the television in the living room, so she sat down in the study, opened up an old photo album, and let nostalgia take hold as she flicked through the photos of their last year at high school.

They'd been a tight group; she and Tilly and Sophie Cartwright had been close friends. Tilly had been madly in love with Jeremy Johnson, Kimberley had always had a crush on Quinn, who was a couple of years ahead of them, and Sophie Cartwright and Kent Mason had been a couple. That year had been so much fun; they'd all managed to socialise around study and final exams, but suddenly, everything had changed when the exams were over. Many of them had moved on pretty much straight away. Kimberley had left for university in January, but Tilly had left town suddenly the weekend after the last exam in mid-December. Kimberley had been hurt that she had left without saying goodbye, but her plans had soon taken over.

It would be good to have Tilly back in town. They had been good friends, and she'd always regretted losing touch.

Kimberley stared at a photo of Jeremy and Tilly at the Year Twelve formal.

She hadn't heard anything back from Jeremy since she agreed to be his referee, and she wondered if he'd been successful as well. Tilly hadn't mentioned Jeremy, but Kimberley wasn't sure what that meant. She'd be careful what she said when they met in the morning.

##

Kimberley walked into the tea room mid-morning on Saturday. There were no empty tables, and she wondered if Jenny Riley had remembered to book a table for their lunch meeting. Jenny had seemed distracted lately.

Since Jenna renovated dear old Reg's house and opened the tearooms, it had become a popular meeting place for locals and a popular highway stop for tourists and grey nomads travelling along the Matilda Highway.

Kimberley smiled as she spotted Tilly sitting at a table on the side verandah. When Kimberley walked over, Tilly stood and held her arms open, and they shared a big hug.

'Oh my goodness, Tils, it's so good to see you. It's been such a long time, and you know what? You don't look any different.'

'Neither do you, Kim.'

'I wish,' she said. 'I feel like I've aged twenty years since I took on the assistant principal role this year.'

'You look fine. How long have you been back in town?' Tilly asked as they sat opposite each other.

'I came back a couple of years after I finished my teaching degree. I did some casual work in Brisbane, but I've been back here over six years now.'

They sat at the table and waited for their order to be taken. Tilly looked at her and said, 'How long have you and Quinn been married?'

'Six months. We didn't want the whole shebang and the cost that goes with it, so we eloped. We were home about three weeks before anyone twigged, and then we had a quiet dinner at the pub with our closest friends.'

'And are you happy living on the farm out of town?'

'How did you know we're out on the property?'

Tilly smiled. 'I knew that Quinn's family had land out there. It's all you used to talk about. I was so pleased to hear you ended up together. But to answer your question, Alice Templeton at Choice for Youth told me that the Easter camp is out there near your farm. I didn't know there was a campsite out there.'

Kimberley frowned. 'There have been some big changes in the district over the past six months. We've got these generous new people in town who are injecting so much money into different projects. Remember the lake we camped at for our Year 12 retreat? They've built a proper camp there.'

Kimberley watched as Tilly's expression changed.

'That lake? I didn't know that's where the Easter camp was being held. I don't remember that camp being near Quinn's place.'

Kimberley nodded. 'It was. Don't you remember how

much I was hoping that Quinn would turn up even though he wasn't in our year? I thought at the time he might because the camp was close to their farm. And I was so disappointed when he didn't come.'

'I'm sorry.' Tilly shook her head. 'I don't remember that.'

Kimberley almost commented that Tilly had been too wrapped up in Jeremy to notice much back then, but she held the words back.

'I went over and had a look last night. The buildings are rustic inside, with an American redwood forest-type look, and the outdoor areas are fantastic. But you'll see it when you're out there at camp.'

'I think we're going out there to have a look next week.'

'It's fantastic, Tilly. Wait till you see it.'

'Hi, ladies, are you ready to order?'

Kimberley looked up at Ellie as she waited with pen poised. 'I'll have a flat white, thanks. Tilly, how about you?'

'I'll have the same, thank you.'

'Ellie, do you know if Jenny Riley booked the table for lunch?'

'Table's booked for eleven. Amelia rang up yesterday.'

'Great. Jenna's not around today?

'No, she and Joshua have gone out somewhere for the day. I'm the boss.'

'You're a good girl, Ellie,' Kimberley said. 'Even though it makes me feel old seeing you working.' She grinned at Tilly as Ellie chuckled and hurried back to the counter. 'I do feel old. That's Ellie Wilson, Craig and Lorraine's daughter. She was in Year Six at the school when I started there. Now she's finished high school and working.'

'Time goes quickly,' Tilly agreed.

Kimberley sat back as they waited for their coffees. 'Tell me what you've been up to, Tilly. We lost touch when you left town so quickly after we finished our exams, and then I didn't know where to get in touch with you.'

Tilly stared at her; her mouth set in a straight line.

'Then your mum and dad left soon after, and we had no forwarding address and no way to contact you.'

Tilly spoke slowly. 'It was a difficult time for me, Kim.'

'What happened to you and Jeremy? I thought you guys were made for each other. You always used to talk about each other being your soulmates.'

'I thought that too, but when it came to the crunch, he didn't support me.'

'What do you mean came to the crunch? You weren't pregnant, were you?' she asked.

'Oh, God no, Mum and Dad would've killed me if I'd been pregnant at eighteen.'

'Are you able to tell me what happened, or is it private?'

'I know you won't judge me, Kimberley, because you knew me well enough. I should have told you back then, but I was so upset, I wasn't thinking straight.'

'Upset? What happened?'

'It was a hard time. Remember how I was working for Jeremy's parents on weekends, out at that store on the road to Wardville?'

'Yes, I do. The general store just on the edge of town.'

'Well, I worked all day the Saturday after my last exam. Remember that day? The boys were all at the pub, celebrating being eighteen and the exams being over. By the time I finished work, Jeremy had gone home and had an early night, and I didn't see him.'

'I do remember that. Some of the girls were there for a couple of hours, and I remember you were at work. Old Sarge made sure none of the boys drove home.'

'I went to work on Sunday morning to do the morning shift. The Johnsons stayed open for the Sunday papers when they came in on the plane, and then we closed at lunchtime. I was there by myself for a couple of hours because Mrs Johnson wasn't feeling well, and Mr Johnson never worked on a Sunday.' She put her head down and looked at her hands folded in her lap. 'He came in that day. And that's when it happened.'

'What? What happened?' Kimberley asked.

Tilly paused as Ellie brought the coffee to the table. She stared past Kimberley and gave a brief nod as her coffee was placed on the table. When Ellie had walked away, Tilly continued, her voice flat and expressionless. 'I'd always felt uncomfortable around Jeremy's dad. He used to like to stand close to me and was a bit touchy when there was no one else there. When Mrs Johnson or Jeremy were there, he barely acknowledged me. So he came in mid-morning on that Sunday, and he actually . . .'

'He actually what?' Kimberley asked.

'He put his hand on my breast,' she said.

'What? What did you do?' Kimberley widened her eyes. 'Oh Tilly, that's awful.'

Tilly's lips lifted in a slight smile. 'I kneed him in the place that it hurts and told him to never touch me again.'

'Good on you, girl. And who did you tell? Did you report it? What did Jeremy say?'

'That's the problem,' she said. 'I knew no one would believe me, so I just didn't say anything.'

'But that's assault. Sexual assault.'

'Well, I suppose I assaulted him back. When I kneed him, he doubled up, but he told me not to say anything or he'd make sure I was sorry.'

'I can believe that. He always was a hard man. I remember.'

'Jeremy had issues with him too. They used to fight a lot, but I never got involved, and I never said anything.'

'So what happened? Why did you leave town? Were you embarrassed?'

'No, I went in on Monday morning, and Mrs Johnson accused me of stealing a thousand dollars from the till when I was there by myself the day before.'

'What? I don't believe a word of it.'

'She told me that they'd already contacted Sarge and that the word was around town. I was mortified. I'm surprised you didn't hear about it. I'm sure they bad-mouthed me after I left. Even Dad sat me down and told me to tell them the truth and asked what I wanted the money for! That was the breaking point for me. I left Augathella, and I was on a Greyhound bus to Brisbane the next day.'

'Oh, Tilly, really? You should have come to me.'

Tilly lifted her head, and her eyes were sad. 'And you know the worst part of all? Jeremy believed them, and he didn't even come to see me. He totally wiped me. And the first time I've seen him since then was when I ran into him in Charleville this week.'

'Oh, sweetie, are you okay?'

Tilly shook her head and her eyes filled with tears. 'You know what, Kim? I've spent the last ten years convincing myself that I was over Jeremy. I've tried to have other relationships, but every time I think I'm getting close to a guy, it feels wrong. No matter what Jeremy did, and not matter that he didn't trust me or come to see if I was all right, I've spent ten years still hoping that he still loves me. It was as though we were connected. He was my soulmate, and no one else has ever come close.'

Chapter 17
Bec

Matt was already up and working when Bec woke up. The trip to Roma, the two intensive days of professional development, and then the long drive home last night had been exhausting. She was surprised to see it was almost ten when she woke up. She quickly jumped in the shower, then dried her hair, found an ironed dress in the wardrobe, and applied a coat of lip gloss.

'Good morning, sleepyhead.' Matt looked up from his computer as she came into the kitchen. He was at the table surrounded by piles of paper and two shoeboxes overflowing with receipts.

'Craig Wilson?' she asked with a sympathetic smile after she kissed him.

'Yep. I'll be here all day.'

'Do you mind if I go to Jenna's for this meeting?' she asked. 'Or is there something I can help you with?'

'Thanks, sweetheart, but no. I really need to finish this return for him today. He gave me his receipts and things a bit late,' Matt replied. 'I feel bad because we haven't seen each other for a couple of days, and I'll be here most of the day.'

'All good. I've got a masquerade ball planning meeting at Jenna's at eleven, and I need to get some groceries first, not to mention the huge pile of washing to tackle when I get home. I'll only be gone for an hour or two,' she assured him. 'I'll bring you some lunch home.'

'Another ball meeting? Didn't you have one a couple of weeks ago?'

'We did, but Jenny Riley called a few days ago because

she wants to hand over the reins to someone else.'

'That's unusual for Jenny. She's usually the one leading these events,' Matt commented. 'What's the ball for anyway? And why is it being organised so early?'

'Jenny has had some great ideas, and starting early means a good lead time for everything, but I am a bit worried about her.'

'I was talking to her at the supermarket the other day, and she didn't seem like her usual bubbly self,' Matt said. 'I hope she's okay.'

Bec leaned over and kissed him again. 'I'll suss her out, and I'll see you later. Let's have a nice dinner tonight and spend some time together. Do you think you'll be finished with Craig's BAS by then?'

'I can only hope,' Matt replied. 'Have fun and say hello to everyone for me.'

'What would you like me to bring home from Jenna's?'

'A hamburger? With the works?'

'Will do. See you in a while.'

A few minutes later, Bec parked at the side of Jenna's Vintage Tearoom. As usual, the car park was jammed with caravans and motorhomes, but when Bec parked, she recognised a few of the local cars. As she locked the car, a small sedan passed her, and she recognised Tilly Tingle. By the time she realised it was Tilly, it was too late to wave. Alice had told her last night that Tilly had been in to work for the last two days.

Bec ran lightly up the stairs and glanced across to the shaded veranda. A dozen local women were already sitting at the table drinking coffee.

'Hi, Bec.' Kimberley waved her over. 'Sit here next to me. How's your week been?'

Bec sat on the vacant chair beside Kimberely and smiled. 'Busy. Interviews and a two-day course in Roma. How about you?'

'Really good, busy as usual at school.'

'How did you go with the interviews? I know Tilly's already started. I just had coffee with her.'

'I thought it was Tilly driving out when I got out of the car.'

'Am I allowed to ask who got the other position?' Kimberley asked.

'Sure, not a problem at all. Both have been signed up, and the unsuccessful candidates have been advised and put on the eligibility list. You'll be pleased to hear both your friends you gave references for have been appointed.'

Kimberley frowned and answered slowly. 'Oh. I guess Jeremy will be pleased too.'

'You've all been friends for a long time, obviously?'

'Yes, you could say that. We were all in the same year at school. Bec, look, I hope I'm not speaking out of turn, but keep an eye on Tilly. When she rang to ask me about being her referee, she asked me if Jeremy still lived in town. I don't think she knew he was going for the job too.'

'Okay, thanks for the heads up.'

'I won't breach any confidences, but as long as they get on, that's the main thing.'

Bec nodded and wondered if she'd made a mistake. Everything was going so well, and she hoped there wouldn't be a conflict between her two new youth workers.

Amelia stood at the end of the table and hit her cup with a spoon. 'Everyone ready to order?' she called out over the loud buzz of conversation.

Bec stood and Amelia's attention. 'Amelia, I'll go over and tell Ellie we're ready to order.'

'Thanks, Bec. We'll talk while we eat. I need to get home early because Ben has to go out to Charleville when I get home.' Amelia blinked as she held Bec's gaze.

Something wasn't right.

Kimberley turned to Bec as she moved to the counter. 'Bec, have you got time to have a bit of a talk after the meeting?'

'I do. What's up?' Bec looked at Kimberley curiously.

'I'll tell you later,' Kimberley whispered.

Chapter 18

Ellie had been too busy to come to the table to take their orders, so Amelia had marked them in pencil on one of the laminated menus.

As she waited at the counter, Bec walked over.

'How are you, Amelia? Is Jenny okay?'

'I'm good, but Jenny had to go to the hospital with Tom.'

'Oh, I hope everything is okay.'

'Well, not exactly, but keep it between you and Matt. Tom's going to have some tests to see if he needs to see a specialist in Brisbane.'

'Oh, I'm so sorry to hear that. Tom's a lovely guy.'

'Yes, he is. I'm worried about Jenny, she's not coping well at all.'

'Jenny was really looking forward to organising the ball, but Tom's health certainly takes priority. I'll keep an eye out for her.' Bec reached over and touched Amelia's hand. 'And you and Ben, too. That's what friends are for.'

The meals were out in twenty minutes, and Amelia stood and waited for the girls to stop chatting.

'First, we've set the date of the ball. It's the last Saturday in August, and it will be called the Spring Ball. Is everyone happy with that?'

Nods around the table confirmed that there was no disagreement, so Amelia continued.

'We've talked to Harry at the hospital, and they're delighted that the hospital is going to be the major fundraising recipient. Most of the funds raised will go to the maternity wing. It's fantastic to see the wing open again, but Harry indicated it will take more funding to keep it open.'

Callie spoke up. 'I agree. It's great that all the new mums

don't have to travel to Charleville, and with all the new young couples in town, there will be even more of a need.'

'Okay,' Amelia said. 'Jenny's asked me to get some creative ideas for the ball from all of you today . . . for a theme. What does everyone think? Should we have a theme, or what's the best way to go about it?'

The silence at the table lasted for a while as they all thought, and then Callie, Sophie and Rosie started to speak at once. There were some chuckles, and Callie and Sophie sat back, and indicated for Rosie to talk.

'Go ahead, Rosie,' Callie said. 'We love your ideas.'

Rosie's eyes lit up. 'Well, before we moved to Australia—I know it's very different because of our history over in the UK—but we had a Masquerade Ball in the village hall, and it raised a lot of money for our local community. Our masquerade had a sort of theme with costumes from the last century, and everyone had to wear a face mask.'

Bec looked across the table as Gladys Tingle gave a disapproving grunt. She smiled at Rosie and nodded, encouraging her to go on.

Rosie spoke quickly. 'The best thing was that we held craft afternoons in the weeks leading up to it, and we all got together and made different masks. Then the masks were all swapped around, sort of drawn out of a hat, so no one knew who got what mask.'

Amelia smiled. 'I like that idea. What does everyone else think, Callie, what about you?'

Callie Cartwright leaned forward. 'I think it's a great idea, but instead of having a British historical theme, why don't we have an early "set in Australia" theme and we could have all different masks?'

Sophie Mason got on board. 'We could even have masks of Australian animals and birds to match our dresses.'

'I love the idea,' Bec said. 'What do you think, Amelia?'

Amelia nodded. 'I think it sounds fabulous, and I think with Jenny being so crafty, she'd love to take it over. She should be back on deck next week . . . we hope.'

There was a bit of an awkward silence. Everyone wondered what was wrong, but no one asked—not even Gladys.

Amelia continued. 'So, will we assign some committee roles? Jenny is the chair of the committee. I suppose we should take some notes about this.'

Sophie whipped out her phone, 'I'm happy to take the notes as secretary. I can record it here and email it to you all later when I check it.'

'Great, we have a secretary,' Chloe said. 'Do we need a treasurer?'

'Probably not just yet,' Amelia said. 'But once we get closer, we might need to look at how we're going to raise extra funds on the night.'

Gladys Tingle hadn't spoken since she'd given her disapproving snort, and Bec tensed as she spoke.

'Perhaps we could have a raffle and sell some tickets in town. We could make some crocheted rugs and doilies. And maybe Jenna would be happy to sell the tickets at the counter here?'

Bec's shoulders relaxed. 'Great idea, Gladys.'

'The problem is, with raffles, we do need one valuable prize,' Sophie chimed in.

'I think a raffle sounds like a great idea,' Amelia said. 'We need to get someone to approach the local businesses and see if we can get some donations.'

Chloe put her hand up. 'I'm happy to do that, but let's ask statewide too. The better the first prize, the more tickets we'll sell. We've got plenty of time.'

'Seven months,' Gladys said.

Sophie nodded. 'Good idea, Chloe. I'm happy to write to a heap of businesses. Bec, I know you're busy with the youth centre at the moment, but would you be happy to help me? You're such a good grant writer. Maybe we could get together and write some letters to some of the bigger corporations, maybe get holiday prizes and things like that.'

'Sounds good to me,' Bec said. 'Yes, I'm happy to help you.'

The conversations went on for another half hour, and Amelia finally sat back with a smile. 'I think Jenny's going to be very pleased with that. So did you get all that down?' she asked Sophie.

'Noted it all, I'll type it up when I get home. I think I've got just about everybody's email here except for Gladys and Beryl.'

Gladys shook her head. 'I don't have one, but maybe Tilly does? She could print it out for me.'

'Me either,' Beryl added.

'That sounds like a plan,' Sophie said. 'I'll get the minutes to you both somehow, even if I print them and drop them in.'

'One copy will do,' Gladys said. 'We'll have the same address from next week when I move into the facility.'

'Shall we set the date for the next meeting?' Amelia asked. 'How about four weeks from today?'

'Sounds good.' There was a lot of nodding as Ellie came over to clear away the lunch dishes.

With calls of 'goodbye' and 'see you soon', the group broke up and headed down the stairs and out to their cars. Bec waited for Amelia to come down the stairs. When she'd been working at the hospital, she and Matt had had a couple of weekends away camping with Ben and Amelia.

Amelia caught up to her in the car park.

'Are you okay, Amelia?'

'Yeah, I'm coping. Just dreading going home to Ben and finding out what the verdict is today.'

'So Tom's test results will be back straight away?'

'Sort of. I think we all know that something is wrong. He's becoming very forgetful, and he's losing track of time. Jenny suspects he's in the early stages of dementia. Ben's not coping well.'

'Oh no, Tom's young.'

'Yes, apparently, it can impact people of all ages. Tom's only fifty-nine.'

'Thanks for taking over. I was getting a bit choked up there.'

'I saw that, and that's what friends are for.'

Bec hugged Amelia as her eyes filled with tears. 'You and Ben know where to find us. Come around anytime you need a break or just need to talk.'

'Thanks, Bec. We will.'

Chapter 19
Bec - Jenna's Vintage Tearoom

'I'll have to be quick, Kim. I told Matt I wouldn't be long, and I've got a stack to do this afternoon.'

'Me too. Quinn's waiting for me to get home. We're going out this afternoon with the trailer to get some firewood in. It's going to be cold soon.'

"What's wrong?' Bec asked as they walked down to the car park. It had emptied out as the lunch crowd had gone, and the only ones left were Gladys and Beryl. Gladys was helping Beryl put her walker in the back of the small car.

'I've been thinking more about Jeremy and Tilly and what I told you. I'm going to catch up with Jeremy as soon as I can and see where he is.'

'What do you mean? Where he is?'

'Where he is in terms of his relationship with Tilly. They were a very tight couple, and I know Tilly still has feelings. If Jeremy is still interested, I am going to play matchmaker. Do you want to help me?'

Bec smiled. 'I think they would make a lovely couple.'

'They did,' Kimberley said sadly. 'But something happened. I won't share it with you, as Tilly told me in confidence, but I'm determined to suss Jeremy out.'

***

'Jeremy, it's Kim here, Kimberley Calthorpe. I believe congratulations are in order.' Kimberley lifted her shoulder and tucked the phone to her ear as she wiped down the kitchen countertop after lunch on Sunday afternoon. She'd given a lot of thought to what Tilly had said.

'Hi Kim, how are you?'

'I'm good.'

'Thank you so much for the reference. I'm assuming it

was a pretty good one because I got one of the jobs at Choice for Youth.'

'Yes, I asked Bec when we were at a meeting yesterday. I hope you don't mind the news being out there already. It's probably right around town by now.'

'No, that's fine. I'm looking forward to starting.'

'When do you start?' she asked.

'Tomorrow morning. I nipped back to St George on Friday, and I'm just unpacking at the flat I've rented in Charleville.'

'We're having a barbeque tonight. It might be too far for you to drive, but we'd love you to come. There'll be a few of our friends from school here.'

Jeremy was quiet for a moment. 'Will Tilly be there?' he asked.

'Tilly Tingle? No, she won't. Just a few couples. I'm sure you remember Kent Mason and Quinn, of course. Everyone wants to catch up with you. Would you have time to drive up? It won't be a late night. We'll kick off around four o'clock.'

'That would be great, thank you.'

'Excellent.' Kimberley quickly gave Jeremy the road address of their farm so he could put it into his GPS.

'I'll see you around four. What can I bring?'

'Just yourself.'

As soon as she disconnected, Kimberley called the Ingrams, the Masons, and Bec and Matt.

Maybe seeing happy couples might get him thinking.

For only a brief moment, Kimberley wondered if she was doing the right thing. Then she remembered Tilly's eyes brimming with tears, and she knew she was.

She filled Quinn in when he came in from the shed. 'We're having a barbie tonight, love. Jeremy Johnson's coming too.'

He raised his eyebrows. 'Am I suspecting an ulterior motive in this? It's not like you to organise a barbecue on such short notice.'

'Yes, I need to get to the bottom of something before tomorrow.'

'Bottom of what?' her husband asked.

'Well, remember Jeremy Johnson?'

'Yes,' he said.

'And Tilly Tingle?'

'Yes, I remember them both.'

'Well, we haven't seen them for ten years, and they're both starting work together at the Youth Centre in Charleville tomorrow.'

'And?' Quinn's eyebrows rose again.

'And I've got a feeling that this needs a little bit of investigation tonight.'

Quinn stared at Kimberley as she filled the kettle. 'You're not treading on toes, are you, Kim?'

'No, it's something I feel strongly about. I've had a good talk with Tilly, and I think this is something I need to do. I need to talk to Jeremy and find out whether he knows she's starting work with him tomorrow and then suss out his feelings. Both of them are still single. Doesn't that tell you something?'

'It tells me they've been busy.' Quinn grinned at her.

'I'll give you busy,' she said. 'How about you go out and get the firepit sorted, and I'll bring a cuppa out to you?'
At four o'clock, the fire was well alight, and the kitchen bench was covered with bowls of salad and the meat that Quinn had brought over from the big refrigerator in the shed.

Kent and Sophie were the first to arrive with baby Rosie, followed by Bec and Matt. Fallon and John arrived soon after with little Ryan, and soon they were sitting around the fire chatting. The sound of a car pulling into the driveway caught Kim's attention, and she jumped up.

'That must be Jeremy now. I'll go and meet him.'

She took off before anyone could come with her. She wanted to have Jeremy to herself for a while and find out what she needed to know.

Chapter 20
Tilly

Because Nana was busy at a meeting on Saturday, Tilly went back to Charleville after she had coffee with Kimberley and called in to one of the real estate offices. She was disappointed to find out that there was very little available to rent.

'Check with Bec Hunter,' the receptionist said. 'I think Damien, our property manager, told her about a couple of flats available when she was asking last week.'

'I will, thank you.'

Tilly frowned as she headed back to the hotel. Perhaps she could stay in the hotel over the weekend and talk to Bec on Monday to see if she had any suggestions. And if the worst came to worst, there was always Augathella. Surely, there would be something up there. So, having had no luck, she settled into her hotel room and had a relaxing weekend. She tried to push any thoughts of Jeremy Johnson from her mind and was successful—for some of the time.

On Monday morning, at 7:45 a.m., Tilly unlocked and pushed open the door of the Choice for Youth Centre.

Even after two days at the hotel, she felt at home in the office. Maybe it was because she had been there by herself and hadn't had to share the office with anybody. But she felt comfortable there. Today would be different, but she was still looking forward to the work ahead.

She crossed to the desk she'd chosen, opened the drawer, and put her car keys in there. When she turned around, Bec was walking through the door.

'Welcome, Tilly. An official hello.' Bec smiled at her. 'I'm so sorry you were here by yourself on Thursday and Friday. Poor Alice is still a bit shaky on it. She said she was going to try to come in today, but she still doesn't feel well enough. She assures me it's not COVID, she just has a head cold.'

'I was fine,' Tilly said. 'It gave me a good chance to read everything and get to know a bit about the place. With the centre up and running only a couple of months, you've certainly got a lot done.'

'Yeah, it's been good. I'm really enjoying it. Bit different from my last job. I did love that one, too, but it just got too hard after a while.'

'You worked at the hospital in the dementia wing, didn't you? My grandmother mentioned it.'

'Yes, I did. I did love the oldies, but I used to take a lot of the worry home with me. Especially those whose families weren't a bit interested in coming to see them. They were so lonely, it broke my heart.'

'Not that youth work is any easier,' Tilly said. 'A lot of the time in Brisbane, I think if I'd had a bigger home, I would've ended up fostering a few kids. Some people should never have children. A lot of them do it hard, and we had so many homeless kids that we ran a soup kitchen there three days a week, and we were always full.'

'Yes, I'm already worrying about some of the kids who come here. You'll meet them this afternoon. I forgot to mention that we're having a welcome afternoon to greet you and Jeremy.'

Tilly froze and stared at Bec. 'Jeremy?'

'The other new youth worker. I'm sorry I thought you knew, but then, of course, Alice wasn't here, so she wouldn't have told you.'

'Oh. What's his last name?' she asked casually.

'Johnson. He starts this morning.'

'Jeremy Johnson,' Tilly repeated.

That's why he was in town on Wednesday.

Thoughts were running furiously through her mind. He had been in town on Wednesday, but he said he was there for an appointment. He didn't say an interview. And as far as she knew, he was a nurse. Surely, he hadn't retrained as a youth worker.

But he must have.

Oh, God, how was she going to cope with working with him?

Bec was looking at her curiously. 'Is there a problem?'

'No, no, just coincidental. I bumped into Jeremy in town on the day of the interviews. We were friends at high school.'

Friends? Not really the right word for the relationship they'd had in their teens.

Her hands were shaking, and her mouth was dry. She resisted giving any indication that there was a problem with working with Jeremy. She didn't want to jeopardise this job, so she would talk to him and deal with it.

She forced a chuckle. 'Well, what a coincidence. We've both come back to the region. And we both trained as youth workers. We haven't seen each other for years.' Her voice was flippant as she hid the turmoil within. She tried to change the subject.

'Oh, Bec. While I think of it, I went to the real estate agency to find somewhere to live, and they suggested you might know of a flat.'

Tilly frowned as a strange expression crossed Bec's face.

'I do,' she said. 'The shire asked the agency to put aside two flats in case some of the new staff needed something. I'll show you later.'

'Thank you, sounds good.'

'Okay,' Bec said, 'Come and I'll show you what we're doing today. As soon as we get Jeremy through the orientation process, we'll go out to the campsite; it shouldn't take too long. You're probably an expert, considering you did your own on Thursday and Friday.'

Tilly smiled back, finally starting to calm down a little. 'Honestly, I didn't mind. It was a good introduction to get to know the place.'

'Well, once we've taken him through that and given him his key and everything, we're going to go down to the council and have a look at a couple of buses that they've got. It all depends on how many kids we decide on. Did you have a look at the applications that Alice left?'

'Yes, I did. I did recognise a lot of the names from school.'

'Some are new to Augathella too,' Bec said. 'Our main goal today is to go out to the campsite. The generous benefactors who are letting us stay at the retreat, I might add, for no charge, are Chloe and Rosie, who I'm sure you'll meet if you spend some time in Augathella. Anyway, they rang me over the weekend to say that the buildings are all finished.'

'Is that quicker than you expected,' Tilly asked.

'It was a big shock, I can't believe it. They only bought the land a couple of months ago, and not only did they have to go through the appropriate paperwork and permissions and get everything approved by the council, but they also had to find a builder to build the bunkhouses, an amenities block and a cookhouse.'

'That is fast. I can't wait to see it.' 'We need to look at the layout before we decide how many kids are going to come. Once we take a look, we can come back and get this camp organised.'

'Sounds good to me. So, it's only you, Alice, Jeremy, and I for the camp,' Bec said. 'We really need to look at numbers. We do have some volunteers from Augathella—two or three couples who are going to come out and do some of the activities and help with the cooking. My only worry is that they won't have as much time as they think because Easter is big in Augathella.'

'I remember,' Tilly said. 'The billy cart derby, the rodeo,

and the races. It was a lot of fun when we were in high school.' Her head flew up as the door opened, and Jeremy walked in, his eyes wide when he saw her standing there.

'Tilly!' he said, his brows drawing together in a frown.

'Jeremy!' she said, taking total control of her emotions. 'What a coincidence. Both of us starting the same jobs in Charleville.'

Bec stepped forward with a wide smile. 'I believe there are no introductions needed. Tilly tells me that you both know each other from high school.'

'We did,' Jeremy said, his voice wary. 'We knew each other quite well at school, didn't we, Tilly?'

'Yes, we did, Jeremy,' she said.

'Fabulous,' Bec said. 'Tilly, I'll get you to go through the applications again and sort them into age groups for me. Jeremy, I'll give you a quick look around the place, get you a key, and get you to take a look at the orientation package. And then we're going to jump in the council car, check out the buses and head out to our campsite.'

Tilly watched Jeremy as he absorbed what Bec was saying.

He nodded slowly. She couldn't help but think what a good-looking man he had become; he had been a handsome teenager, and she knew every inch of his face. It had been imprinted on her memory for ten years. He'd always worked out and kept himself in good shape, and it looked like he'd continued that. His hair was a bit short now, but Tilly's thoughts raced through her mind, and she pulled herself up short.

What the heck was she thinking? She had to remember what he had done to her, how he had really hurt her. It was all coming back to her now. Tilly clenched her hand, vowing to never forgive Jeremy Johnson as long as she lived.

No matter what her heart told her.

Chapter 21
Tilly

Bec sat in the front of the four-wheel drive with Jeremy at the wheel, while Tilly and Alice sat in the back. Tilly stared out the window at the passing landscape, trying not to look at the curls that brushed Jeremy's collar.

So far, they had maintained a friendly tone with each other. They had avoided personal topics and kept their relationship professional throughout the morning. When Bec asked if everyone was happy to visit the campsite after their morning tea break, they agreed to all travel out in the council's four-wheel drive.

Bec turned to Jeremy and asked, 'Did you finish filling out all those forms for driving? And did you leave a copy of your license with the shire office?'

Jeremy nodded. 'Yes, everything is in order. But if anyone else wants to drive, don't feel like we have to stick with me.'

'You can drive, and we can chat,' Bec said.

'Okay,' Jeremy replied with a laugh.

Alice was quiet with Tilly in the back as they headed northwest. They were on the road to the Calthorpe's property, but they would turn off about five kilometres before the gate and go around the lake to the other side.

Apparently, the New Life company had built several new buildings there, including a camp kitchen, and a couple of breakout rooms, as well as the two bunkhouses. Tilly imagined it would be a lot fancier than the tents they'd camped in during the Year 12 retreat.

As Jeremy accelerated along the road, Alice turned to Tilly. 'I'm not being rude, but I'm just going to rest for a bit. I'm still not fully awake. The antihistamines I took to stop my nose from running always make me sleepy.'

'No problem at all,' Tilly replied. 'I'm happy to enjoy the scenery.'

The scenery that was so familiar to her. All she could think of was the time she had spent out here with Jeremy at the Year 12 retreat.

When they had still been a couple and were making their plans for the future,

She wondered if he was thinking about it, too. He'd been quite aloof since he had discovered they would be working together. She wondered if he was going to find it as hard as she was already.

Tilly knew she had to put the past behind her.

In the front, Bec and Jeremy were talking occasionally, but the sound of the wheels on the road drowned out most of their conversation. Tilly leaned back, closed her eyes, and tried not to dwell too much on the situation.

She knew she had to maintain professionalism and treat both Jeremy and herself as fellow coworkers. They were different people now than when they were teenagers, and she needed to focus on that. Jeremy was simply the other new youth worker at the centre, and she would deal with it.

After another fifteen minutes of driving, they arrived at their destination. Alice still wasn't looking well, and Bec suggested that she shouldn't have come.

'I wanted to see what Chloe and Rosie have done out here,' she insisted, her voice thick. 'I think it's the tablets rather than the cold making Alice sound like that,' Tilly reassured Bec.

'As long as you're better by Easter. It will be all hands on deck that long weekend,' Bec said.

As they drove closer to the lake, Tilly's memories flooded back. The road was familiar, and they passed a couple of old sheds and a windmill that she remembered from the bus trip out here in Year 12.

An unbidden smile tilted her lips; they had been happy

days, and in a way, she was pleased she was back here.

She and Jeremy would just have to make their peace.

Chapter 22
Ten years ago

Their school classroom was set up with rows of desks, but tonight, in recognition of the camp's bonding goal, the Year 12 students sat in chairs placed in a half circle. It was the last night of the senior school retreat, and the group of Year 12 students was gathered to learn some valuable study tips before heading into their final exams. It was probably going to be the last time many of them would be together.

Mr Thompson stood in the middle of the circle in front of the data projector, which was connected by two extension cords along the grass to the single power point in the old camp kitchen. The light illuminated his face, displaying a slide titled "Top 5 Things You Need to Know About Successful Study."

'Rightio, everyone.' Tilly nudged Jeremy as Mr Thompson began. Unbeknownst to the elderly teacher who was teaching his last class before retirement, the students called him Mr Rightio because he began every sentence with that word. 'Let's go through these tips. I promise they're worth your attention.'

Tilly and Jeremy sat next to each other, Tilly's iPad in her lap, Jeremy's pen tapping absently on the side of his chair.

'First.' Mr Thompson pointed to the slide that was displayed on the side of a tent. 'Plan your study time. Make a timetable and stick to it. Scheduling is the key.'

Jeremy leaned closer to Tilly, whispering with a grin. 'Rightio, Tils. How's your timetable looking?'

'I'm working too many hours at the store.' She smiled, her cheeks flushing a little. 'I might need some help with that.'

Mr. Thompson continued. 'Second, find your study style. Some people are visual learners; others are auditory. Figure out what works best for you.'

Tilly typed a note, and Jeremy scribbled a quick diagram of different learning styles. They exchanged looks, knowing they had very different approaches to studying.

'Third, take regular breaks. Your brain needs time to process information. Don't cram the night before!'

Tilly nudged Jeremy playfully. 'Hear that? No more last-minute all-nighters for you.'

Jeremy grinned, shaking his head. 'I'll try, but no promises.'

'Fourth,' Mr. Thompson said, 'Practise past papers. You can get them on CDs from the school library.'

'And on the education website,' Tilly whispered. 'He's so old-fashioned.'

Mr Thompson looked over the top of his glasses at her.

'Sorry,' she mouthed.

'They're the best way to get used to the exam format and timing. Multiple-choice questions first, then the short answer ones, and then the essays. Work out how much time you need for each, and stick to it when you practise.'

Both Tilly and Jeremy nodded, making more notes. They'd heard this tip before, but Mr. Thompson's emphasis made it seem more urgent.

'And finally,' Mr Thompson concluded, 'look after yourselves. Eat well, sleep well, and get some exercise. No late nights.' He tapped the side of his nose. 'And no end-of-year parties until after the exams. A healthy body means a healthy mind.'

The session wrapped up, and the students dispersed for dinner. After the meal, Jeremy was on scullery duty with the other male students, and Tilly wandered down to the water's edge. She knew he would follow her when the camp kitchen was clean.

When he appeared beside her, he held out his hand, and

she laced her fingers through his.

'Soft hands,' she giggled.

'Dishpan hands,' he retorted. 'I had to scour the pot the spag bol was cooked in. I vote we get a dishwasher when we set up our flat in Brisbane.'

'Waste of money,' she replied.

Tilly looked away over the water. Jeremy's family was well off. His dad was a hard businessman, owning three shops in town. Her dad was a farmhand, and they rented in Augathella. She knew that Mr Johnson didn't like her, and she always felt uncomfortable when she was alone at the store with him. She knew that he looked down his nose at her family.

Tilly and Jeremy walked hand-in-hand towards the lake. A fat yellow moon was rising, casting a shimmering path on the water.

'It's beautiful,' Tilly said, looking at the moonlit lake.

'Yeah,' Jeremy agreed, his voice soft. 'Really beautiful.'

They walked in silence for a while, the sounds of the camp fading into the background. When they reached a secluded spot by the water and stood in the dappled shadows of a huge tree, Jeremy turned to Tilly.

'I'm really glad we came to this camp,' he said. 'It's been . . . nice, spending time together. Better than being at school. Or seeing you when you finish at our shop.'

Tilly nodded, her heart beating faster. 'Yeah, me too. It feels like old times. Before, we were worrying about our final exams.'

Jeremy looked at her, his eyes reflecting the moonlight. 'I love you, Tils.'

Before Tilly could respond, Jeremy gently cupped her face with both hands. They stood there, the lapping small waves from the gentle breeze, the only sound breaking the silence. Slowly, Jeremy leaned in, and Tilly met him halfway. Their lips touched in a soft, lingering kiss, a gentle promise of what was ahead.

When they finally pulled apart, Tilly smiled up at him as he held her hands in his. 'That was pretty special.'

Jeremy grinned, his thumb brushing against her palm. 'I can't wait until we've moved to Brisbane together.'

They stood there a little longer, the full moon watching over them, their futures stretching out before them like the shimmering path on the water.

Chapter 23
Tilly – Choice for Youth office

Three weeks later

'Tilly, are you still good with spreadsheets?'

Jeremy stood by her desk. She looked up, managing to keep her heart rate at a normal pace. Being in the office with him and working with him had become easier over the past three weeks, and they had slipped into an almost easy collegial relationship. There was no personal conversation and no socialising, but when they were in the office, it was as though he was simply someone she worked with. She managed not to think about her feelings; she learned to switch them off when she left the flat each morning, but she suffered for doing that as Jeremy filled her thoughts and dreams as soon as she got home each night.

She'd finally got over the shock she'd had when she'd discovered that Jeremy had moved into the same block of flats as she had.

At least he wasn't next door; he was at one end, and Tilly was at the other. But it made it hard because sometimes, from her window, she'd see him going out to the bin, the mailbox, or backing his car from the carport. It was as though he was with her twenty-four hours a day. She knew when he was home, and she wondered where he was when he went out and listened for him to come home. It was doing her head in.

At the end of the second week in the office, Tilly drove up to Augathella to help Nana move and had some respite from her thoughts of Jeremy. Nana had been happy, and they'd shared some laughs as they'd ferried some of her belongings to the aged care facility.

Tilly snapped back to the present, aware that Jeremy was waiting for her answer. She looked up at him before quickly looking away. He was staring at her, and his expression was strange.

Almost yearning.

'Yes, what do you need?' she asked briskly, opening Excel on her computer.

'I'm having problems with the formula for the budget graph.'

'Okay, let me show you.' She quickly demonstrated the steps. He nodded and went back to his desk.

For the rest of the afternoon, Tilly couldn't forget the way Jeremy had looked at her. He'd looked miserable but hopeful. Maybe he was finding it hard working in the same office, too.

Alice was Bec's second-in-charge and mostly stayed in the office. Bec rostered Jeremy and Tilly together to go out to the various homes, where they checked on some of their clientele. Anything related to the centre and the camp organisation meant they were in the council four-wheel drive together.

In one way, it was good. It made working with Jeremy so much easier because they were used to spending time together again, as *colleagues,* not as ex-friends and certainly not as lovers.

Luckily, they hadn't had to go back out to the lake together.

Yet.

Memories of that night by the lake ten years ago wouldn't leave Tilly, and in a way, she was dreading being out there over Easter, which was now only a week away.

She jumped when the door slammed loudly.

Bec strode into the office, a thunderous look on her face. 'Alice, Jeremy, Tilly, drop whatever you're working on. We need to talk now. In the meeting room. Please.'

Alice caught Tilly's eye as she left her desk. Tilly raised her eyebrows and shook her head as she followed Alice and

Jeremy into the meeting room.

'What's wrong, Bec?' Jeremy sat with his hands folded on the table in front of him, and Tilly looked away.

Stop looking at him, she told herself sternly.

'One of our councillors has read an article in the media about a camp in Western Australia being fined $100,000 because a couple of kids ran away from the camp one night,' Bec explained.

Jeremy and Tilly looked at each other, and Tilly could swear she saw a small smile form on his lips.

'So, how does that impact our camp?' Alice asked.

'Well, Mrs Cahill has asked that it be cancelled until she can find out more information. She's raising it at the council meeting tonight.'

Tilly shook her head. 'Why? We've had all this wonderful stuff donated for the camp. I mean, the buildings and everything, and we're not paying for them. She should be grateful for the opportunities being provided for us.'

'What can we do?' Jeremy asked.

'Three things,' Bec said. 'Alice, I want you to go through all of our documentation, all of our risk assessments. All of the kids' applications. Check that all their medical stuff is definitely listed. Check if we've missed anything there in terms of medication. You know the drill.'

Alice nodded. 'Okay, what else?'

'That's all for you. I'm going to meet with Mrs Cahill and see if I can talk some sense into her before the meeting. She's talking about going to the media. The mayor is just rolling his eyes. He's supportive of all our initiatives, but she likes to cause difficulty.'

'Jeremy and Tilly, I want you to drive out to the campsite. I've called the builders and the New Life team. They'll meet you there. Go over anything that you think needs more explanation, and check that we've got all of the warranty documents, hot water systems, cooktops, heaters, and anything else you can think of. This is absolutely doing my head in,' Bec said, slumping back in her chair.

'There'll be so many disappointed kids if the camp doesn't go ahead,' Jeremy said. 'The kids have all been buzzing about it.'

'You've got it there, Jeremy. They are. Let's look on the positive side.' Bec sighed. 'We've crossed all our Ts and dotted our Is. If you guys can just do that for me— what time is it now?' Bec glanced down at her watch. 'It's almost noon now. By the time you get out there, have your meeting, and get back, it'll probably be about four hours. Alice, anything that's missing, chase up. I'll go and see Mrs Cahill now. Let's plan on meeting back here at four o'clock. We'll bring all of our documentation back together, make sure it's all fine. I'll get it all sorted, and I'll go to the council meeting. I'm sure she's going to raise it. If we're prepared, we'll be right, and the rest of the council should be fine, but we just can't afford to leave any stone unturned.' Bec grabbed the keys and was out the door before they could blink.

'Right, I'll get the paper trail in place. I'll see you at four,' Alice said, heading to her computer.

'You ready to go now, Tilly?' Jeremy looked at her.

'Yes, I'll grab my lunch out of the fridge. I'm starving. I was just about to go and get it when Bec arrived.'

Tilly nodded to herself. *Look what normal conversations we can have.*

'Yeah, I'm hungry too. I was going to go down to the bakery, but I won't have time now.'

Tilly stared at him and then dropped her eyes as Jeremy held hers. 'I've got two sandwiches. I'm happy to share.'

'Thank you. And I've got a couple of apples. I'll throw them in. We'll have a picnic in the car on the way out.'

Tilly nodded and disappeared into the kitchen. Well, she'd known she was going to have to face being out at the lake with Jeremy eventually. She was better off getting it over and done with before camp started.

Their conversation was light as they shared their food in

the car as Jeremy drove out to the lake. Passing him a sandwich and then one of his apples as he drove brought back old times when they would go driving in his old Land Rover ute on weekends.

Not only was the builder onsite when Jeremy parked outside the bunkhouse, but two other cars were parked beside him. Chloe and Rosie, and their husbands were talking to Rod, the builder, on the veranda of the cookhouse. Chloe turned around and smiled at them. 'Hi guys, a bit of a hiccup, I hear.'

'But I'm sure we'll get it sorted,' Rosie chimed in.

'I hope so. There will be a lot of disappointed kids if we don't,' Tilly replied as they walked up the steps.

'It's really sad that one person can be like that,' Rosie said.

'It is,' Chloe said, 'but she obviously has other problems that make her unhappy, and this makes her feel good about herself. She's making sure everything is right for the kids.'

Rosie shook her head. 'You're a good person, Chloe. Kinder than I am.'

It took a couple of hours to go through all of the documentation with Rod. He showed them how to switch off the hot water system and demonstrated the fire extinguisher, although they all knew how to use it. They decided to do it anyway.

'We were all going to come out the night before the camp started,' Chloe said. 'Is that okay with you?'

Jeremy nodded. 'I'm sure it'll be okay with Bec. After all, it's your land and buildings. You don't have to ask our permission.'

'No, it's a community facility,' Chloe said.

'Okay, I think we've got everything. Do you guys have all the paperwork from Rod?'

This time Tilly nodded. 'We do. So, we'll see you soon. I guess you're going to the council meeting tonight to support Bec. We'll all be there.'

'Rosie and I will be. The guys have to go back to take over at the store. We're opening for late-night shopping tonight. A trial run.'

Tilly grinned. 'You guys are amazing, not only a department store in Augathella but late-night shopping too!'

The three vehicles left. Jeremy and Tilly stood as they drove out. All of a sudden, it seemed very quiet with just the two of them. A crow cawed in the tree above them, and Tilly jumped.

'I think there's one thing that we need to do,' Jeremy said. 'I'm happy to go and do it unless you want to come for a walk with me.'

'What's that?' Tilly asked. His eyes were still on her, and she looked up at the crow.

'Considering the nature of Mrs Cahill's concern, I think we need to have photographic evidence for the council tonight, seeing her biggest worry is that the kids are going to wander off. I thought I'd go down with my phone and take photos of the fences that are on either edge of the camp, the gates, and how I've got padlocks on them, and also that we've got some kayaks and life buoys down on the edge of the lake. That way, she can't talk about kids disappearing down by the lake.'

Tilly bit her lip. 'We probably also need to make up a roster for the camp. I know we've got rosters for supervision, but it ends at lights out. And we need to—'

She stumbled over her words as she remembered why she'd thought of this and then took a deep breath. 'I think we need to have a roster for after the kids have all gone to bed because we do have some 16 and 17-year-olds here. I think someone needs to be stationed down by the lake at night.'

Jeremy's eyes met hers, and held. They both knew exactly what she was talking about. That night, down by the lake, which had started with a lingering kiss and more planning about moving to Brisbane, had ended up with a lot more; they knew firsthand what teenagers could get up to at the lake.

Jeremy grinned at her. 'More than most, perhaps?'

Suddenly, a load lifted off Tilly's shoulders. They were on the same wavelength. She understood Jeremy, and she knew exactly what he was saying.

She always had.

Tilly began to think about her opinion of Jeremy. No matter that she had had issues with his parents, the Jeremy she'd known then, and the Jeremy he had grown into as an adult, had been and was still a good person.

He wouldn't have abandoned her.

If she'd stayed in town longer, he would have come to see her, so Tilly knew she had to take some of the blame.

'Jeremy, I'll come down to the lake with you, but I also want to talk to you.'

'Talk to me?' he asked.

She nodded and kept her eyes on his. 'Yes, we really need to talk.'

She smiled as relief softened his features.

'I like the sound of that. We do need to talk, Tilly.'

Chapter 24

It seemed fitting to Tilly that she and Jeremy were going to try to resolve their issues by the lake; the lake where they had made their future plans and shared a night of passion together.

This time, as they walked through the trees to the water, they weren't hand-in-hand, but Jeremy kept glancing over at her and Tilly could see the happy anticipation on his face.

She felt a lot lighter too. Hopefully, once they talked it out, their time working together would be a lot easier.

She thought as they approached the last stand of trees leading to the lake's shore, that perhaps they could even be friends.

Six barbecue tables with bench seats had been placed along the lawn at the edge of the water.

Since their last visit here with Bec, gardens had been built, some with rock edges and some with timber benches in a square around the edges of the plants.

'I can't believe Chloe and Rosie and their group did this. It looks like these gardens have been here for years,' she said. A fully established tree was in the centre of each garden.

'They are amazing, and they do so much for the community. That's why we really have to have this first camp. I heard Bec mention the other day that there is a surprise ceremony with the mayor presenting them with a certificate on the first night.

They sat at a table closest to the water, opposite each other, and Jeremy placed his hands on the table in front of them. This time, Tilly looked at them without feeling self-conscious.

'What did you want to talk about, Tils? Us?'

She nodded. 'Our new relationship.'

'New?'

'As work colleagues. I'd like . . . I was hoping we could be friends too.'

Jeremy shook his head and looked away, and Tilly's heart fell. When he turned back, his eyes were intense.

'I can't be just a friend to you. That's not enough for me.' His voice shook. 'I still love you, Tilly. I've never stopped loving you.'

She went to speak, but he put his hand up. 'Let me finish.'

When Jeremy reached over and took her hand, she didn't pull away.

'I've never forgiven myself for not coming to see you that night. My father forbade me to leave the house, and I listened to him. I tried to text you, but there was no answer. By the time I got to your house the next morning, you had gone. Your parents wouldn't tell me where you were; even your mother would barely speak to me. They obviously thought I was like my father.'

'It's okay, Jeremy.' Tilly was still trying to process what he'd said about loving her. A kernel of warmth had formed in her chest and was slowly spreading through her whole body. 'I was young and impulsive, and I was so embarrassed. I thought somehow I'd brought it on myself.'

'What? The accusation of being a thief?'

'No, the other, and retaliating.'

Jeremy frowned and stared at her, and she *knew*.

'Retaliating to what?' he asked.

She took her hand away from his and waved it in a dismissive gesture. 'It doesn't matter. You don't need to know.'

'I do. What you need to know is that I have been looking for you for so long. I couldn't find you on social media; your parents moved away, and no one would tell me where you'd gone. What you need to know is that I didn't speak to my father again before he died.'

'Oh, Jeremy, that is so sad.'

'No, he was a hard man. I've often thought of changing my name.'

'Changing your name?' Tilly frowned. 'Why?'

'I found out that weekend that I was adopted. I'd never known. That made it so much easier for me to leave. I'd never got on with him. He was a cruel and hard man. So I want you to tell me *exactly* what happened.'

'He assaulted me. He squeezed my breast, and he hurt me.'

Jeremy's face was white. 'The bastard.'

'I hurt him back,' Tilly admitted. 'I kneed him in the "you know whats". And then I fled and the next I heard he rang up and told Mum and Dad that I stole from the store. I've always thought you believed that I did.'

Tilly stood and walked around to the other side of the table. She placed her hands gently on Jeremy's shoulders. 'Did you really mean what you said about not being friends?'

'Telling you that I love you?' He stood, and his arms went around her. 'I did, and the way that you're looking at me gives me hope that you still love me. Even though it's been ten years? Ten long and lonely years.'

'You are my soulmate, Jeremy. You always have been, and yes, I do love you.'

Jeremy's head lowered, and they shared a brief but sweet kiss before he pulled back. 'As much as I hate to say it, we have to go. Bec and Alice will be waiting for us.'

Epilogue

With everyone's support, Bec was victorious, and the Easter camp went ahead. On Saturday night, the mayor presented the new Augathella residents with certificates of appreciation at a function. Half the town came to the night by the lake, and with their usual generosity, Chloe and her friends put on a free barbeque for about two hundred people. Even Councillor Cahill attended and was seen to smile.

Everyone was there. Matt Randall and Ben Riley were on the temporary stage singing to the crowd.

The three Cartwright boys whooped around because they had each won their age group in the Billy Cart Derby that morning. Their half-siblings, Megan and Munro, sat in their prams and whooped as loudly.

Callie put a hand to her head. 'I can't believe that pair can yell as loud as their brothers.'

'And Meggie is the loudest,' Braden said with a laugh as he put his arms around Callie.

Fallon Ingram grinned at Callie. 'So the family is complete?'

Callie looked up at Braden, and they shared a secret smile.

'What about you two?' she asked Fallon.

Fallon put one hand on her stomach. 'I think Augathella is going to need a larger school.'

Jenny Riley was there with Tom, all smiles as they chatted to their friends, and shared their good news. Tom had been diagnosed with an illness that presented the same symptoms as dementia, and the treatment had worked.

Kimberley and Quinn Calthorpe's news of a baby on the way had been met with great joy.

'We're due on the same date,' Sophie Mason announced.

No one noticed, but Laura and Dr Harry shared a quiet smile. Their news would be around soon enough.

Gladys Tingle stole the show when she marched up to Jeremy and put her arms around him. 'About time, boy. Welcome to the family.'

The biggest announcement that night was when the mayor announced the date for the Spring Masquerade Ball.

After the town residents had left, Alice, Bec, and two volunteers went to the water to check for anyone who may have left the bunkhouses.

Jeremy smiled at Tilly, tugged her hand, and led her in the opposite direction to the dark side of the lake—the side where they had been before, ten years ago.

Tilly turned to him with a smile, and Jeremy pulled her into his arms, fitting together as if they had never been apart. He kissed her—a tender, lingering kiss that spoke of all the years lost and their future together.

290

An Augathella Masquerade Ball

ANNIE SEATON

Augathella Short and Sweet: 7

Chapter 1
The Cartwrights - Kilcoy Station

Braden Cartwright rolled over, forced one eyelid open and groaned when the red numbers displayed on the bedside clock radio showed it was well past time he should be out of bed. With both eyes still closed, he reached over to cuddle Callie, but her side of the bed was cold and empty. He rolled onto his back and slowly forced both eyes open. The twins had both woken up at three o'clock, and he'd managed to get to the nursery next to the master bedroom before they'd disturbed Callie.

Callie needed her sleep; she'd had a head cold all week and had insisted last night that she was well enough to go back to work today. 'I've got some special sports thing on today. I promised my class it would be today, and they're so looking forward to it,' she said. 'Plus, there's a masquerade ball organising meeting straight after school, and I've somehow ended up as president.'

Braden had quirked an eyebrow. 'Somehow?'

'Well . . .'

'It's just that you love to help wherever you can. No wonder you're tired and picking up everything the kids bring home from school.'

Callie had smiled. 'Bring home? I'm there too.'

'I know. But you can't go in with a cold,' he said.

'It's almost gone. My throat's not sore anymore. I haven't got a headache, and my head's pretty clear. I'll just dose up on some antihistamines to stop my nose running all day. And don't worry, I've done two COVID tests, and they were negative. I think the twins have passed the bug on to me after they caught it off Ryan Ingram at Ruth's last week.'

'Well, as long as you feel well enough in the morning,'

Braden said when they went to bed. 'You know you can't overdo it. Not only with the boys and the twins to look after, you have to think about the baby on the way, too.'

'And about you too, my sweet,' she said, patting his cheek.

'A tough cattleman doesn't need looking after,' he teased her.

Callie didn't reply. She was asleep as soon as her head hit the pillow.

So, when Braden heard the twins stirring in the early hours, he quickly got out of bed and closed the door. Megan and Munro were both teething, and all they wanted was a bit of a cuddle. He changed their nappies and rocked them both back to sleep, managing not to have to do the whole bottle thing.

When Callie got up, he must have been out like a light. A glimmer of light shone from the kitchen end of the hallway as he climbed out of bed, pulled on his jeans and flannelette shirt, and then padded barefoot to the kitchen.

On his way past, Braden glanced into the nursery and was pleased to see that everything was quiet; two little mounds were still under the blankets in both cots. Nigel and Petie were still sound asleep in their room, but Rory's bed was neatly made. As Braden approached the kitchen, his eldest son's voice reached him.

'He's a cool kid, Mum.'

'I don't know him,' Callie said. 'When did he start at the school?'

'When you were home sick,' Rory said, smiling when he saw Braden come in the door. 'Morning, Dad.' He turned back to Callie. 'He's a really good footballer. I reckon he'll play for the NRL one day.'

Braden went over to the coffee machine and switched it on. 'Who are we talking about?' he asked, rubbing his hand over his face. He'd forgo a shave this morning since he'd slept in.

'Sit down, Braden, and try to wake up. I'll make your coffee for you.' Callie came over as soon as he sat at the table and dropped a kiss on the top of his head. 'Thanks for getting up and seeing to the twins. I thought you'd sleep a bit longer.'

Braden wasn't a morning person, which wasn't a good thing for a cattleman, but he would be okay as soon as he had his coffee hit. 'What are *you* doing up so early?' he said.

'Well, I'm feeling much better thanks to an unbroken night's sleep, so I'm going to school, okay?'

Callie did look better than she had last night. She crossed to the coffee machine.

'I've got a lot to prepare for my class this morning, so I want to get into town early. I texted Ruth last night on the off chance that I'd be going in, and she said it's fine to bring the twins in as early as I want to. Rory, you three boys will have to sit in the staffroom for the first half hour when we get to school.'

Braden shook his head. 'It's okay, Cal. I have to go into town and meet Jon Ingram at the rural store this morning. He's dropping Ryan at Ruth's because Fallon is mustering today. She has to drive to Charleville for the helicopter. I'll run the boys in.'

'That'd be a great help. Thank you, sweetheart.'

'So, what's the plan? Lamb shanks for dinner?' He spotted them thawing out on the sink.

'Yep, I'll put them in the slow cooker before we go. Rory, there's a load of towels in the machine. While I have my shower, can you peg them on the line in the breezeway for me, love? And then get them in this afternoon? I've got a ball meeting after school.'

'Yes, Mum. But you haven't answered my question…'

'Sorry, I got sidetracked.' Callie reached up and pushed her hair back as she stirred the porridge. 'Tell me more about this new friend.'

'He came to school last week, and we're good mates already. I said he might be able to come out and play footy after school this afternoon. He could come home on the bus with me unless you're picking us up, Dad.' Rory turned to Braden with a hopeful look.

'Yes, I am, but remember, we're a long way out. If he comes here, we've got to run him back into town unless his parents pick him up. Who are they? Where do they live?'

'He hasn't got a mum. He said his carer would be happy to come out here and pick him up,' Rory said as he put a bit of bread in the toaster. 'Do you want some toast, Dad?'

'Thanks, mate, that would be great.'

'Who's having porridge?' Callie asked.

'I will,' Braden said. 'I'll start with toast with my coffee.'

'So, keep going,' Callie continued. 'What's his name? Whose class is he in?'

'His name is Beau, and he's in Mr Cooper's class. He's had a couple of days off since he started at school because his carer makes him work around the house,' Rory said.

Braden and Callie's eyes met over the top of Rory's head. Rory tended to pick up the needy kids at school, and Callie kept a close eye on him. He'd been burned a couple of times. The last time they'd discovered, he'd been buying lunch at the canteen for a student who hid his lunch so Rory would buy him a pie. It happened every day for a week until Ros at the canteen told Callie what was going on. The only day the boys bought their lunch at the canteen was Monday, so Rory took money out of his money box and bought lunch for someone he thought was a needy student.

'It's not going to be Lucas Jones all over again, is it?' Callie asked.

'No, Mum. Beau's a really good guy, and like I said, he plays football, and we hit it off like a house on fire.'

Braden smothered a smile. 'Well, Mum can suss it out today and find out what the story is with getting picked up. Maybe Beau can come out on the weekend,' he said. 'Today's a bit short notice to organise him getting home.'

'Okay, I guess that's alright. I'll go and hang that

washing out now. Here's your toast, Dad.' Rory laughed as Braden lifted his hands just in time to catch the piece of toast Rory frisbeed across from the toaster.

'Good catch, Dad.'

'Eat your porridge before you hang the washing, mate,' Callie said.

'Aw, Mum. You know I hate that gluggy stuff.'

'It's good for you.'

'I like porridge,' Nigel muttered as he came into the kitchen and sat at the table.

Callie grinned as she poured Braden's coffee. Nigel took after his father; he was not a morning person. Sometimes, he managed to eat his entire bowl of porridge without opening his eyes.

'Okay, I'll go and get ready. Now,' she said as she put the mug of coffee in front of Braden. 'Rory, don't forget the towels. And Nigel, you can feed the dogs for Dad this morning.'

'What about Petie? What's his job?' Nigel muttered crossly. 'I wish I was the baby of the family.'

'Petie's not the baby anymore, dumb-arse.'

Callie drew in a breath. 'Rory Cartwright, I beg your pardon. What did you say?'

Braden reached out and pulled Rory over to him. 'That's not a word we use in this house, Rory.'

'It's just a word,' Rory said defiantly. 'Just a mix of letters.'

'It's rude, and it wasn't good to call me that.' Nigel was wide awake now.

'I'm sorry. I take it back,' Rory mumbled.

'Good, now eat your porridge and then go and hang those towels out for Mum.' Braden caught Callie's hand as she hurried past. 'Slow down. Are you sure you're well enough to go to school?'

'I am.' She smiled at him. 'I'm going for a shower. Cross your fingers that the twins sleep a little bit longer.'

Chapter 2

Getting six-year-old Petie out of bed on cold winter mornings was a chore in itself. By the time Braden had the three boys ready to go to school, their lunches packed, the dogs fed, and the twin cab ute backed out of the shed, they were running late. He tore off down the dirt road and was pulled up by his youngest son within seconds.

'Dad, you're going too fast. Mum said you always drive too fast, and she's not here, so I'm telling you to slow down. Got it?'

Braden bit back a grin and nodded. 'Sorry, Petie. I *was* going a little bit too fast. I'll slow down. If you're late for school, you're late for school. So be it.'

That started a fight between Rory and Nigel in the back seat. 'If we're late, I'm taking the football back into the sports storeroom when the bell goes,' Rory said.

Nigel shook his head, and Braden heard a thump from the backseat.

'No, you're not. It's my turn to do that.' Nigel was building up to a whine.

Braden threw a glance over his shoulder. 'If we're late, we'll miss the bell, and I'm sure the football will be put away by then anyway. Besides, that's not a thing to fight about, okay?'

All was quiet for about ten minutes, and then Rory leaned forward and put his hands on Braden's shoulders from the backseat.

'Dad?' he said.

Braden waited. By the tone of his voice and the soft touch of his eldest son's hands on his shoulders, he knew a favour was about to be asked. 'Yeah, mate, what's up?'

'I was really hoping Beau could come out and play football with me this afternoon. What do you think about that? Mum will be at her meeting, and the dinner's cooked, and he can help me with the chores before we play footy.'

'Can I play footy too?' Petie asked.

'No, Beau's my friend, and you're still too little. We can't tackle you,' Rory said.

Petie grunted.

'What's Beau's last name?' Braden asked. 'Does he live in town or on a property? Depends where he has to go home to.'

'I don't know his last name. I never took much notice. I only hear the first name in class when they mark the roll.'

'Well, I don't know if I know his family.'

'You won't know his parents. He hasn't got any family.'

Braden sat up a bit straighter and paid more attention. 'What do you mean? He hasn't got any parents? Who does he live with? You talked about his dad when we had breakfast.'

'No, I didn't. You were half asleep, Dad. I said his *carer*. And Mum heard what I said because I saw the look she gave you. Anyway, this is different. I was just helping Lucas when I thought he was hungry, but I'm real friends with Beau already.'

'So what's the carer story?' Braden asked.

'Well, they've just moved to town, and he said he lives with this bloke who wants to be his dad. He said he doesn't want him to be his dad, and he called him a dumb arse. That's where I heard that word.'

Braden was trying to think of a suitable reply when Rory rushed on. 'Okay, so when can Beau come out?'

Nigel leaned forward. 'I don't like him. He smells.'

'Well, he's not your friend, so what you think doesn't matter, dum—I mean, you can go and watch TV while we're playing football,' Rory said. 'And maybe his clothes don't get washed, so it's not his fault.'

'If my clothes smelled and we didn't have Mum, I'd wash

my own,' Nigel chipped in. 'I know how to use the washing machine.'

'You would not, you—'

'Dad, he was going to call me a name again,' Nigel yelled.

The sound of another muffled thump came from the back seat. 'Dad, Rory just punched Nigel,' Petie said.

'Okay, calm down. Thanks, Petie. Rory, I've told you about punching.'

The last six months had seen a change in the family dynamic. Petie was as sweet as ever, but Braden was sure that one day he'd grow out of that too and enter that horrible time between ten and twelve, which Rory and Nigel had just respectively reached.

Almost ten-year-old Nigel had been the difficult child since the boys' mother and Braden's first wife, Julia, had been killed in an accident before Braden had met and married Callie.

It was almost as though a switch had been thrown the day Rory turned eleven. He must be developing hormones or something because he'd been an absolute pain in the butt over the last few weeks, constantly niggling at Nigel. To Nigel's credit, he hadn't flared up as much as he would have done a year or two ago.

'Okay, the first thing is that you pair stop fighting in the back, or no one will be coming to play football. This behaviour, name-calling and punching, is not how we work in our family, and I'm certainly not letting anyone come to play at the station while you two carry on like that. You pair need to show a lot more respect to each other. Got it?'

A couple of mutters came from the back seat.

'I said do you get it?' Braden's voice was louder.

'Yes, Dad.' Two meek voices answered him.

'Good. Second, if you can show me you can behave, Beau can come out one day. But I'm not promising anything, okay? And I'll need to talk to your mum about it. She's been tired lately.'

Pete's sweet little voice came from the backseat. 'That's because you've got twins, and Mum's having another baby. Will we have enough bedrooms when you finish having babies, Dad? Or will we build a bigger house?'

Braden's lips twitched. 'I think we're finished having babies now. When the new one's born, I mean.'

'You might be. You never know what might happen. Penny Wilson told me—'

Braden tensed, but Rory had obviously elbowed Petie. 'Shut up, Pete. We don't wanna hear about all that romance-type stuff. Penny talks about making babies all the time.'

Braden rolled his eyes; his boys were growing up too fast.

The last ten kilometres of the drive into Augathella seemed to take forever. The arguments continued—albeit quietly. Occasional muffled thumps came from the back, and when he finally pulled up outside the school and got out of the ute, he leaned down and kissed Petie on the cheek. 'Off you go, mate.'

Petie ran off happily.

'Right, you pair. I want to talk to you. That behaviour in the car on the way in was unacceptable. I hope you don't behave like that when Mum drives you to school.'

'No, Dad, it was just that—'

'Enough, Rory. I don't want any excuses. I want you to know that from now on, I won't put up with any of that behaviour. I'm going to talk to Mum, and if I find out that you do that when she's driving you to school, there'll be big trouble. And I mean big trouble. Okay?'

Rory and Nigel wouldn't meet his eye, and they lowered their heads, kicking at the dirt.

'Okay?' Braden said.

Nigel looked up and held his eye. 'Dad, I respect that.'

'Rory?'

'Yes, Dad, but it wasn't me.'

Braden refrained from roaring. Instead, he bent down and

squeezed both their shoulders. Rory and Nigel maintained they were too big to be kissed by their parents outside the school. 'Have a good day, okay? And be good!'

'Yes, Dad,' Rory said politely. 'We will. Won't we, Nige? And Dad? Don't forget to ask Mum about Beau coming out. You could send her a text maybe,' Rory suggested hopefully.

'We'll see what happens.' Braden gave them a wave, climbed into the ute, and switched his mind to work mode as he headed to the rural store to meet Jon Ingram.

Chapter 3
Alice

'Wow, you've got the Audrey Hepburn look going today, Alice. Looking pretty swish.'

Alice smiled at Bec, the team leader at Choice for Youth in Charleville, as she put her handbag on the kitchen counter. Bec was making her first coffee of the day.

'I've got a meeting this morning, remember?' Alice patted her hair. She'd pulled it back into a chignon to match her professional suit.

'Oh, that's right. I really appreciate it. I'm tied up with this other initiative. I can't tell you about it yet, but hopefully, I might hear today. And that's the first time I've seen you with your hair up. You look very sophisticated.'

Alice laughed. 'As long as I look the part. Doesn't feel like me. The last time I turned up at one of the meetings in my youth worker clothes, jeans, and a T-shirt, one principal looked at me as if I had crawled out from under a rock.'

'I appreciate you taking my place today. The local commanders of the three police regions and five high school principals from the school region will be there, as well as the three local schools. With your matching blue shoes and the pearls, the chignon is perfect.'

'Like I said, as long as I look the part. I can take notes for you. I won't have to say much, will I?'

'No, just a presence is fine. You look lovely today, and thanks for going to the meeting for me. Let me know how it goes. I wish I had my news to tell them before then, but I the phone call hasn't come through yet.'

Alice was intrigued. Bec had been very quiet this week, and every time her phone rang, she picked it up immediately.

The meeting went well, and she got back to the office just in time for her lunch break. The last few days had been showery and cold, but the sky had cleared to a brilliant blue when Alice set out for work this morning. Now, it was warm enough to take her cardigan off as she and her co-worker, Tilly Tingle, headed to their favourite coffee shop on the main street of Charleville for lunch. The morning had been busy; the phones had rung non-stop, and the leader of their team at Choice for Youth, Bec, had been closeted in her office most of the time. The three other youth workers, including Tilly's fiance, Jeremy, had headed out to visit a cattle station that had agreed to be part of a program for local youth. Alice and Tilly decided to spend their break at the table outside the coffee shop.

'Thank you.' Alice smiled at the waitress as she brought their baguettes to the table.

'Coffees won't be long. Do you want me to leave the takeaway one until you've finished your lunch?' the young girl asked.

'Yes, please.' Tilly nodded and then looked at Alice. 'I wonder if Bec's off the phone yet?'

Bec had been bursting with excitement all morning. Alice had been going to pump her to see what was happening over lunch, but the call Bec had been waiting for came through as they were about to leave. She waved them off and mimed bringing her a coffee back.

'What's going on, I wonder?' Tilly asked as she reached for her chicken and avocado baguette.

'I don't know,' Alice replied. 'She's been on the phone constantly for a couple of days. Something's happening. At least we know we don't have to worry about our jobs, with Chloe and her group funding the youth centre.'

'That's true. I'm sure Bec'll tell us when she's good and ready.' Tilly lifted her hand and pushed her hair back as the slight breeze caught it. The mid-morning sun glinted on her engagement ring.

'Jeremy certainly didn't waste much time putting a ring on your finger,' Alice said with a smile.

Tilly looked down at the diamond and sapphire ring gracing her finger and smiled back at Alice. 'He reckoned he'd waited long enough. We came down to the jeweller here straight after the Easter camp. Jeremy said he wasn't going to risk any more misunderstandings.'

'You've certainly hit the jackpot there, Tilly,' Alice said. 'He's a top guy.'

'That he is, and yes, we did waste a lot of years, but that's all water under the bridge now. We've sorted everything out. And you know one of the best parts? We're both back living where we want to be.'

'I won't say you're lucky because you went through a tough time until you finally got together, but I am envious.' Alice reached for her coffee cup.

'Envious?' Tilly frowned.

'Oh, don't get me wrong. I'm not in love with Jeremy or anything like that. I'm really happy for you guys. I wish I could find someone like him—a guy with a profession who likes the same things I do. Developing a relationship, falling in love, setting up a home together, and having a family are all I've ever wanted. But I think it's too big an ask. Life's passing me by.'

'What makes you say that?' Tilly put her hand gently on Alice's wrist, and Alice looked away as the beautiful ring sparkled. She wasn't going to take away from Tilly's happiness.

'I saw the happy marriage my mum and dad had. God bless their souls. They're both gone now. They married late in life, and I lost them when I was in my early twenties. I wanted to get married and have kids before I got too old.'

Tilly stared at her. 'How old are you now, Alice? I thought you were that age now.'

'You're my new best friend, Tilly,' Alice chuckled. 'I'll be thirty-three next birthday.'

Tilly's eyes widened. 'Well, that surprises me. Have you always lived here?' she said. 'I don't remember you from high school. You wouldn't have been that far ahead of us.'

'Yes, I grew up out past Allenvale. Dad had a cattle property there. I left high school in Augathella when I was about fifteen. Mum and Dad sent me off to boarding school. Dad wasn't well, and they were thinking about selling the farm. I was an only child and had no interest in the land.'

'Ah, I would still have been at the primary school then. Did you like it? Boarding school, I mean.'

'No, I hated every minute of it,' Alice said. 'I went to a girls' school in Toowoomba. I was a handful back in those days. I did everything I could to get expelled. Sometimes, I think how I was at school helps me understand the kids we deal with. They think they know all the tricks, but I'm usually one step ahead.'

'And you came back to Augathella after high school?'

'I did. I lived in a flat and worked at the IGA here for a couple of years after I lost Mum and Dad. There wasn't much left when the mortgage was paid out on the farm. When I'd saved enough, I went to university and got my social work degree. I did some of it externally and worked to support myself in Brisbane, and then I finished it off at Griffith University.'

'We must have lived in Brisbane at the same time.'

'Maybe. It's a big city, but I did leave for a few years to travel overseas. I've been back in Charleville for about four years now. One day, I'd like to buy a place in Augathella. I love interior design, and I'd spend a lot of time in the garden. Maybe I could buy and renovate houses if I ever get sick of this work.'

'That would be a shame. You love your job, and you are so good at it. I've learned a lot watching you work. Especially at camp.'

Alice chuckled. 'And here was I thinking you were focused on Jeremy that weekend.'

Tilly's cheeks flushed. 'I had time to watch you and Bec work, too. Have you ever had a partner?' Tilly asked. 'I hope you don't mind me asking.'

'I had a close friend at uni who ticked all the boxes, but he wasn't interested in developing a relationship. And I guess there wasn't a spark, so he was right. Then, when I was travelling, I met this Spanish guy in Europe, and we stayed together for a while, but Rafe didn't want to settle down. I told myself we'd stay together; I thought we were pretty serious, but he never wanted to discuss a future together. All he wanted was to do adventurous things: skiing, snowboarding, climbing mountains, etc. I used to sit around and wait for him on the tours, and then he decided he wanted to go and live in Iceland for a while; he was intrigued by volcanoes. That was when I woke up to myself. I knew I didn't love Rafe enough because if I had, I would have gone with him wherever he wanted to go. It was the thought of a relationship I wanted rather than the man himself.'

'It's good that you didn't make the wrong choice,' Tilly said. 'Sounds like we need to do some matchmaking here.'

Alice chuckled. 'No, don't you start. The problem is, there's no one suitable around here. If I want to find someone, I might have to sign up to one of those online sites or move to a city and start going to pubs and nightclubs. Maybe I've waited too long for Mr Right to appear.'

'No, you don't have to do that. I'm a great believer in fate. Someone is waiting for you. One day.'

'One day?' Alice chuckled. 'As long as I don't have to wait twenty years. I'd love a family.'

'It'll happen. Be positive. I thought I'd spend my life alone, but look at me now.'

'You always knew Jeremy was the one?'

'Yes, I did. The few relationships I had in Brisbane just didn't measure up to what we'd had, and Jeremy says the same thing. That's why he put a ring on my finger within a couple of weeks of reconnecting.'

'And a lovely ring it is,' Alice said, pushing away her plate. 'Anyway, as much as I'd love to chat in the sun, I promised the girls at Augathella I'd get some craft samples from the discount store for the ball planning meeting this afternoon.'

'Crumbs, I forgot about that. I hope Nana wasn't too pushy when she talked you into joining the committee.'

'No, I love being involved. Although the time is going quickly, and we have a lot to do.'

'Yes, spring will be here before we know it; the wattle's coming out already. But it's a great initiative. Being on the committee and moving into the aged care facility seems to have given Nana a new lease on life.'

'She was very persuasive when she heard I like making things.'

'And when Bec told her you also make all your clothes, she was determined to get you on the committee.'

'Are you right to take Bec's coffee back, Tilly?' Alice asked as she stood and picked up her cup and saucer to take back to the counter.

'Yeah, not a problem.'

'I've still got half an hour left on my lunch break, so I'll go back and have a good look at the craft stuff I was looking at when I raced through the other day when I went down to get supplies to top up the lolly jar in the office.'

'Okay, I'll see you back there. Don't worry about taking those cups in.' Tilly reached over and took them. 'I'll take them in while I get Bec's coffee. See you in a while. Bye.'

Chapter 4

When Alice left Tilly at the coffee shop, she headed to the huge discount store to look in the craft section for some decals that might be useful for making masks. Gladys had told Tilly that the main task for tonight's meeting was to ensure she passed that on to Alice.

Tilly's busybody grandmother seemed to have taken over the agenda—and the committee—even though she wasn't president or secretary. Callie Cartwright and Sophie Mason had taken on those roles, and now that Jenny Riley's husband was better, Jenny had returned and resumed the treasurer's position.

The discount store was at the other end of the street, and Alice strolled along slowly, enjoying the sun's warmth on her shoulders. It had been a cold winter, and Alice was looking forward to spring, but she knew they still had a lot of planning to do. Tonight's meeting was necessary; it had been a few weeks since they'd last met. Everyone was busy with work and families, and the months had flown by. Working at Choice for Youth with Bec had kept Alice busy, and the time seemed to pass more quickly every week. However, the workload had lessened since Jeremy and Tilly joined the team.

Alice pulled a face; she had more time to herself again. Well, at least she had work to keep her occupied, and the upside of living alone was that she'd have plenty of time to make the masks for anyone who wanted her to. Not only was it time to make some decisions about the ball, but it was also time to make some decisions about her future. Would she stay here, or would she move on in the hope of meeting the right man?

Alice took a deep breath. She walked past the revamped butcher shop, the spicy smell of Smokin' Joe's marinade drifting out into the street. On her way back, she'd call in there for a steak and store the meat in the fridge at the youth centre, ready for her dinner tonight. Some of the marinades in the shop were addictive, especially on these cold winter nights.

Another dinner alone, she thought. Sitting with Tilly and looking at her ring and her happy expression had made Alice realise how lonely she was.

She had a great job and worked with good people, but going home to her empty flat every afternoon, having dinner alone, watching television, or reading a book didn't satisfy her. It's not what she'd imagined for her life. She thought by her early thirties, she'd be happily married with a couple of kids, running them to daycare or school, but here she was, still alone.

With a sigh, Alice walked into the discount store. She needed to give her future some serious thought. She wasn't going to meet anyone here in Charleville. Most of her clientele were already married or in relationships, and everyone else she worked with was still in their teens.

I've got a great job, I'm doing a great job, and I've got to accept that makes me happy enough and stop hoping for the impossible.

The discount store was in one of the biggest buildings in town, and you could find anything there.

'Hi, Cherie,' she said to the young girl at the counter.

'Hi, Alice, how are you?'

Cherie had been one of her successes at the youth centre. She'd run away from home and had struggled with motivation and making ends meet. She wandered into the youth centre one afternoon, and Alice had taken her under her wing. Alice had found her somewhere to live and this job. She'd been working now at the discount store for about three months, and Alice could see the happiness in the young girl's face.

'I'm good. How about you, Cherie?'

'Really good. I've been going to the farm, and I've sorted things out with Mum and Dad. I took on board what you said about families being there for each other.'

'That's great news.' She smiled at the young girl and headed down the back of the store to the craft section.

Browsing along the shelves made her smile. They had decided to have an early Australiana theme for the masquerade ball, and that could mean anything from native animals to the dress of the nineteenth century. Alice stood and looked at the cardboard cutouts of various mammals—a platypus, a kangaroo, and an echidna—and wondered how they could be shaped into masks. There were a couple of very creative, crafty girls in the group. Sophie had surprised her. She'd known Sophie for a long time but hadn't realised what skills she had.

Moving to the end of the aisle, she picked up one of the red plastic baskets and wandered along, picking out a selection of the cardboard faces. There was a brightly coloured parrot cutout on the top shelf, and she stood on her toes, reaching for it.

'Oomph.' A teenage boy trod on her right foot, and Alice yelped as her basket tipped and the contents spread on the ground.

He looked up from his phone. 'Oh, sorry, I didn't mean to do that,' he said, but instead of helping Alice collect the cardboard and cutouts that had fallen on the floor, he took off towards the lolly section at the back of the store.

She shrugged and bent down to fill the basket. Seeing him head that way reminded her she needed to stock up on the lolly jar at the youth centre.

Again.

That was one of her jobs at the centre. In this cold weather, the small wrapped chocolate bars were quickly disappearing, and she suspected that Bec, Jeremy, and a couple of the other youth workers were more responsible for them going down than any of the kids coming after school.

She hitched the basket over her arm and turned into the aisle. There was a wide selection of chocolates and lollies. A movement to her left caught her eye, and she glanced to the side just in time to see the teenage boy who'd trodden on her foot slip a Mars bar into the front of his hoodie. Alice looked away, wondering what to do. Maybe he was putting it there until he got to the counter. She shouldn't make assumptions, but he had looked around furtively before he headed along another aisle. He had a school bag on his back, and that raised her suspicions.

She walked towards the checkout and jumped when the young boy pushed past her. She caught a whiff of stale clothes, and when she looked down, she could see mud on his thin legs. Alice knew most of the kids who hung around town and hadn't seen him before. She might strike up a conversation with him at the checkout, but there was no sign of him when she reached it.

Alice shrugged. Maybe he'd gone to get something else.

She queued up behind an elderly lady paying for her purchases—balls of wool and knitting needles—and listened to Cherie engage the woman in conversation. The young girl had grown in confidence. As Alice reached down to pick up her basket and put it on the counter, an elbow pushed her against it, and she almost stumbled again.

'Hey,' Cherie called out. 'Do you have anything to pay for?'

The same young boy shook his head and kept walking. 'Nope, couldn't find what I wanted,' he muttered before disappearing.

'I'll bet he did,' Cherie said. 'I always doubt them when they come in with a hoodie on.'

Chapter 5

'You okay? He fair shoved you, Alice.'

'I'm okay, just in a bit of a hurry. I have to get back to the office. I took too long in the craft section.'

The shop assistant smiled at her and quickly put Alice's purchases into a plastic bag she held open.

'Have a good day, Alice.'

Alice took her change and turned to leave. She looked back at Cherie. 'Have you seen that boy around here before?'

Cherie shook her head. 'No, I haven't.'

'Okay, thanks,' Alice said. 'Have a good day.'

She picked up the bag of craft supplies and hurried to the door. As she stepped out onto the footpath, she looked along the street. The boy was sitting on the seat at the bus stop at the corner.

She glanced at her watch; she still had a few minutes before she was due back in the office, and besides, she had a feeling this was going to be a necessary interaction that was part of her role in the town. She put the bag over her arm, checked that her purse was securely over her other shoulder, and casually walked up to the corner.

The hood was half covering his face, but she knew it was him. As she got closer, she could see the Mars Bar wrapper curled down over the chocolate bar as he scoffed it.

Something wasn't right. He was too young to be out by himself, and she knew he'd shoplifted the Mars bar. As she approached the seat, she walked over to the bus timetable in the Perspex cover to the right of the seat and pretended to look at the bus times.

With a nod, she walked across and sat at the other end of the seat next to him. He barely glanced at her.

'What bus are you waiting for?' Alice asked, keeping her voice even. She looked down into her bag of goodies, so he didn't feel like she was looking at him. 'Have you noticed if the bus to Augathella has come yet?'

He shook his head, but he did turn to her, and she could see his mouth was full as he chewed. When he'd finished eating, he shoved the chocolate wrapper in his pocket and shook his head again.

'I'm supposed to catch the bus home, but I haven't got enough money,' he said.

'Where is home?' she asked.

'Augathella.'

'It's about five dollars, I think. How much have you got?'

He shrugged.

'Not at school today?' she asked. This time, he turned his head and stared at her. Chocolate smeared his lips.

'I had to go to the dentist,' he said.

'Too many Mars Bars?' she asked with a smile.

'No, just a check-up.'

'How did you get down here?'

'I caught the bus.'

'And how come you haven't got enough money to get home?'

His face reddened, and he shook his head for the third time. 'I lost it,' he said.

She stood and walked over to the bus sign again. 'So the Augathella bus leaves at three-thirty. What are you going to do until then?'

'I can't wait that long,' he said. 'I have to get back before the end of school; I'm getting picked up.'

'The bus doesn't leave until after the school bus picks up the kids at the Catholic high school and takes them back to Augathella.'

'That's not on the board,' he said.

'No, it's the school bus,' she said.

His eyes narrowed. 'Are you a teacher?'

'No, I'm not a teacher, but I know the bus schedule. I work with kids. What about your parents? Did they let you get the bus down by yourself?'

He nodded slyly.

'How old are you, mate?'

'Nearly thirteen,' he said.

'Fair enough. So you'll have to hang around town for a while.'

'I guess I do.'

'You want to come back to my work with me?'

His eyes stayed narrowed suspiciously. 'Why would I want to come back to your work?'

'Because I work at the youth centre, and we've got a kitchen and a room with computers.'

His eyes lit up. 'There was a youthie at home.'

'Where was home?'

'Kununurra.'

'In the Northern Territory?'

'Yeah. Could I wait there until the bus comes?'

'It's a drop-in centre for kids before and after school. And also for those who don't go to school sometimes.'

'I told you I had a dentist appointment.'

'Well, you're quite welcome to come back to the centre with me until your bus arrives.'

'I'm going to be in deep shit.'

'Why?' Alice asked.

'I'm supposed to be back there to get picked up after school. How long does the bus take to go back? It took a long time to get down here.'

'It takes the same time as it did to get here. You'll get back to town about quarter past four.'

'Jesus,' he said.

Alice's eyebrows rose. 'Your parents didn't know what the bus times were? Are they at work?'

'I haven't got any parents,' he said. 'My mum's gone, and *he* took me away and brought me here.'

Alice's chest warmed with sympathy. She'd known he had a story behind him, and she would keep her eye on this kid before he slipped through her fingers. She would follow up on this once she made sure he was safe. 'Are you hungry? How about you come back with me now, maybe have some lunch. And then I could ring your dad if you tell me where he works, and we can get you a lift home to Augathella in time to get picked up.'

'He's not my dad,' he said.

'You have a carer then?' she asked.

'I just live with a guy.'

'A guy. Who's he?'

'Just a bloke.'

Warning bells rang inside her head. 'So maybe I can call him and get permission to drive you back to town.'

'He wouldn't care,' he said. 'You can do what you want, but it'd be good to get back in time so I don't get into trouble.'

'What sort of trouble?'

'Probably cop a hiding,' he said. 'I do all the time if I don't do the right thing.'

Alice stood and put the bag over her arm. 'Come on, I'll take you back, and we'll get you sorted,' she said.

Chapter 6

Callie's day at school sped by. Between teaching her class, organising a room for the visitor coming for a sports talk this afternoon, and getting ready for the meeting at Jenna's, she was exhausted.

She combed her hair with her fingers mid-afternoon as Kim Colthorpe came into the staffroom.

'You look tired, Cal. Are you okay?'

'It's just pregnancy tiredness,' she said. 'Plus, I had a cold last week, and that took a bit out of me, and the twins haven't been sleeping well. They're both teething. However, thanks to my gorgeous husband, I got to sleep through the night because he got up and looked after them at three o'clock this morning.'

'Do you think you came back to work too soon?' Kim asked.

'No, it's just normal. The first three or four months of pregnancy is tiring. It was like this for me with the twins, although I was doubly tired then, carrying the two of them.'

'Do you know what you're having this time?' Kim asked.

Callie gave her a look. 'We sort of do, but we're not saying anything.'

'Fair enough,' Kim said.

'What about you?'

Kim chuckled. 'We're the same. As long as the bub's healthy, I'm happy.'

'It will be like a crèche in town once we all have the babies. As well as us, Fallon, Sophie, and Amelia are having babies, plus we've got the littlies from Laura, Chloe, and Emily.' Callie grinned. 'Must be something in the air out here.'

'It's certainly making the town grow, isn't it?' Kim said, tucking in the chairs at the desks in the front row of the classroom.

'It's the best thing that ever happened to Augathella. Chloe and her group moving here have added to it, too,' Callie said.

Kimberley looked at Callie as she spoke. 'One of the best things for the community and the school was you walking down that road, leaving your suitcases in the ditch, and being rescued by Braden.'

Callie laughed and shook her head. 'Don't remind me. That feels like a different world to me. It wasn't that long ago, though.'

'It wasn't.'

'Packing up and leaving Brisbane and moving out here was the best thing I ever did. It's a wonderful life.'

'Sure is. Now, what's happening with the meeting at Jenna's this afternoon? What time are we supposed to be there?'

Callie looked at her watch. 'Sophie called me before and said Jenna is closing the tea room to the public early this afternoon. So if we could all be there by four, we should be finished by five or five-thirty at the latest, and we won't get home too late.'

'That was good of her. She knows that some of us have got a fair drive home. It'll still be dark by the time we get away anyway,' Kim said.

'Yes, we'll have to watch out for roos on the road,' Callie agreed.

'What about the boys? Are you taking them home today?'

'No, I just texted Braden to remind him about the meeting, and he's coming back through town because he's been out at Jon Ingram's place all day. They've been mustering, so he's going to swing by and pick them up. I might even head off early if that's okay with you. I'm finished with class now.'

'Yeah, that's fine.'

'I've got to pick up some things at IGA and whack them in the car fridge, and then I might head out to Jenna's and rest before we start the meeting. I imagine it will be interesting if Gladys Tingle's there.'

'I think it will be. And she'll be there for sure.'

'She means well, but she's hard to get along with, isn't she? Something must've made her like that.'

'She does. We have to humour her and keep her onside. Make her feel valued. I'll head off now and see you there, Kim. Can you keep an eye out and make sure that Braden gets the boys?'

'Not a problem at all.'

'And before I forget, what do you know about the new boy in Tom Cooper's class? Beau? According to Rory, he arrived last week when I was off sick.'

'I haven't met him yet. I was on a professional day when he was enrolled. He wasn't at school today. I was going to call his Dad and ask him to come in so we can find out where he's up to with his schooling. He started last Thursday. He's come from interstate, and he's almost thirteen. I'm not sure why he didn't go to the high school. There's no mum on the scene, apparently.'

'Rory asked about having him out to play football at home and said he's a really good footballer.'

'Well, kids pick up quickly who's good at what before we even get to know them, don't they?'

'Okay, I'll talk to Braden about it, and we'll have him out.'

Callie picked up her class folder, grabbed her bag, and headed to the Land Cruiser. The twins would be staying at Ruth's while she was at the meeting. Ruth was their wonderful babysitter, who seemed to be babysitting half the babies in town. Callie shook her head. She didn't know how Ruth managed it, but everything was always calm and clean in her house, and the twins were always happy when she picked them up. Even the three boys loved going there; there was always homemade cake and lemonade.

Callie headed to the IGA to pick up some milk to take home, plus four loaves of bread for the freezer. Dinner was sorted, and she added a pack of garlic bread to the basket because she certainly wouldn't feel like cooking vegetables when she got home. Garlic bread and lamb shanks would do them for the night. Or frozen peas; at least the boys would get their greens that way.

She drove out to the highway and turned into the parking area for Jenna's Vintage Tearooms, the most popular eatery in town. A car towing a caravan was driving out, and there was plenty of room left to park.

Callie sat in the car momentarily and took a deep breath, closing her eyes and grounding herself. It had been such a busy day. The baby had moved for the first time today. She hadn't texted Braden yet, but it was one of those moments when you finally realised that you've got another human being in there making little butterfly flutters. Strangely, her eyes filled with tears. Five years ago, if someone had told her she'd be living out on a cattle station, stepmother to three boys, mother of twins, and another baby on the way, she would have told them they were crazy.

Her friend, Jen, from Brisbane, often told her on the phone that she was a mad woman. 'You had a wonderful life here—sports car, great money, beautiful home on the river. And where are you now? You're out in the red dirt.'

'But, Jen, I'm so happy.'

'I know you are, love, and it's great to see. I was teasing.'

Callie asked her when they were coming out to visit, and Jen had been quiet for a moment. 'Jen? Everything okay there?'

'Yeah, sort of. Phillip is so busy at work, the kids are growing up, and I spend a fair bit of time at home by myself now.'

'Well, if the kids are old enough to look after themselves,

why don't you jump on a plane and come out for a visit?'

'Really?'

'Yeah, if the kids stay home, you don't have to worry about waiting until the school holidays. Phillip can look after them for a week or so, couldn't he?'

'You know what, Callie, you're a lifesaver. I think it's just what I need. Are you sure about the invitation? You're not too busy with work and the kids?'

'Not at all, and you still haven't seen the twins. I'd love you to come out and visit. I know, you could come out for the Masquerade Ball.'

'Okay, you got a deal. I'll do some sussing out with Phillip and the kids, and I'll give you a call in the next week or so. You can tell me all about it then.'

'Sounds good.'

Callie blinked as the sound of a car door closing beside her brought her out of her thoughts. She had almost gone to sleep sitting there.

Sophie was parked beside her. She climbed out and came around to Callie's door.

'You okay there, Callie? I thought you were asleep when I pulled up.'

'I'm just having a two-minute break. It's been a big day.' Callie reached for her bag across the passenger seat, put the car keys in her pocket, and climbed out of the car. She hugged Sophie. 'I haven't seen you for a week or more.'

'I know, it's hard to believe. We've been busy, too, even though I'm not working. Between Kent and Ruby Rose, I never seem to have a spare minute in the day. The highlight of my day is being here without a baby and being able to sit in grown-up company and have a cup of coffee.'

'It will be good company,' Callie said. They looked at each other and chuckled.

'Despite poor Gladys Tingle,' Sophie said as she put her arm through Callie's.

They walked up the stairs to the tea room. Jenna was

already sitting at the table with a cup of coffee, talking to Ellie, her offsider.

'The last customer has just left, and I was putting my feet up for a minute,' she said.

'You're entitled to do that,' Sophie said. 'Not like us ladies of leisure,' she chuckled.

'Speak for yourself, Sophie. I go to work,' Callie said with a grin.

'I know you do. I was joking.'

'Hi, Ellie, how are you?' Callie asked.

'I'm good, Mrs Cartwright,' Ellie said.

Callie rolled her eyes. 'It's not Mrs Cartwright, it's Callie.'

'What would you like to drink?' Ellie asked.

'Just the usual, thanks,' Sophie said.

'Me too,' Callie said. 'A skinny cappuccino would be lovely. I want to avoid sugar, though, as I'm trying not to put on too much weight.'

She leaned back and smiled as footsteps pounded on the stairs. 'Here's Gladys and Beryl.'

Chapter 7

The whop-whop thumping of the helicopter landing filled the air and stirred the cattle as they moved around the paddock. Red dust swirled, and Braden ducked his head and pulled his hat down over his face. Jon and Billy Burke did the same.

The new stockman was a quiet bloke, and Braden had tried a couple of times to engage him in a conversation, but he hadn't been very forthcoming. After six hours on horseback and three tea breaks in his company, the only thing he knew about him was that he was from the Northern Territory.

At one point, he spoke to Jon on the side when Billy went off to water his horse and asked about him.

'Good bloke, good references. I knew him briefly when I was up there a few years ago, and I never had a problem with him. He's a bit quieter now than he used to be. I don't know what's happening in his life, but he's one of the good ones, mate. He's also an excellent cattleman, and he has a degree in agriculture, so he's right up there with the latest chemicals and fertilisers. He's taught me a bit already.'

'Okay, that's all I need to know.'

'He's got a kid too. He wants to be done here by three so he can pick him up from school.'

Braden looked up at the sun. 'What do you reckon? We'll be done? I'm hoping to pick the boys up, too.'

'That's not a problem. Once Fallon gets up there, we'll only have that last mob to do. We'll have them all in by two.'

'That's good. I'll go at the same time. Callie's got a meeting at Jenna's. This blasted ball seems to be taking over everything.'

'Sophie's there too. I'm picking Ryan up from Ruth's.

Are you going to the ball?' Jon asked with his face screwed up.

'Mate, if you think you're going to get out of going to the Augathella Masquerade Ball, which is going to be the event of the century, you've got another think coming.'

'Someone will have to stay home and mind the kids,' Jon said with a grin.

'Ha ha, didn't you hear that one? Ruth Mason and Beryl are running a crèche. All we have to do is bring a cot, pram, or whatever, and they'll look after all the kids at the venue.'

'Well, I suppose the music will be loud enough that we won't hear all the screaming,' Jon said with a grin. 'I'll offer to help them. I'd rather look after crying babies than dance any day.'

'You got Buckleys, mate.'

Braden looked up as the new stockman led his horse across from the creek.

'Have you heard about this big ball, mate? Will you still be around here in spring?'

'I haven't heard of it, but I should still be around. I'll be here for a while, I hope.'

'Jon told me you've got a young bloke in primary school.'

'Yep.'

'My wife's a teacher there.'

Billy didn't reply, just nodded. Braden caught Jon's eye, and Jon shrugged.

'Okay, guys, back in the saddle. Fallon just came down to refuel, and she's right to go now.'

'She does a good job,' Billy Burke offered.

'She's the best,' Braden said. 'Did you know Fallon up in the Territory?'

'Yeah, I heard about her several times but never met her. She had a good reputation up there, too.'

It didn't take long before the cattle were secured in the home paddock, ready to be collected by the trucks tomorrow.

Fallon came over, and Jon introduced her to Billy. She stood on tiptoes and kissed Braden's cheek. 'Hey, Braden, I haven't seen you for ages.'

'I know, we've all been busy.'

'Okay, I'll head back to Charleville and see you at dinnertime. If I get back to town in time, I'll swing by the ball meeting.'

Jon and Braden both rolled their eyes.

'What's wrong with you pair? It's for a good cause.'

'Is it still for the hospital? I heard there was some discussion about that.'

'No, just Gladys Tingle putting her two cents' worth in,' Fallon said. 'It'll get sorted. I'll swing by there if I have time, but if not, I'll come straight home. I took some steak out for dinner, Jon. If you do the veggies, that would be great.'

Braden knew that Billy was watching Fallon and Jon's conversation, but Billy's expression was difficult to read.

'Okay, guys, I'll see you later.' It wasn't long before the helicopter rose above them; the dust settled, and Fallon's helicopter disappeared into the distance.

'Right, guys, we might head into town now. Do you need a lift, Billy? Where are you living?'

Jon looked at Braden. 'Billy's living in the old house down the back of my place.'

'I'll ride back to the house and jump in my car. Thanks for the offer, though, Braden.'

It was the most that Billy had said for the whole day.

'Not a problem, mate. See you around.'

Chapter 8

When Alice got Beau settled in the small games room at the back of the youth centre, she went to their office and spoke quietly with Bec.

'I think he's got some issues. I'm not sure about where he's living. I can't get anything out of him, but he's very thin. Plus, he's not very clean, and he claims he needs to get back to Augathella because he's getting picked up by someone.'

'Someone?' Bec's forehead wrinkled in a frown. 'Sounds like intervention is needed, perhaps.'

'Yes, what do you want me to do?' Alice said.

Bec tapped a pencil on the table for a moment. 'You're going up there this afternoon, aren't you?'

'Yes, a little bit later. Tilly and I are going to a ball meeting. Aren't you?'

'I was going to try to get there, but I'm not sure if I'll be able to get away in time. You can't get anything out of him, and we can't get permission, but if he says that's where he lives, we'll get him there, and you can wait to connect with his parents and see if an intervention is needed.'

'Okay, I can do that. I might leave early once he's had something to eat. He's settled down at the computer now. Is that okay with you?'

'Yes, go as soon as you and Tilly are ready. You don't know how long it's going to take to get him sorted.' Bec's face lit up. 'And on a different subject, Alice, I've got some great news.'

'We wondered what was going on. Tell me.'

'Well, you know how Chloe and her group have funded most of our stuff?'

Alice nodded. 'Yes.'

'Well, I applied for an expansion grant, and I was able to say how well it's going here and what an impact we're having on the kids. And provide evidence. It's been approved.'

'Oh wow, what does it mean for us?'

'It means we can open up a centre in Augathella.'

'Oh my goodness, that's fantastic news.'

'More staff and a service for the kids up there. We just have to find a location, and we can get started.'

'Well done, congratulations. That's great.'

'I'm excited,' Bec said.

Alice went into the kitchen and made herself a quick cup of coffee. She pushed the good news to the back of her mind, although she would ask Bec if she could work at the centre up there. She was well placed financially now and had been looking at houses for sale around Augathella.

At the moment, her concern was for young Beau, and she needed to focus while finding out what was going on there. At least she'd have Tilly in the car with her, and there'd be no issues with child protection if anyone queried Beau's being in a car with her.

She made her coffee and wandered through the room, which contained a couple of old lounge chairs and two computers.

'How are you going, mate? Would you like something to eat?'

He turned and looked at her. 'Thank you, but the other lady gave me a sandwich and a drink.'

'That's good. That's Tilly.'

'Yeah, that was her name.'

'I've got some good news for you, mate. We'll be able to give you a lift up to Augathella. We have to go to a meeting up there, so what do you think about that?'

His eyes lit up. 'Oh, that's really good. I won't get into trouble now. Can you drop me at the primary school?'

'Why the primary school?'

'Because that's where I'm getting picked up.'

'Do you go to the primary school or the high school up there?'

'I go to the primary school,' he replied.

Alice was sussing him out. She knew the names of all the staff from a few meetings.

'Who's your teacher?'

'Coops. He said I could call him that, but his name is Mr Cooper.'

'So you're in year six?'

'Do you know the school and the teachers there?' He leaned back from the computer and looked at her.

'I do. I went to school there. I thought you looked older. I thought you were maybe in high school. How old are you?'

He lowered his eyes. 'Almost thirteen. I should be in high school, but we moved a bit.'

'We?

'Yeah, us.'

Alice had enough experience with kids when to know not to push it. 'Okay, fair enough. So do you need to have a drink or go to the toilet before we go?'

'No, I'm ready. What sort of car you got?'

'Government car. Just a sedan, nothing flash.'

'That'll do, as long as I get there on time and I won't get in trouble.'

Alice went into the office looking for Tilly. 'Are you okay with going up now? Bec said it was fine.'

'Yes, I'm right to go. What's the story there?' Tilly asked.

'I don't know, but we're going to do our best to find out. We need to suss out his home situation, I think.'

On the drive up, Beau sat in the car looking out the back window the whole trip and didn't say anything after the first few questions. Alice and Tilly looked at each other and gave up. He wasn't forthcoming, and they were no more informed than they had been when they left. They turned off the highway, and finally, a voice came from the backseat.

'Do you remember where the primary school is?' he said.

'I do,' Alice nodded. 'I'm not that old.'

'Good, just drop me there.'

'Before we do, mate, we need a few more details. What's your last name?'

'Beau Burke.'

'And you're twelve years old, and you've been at school since last week, and you've moved a bit.'

'That's right.'

'Okay, sounds good. Who's picking you up at the school?'

'Why do you need to know?'

'Well, we can't just leave you there in case there's no one there to get you.'

'I told you I was getting picked up. Don't you believe me? Do you think I'm a liar?'

'No, mate. Your safety is our main concern. We work at the centre, and it's our job to look after youth.'

'Okay, Billy is picking me up, and he'll be at the school.'

'What sort of car has he got?'

'A white ute.'

Alice and Tilly looked at each other again. There were probably twenty white utes parked outside the primary school as property owners came to pick up their kids. Taking the bus home took longer, and many of the parents also took the opportunity to do business in town.

They turned onto the main street, then left into Bendee Street, and pulled up next to the school oval. The back was open before the ignition was off, and Beau was off like a shot.

'God, that was quick. I still don't trust him,' Alice said as she quickly opened her door. 'Okay, let's follow him and see where he goes.'

But by the time they were out of the car, there was no sign of Beau; he had disappeared.

Chapter 9

Billy Burke sighed as he swung around the corner and parked opposite the sports field. The street outside the school was jam-packed with cars and buses. He'd told Beau this morning he'd pick him up where they lined up for the bus.

The school bell rang as Billy climbed down from the ute, tucked his phone and keys in his back pocket, and headed along the street towards the school's front gate.

Beau had had one of his quiet mornings as they'd eaten breakfast together, and Billy had kept his phone handy all day, waiting for the school to call about a meltdown. To his surprise, the boy had lasted all day at school. At Kununurra, the phone call had been a daily event, and in the end, it was easier to keep Beau home from school and take him out to the cattle stations where Billy was working. That's when the social worker became involved and told him that action would be taken.

Moving to Augathella gave them a chance for a new start. Picking up the job with Jon Ingram and the bonus of a house at the back of the property to live in had been a godsend.

All they had to do now was get Beau settled in. They'd arrived too late in the season for him to play in the local junior rugby league team; there were only a couple of games left before the end of the season finals. Beau was already talking about joining next year. His love of NRL football bordered on obsessive, but at least it gave them something to talk about. Apart from that, there was little conversation. If Billy asked Beau, "Did you brush your teeth?" he was rewarded with a dismissive glance. At least watching football on television gave them something to do together in the evenings and on weekends and occasionally—very occasionally—resulted in a conversation of more than two sentences.

Billy found caring for the young boy hard, but he'd had no hesitation when Mary called him home. A pang of regret lodged in his chest. If he'd stayed in Mt Isa, he might have established a relationship with Beau before his sister left them.

Billy hadn't seen him since he was a baby, and now he was his only family. Being the sole carer of an almost teenager had him on a steep learning curve, but Billy was determined he would make a success of it.

Beau had always lived in Mount Isa, and with everything else, the move to Kununurra had messed with his head. Setting up home here in southwest Queensland in another unfamiliar place had been the final straw, and Billy had tried to talk to Beau about seeing someone and getting help to deal with his feelings. That was if you could call sitting in front of the television with no response talking.

He'd had nothing to do with kids, so he had no idea what to do. The social worker in Kununurra has been intrusive, and it was one of the reasons Billy had thought about moving south. When he'd heard that Jon Ingram was looking for a stockman on his new station out of Augathella, the decision was made. One phone call, and they were on their way.

Billy knew Beau was a good kid—he always had been; Mary had kept him in the loop. It was just a matter of finding the right place, the right friends, and getting him back on track.

As Billy rounded the corner near their arranged pick-up place, he paused as a stream of kids in school uniforms came pouring through the front gate. Three female teachers stood near the buses, and each looked at him as he walked past.

'That's not bad to see,' he thought. They were keeping an eye on anyone they didn't recognise.

He approached the woman who appeared to be in charge. Her badge said Mrs Colthorpe, Deputy Principal.

'Good afternoon, Mrs Colthorpe. My name is Billy Burke. I'm here to collect Beau.'

He never tagged himself as a carer, stepdad, or uncle because Beau seemed to prefer that. He refused to call Billy anything—not uncle, not Billy. They were still getting used to each other. Billy knew he'd gone a bit soft on the kid, but hell, he'd been through a lot for a twelve-year-old.

'Hello, Mr Burke. It's good to meet you. He's not catching the bus home today?' the deputy principal asked. 'He hasn't come out yet. Ah, here's his class now.' She gestured to a group of students around Beau's age.

'Yes, he was a little bit upset when he left this morning, and I've been half-expecting a phone call from you all day, but he obviously settled in okay.'

They waited until the group lined up, and Mrs Colthorpe frowned. 'He's not with his class.' She turned and spoke to the woman on the other side of the gate. 'Penny, have you seen Beau Burke?'

'He's not here today,' the woman replied. 'When I checked the roll at drama this afternoon, he was marked absent.'

Mrs Colthorpe took his arm and pulled Billy to the side, away from the chatter of the children lined up.

'Are you sure he got the bus this morning, Mr Burke?'

'He didn't get the bus today. I had to come to town, so I dropped him off and watched him go in the front gate. He must have misunderstood where I said I'd pick him up. I'll call him. Hopefully, he's got his phone on.'

Billy pulled out his phone and thought carefully about what to say when Beau answered. He didn't want to sound angry because then he would take off. He'd done it before in Kununurra, and the first time he went missing for two days, the authorities got involved, and that useless social worker had taken him on her caseload. The last thing he wanted was for Beau to go into care. Mary had been very explicit: Beau was to stay with Billy until he reached eighteen. Luckily, she'd been to see a solicitor, and it was all in black and white.

He waited for the phone to pick up, but it went to voicemail. 'I'm here to pick you up, mate. Where are you?'

He waited for his phone to ring or ping with a reply, but it stayed silent.

'What does she mean he was marked absent?' he asked. 'Absent from drama class? He'd hate that.'

'No, it means he wasn't in class when the roll was marked this morning. Maybe he's on the premises, but it appears he didn't stay with his class for the day. When I was on playground duty at lunchtime, I didn't notice him on the football field either. And that's where he's spent most of lunch and recess for the week or so he's been here.'

'He loves his football,' Billy said, reaching in his pocket for cigarettes before he realised it was inappropriate to light up here, and besides, he didn't have any. He'd given them up a fortnight ago, after one night when Beau accused him of being addicted. He'd managed not to smoke for two weeks now, but the stress of wondering where Beau was had had him reaching for one without thinking.

'Do you have any idea where he might've gone? Does he have any other friends in town?' Mrs Colthorpe asked, concern etching her features.

'We don't know anyone yet. His only friends are at school, if he's made any, that is. Shit. I watched Billy go into school this morning, so his well-being is then the school's responsibility.'

'Yes, it is,' she said. 'Wait a moment, please, Mr Burke.' She hurried across to one of the other teachers.

As he waited, he sent Billy a text.

I'm at the bus lines, mate. Where are you?

As Mrs Colthorpe came back over, Billy glanced down at his phone.

'It looks like he's out of range,' he said. There was a red symbol beside his message saying not delivered. His concern ramped up a notch. Beau's phone was always fully charged, and he always had it on.

'Come into the office with me, please, Mr Burke.'

They walked through the front door and along a corridor. The deputy principal stopped and tapped on a door marked Principal. She opened the door and took a step so she was just inside the door.

'Sorry to interrupt, David, but we've got a bit of an issue here. One of our new students is apparently wagging today, and we don't know where he is. I have his father with me.'

'Come in, please,' a male voice responded.

'Mr Burke, this is David Foy, our relieving principal,' the woman said.

A short man with a ruddy complexion stood, came around the desk, and held out his hand to shake Billy's.

The look of disdain on his face when he shook Billy's dusty hand filled Billy with instant dislike.

'It's good to meet you, Mr Burke. I was away last week when your son enrolled. I'm relieving here at the moment, and I like to meet our parents. Now tell me what's happened.' He gestured to a table with four chairs around it.

Billy ran his hands through his hair before he pulled out a chair and sat down. 'He's had a head start. If he's decided to take off again, he could be halfway to Brisbane by now. I'd like to know why the school didn't let me know he wasn't here.'

'Don't worry, we'll sort this out. Kim, who's Beau's teacher?' the red-faced man turned to the deputy as he wiped his dusty hand on an ironed handkerchief.

'Mr Cooper,' she replied.

'I'll ring the staffroom and see if he's still here.'

He walked to his desk and picked up the phone. 'Coops, could you come to my office, please? Don't worry. It's not serious.'

He put the phone down and came back to the table. 'He's on his way.'

'Nothing serious?' Billy held back his temper as best he could. 'It's damn serious, mate.'

'I didn't want my teacher to think he was in trouble.' His stare was cold.

'I don't give a flying fig what he thinks. My boy is missing. And we're wasting time sitting around here.' Billy stood up so quickly his chair fell over.

Mrs Colthorpe stood and put her hand on his arm after he'd picked up the fallen chair. 'Calm down, Mr Burke. He won't be far away. We'll look for him as soon as we talk to Mr Cooper. I'll ask him to get a group of teachers together as soon as we establish what he knows. There are a few things we can do.'

'Like what?' Billy asked.

'Just give us a moment,' she said. 'Can I get you a cup of tea or some water?'

'No.' Billy turned to head for the door, but it opened before he reached it. Another teacher walked in.

'Mr Cooper, we need to know as much as we can about Beau Burke's routine,' Mrs Colthorpe said. 'It looks like he's wagged school, and we're unsure where he is this afternoon. This is his father.'

Billy didn't correct her.

'I'm sorry, Mr Burke,' the male teacher said with a frown. 'He told me yesterday he wouldn't be here today because he was going to the dentist, so I marked him as sick.'

Billy frowned. 'No, he wasn't going to the dentist.'

'Who has Beau palled up with, Coops?' Mrs Colthorpe had taken control, and the bloody principal sat there, flicking through papers on the table. Billy held back his anger, but it was hard. If they didn't get moving, he'd go looking himself. The problem was he had no idea where to look.

Mr Cooper was still frowning. The more he heard, the more Billy wondered if this school had been the right choice. 'He's very friendly with Rory. They're together every day before and after school, at recess and lunch.'

'Hopefully, Rory's still out there. He was on the oval waiting to be picked up. We can ask him what he knows,' Kimberley gestured for Billy to follow her.

'Right. I'll come with you.' Billy followed her down the corridor.

Chapter 10

Braden parked behind the school on Nelson Street, on the other side of the sports oval, and cut through the vacant block to the oval. There was never any parking out the front, and the boys enjoyed kicking the football around while they waited for him.

He spotted the boys near the shed at the side of the oval. They were kicking a football around with a boy he assumed was Rory's new best mate.

He whistled and waved to let them know he was there. Rory raced over ahead of Nigel and Petie, and the unfamiliar boy followed them across to where Braden waited.

'Hey guys, ready to go home?' He looked at the newcomer. 'You're new to the school, I hear, mate?'

'Yes, sir,' the boy said.

'Dad, I talked to Mum before, and she said that Beau could come home with us this afternoon. He'll get picked up later.'

Braden raised his eyebrows. 'She didn't message me about it.'

'She said *I* could tell you, Dad.'

'Okay, I'll send her a text now.'

'No, there's no need. She said Beau could come today, didn't she, Nigel?'

Nigel looked at Rory, his eyes narrow. 'Yeah, if you say so. I wasn't listening.'

'Is that okay with your parents, Beau?' Braden asked.

'Yeah, I can go to your place and get picked up later.'

'Okay. I'll still text Mum and see what she's arranged.'

'Don't you trust me, Dad?' Rory held his gaze steadily.

'I do. You have never given me any reason not to. I'll

send her a quick text to see the pickup arrangement.'

Braden took out his phone and texted Callie. He waited for her to reply, but there was no answer. With a shrug, he said, 'Okay, Beau, come along. We'll sort out how you're getting collected later.'

As long as he didn't have to drive back into town to bring him back. Braden had a few jobs to do when they got home. As they drove home, he was unsettled. It wasn't like Callie not to let him know, and he wondered whether he'd done the right thing, but he knew she'd had a busy day. Rory had been very persuasive, and as he'd said, his son had never given him any reason not to trust him.

Half an hour later, they turned into the drive and approached the house.

'Wow, not a bad place.'

Braden glanced in the rear-vision mirror. Beau's eyes were wide.

'We've got a great area at the back too, great for playing footy,' Rory said. 'Dad's mowed it and put goalposts in too. Wait until you see it.'

'How about some afternoon tea before you play footy?' Braden said when the ute was in the shed. 'There was some cake left after I packed your lunches this morning.'

'That would be good,' Beau said. 'Thank you, Mr Cartwright.'

The boy's manners were fine, even though he looked a bit scruffy. He seemed like a nice enough kid.

'Rory and Nigel, show Beau the bathroom. You can all have a clean-up, and I'll get some afternoon tea and milkshakes.'

The three boys threw their bags in the breezeway and shot up the hall, Beau behind them; he must have left his bag in the ute. Rory still had his football under his arm. Braden whistled as he went into the kitchen.

Chapter 11

Screams of laughter and the barking of three dogs drifted across the house as the boys played football. Petie was out there, too, but Braden knew he'd be more interested in playing with his dog, Apricot, than football.

He was about to head out to the shed when the landline rang in the study.

'Hi, love, it's me,' Callie said. 'I'm about to leave town. Is there anything we need?'

'Not that I can think of,' Braden said.

'I've picked up some garlic bread for tea and thought we could have frozen peas with the lamb stew. I put some potato and carrots in it. Can you check the slow cooker for me? I'll be about half an hour.'

'I will. How come you're calling the landline?'

'I tried your mobile, but it rang out.'

'That's strange.' Braden walked back to the kitchen and picked it up off the countertop. 'Ah, I must have switched it to silent accidentally. Looks like I've had a few missed calls.' He frowned. 'A couple from the school. I'd better call them and see what's up. Did you see my text, Cal?'

'No, sorry, I haven't looked at my messages. What's up?'

'Rory said it was okay for this new mate of his to come out this afternoon. He said he squared it with you.'

There was silence on the other end of the phone. Callie's voice was firm when she finally replied.

'Then I'll have to have a talk with Rory when I get home. We didn't have any conversation about it.'

'He lied to me.' Braden's jaw tensed.

'If he told you that he'd spoken to me and I gave him permission to have a friend over this afternoon, I guess that's what you call it. I didn't see him through the day, and I certainly haven't spoken to him.'

'Little bugger,' Braden said.

'So what's happened?' Callie asked. 'Is he there?'

'Yes. Beau came out of school with them. Rory said his carer was going to come and pick him up afterwards. Wait until I get my hands on that little—'

Callie cut him off. 'There will be a consequence for the lie, but if this boy has no friends, I guess Rory was trying to do the right thing. Leave it until I get home, Bray. What's he like?'

'He's got manners. He said his pleases and thank yous and called me sir a couple of times, which made me feel old. They're out playing footy now. I've been keeping an eye on them through the kitchen window, and everything *seems* fine.'

But Callie said, 'I can hear the "but" in your tone.'

'He's pretty scruffy and very thin. Between you and me, he looks a bit neglected.'

'Have you given him something to eat?'

'Yes, he had two pieces of cake, and I made them chocolate milkshakes. And some fruit.'

'Did he say anything about his parents?'

Braden shook his head. 'No. I'll call the school. Maybe that's what they called about.'

'Okay, it sounds like Rory's a good kid. I'm coming straight home.'

'Yep, but I hate that he lied to me about talking to you.'

'Leave it till I get there, and we'll sort it out. It's getting dark now, so I hope he told someone he was coming to our place. Otherwise, they'll be worried when he doesn't go home.'

***

Billy was more than worried; he was trying to hold his worry in, and the more he did, the more anger took over. By the time they'd gone out to the front of the school, there was no sign of this Rory or his father. And now, half an hour later, Beau still hadn't turned up. The school hadn't been able to get in touch with the boy's father either.

'I think it's time to call the police,' Kim said. She'd insisted he call her that, and she looked as concerned as he was, which made Billy worry more.

He ran his hands through his hair again. 'Give me a minute to think about it. I'm trying to think where else he could've gone.'

His words were interrupted by the ringing of the phone on the principal's desk.

'Yes, thank you,' David Foy said. 'Please put him through.' He listened carefully and nodded sagely. 'That's excellent news. Thank you very much. Yes, Mr Burke is here now looking for him. I'll put him on in a moment after I tell him.' He put the phone down on the desk and looked at Billy. 'Beau is out at a property half an hour out of town. He apparently went out there after school to play football.'

Billy kept his face expressionless as relief flooded through him. At least Beau was safe, although he would be in trouble when he got his hands on him.

He calmed down before he took the phone from the principal; that wasn't the way to handle a situation like this. One thing that the social worker had told him was to stay calm and try to talk things out rationally with Beau.

'Braden Cartwright would like to talk to you and organise for Beau to be collected,' the principal said.

Billy sat up straight. 'Braden Cartwright?'

'Yes, that's Rory's father.'

'I worked with Braden at the Ingram's property today.' His heart rate slowed as relief built. 'He's obviously in good hands.'

'I can't comment,' the red-faced principal said. 'I don't know them.'

'He's one of the best,' Kim said. Billy caught the disgusted look she shot the principal's way.

'You couldn't ask for a better place for him to be,' Mr Cooper said. 'The Cartwright boys are top kids, and Callie, their stepmother, is actually a teacher here at school.'

'I'll put you onto Mr Cartwright now, and you can work something out.' He looked at the other two teachers. 'We'll give Mr Burke some privacy.

Billy took the phone as the three teachers walked out of the room. 'Billy Burke here. Braden?'

'Yeah, mate, it's me. I didn't think I'd be talking to you again so soon. Apparently, there's been a bit of a mix-up, and we've got your young bloke out here. I suspect the boys cooked it up themselves.'

'So I believe.'

'Do you know your way out here? Do you know where we are?'

'No, I don't,' Billy said.

Braden gave him directions on the way to head out of town. 'After you turn at the intersection, turn right there, and then you'll see the *Kilcoy Station* sign, mate. It's getting late. We've got plenty for dinner. Stay for dinner and meet Callie and the rest of the family.'

'Thanks. We'll talk about it when I get there. I'll see you in a little while.'

Chapter 12

As Alice locked the car, she spotted the school bag on the back seat.

'He's gone without his bag,' she said.

'Tilly, you go that way across the football field, and that'll put you up in Nelson Street. I'll go from here along the front of the school, and we'll meet up at the corner. He has to be here somewhere. I want to make sure he's okay. Did you think he looked neglected?'

Tilly nodded. 'Yes, and his clothes smelled dirty. There's something not right there. I wonder if he's really getting picked up. We know his name and what he looks like. If we don't find anyone, I'll go and see the school principal and see if they know anything. Actually, Kim's out front now on bus duty, so I'll have a chat with her if we don't find him.'

'I might have a chat if we do find him,' Alice said.

'I'm off.' Tilly scooted across the football field as Alice made her way towards the school. There were all manner of vehicles parked along the road, and she recognised lots of faces as she glanced into them. Trying not to get into conversation, she waved and kept walking. Kids she used to go to primary school with now had their kids in kindergarten, and she ignored the pain that hit her chest. She was here to look for someone else's child, and it wasn't the time to regret not having kids yet.

She walked to the corner carrying the bag, but there was no sign of Beau. Tilly was walking towards her and raised her hands as if to say she hadn't seen him either. Alice stood there for a moment, amazed at how quickly the school crowd had cleared. The last bus had left, and the teachers went back inside. Now, there were only a couple of cars parked around the corner.

'How about we walk down to Main Street and see if he's gone there? The library's open, and he could have gone to IGA or the football field,' Alice said.

'Or he could have been picked up,' Tilly said.

'Yes, but they would probably have hung around looking for his bag.

They each took a side of Main Street, and half an hour flew by as they looked in the shops and the library, and Alice checked out the park.

Tilly looked at her watch. 'I'm going to have to go, Alice. 'I promised Nana I'd go with her and Beryl to the meeting.'

'That's fine. I'll call into the school office and drop his bag in. I'll see you at Jenna's.'

As Alice headed for the front gate of the school, a voice came from behind. 'Hey, who are you?'

She turned around to see a tall guy in dusty work pants standing with his hands on his hips. A battered Akubra hung from one hand. She frowned and walked over to him.

'Excuse me, were you calling me?'

'Well, no one else is around, is there? Do I know you?' he said. 'What I want to know is, what are you doing with that bag?'

She looked down at Beau's bag still in her hands and frowned. 'Why? What's it to you?'

'Because that's Beau's bag. It's got his initials on it. See, B.B. And you're holding it,' he said.

'Beau?'

'Yes, Beau. What are you doing with his bag?'

'He left it in my car. I'm looking for him to make sure he gets his bag back and that he's okay.'

'And why wouldn't he be okay?' he asked. 'Exactly who are you, and why did you have Beau in your car?' His eyes narrowed suspiciously.

He took an instant dislike to her. Her hair was perfect, her makeup flawless, and her navy blue suit wasn't creased. She looked just like one of the social workers from Kununurra, the ones who'd caused all the trouble for them.

Her eyes widened, and she drew in an audible breath. 'My name is Alice Templeton, and I work at Choice for Youth in Charleville.'

He'd been spot on. 'What's Choice for Youth?'

She stared at him, and Billy felt as though he was being assessed—and found wanting—as her gaze slowly raked him from head to toe. His eyes stayed on her, and he kept his expression bland.

What was that woman's name from Kununurra? This one even looked like her, not in looks but in the way she checked him out. She was younger and better looking, but still, she got his hackles up.

'I bumped into him, literally, in a discount store in Charleville around lunchtime.'

'Charleville?' Billy groaned out. 'What the hell was he doing in Charleville?'

'You tell me,' Alice said. 'Beau was not forthcoming when I questioned him.'

'Not forthcoming, hey? Who gave you permission to question him?' Billy said.

'I saw a boy who was quite distressed, obviously hungry, and he told me he didn't have enough money for the bus to get home after his dental visit.'

'Dental visit? He wasn't going to the dentist.'

'Are you sure?' she said calmly.

'Unless he made the appointment himself and jumped on the bus this morning, but he wouldn't have had any money to pay for it. He hasn't even got a Medicare card yet.'

'And why would that be?' Alice asked. 'Is he your son?'

'I don't think that's any of your business,' he said. 'Now give me his bag, please.'

'Not until I know who I'm talking to and if you actually have a right to take his bag.' Her chin shot up, and her eyes challenged him.

Chapter 13

With a smile that had no friendliness, the guy held out a hand stained with grease. 'Billy Burke. Who are you?'

'Alice Templeton.' Alice winced as his dirty hand held hers; his grip was so firm it hurt. If it weren't for his dour expression and the aggression coming off him in waves, he would've been a very good-looking man. Her face had heated when he'd caught her checking him out. Snug-fitting, dusty denim moulded muscular thighs, and a tight navy blue T-shirt showed well-developed arms and broad shoulders.

Alice cleared her throat. 'Okay, let's start at the beginning. I work down in Charleville. At lunchtime today, I happened to be in a store and came across Billy. A few minutes later, when I went outside, he was sitting at the bus stop, and he was a bit upset because he didn't have enough money to get home.'

She didn't mention the shoplifting.

'How the hell did he get to Charleville? He was supposed to be at school. I dropped him off this morning.'

For the first time, his expression softened. 'I'm sorry if I appear curt, but I've just spent the last hour looking for him.'

'You and me both. He shot out of my car when I parked. I wanted to make sure he was telling the truth and was really getting picked up.'

'He was, but he wasn't here. I know he wasn't at school today, and I know where he is now, so everything is okay. He's safe. Did you offer to bring him here?'

'It's fine.' Alice nodded. 'It was discussed with my boss, and I had permission. There was another youth worker in the car with me. It was either that or leave a kid sitting in a town with no money, no food, and looking quite vulnerable.'

'So you decided to be a good Samaritan and take him

wherever he wanted to go.'

'Yes. He was distressed because he had told me he'd been to the dentist, had gotten the bus down, and had spent all his money. He didn't have enough money to get home, so I drove him back. However, as soon as I pulled up, he got out of the car and took off, and he left his bag behind. Where is he now?'

'Well, he's pulled a fast one again. I came here to pick him up, but he decided he was going to go home with one of the kids to play footy apparently.'

'Are you sure he has?'

'Yes, I've spoken to the guy who took him home.'

'May I ask you one thing, Mr Burke? Are you his father?'

'Is that any of your business?' he said.

'It is, actually. I'm a youth worker down in Charleville, and I have some concerns about Beau's care.'

His jaw tightened, and he glared. 'Well, Miss Templeton, that's none of your business. I can assure you that Beau is fine. He's well cared for, he gets fed, he's got a bed to sleep in at night, and he's going to school. And that's about the best anyone can do at the moment in these difficult circumstances. So how about you butt out?'

'No, I'm not quite sure about this. Do you know that in my position, if I have concerns about the care of a child, it's mandatory that I make a report?'

'A report? Why the hell would you need to make a report? Beau wagged school, he's been caught out, and he's going to face the consequences. He's safely home, thanks to you, and I appreciate that. I'm pleased that you looked out for him—it could've gone very badly if he hadn't met the right person. So thank you, Miss Templeton. However, I can assure you that there is no need for you to worry at all about Beau.'

'I'll be sure of that when I see him,' she said.

'Is it really any of your business?'

'I've already told you, and yes, it is my business. And if necessary, I will make that report. I want to be sure that Beau is alright.'

He sighed visibly and took a deep breath. He reached out and picked up the bag from the ground. 'Okay, you're from Charleville, so you probably don't know the local people, but he's gone to *Kilcoy Station* and is currently in the care of one Braden Cartwright, who I have just spoken to on the phone. I'm going out there to pick him up now. And between you and me, he's going to face some consequences: one, for wagging school; two, for lying about going to the dentist; and three, for putting himself in a position of not being able to get home and relying on the goodwill of someone; and four, for not waiting for me when he was supposed to get picked up and deciding to play at someone's house, which is about thirty-five kilometres away from where we are now.'

'I know exactly where Braden Cartwright lives,' she said, 'and I do know the Cartwrights. They're very good people.'

'So I've been told. Thanks again for looking out for him, but that's the end of the matter.'

'I'm still not satisfied,' Alice said. 'I won't make that report, but I would like to meet with you again and see where you're living.'

His eyes fixed on hers, intense. 'If that's what it takes, we can meet. Do you have a phone number?'

'Yes, I do. Please text me your phone number, and I'll reply. Then I want you to tell me where you live. I'll come out and see where you are, and if I'm reassured, I'll leave you in peace.'

He removed his phone from his back pocket and showed her the number.

'Okay? I'll text you and make sure that's right.'

'For God's sake, is there anyone you trust?' he said.

'Not when the care of children's involved.' She put the number into her phone, texted him and nodded when his phone pinged.

'Good.'

'Happy now, Miss Templeton?'

'Yes, I am. I'll be seeing you soon, Mr Burke.'

Chapter 14

Alice was seething. She had met some rude and uncooperative people in her life—it went with the job—but never had treated anyone her with the disdain that Mr Burke had.

She took an instant dislike to him. He was rough and ready, and his manners needed attention.

He put his Akubra on and then tipped the brim. 'I'll wait for your call, Miss Templeton.' He turned on his heel and headed to a white twin cab ute that had seen better days. She stayed there watching until he drove around the corner. At least she knew Beau was okay; he'd been fine with the Cartwrights. But there was a lot more to the story, and she would get to the bottom of it. Why had Beau taken himself off to Charleville?

Alice was thoughtful as she drove to the meeting at Jenna's tearoom. She thought she was early, but when she looked at the clock on the dash, it was already heading towards four-thirty.

She turned off the highway to a full car park. Chatter and laughter met her as she climbed the steps up to the beautiful tea rooms. Every time Alice came here, she appreciated what a great job Jenna had done. When she'd grown up in Augathella, the old house had been a local eyesore. When Reg had lived there, the weatherboards had been faded and rotting, and the block had been covered with long grass.

Now, it was a pretty cottage. Jenna's Tea Room sign was written in old English script, and the roses that Jenna had planted the first spring she'd been there now tumbled down the railing of the steps and across the fences—the smell of early blooming jasmine carried on the breeze. The whole feel of the tea room made you want to relax, smell the roses, and let calm fill you.

That wasn't a bad idea, Alice thought to herself. For some reason, she'd let that Billy Burke really upset her. She wasn't satisfied that things were okay, but there were processes to follow. Perhaps she was wrong; hopefully, she was.

Conversations filled the room as she walked into the tea room. There were about a dozen women already sitting at the long table along the window that overlooked the rose garden.

'Hi, Alice, come and sit down,' Callie called out. 'We're about to start the meeting.'

Tilly was sitting beside her grandmother on Callie's other side.

Alice smiled at Gladys Tingle and Beryl as she sat opposite them in one of the two vacant chairs.

'I thought I was early, but the time got away,' she said.

Gladys smiled, which was quite out of character. 'Hello, Alice. How did you go with those samples you were going to bring up for the masks?'

'They're in the back of the car,' Alice said, not letting on that she had totally forgotten about them after encountering Billy Burke. 'I'll run down and get them.'

'Leave it until we're ready to talk about the masks later in the meeting.' Callie caught Alice's eye, and Alice knew that Gladys would take over when she brought the craft supplies up.

'Okay, I'll just grab a coffee now,' Alice said. Maybe that would help settle the trembling feeling in her arms and legs.

Ellie took the last of the coffee orders, and when she and Jenna brought the drinks over, Jenna joined the meeting, and Callie tapped her spoon on the side of her teacup.

'Are we ready to start?' Callie sat at the head of the table. 'Ladies, thank you all for coming. Let's get this meeting started. Thank you to those of you who emailed me with items to discuss. I've got a bit of an agenda here. I'll read it to you, and if there's anything that you think we don't need to talk about today, just let me know when I finish, or if there's anything else that we've missed, please let us know. We've only got an hour. I know it's a terrible time in the afternoon, but it suits those of us who work. Plus, thank you to Alice and Tilly for driving up from Charleville.

'Right. The first thing that we really need to talk about—actually, no, instead of going through them one at a time, I'll list the things that I've got, okay? I've got fundraising—that is, who we're fundraising for—the ball theme that we discussed, and we need to talk more about that. We need to talk about who's eligible to come to the ball. Plus, the venue and catering.

'Is there anything else that's pressing that we missed?'

'We need to discuss the ticket price, but that will depend on the fundraising goal,' Amelia Foley said.

'I'll add that to the agenda,' Callie said. 'It's a good point, thanks, Amelia. So, how about we start with fundraising, as that will drive a lot of what we do? Jenny? Your thoughts?'

Jenny Riley had worked as treasurer on quite a few other committees over the years, and she had been appointed treasurer at their first meeting. She'd had to take some time out when her husband was ill, but she was back on board and raring to go now that Tom was well again.

'We had decided that it would be for the hospital to develop the maternity wing, but since then,' Jenny looked across at Laura with a smile, 'Dr Harry tells me that the government has looked at recent data. Because of the increase in births locally, they've agreed to increase funding for the hospital next year.'

'So what you're saying,' Gladys said, 'is that the need for funding for the maternity wing is not so pressing.'

'Yes, that's correct, Gladys.' Jenny looked around the table. 'What does everyone think?' A robust discussion took place, and especially as there were so many pregnant women in the group, some good points were raised, but the general consensus was that more funding for the maternity wing was not really needed at this point.

'Maybe we could just have a ball and not have it for fundraising,' Beryl suggested tentatively.

Gladys turned sideways and gave her an icy look. 'The point of the ball is to raise funds for the community. Isn't that right, Callie?'

'As chair, I'm open to all suggestions. It's then up to us all to vote as a committee. It's not my decision,' Callie said. 'What does everyone think? Has anyone got any other suggestions for worthy fundraising? Alice, what do you think? You know a fair bit about the region. How do we compare with Charleville and some of the other local towns with funding for various initiatives?'

Alice thought for a moment. 'Well, there are sporting clubs, schools and the hospital. Our aged care facilities can always do with more funding. I don't know if anyone else has got any other thoughts.'

Chloe put her hand up, and Callie nodded. 'Chloe?'

'Well, I can tell you that at the moment, we've got some initiatives in place for the football club and the cricket club.'

'What about the school, Callie? Is there anything that they need to purchase?' Jenny asked. 'Something in the way of resources or equipment rather than staffing.'

'Well, we're pretty lucky. We've just received more funding from the federal government rural school bucket, and we're pretty right with sporting equipment again, thanks to Chloe and her group for their kind donations over the last twelve months. The only thing I can think of is maybe some cultural activities, but that means we need to fly in people like illustrators, authors, and motivational speakers. There is a need for motivational speakers in education, particularly for teachers who are suffering a little bit of stress. I know of a really good speaker who talks about depression and balancing your work-life, and I think something like that would be worthwhile. But I know the speaker I have in mind charges a four thousand dollar fee plus accommodation and travel costs to get him here.'

'It sounds like a good possibility,' Sophie said. 'Our teachers are important to us.'

'Alice, what about the youth centre? I've heard a whisper that there are some changes there,' Rosie asked.

Bec was late to the meeting, and Alice hesitated, unsure whether the expansion was public knowledge or not. To her great relief, footsteps sounded on the stairs, and Bec came through the door.

'Hi, everyone, sorry I'm late.'

'Great timing,' Gladys Tingle said. 'We just asked Alice a question, but she seems reluctant to answer.'

Alice turned away and rolled her eyes. Given her mood this afternoon, it would be easy to snap at Gladys. She was an astute old bird, but she could be painful to deal with if things didn't go her way. Tilly, her granddaughter, seemed to cope with her snarky words, but Alice didn't have the patience these days. Her patience was all expended on the local youth.

And Billy Burke.

Bec sat down, and Ellie got up to get her a coffee. 'Flat white?' she asked quietly.

'Yes, please, the usual,' Bec said. 'What can I help you with, Gladys?'

Gladys gestured for Callie to answer.

'We're looking at the fundraising recipients from the ball,' Callie said. 'The hospital's not in need of funding for the maternity section anymore. We talked about a few possibilities. The school has no need, apart from maybe some mental health funding for staff professional development. Sophie asked about your youth centre, Choice for Youth—'

Gladys interrupted Callie before she could finish. 'But *I* don't think it qualifies as it's in Charleville. This ball and all funds raised are for the *local* community.'

Bec caught Alice's eye as she leaned back, and her grin

was wide. Alice knew that she was about to spill the news.

'Well, everyone.' Bec looked along both sides of the table. Alice noticed Gladys lean forward, her eyes gleaming as she prepared to pounce on any words she didn't want to hear. 'I've got some very good news for Augathella this afternoon. I finally received the phone call I was waiting for today and got the final confirmation that we're opening a branch of Choice for Youth up here in Augathella.' She turned to Alice. 'Thanks for not spilling the beans before I arrived, Alice.'

There were some positive nods and murmurs around the table. Gladys' mouth dropped open as she stared at Alice with narrowed eyes.

Alice bit the inside of her cheek so that nothing rude came from her mouth, but she could still think about it.

'That's great news,' Jenny Riley said.

'So, if the centre's starting here, what's being funded?' Beryl asked.

She was certainly getting gamer these days, Alice thought.

'Well, mainly leasing a building and getting some more staff, but we won't have anything to put in it, you know, like computers, lunchroom facilities, meals for kids on the weekend,' Bec said. 'The sooner we can resource it and start activities up here, the more it will benefit our local youth. At the moment, we can bring some of our resources up from Charleville, but that will probably mean opening only a couple of afternoons a week.' She looked at Alice, who nodded. 'But if we knew that more funding was on the way, we could split the resources equally across the two centres until we had funding for the Augathella centre on its own.'

'Well, I think that's a great idea.' Callie smiled widely. 'Thanks so much for letting us know the details, Bec. Now that we know the youth centre is opening, I think we should provide some funding for all the things you might need to make it a top-notch place. What do you think, everyone?'

Callie asked.

Gladys Tingle shook her head. 'I don't think so. We need to be looking at the aged care facility. We need stuff there. There are not enough books to read in the library. The food isn't very good, and none of us have televisions in our rooms. We have to go out to the lounge to watch television.'

Everyone was quiet as they considered that.

'Okay, well, we've got two possibilities to consider,' Callie said. 'Let's not decide tonight. We don't have to do it until we start printing tickets and publicising the ball. We don't really need to say what it's for yet, so let's give it a couple of weeks until our next meeting. That gives everyone a chance to think about what they prefer.'

Sophie caught Callie's eye across the table with a small smile, and Alice thought to herself that Callie had handled that very well. She could teach Alice how to be diplomatic. The image of that damn stockman came back to her—again— and she closed her eyes.

Why wouldn't Billy Burke stay out of her head?

The rest of the meeting was spent discussing the other items on the agenda, and just after five, Callie stood. 'Okay, everybody, that's been a great meeting. Thank you, Alice, for bringing those craft items. It's given us some fabulous ideas. Thank you, Sophie, for offering to sew some costumes. So, if everyone puts some thought into what we discussed today, when shall we have our next meeting?'

'A fortnight,' Jenny Riley suggested.

'Does that suit you, Jenna, if we have it at the same time? Four o'clock back here?'

Jenna nodded. 'All good.'

Callie raised her hand to quiet the chatter that had started. 'One last thing. I forgot to thank Jenna for providing the coffee for everyone and not charging us. You didn't have to do that, Jenna.'

'That's my contribution,' she said. 'Plus, if we have raffle prizes on the day, I'll be happy to donate some lunches and afternoon teas for that, too.'

'We didn't even talk about raffle prizes,' Sophie said.

'Next meeting. I'll send out an agenda in about a week. If you think of anything, email or call me.' Callie said. 'Okay, everyone, thank you so much for coming and for all the ideas. We've made great progress today. This way, we'll all be home before dark.'

Alice stood and waited for Tilly to say goodbye to her grandmother before they drove back together. Being in the company of the other women and thinking about things broader than her job had calmed her a little, but a niggle of anger still tugged at her as she thought about Billy Burke. Her first job tomorrow would be to make an appointment with him.

Chapter 15

It was almost five o'clock by the time Billy turned at the *Kilcoy Station* sign. He looked around with appreciation; the cattle were fat and in top condition, and the paddocks were lush and green. The drive down to the house was about a kilometre long. As he approached the red brick building, he could see the boys playing football in a paddock that looked like it had been marked out as a football field.

As angry as he was with Beau, he was pleased that he had actually connected with some kids. Good kids, by the sound of things. When they'd stayed at Mt Isa for a few months after Mary's funeral, Beau had turned into a loner. Then, the move to Kununurra had made that even worse.

Even if Beau had wagged and lied to get here, seeing him playing football with kids his own age tempered Billy's anger.

A little bit.

Beau was still in big trouble and would suffer consequences for what he'd done. They'd sit down tonight and have a very serious talk. Billy had decided to let it go this afternoon. This wasn't the place to discuss it, but Beau had to be taught about risk-taking behaviour.

Billy also wanted to find out what happened in Charleville with that woman who had bailed him up this afternoon. He was still angry about the way she'd spoken to him as she vocalised her doubt in his ability to care for Beau.

What did she know about their circumstances, and how dare she form an opinion?

God knows it had been hard enough, but he was doing his best. He was trying to deal with a battle he hadn't had time to fight. The situation was caused by his dropping Beau off at school early so he could meet Jon at the rural store. Maybe if he'd told Jon he had a kid, he could have made different plans. He and Beau had kept to themselves since they'd moved into the old farmhouse about five kilometres from the Ingrams' new house.

But one thing that Billy wouldn't do was rely on other people. They needed to be independent. They had each other, and that was all that mattered. If Beau had gone off the rails for one day and someone thought he looked neglected, dirty, and hungry, well, that was something that he'd be addressing, and he wouldn't hold back in telling Beau what she had said.

The boys heard his ute approaching, and a football bounced on the road in front of it as four boys ran over. At the same time, Braden came out of the big shed to the left of the house. Billy drove over to the shed, parked there, and reached over to shake Braden's hand.

'Braden, was your son at school today, or did he wag school with Beau and go to Charleville?'

'What? Charleville?' Braden said. 'Hang on a moment.' He hurried out of the shed, and the next minute, he roared, 'Rory Cartwright! Get your butt in here right now. By yourself.'

Braden was speaking so loudly Billy could hear every word. 'I don't want you to lie to me. I want the truth, mate. Did you go to school today?'

'Yeah, Dad, you saw me go. You dropped me off there, and you picked me up.'

'But did you *stay* at school all day?'

'Of course I did. Where else would I go? There's nothing else to do in town.'

'Are you telling me the truth, mate?'

'Yes, of course I am.'

'Okay. Do you know if Beau was at school today?'

There was a long silence.

'Okay,' Braden said. 'You guys just keep playing. We'll talk about this later when Mum gets home.'

'Have you talked to her yet?' The boy's voice quavered.

'Yes, I sure have, and there are going to be consequences. That is one thing we don't do in this family—tell lies to get our own way. Outside now, Rory. We'll talk more later.'

Braden came back into the shed, shaking his head. 'It sounds like we've both had a bit of a day with the kids,' he said.

'Yep,' Billy replied.

'Apparently, Rory *was* at school. He tells me he was, and I tend to believe him. I don't know what else has happened. Do you want to talk about it while you're here?'

'No, I'll sort it out with Beau once we get home. I'm sorry if he's been a nuisance, Braden. I didn't expect that to happen.'

'No, not at all. They're having a good time, and I'm sure I did similar things when I was a teenager.'

'And me too. It's the beginning of hard years for both of us, I would say.' Billy ran his hand through his hair. 'Thanks, mate. I owe you. Beau's gone off the rails today, from what I can tell, but he ended up safe, and I'll sort it out with him. The best thing is seeing that he's made some friends and is interacting with others like a normal kid. There hasn't been a lot of that.'

'Mate, I'm guessing you've had some tough times,' Braden said. 'If you ever need to talk, I'm a willing ear. 'There's a beer fridge in this shed and many a problem has been sorted here.'

'I appreciate it, mate. I might take you up on that. Looks like you've got some experience with kids.'

'Speaking of which, here they come, and two of them are looking very sheepish,' Braden said quietly. 'Is Billy okay, or would you prefer Mr Burke?'

'God, no,' said Billy. 'Billy is fine.'

Braden put his hand on the tallest boy's shoulder. 'Billy, This is my older son, Rory. He's the same age as Beau, I believe, and this is Nigel, and this is Petie.' He looked proud when each of the boys shook Billy's hand. 'Good manners, boys, thank you.'

'What time is Mum coming home?' Nigel said. 'I'm hungry.'

'Mum will be about half an hour,' Braden looked at Billy. 'I think I told you Callie's a teacher at the school, but she had a meeting about this fundraising ball this afternoon. She'll be home in a little while, and she'll have our other two kids with her.'

'Two more? You've got five kids all together?' Billy said, running his hands through his hair.

'Yeah, mate. Our youngest are eighteen-month-old twins.'

'And I think I've got my hands full with one.' Billy looked over at Beau, who was looking very nervous. He went over and put his hand on his shoulder. 'Good to see you home safe, mate. We'll have a chat later, fair enough?'

Billy felt Beau's shoulders tense as he continued speaking, but he didn't move away. 'I'm actually Billy's uncle, but he's now my adopted son, and we're learning how to get along together.'

'Our boys can help him. Callie is their stepmother, and we all had lots of learning to do.'

'Mum left her bags in the drain, and they nearly drowned. Dad saved them, and they fell in love. Callie and Dad, that is, not the bags. We got a new Mum,' Petie said.

Billy got the general gist of the story and smiled.

Braden gestured to the shed. 'It's still light enough for the boys to play a little bit longer. Can I offer you that beer? I've got light beer.'

'I'd appreciate that, mate.'

'And think about what I said. Dinner's on offer, too.'

'Can we stay for dinner?' Beau said. 'Their mum is a really good cook, and it's lamb night.'

'We have to get home, Beau. We've got some talking to do, and I've got an early start again tomorrow.'

'Maybe you could stay the night here,' Petie piped up. 'We've got plenty of spare beds.'

Billy laughed and ruffled his hair. 'Thanks for the offer, mate.'

'Maybe Beau could come out and stay with us one weekend,' Braden offered.

'We'll have a chat about that. Sounds good,' Billy said. He glanced over at Beau, who had a grin from ear to ear. It was the happiest he'd seen him look for at least twelve months.

Maybe he'd go easy on him tonight. If it was okay, they might stay for dinner. It might mellow Beau a little bit more.

Chapter 16

Callie took the drive home slowly. It was that awful time of the afternoon when she hated driving—the sun had set, but it wasn't quite dark. The fading light made it hard to see kangaroos on the road, and she also had to dodge corrugations along the way. At least the twins were well-behaved. Ruth had given them early dinner and bathed them. She was an absolute gem.

It was almost six when she turned into the driveway and wondered whose ute was parked outside the shed. The big shed lights were still on as she put the car away in the garage on the side of the house. She rolled her eyes as the washing flapped on the line.

'Thanks, Rory,' she muttered. As she got out of the car, a sharp twinge pulled in her lower left side, and she caught her breath.

'Just the baby stretching my muscles,' she reassured herself. She stood there until the pain eased and was gone as quickly as it had come. The washing could stay out for the night; it would be damp again by now; at least Rory—or someone had hung it out.

She'd hoped that Braden would have heard the car, but there was no sign of him.

'Come on you, pair, bedtime.' Seeing they'd had their dinner, it would only be a matter of a bottle each, and they could go straight to bed. She lifted the small bag of groceries and the two strollers out of the back of the Landcruiser; the twins were too heavy to carry at the same time now. She strapped them in; her bag and school stuff could wait until later.

From the breezeway into the house, she could hear

laughter, and couldn't help her smile as the sound of a Nintendo game drifted down the hallway. She hoped they'd done their homework. Although, by the sound of things, that young fellow Beau was still here, and she assumed the car must belong to his father. The talk with Rory could wait until after they'd gone.

When the twins were out of the stroller and sitting happily in the old-fashioned wooden playpen in the corner of the kitchen, she lifted the lid of the slow cooker. A tantalising aroma of lamb and herbs filled the kitchen. The casserole was bubbling along gently. She turned the cooker off and flicked the kettle on, ready to boil water for the peas and pasta. She headed up the hallway and stuck her head into the games room. Petie called out and raced over, throwing his arms around her legs.

'Hi, Mummy. Where's our twinnies? You didn't forget them, did you?'

She ruffled his hair. 'No, sweetie. They're in the kitchen.'

He took off down the hallway, and Callie smiled. Petie would sit for ages, playing peekaboo with the twins around the playpen. The smile disappeared when she walked into the games room; she was disappointed with Rory's behaviour. It was so out of character; she couldn't remember him ever lying before, and that made her wonder about this new friend.

Rory and Nigel were sitting in their beanbags, and an unfamiliar boy was sitting on the floor between them.

'I'm home,' she said loudly over the noise of the game.

'Hey, Mum,' Rory took his eyes off the screen for a second. His eyes met hers and skittered away as she raised her eyebrows.

'Perhaps you'd like to introduce me to your new friend, Rory.'

'Sorry, Mum, this is Beau. You were off school when he arrived last week.'

'That's right. I haven't met Beau yet.'

The young boy pushed himself to his feet and, to his

credit, came over to her. 'Hello, Mrs Cartwright. It's very nice to meet you. Thank you for letting me come out to your house this afternoon.'

Nigel jumped up and said, 'Dad's invited Beau and his dad for tea. Is that okay with you, Mum?'

Callie nodded, although the last thing she wanted was visitors. She was exhausted. 'If Dad actually did say that, they are more than welcome to stay.'

Rory looked at her again and then looked away.

'I'll go over and see Dad and meet your dad, Beau. Ten more minutes, boys.'

'He's not my dad,' Beau said.

'Oh, okay, I'll go and see them then,' Callie said, wondering what the story was.

Petie was still playing peekaboo with the twins, and she smiled as laughter and giggles filled the kitchen.

'Can you stay there, please, Petie? I'm just going out to the shed to see Dad. Dinner's nearly ready.' She wouldn't put the peas on until she knew if the boy and his father were staying.

'Yes, Mummy.' Petie giggled as Munro reached out and grabbed his hair. 'Ouch, that hurt, Munnie.'

'Don't get too close. He's getting very strong.'

Callie headed out to the shed. Braden and an unfamiliar guy were sitting in the little den he had built at the back of the shed near the beer fridge.

'Hi, Callie, I thought I heard you drive in. We were just about to come inside. This is Billy Burke,' Braden said.

Billy, who was a very good-looking man, came over and extended his hand.

'Please excuse the cattle dirt on me, Mrs Cartwright,' he said, his voice deep and low.

'Callie, please. It's fine. I know you've been working with Braden and Jon all day. I'm more than used to it, so don't worry.'

'Callie, I've invited Billy and Beau for dinner. Is that

okay with you?'

'Yes, of course it is. I met Beau. Of course, you're more than welcome,' she said to Billy with a wide smile. 'I've boiled the water for the peas, the lamb's ready to go, and I'll get the kids to set the table while I put the twins down.'

'I can do that. Let them keep having a good time. They've been really well-behaved this afternoon,' Braden said.

'Beau is very polite,' Callie said to Billy.

He chuckled. 'When it suits him. It is good to see him having a good time and being polite. I'm sure you've heard about the dramas today at the school. Braden and I have been talking about it. Beau wagged school. I'll be having a good talk with him when we get home.'

'And we'll be talking to Rory later, too,' Braden said.

'Please stay for dinner, Billy. It will be too late once you drive home.'

'Thank you, I appreciate it,' he said. 'I'm sure Billy will be, too, because I'm not much of a cook.'

Callie hesitated. 'So I don't put my foot in it, may I ask about Beau? He said you're not his dad?'

'That's right. I'm his uncle, but I do have legal custody of him. My sister passed away last year.'

'Oh, I'm so sorry to hear that.' Callie leaned over and kissed Braden's cheek. 'I'll go and put the twins down. Can you pop the frozen peas in the water before you set the table, please, love?' She walked to the door. 'It's an easy tea here tonight, Billy.'

Chapter 17

'They're good people, aren't they, Billy?'

Billy stared ahead, his hand clutching the steering wheel. He was looking out for roos.

It was good of Braden and the others to suggest they stayed the night, as it had been late by the time they finished dinner and chatting.

'They are.'

It was quiet again for a few minutes as they approached Augathella and then headed west past the airfield.

'We need to have a chat.'

'Yeah, I know.'

Billy forced his hands to relax on the steering wheel. 'I'm not going to write you off, mate, but I want you to listen to me. Your mum put you in my care, and you are my responsibility. If you had any idea of the worry I had today when I thought I hadn't looked after you properly and then I'd lost you, you might understand what I'm trying to do. Now tell me why you went to Charleville?'

'I don't know. I don't like the school.'

'But you've got mates there. You seem to be getting on really well with Rory and his brothers, and I know you're playing football, too.'

'Yeah, but I can't do the work, and I feel stupid when I can't do it, so I don't want to be in class.'

Billy's heart clenched. 'You missed a lot of school when your Mum was sick. We can sort something out about that, mate. Nobody has to know.' Thinking about Mary made his throat ache. She should be here with them, watching Beau grow up. All was quiet for a while as they left Augathella and then headed west towards Jon and Fallon's place.

Billy broke the silence once he had his emotions under control. 'I don't want to lose you, Beau. Because Mum—'

His voice trembled. 'Because Mum made you promise to look after me.'

'Yeah, that's a big part of it, but also because you're my nephew, and I'm the one who's going to look out for you as you grow up. I want to make sure I do the right thing. I was worried that I hadn't been doing it properly for you.'

'You do alright.'

Billy supported himself with his hands on the steering wheel, and his shoulders sagged in relief. 'We are sort of poking along alright together, aren't we, mate?'

'Yeah, we are. Can we watch the footy tonight?'

'I think we might have missed it, but we can watch the replay on my phone.'

Silence reigned again as they navigated the twenty kilometres of dirt road, past Alan Humphreys' station and down to the Ingram's place. Billy turned his head as Beau said something. 'Sorry, mate, I missed that. What did you say?'

'I said I'm sorry, Billy.'

Emotion clutched at Billy's chest. Maybe Beau doing this had forced a change in their relationship and in both of their attitudes.

'It's okay, mate.'

'Am I going to have any punishment?' Beau asked.

Billy shook his head. 'No, I can see what caused it. I'm just pleased that someone looked after you down there and helped you get home.'

He might be pleased about that, but he certainly wasn't looking forward to meeting with that woman again. He felt like something on the ground under her shoe when she looked at him.

'Alice was nice, Billy.'

That was the first time Beau had used his name since he picked him up.

'Oh, she looked after you well, but she reminded me of that social worker up in Kununurra.'

'No, she was nicer than her. But I've got one thing to confess.'

Billy tried not to smile. 'What else did you do, mate?'

'I left my bag in her car.'

'I know you did, and she gave it to me.'

'Oh, sweet,' Beau said.

Chapter 18

Alice left it until late on Monday afternoon to ring and make the appointment to talk to Beau's carer the following afternoon. She thought a lot about it over the weekend and wondered whether she overreacted. Still, she reminded herself that Beau had left Augathella without permission, travelled on a bus to Charleville, wandered around town, had no money, and had shoplifted a Mars Bar before he realised the error of his ways.

The call was brief and to the point. Billy Burke agreed to meet at the time and venue she suggested—the small meeting room off the bistro in the pub at Augathella. They could have met in Jenna's tearooms or in the room that Chloe had at the side of the department store, but Alice had a feeling that this was going to be a difficult interview, and the room at the pub was more private.

On Tuesday afternoon, before she drove up to Augathella for the meeting, Alice went to the ladies' room at the youth centre. She pulled a face at herself in her bathroom mirror as she carefully outlined her lips with the soft pink lipstick that always made her feel confident. She couldn't understand why her stomach was in knots; for goodness sake, she had done dozens, if not hundreds, of interviews with carers, parents, and families over the past four years since she had been working as a youth worker.

For some reason, Mr Billy Burke, new to town, unsettled her. It wasn't only because he was such a good-looking guy; his confidence and brashness almost intimidated her.

Almost.

Even in his dust-covered stockman clothes and with his Akubra on, it was clear he was a fine-looking man. What had most drawn her attention were his clear, dark blue eyes surrounded by long black lashes. His face was rugged almost to the point of roughness, but that was relieved by the laughter lines fanning out from his eyes. His nose was straight, and his lips were full. If she was honest, even with his ruggedness, he had the sort of looks that you often saw in advertising campaigns.

She shook herself again. His appearance and attitude were no reason to have herself tied in knots.

Her primary concern was supported by the notes she'd made. She identified that Beau had shoplifted. He had told lies about having permission to go out to the Cartwright house, and he hadn't been forthcoming with her when she asked about his situation. Normally, she would've done a notification alone when she had concerns, but she hadn't discussed it with Bec because she knew that Bec would have encouraged her to do it. But there was something about Billy Burke, and the sadness that he carried, had made her decide to give him a chance before she did a notification. Not only would she talk to him, but she would also get his permission to talk to Beau at the school.

Alice had thought long and hard about what to wear that morning before she went to work.

In the end, she chose a pair of black trousers and put on a long-sleeved olive green T-shirt and a set of black chunky beads. Hair up or hair down? She'd compromised and swept her hair back into a high ponytail. There, she looked professional but casual, and by the end of the day working in the youth centre, she would be even more crumpled and relaxed.

Now, she took one last look in the mirror and was happy; her expression was calm and composed. She *felt* professional, and she *looked* professional.

Now, all she had to do was hope that Billy Burke would be as professional within the interview situation as she wanted him to be.

***

'No problem, mate. I'll keep an eye out for him. Hey, I'll ask Fallon to cook some pikelets, and he can come to us. Is that okay?

'Thanks, I'll bring him over before I go. I shouldn't be in town too long. I hope, anyway.'

Billy had mentioned his trip to town this afternoon with Jon when they knocked off from drenching the cattle. He'd given Jon a bit of an explanation about Bea and why the meeting was important.

'I can't afford a whiff of trouble, mate, and that social worker or youth worker or whatever she is looks like trouble.'

'Not Bec Hunter?' Jon said. 'She's great. No need to worry there.'

'No, no, her name's Templeton or something.'

'Yeah, I know Alice. What are you worried about?'

'She looked officious, and she looked like she would follow things to the letter of the law.'

'Well, I guess she does have to follow procedures and policies, but if there's one word that I wouldn't apply to Alice Templeton, it would be officious. She's a young, gentle soul. She gets on well with everyone in town. I've been to a few functions that she's been at. She's working with the girls on this ball, too.'

Billy shrugged. 'We'll see. I'm talking to her in an official capacity. I think most people are different when they socialise.'

Jon took his hat off. 'Going to head to the shed. You got time for a coffee, mate?'

Billy glanced down at his watch. 'Yeah, the school bus won't be in for about ten minutes, if he's on it.'

'Troubles with the boy?'

'He took himself out to the Cartwrights the other afternoon after we'd been mustering. Turned out well. Braden looked after him, and they made me feel very welcome.'

'You couldn't get a better family,' Jon said. 'And the boys will be a good influence on Beau if he's struggling a little bit. You guys have had a tough life, by the sound of things. Do you mind if I ask you? Are you his dad?'

'Oh, hell no,' Billy said. 'I've got no kids.' He split a grin for a second. 'Not that I'm aware of anyway.'

Jon chuckled. 'So you're a carer?'

Billy shook his head. 'No. Beau is my sister's son. Mary passed away last year.'

'I'm sorry to hear that, mate. It must be tough. His dad?' he asked. 'Tell me if I'm being too nosy.'

'Mary was a bit of a girl in her time, and she always assured me that she didn't know who Beau's father was.'

'It's not on the birth certificate.'

'No, and now any chance of ever finding out is gone.'

'How does Beau feel about that?'

'Mary talked with him when she was sick, and she said he was fine with it. He showed no interest, but if he ever does, there's really nothing I can do about it. Mary was only seventeen when she had him, and I was living away. I'm a fair bit older than she was. She was living in Cairns at that time, doing bar work, and she said she had no idea who the father was. As much as I hate to think about it, I think that might've been a way she supplemented her income.'

'Was she sick?'

'Yeah, she knew she was dying. She had cervical cancer. She let it go too late, and by the time it was discovered, it had gone too far.'

'Sorry, mate, you've had a rough trot.'

'It has been hard, Jon, but I'm determined to do the right thing by young Beau. Problem is, I can't get him to respond to anything. The only thing he's interested in at all is football. We watch the football at night on that TV in the house, and sometimes he forgets who he's with and cheers and says things to me like, "Oh, did you see that try?" or "What's the ref doing?" I can honestly say that's the only conversation we have through the whole week.'

'And now you're worried about Alice? What worries you there?'

'She told me she could do a notification because she was concerned about Beau's well-being.'

Jon stared at him. 'But, mate, you look after him well.'

'As well as I can. The little bugger won't shower and won't wash his hair, so he always looks scruffy, and he's always been thin, always a gangly almost-teenager. I didn't fill out till I was in my early twenties. So I know he looks like he's not getting cared for well, but he eats like a horse. I found out the full story about him wagging school the other day. He jumped on the bus and went down to Charleville, and that's where Alice caught him. And then that same afternoon, he lied about having permission to go out to the Cartwrights. By the time Braden rang me, they were already out there.'

'Okay. Like I said, don't rush back, and if you need some time out after the meeting, we can keep an eye on Beau until you get back. We haven't got much on, and that new young ringer needs to work by herself a bit more. If there's anyone with her, any chance to be a bit lazy, I don't know if she's going to last.'

This time, Billy chuckled. 'I noticed that. I wasn't going to say anything yet.'

'What about Beau? Has he ever done the Cattle Cadet program?'

Billy shook his head. 'I don't know. I've asked him. He won't tell me what he's done. If football's mentioned, you can get something out of him.'

'Okay, I might have a chat with him one afternoon. I might "accidentally" bump into him out in the paddock or something.'

'I really appreciate that, Jon. Thanks, mate.'

Chapter 19

Alice reached the pub with enough time to compose herself before the meeting. She parked the car and walked into the bistro. Sean, the manager, was polishing glasses behind the bar and looked at her with interest. He had already asked her out a couple of times, but Alice had politely declined.

'Hey Alice,' he said. 'How are you going?'

'Good, thank you, Sean. I've booked the room next to the bistro for a meeting.'

'Yeah, Billy is in there already, waiting for you.'

Alice glanced down at her watch. 'Already? He's early.'

'Yeah, he wandered in here about twenty minutes ago.'

'Okay, thank you.'

'What can I get you to drink?'

'Is your coffee machine on?' she asked.

'Sure is.'

'Just a flat white, thanks.' She pulled out her wallet.

'No need to worry about it. Coffee's on the house this afternoon—a coffee to celebrate you coming up to run the youth centre here. The whole town is talking about it. Alice Templeton, coming home.'

'Really?' Alice wondered if Sean was working up to ask her out again.

'Yeah. You're a local, born and bred. So the story goes.' Sean turned to the coffee machine.

'But you've been here a long time,' Alice said. 'You were working here before I left town, weren't you?'

'I was working out on a property at Adavale back in those days. Look, you go in. I'll bring your coffee in.'

Alice swallowed and straightened her shoulders as she

walked to the door on the other side of the bistro. Billy Burke was sitting at a table, drumming his fingers—little finger to thumb, little finger to thumb, making a repetitive drumming sound.

'Good afternoon, Mr Burke,' she said.

He looked up, and his eyes widened as he took in her appearance. 'Good afternoon, Miss Templeton.'

'Please call me Alice,' she said.

'Are you sure?' he said.

'Of course.'

'You look much more like an Alice today,' he said.

'What is that supposed to mean?' She bristled.

'Well, the lady in the suit and the pearls and the bun was definitely Miss Templeton, but I think you're an Alice today.'

Alice forced a smile and pulled out the chair opposite. That was some sort of start, anyway.

'So, thank you for meeting me here.'

'I won't say it's my pleasure because it's not,' he said.

Her eyes widened at his brusque response. She put her bag on the floor, leaned forward, and clasped her hands on the table in front of her. His fingers were still drumming on the table.

'Do you mind not doing that?'

'Doing what?' he said.

'Making that noise with your fingers,' she said. He looked down as if surprised that he was doing it.

'Sorry, nervous habit.'

'You're nervous about meeting me?' she said.

'No, not nervous. I can't see the point.'

Alice sighed. She would stay professional and not be cranky.

'Well, Mr Burke, we need to talk about Beau. I need to be sure that he's being well cared for. The situation last Friday didn't really reinforce that for me. Can you tell me what your relationship is with Beau?'

He looked up from his fingers, which had stopped

moving on the table, and his eyes were on her—those blue eyes that she found so compelling on Friday, even when they were full of anger, frustration, and worry. Her mouth dried, and she dropped her gaze. It was ridiculous having that trembling feeling from a client across from her in a professional setting. Maybe it was just nerves.

'Well, Alice,' he said. She looked up and held his gaze again. It was the right way to approach this.

'I'm Billy's uncle. My sister Mary had him when she was seventeen. She never told me who the father was, and there's no name on Billy's birth certificate.'

'So there was no chance of a father taking him?' she asked carefully.

'No. Mary got sick and died about a year ago.'

'I'm sorry to hear that.'

'Yep, it was a hard time. I stayed with her for the last four months, and I saw Beau's grief when he realised that his mother wasn't going to live. Until then, he was always a good kid, but when Mary finally passed away in the hospital, he went inside himself, and he's barely interacted with anyone since then. He's healing, though, steadily. And that's why I'm so pleased to see that he's established a rapport with the football team here and the Cartwright boys.'

'So, is there a formal relationship between you?' she asked.

'Yes,' he said, his voice deep and steady. 'It was all organised before Mary passed away. I've adopted Beau, and it's all legal.'

'And how does he feel about that?'

Billy shrugged. 'Beau's just learning to feel again, I think. It's been less than a year since he lost his mum. We've moved twice in that time, and he's just finding his way. I'll be honest with you, Alice. I've had nothing to do with kids. I knew him when he was a little tacker, and it's a whole new learning experience for me. So what exactly is your problem, apart from him taking off and telling lies, which I'm dealing with?'

'Well, I'll be honest. I was concerned about how thin he was. I was concerned about the state of his clothes and, to put it bluntly, he didn't smell very clean. And that screams neglect to me. Mr... may I call you Billy? If you're calling me Alice?'

'Yes, you may.'

Her heart went out to him as he lowered his head and ran both hands through his sun-tipped hair. He was in need of a shave, but the attractive stubble on his face was quite appealing. She deliberately kept her eyes away from the navy-blue T-shirt that snugly moulded his chest.

Before she could speak, the door opened, and Sean came in with a cup of coffee.

'Here you go, Alice.'

'Thanks, Sean. I appreciate it.'

By the time the barman left the room, Billy had composed himself.

'Okay, let's talk about your concerns about Beau,' he said. 'One, I find it hard to get him to have a shower. I'm lucky if he has one every three days. But short of stripping him down and putting him in the shower myself, which I'm not prepared to do yet unless you say it's absolutely necessary, he's going to look a bit grubby at times. We haven't got a washing machine out at the Ingram's place yet, and I've been hand-washing stuff, but no matter how often I put his clean clothes in his room, he picks up the same dirty clothes every day. And by the time I try to wash them, he's wearing them. And as I said, I'm certainly not going to hold him down and strip him off. Our relationship is too fragile for that. I'm taking it very slow and easy, Alice, as I'm sure you can probably understand.

'As for his size, the little bugger eats like a horse. I'm at IGA every two or three days, stocking up on fruit, meat, and vegetables. And trust me, he eats properly. He burns it up. He never stops. If he's not in bed asleep or sitting at the table eating, he's outside kicking a football or running around. He burns it up. Now, you can either believe me, or you don't. So that's the situation. I'm doing my best.'

Alice nodded and looked away, then reached down and picked up her coffee cup. As she lifted it to her lips, their eyes met again.

***

Sean tried to catch her attention as she left the pub. Billy Burke had lifted his hat, put it on his head, tipped the brim to her, turned on his heel, and left about five minutes ago. It had taken her a good five minutes to calm down; nothing had been achieved in the fifteen-minute meeting.

Billy had explained the things she'd been concerned about with Beau, and she guessed she could understand and probably accept them. He explained the background, and it wasn't her business to check whether he was telling the truth or not. She was the youth worker, and she was concerned. She needed to do a notification, and the powers that be would investigate whether Billy was a suitable carer for his nephew.

At times during the talk, his sincerity had shown through, and she could sense frustration in his words as he explained the difficulties of dealing with a young boy who didn't want to do as he was told. She was still in two minds, but she knew that most of her hesitation about doing a notification was because of Billy Burke himself.

Something about the man attracted her—whether it was his sincerity and willingness to take on a twelve-year-old boy and be a single dad or simply that she found him attractive. It was doing her head in.

She stood and tucked her chair in as Sean called out to her, 'How about a roadie, Alice?'

'Roadie?' she said, confused and shaking her head.

'Before you head back to Charleville.'

'No, I'm staying here tonight,' she said. 'But thank you anyway, Sean.'

'Come and have a drink with me? I'm about to take a

break for a couple of hours.'

Alice shook her head and forced a smile. 'Thank you, Sean. I've got some work to do. I'm actually here working.'

'I thought you were having a date with Billy Burke and that you two had a blue. He didn't look terribly happy when he left. You're certainly not doing handstands. I was going to offer a shoulder to cry on.' He looked hopeful.

'Business,' she said, shaking her head. 'We were just catching up on some business.'

He shrugged and looked at her, but she knew he didn't believe what she was saying. 'You sure I can't talk you into a drink?'

Alice hesitated for a moment. She had known Sean in the early years of high school, and he was a good person, but there was no point in giving him any encouragement. She didn't want to go out with him. The only person she wanted to go out with was someone who could perhaps lead to a long-term relationship, and Sean Barlow certainly wasn't the sort of man she was interested in making that life with, no matter what a good guy he was.

'Thanks anyway, Sean, but I've got some work to do. I'll see you later.' With that, she turned and walked through the door and up the steps to the room she'd booked on the first floor.

Chapter 20

Callie Cartwright tried to organise a craft afternoon on Saturday. But with late notice, Sophie and Alice were the only committee members free to attend.

'Even though it's only the three of us, we're still going to have it,' Callie said when she called Alice to confirm on Friday night. 'Stay for dinner; we're having a bit of a barbeque.'

'Are you sure?'

'Yes, and bring an overnight bag and stay the night.'

Alice thought about it and considered the number of nights she spent home alone in her flat. 'Thank you, Callie. I'll accept; that sounds lovely. I've been talking to Tilly and Bec, and they tell me that I need to get out, so an afternoon and evening at *Kilcoy Station* would fit the bill. What can I bring?'

'Just bring yourself and your craft stuff. I've got a sewing room out on the verandah. Braden's first wife was really into crafts and used to spend a lot of time there, apparently. I've never used it because I'm not crafty.'

'You're happy to have it at your place with your hands full with the kids?'

'Of course. We can get a lot done, even with just the three of us.'

Alice drove into *Kilcoy Station* after lunch on Saturday afternoon. It was the first time she'd been to the Cartwright's station. Her eyes widened as she drove through the gate and looked at the almost manicured paddocks full of healthy-looking cattle. It was very different to the property she'd sold after her parents passed away.

As she drove down the long driveway, a red brick house was ahead, with a huge shed to the side and a few cars parked outside.

As she drove in, she spotted some kids playing football and realised one was Beau, her refugee. She hoped that Billy Burke wouldn't be there, too.

She left her overnight bag in the back of the car until she figured out what the night was going to be like and whether she would stay or not. She carried in her handbag a soft bag of craft fabric,   and the pavlova she'd whipped up last night. Even though Callie said not to bring anything, Alice knew dessert always went down well.

The boys ignored her until she walked to the gate at the front of the long, wide house. She didn't know the Cartwright boys, but it was definitely young Beau. Alice was pleased to see his hair was clean and shiny, and even though his clothes were old jeans and a T-shirt, he looked clean. He stood there watching her for a moment, then smiled and ran over.

'Hello,' he said.

'Hello, Beau, how are you?'

'I'm really good, thank you.'

'It's good to see you looking a bit happier,' Alice said.

You look really different,' he said. 'You look like a girl now.'

Alice laughed. 'What did I look like before?'

'You looked like someone who was in a job.'

'Funny that,' she said. 'I was doing my job that day.'

'What are you doing here? Have you come to work with the cattle like Billy?'

Her breath caught. The worst thing that could happen would be Billy Burke being out here, too.

'No, I've come to help Mrs Cartwright and Mrs…' She paused to think of Sophie's last name. 'Mrs Mason with some stuff for the ball.'

'Can kids come to this ball?' he asked. 'Rory and Nigel were telling me about it. They really hope that kids can come.'

'I'm not sure,' Alice said. 'But probably, seeing it's a

fundraiser. The more, the better.'

'What's a fundraiser?' he asked.

'When we ask people to pay to come and have a good time, and then the money goes to someone who needs it.'

'Like poor people?' His eyes were hopeful, and she wondered what sort of situation he and Billy actually lived in.

'No, more like group stuff. We're talking about the aged care facility, the new youth centre, and things like that.'

'A new youth centre, like the one you took me to down in Charleville? Where you fed me, and where I played on the computer for an hour before you drove me home? I meant to say thank you for rescuing me. I was pretty naughty to do that, and Billy made it clear that it won't be happening again. I'll be in bigger trouble if I do that again.'

'What happened?' she asked, curious, hoping he hadn't had a hiding or anything like that. It was unfair to ask him because she wasn't here in a work capacity, but he looked happy and clean, so hopefully, her talk with Billy had worked.

'No football watching on television for two weeks,' he said, his eyes downcast.

'And that's hard for you?'

'Oh yes,' he said. 'I'm not even allowed to know the results until Monday. He's so mean. He makes me stay in my room, and he watches it with the volume down so I can't hear it. He even took my phone off me so I couldn't watch it.'

'And what did you learn from that?' Alice said as they walked through the gate together.

'Well, I learned if you do the wrong thing, there are consequences, and the consequences usually take away something you really like. You have to spend that time thinking.'

'Sounds like it's been a good lesson for you then, Beau.'

'It has. I'm sorry I did it, but I'm not sorry I met you. You were very nice to me.'

'That's my job.'

'Yeah, it might be a job, but I think you're a nice person too. And looking like a girl makes you look friendlier. Do you play footy?'

'I used to play footy when I was at school.'

'Do you wanna come play with us?'

Alice chuckled. 'I'll take you up on that another time, but at the moment, the ladies are in the sewing room waiting for me. We've got some jobs to do. Good to see you, Beau, and good to see you looking so happy.'

With a wide, cheeky grin, he turned and ran back to join the Cartwright boys. Soon, there were shouts of 'faster, faster' coming from the paddock as she walked to the breezeway and knocked on the back door.

Callie came to the door with one of the twins on her hip.

'Hi, Callie.'

'Hi, Alice, I'm so glad you're here early. I'm sorry I didn't hear your car come in. I'm having a drama with the kids.'

'A drama?'

'Yeah, they ate something they shouldn't, and we've got the resultant nappy mess,' Callie said. 'Munro is all clean. Can you nurse him for me? Sophie is dealing with the other one while I'm cleaning up the mess.'

'Yep, I can hold him. But I'm not used to nursing babies.'

'You'll be fine. Head up the hall with him to the last door on the right. We'll meet you there shortly.'

Alice walked up the hallway with the unfamiliar heavy bundle in her arms. She couldn't remember the last time she'd held a child. In fact, she wondered if she ever had held a baby. Munro reached up and grabbed one of Alice's blonde curls, tugging at it. His fingers headed for his mouth.

'Oh no, you don't, little one,' she said. 'You don't want a mouthful of shampoo and conditioner.'

She freed the hair from the little boy's chubby fingers and smiled down at him.

'More, more,' the little boy said.

'More hair or more food?'

'More yum,' the little boy said, patting Alice on the face with those beautiful fat fingers.

'You're a sweetie, aren't you?' she said.

'Mum, mum, mum, mum.'

'No, I'm not your mum, as you well know.'

She reached the last door at the end of the wooden floor hallway, her eyes wide. The room was full of sunshine, with three sewing machines set up along a bench in the shade. Sunlight poured through windows that ran the whole length of the front wall. She stood there, looking out over the vista of paddocks stretching as far as she could see, and in the far distance, blue mountains rose on the horizon. It had been such a good season of rain; everything was lush and green, and it was a beautiful view to look at.

She wondered how much land Callie and Braden worked and how they managed. It was a long way out of town, but it reminded her of growing up in her parents' place. She swore she would never go back to the land, but now that she had time to think it over, she realised it was because those last few months with her dad not well and the property being rundown had tainted her view.

She'd loved growing up on the farm, the animals, and the wide open spaces. There was no comparison to the small flat where she lived, spending most of her nights alone watching television.

Emotion lodged in her throat as she looked down at the little boy. 'You're just gorgeous, aren't you? If only my life had turned out differently. If only I had met somebody and could have a child like you.'

But it looked like that wasn't going to happen. In the corner was a playpen she hadn't noticed before, with another baby girl sitting there playing with some blocks. Alice carried Munro over and carefully put him in with the little girl. 'I suppose it's okay for you just to sit in here together. You must be Sophie's. Are you Ruby Rose?'

The little girl looked up and smiled, greeting her with two front teeth. 'Well, you're a beautiful girl too.'

She walked back to the window as the two babies settled in and started playing with the blocks again. She was pensive as she stared out the window. She really had to do something. She loved her job and living in this area; she just needed a better personal life to complete it.

She stared out the window, thinking about how much money she had saved and how Bec had agreed that she could come out and run the youth centre here at Augathella. It was time to try and find a place of her own, but if the truth be known, she'd prefer something with a bit of land. She'd have to think carefully about what she was going to buy. Her job was secure now that there was government funding as well as additional seed funding from Chloe's group, so she could afford a mortgage. She just had to work out how much she could afford to spend. Maybe a little house that she could do up on a couple of acres, not too far from town, so she didn't have too far to drive to work.

She jumped as someone spoke behind her.

'Penny for your thoughts,' Sophie said.

'Yeah, I was just looking out at this beautiful view. I didn't realise how much I missed being on the land.'

'You grew up out at Allenvale, didn't you?'

'Yeah, when Mum and Dad passed away, and the farm was sold, there wasn't much left. I had to sell it to pay the mortgage because, at that stage, I couldn't afford it. It took me a while to save up to go to uni.'

'There's no doubt about you being a worker. And I hope you know how much you're appreciated too. We're all really excited that you're coming to town to run the Choice for Youth branch here. So are the kids.'

'The kids don't know me.'

'They know they'll love you. And I've heard you're pretty good. Apparently, Billy's boy has been singing your praises.'

'Young Beau?' Alice chuckled.

'Yep, you made a hit with him when you rescued him from Charleville.'

'He's a good kid. I want to make sure he gets cared for properly.'

'I'm sure Billy cares for him. It's a difficult situation, I believe.'

'I really can't talk about it. I suppose it's gossiping, but it's also my job. Let's say he looks great today, happy, clean, and not so scrawny.'

'You remember Kent when he was growing up?' Sophie picked up her daughter and cuddled her. 'Oh, that's right, you were a couple of years ahead of us.'

'Yep, and when you're in primary school, you don't take much notice of the younger kids. Why? What was it with Kent?'

'Kent was a string bean, would you believe it? Even when we started going out when he was sixteen, he was skinny as, and look at him now.'

Alice called the tall, strong man to mind. 'Well, you'd never know that. He's certainly a big man.'

'We can't judge poor little Beau by his size. He probably eats like a horse and burns it all up.'

Alice chuckled again. 'He wanted me to come and play football with him.'

'No football for you today; we've got some masks to make,' Sophie said.

At the last ball meeting, they decided to move away from the Australian animal theme for the adults and go with colourful masks. Sophie, Alice, and Callie had volunteered to do some sewing. They were going to sell the masks at a stall in town, and Alice had even suggested they do an online shop for those who wanted to order privately. They were making eye masks and full face masks, with a pattern from the internet and all the fabric bought. Today was the day to start putting some together.

Callie walked in the door, holding another baby. 'Alice, this is Miss Meggie, the mistress of disgusting nappies, but she's all clean now.' She dropped a kiss on her head and walked over to the playpen, putting the little girl in with the two other babies. 'Now, you three behave for a while.'

She might as well not have spoken because they were all engrossed in crawling around and playing with the toys.

'So, are we ready to work?' Alice asked.

'We are,' Callie replied.

Chapter 21

By the end of the afternoon, seven masks had been completed. Sophie had made four, Alice had made two, and Callie, between getting up and looking after the kids, the twins, and getting food for the four boys every time they came in saying they were hungry, had managed to complete one. The chatter and laughter had filled the room as they worked, and Alice felt absolutely content. It had been a long time since she spent time with friends like this, and she felt welcomed into their friendship.

The children had been well-behaved, and Alice had found herself helping Callie a couple of times, nursing the children, and actually giving Munro a bottle. She nursed him, sitting in the chair in the corner of the room in the sunshine, as he chugged down a bottle of milk in about two minutes flat. His wide eyes looked up at her. He burped when he finished the bottle, pulled it out of his mouth, and threw it on the floor. 'More.'

'No, young man, you've had one. That's plenty. I'll get you a rusk to chew on.'

'More bottle,' Munro said.

'He's gorgeous, isn't he?' Sophie said. 'He's a little character.'

'I think he's got the energy and the character of the three other boys combined,' Callie said. 'He watches them like a hawk, and you can see he's itching to get out there and play with them, whereas Meggie is the quiet one,' Callie said. 'She sits back and observes. It's going to be interesting watching them grow up.'

'I honestly don't know how you do it, Callie. You've got the three boys, you work, you've got the twins, and now you're having another one. You must have so much energy. You make me feel guilty. I'm exhausted when I get home from a day at the centre. I crash in front of the TV. From now on, I'll be making masks every night.'

'Do you like living by yourself, Alice?' Sophie asked.

Alice thought for a moment and looked up. 'No, I don't. Actually, I've been thinking a lot about it lately. Tilly Tingle is trying to talk me into going on one of those online things, you know, Tinder and those apps.'

'Why on earth would a lovely-looking girl like you need to do that?' Callie asked.

'Picking's pretty slim in the district,' she said.

'Do you ever go out to meet guys?' Sophie asked.

Alice shook her head. 'Not really.'

'So you think you're going to meet someone sitting in your flat all night watching TV? And you work with kids from twelve to eighteen all day.'

Alice nodded. 'I suppose.'

'Well, I think we need to create some social occasions for you. Tonight is the start,' Callie said.

'The start?' Alice chuckled.

'We're going to find you a fella,' Sophie said.

'A fella?' Alice burst out laughing.

'An Augathella fella,' Callie said with a giggle.

'I'm actually moving to Augathella,' Alice said. She was having fun with these girls.

'Really?' Callie said. 'That's great. You can come around a lot more.'

'And you can come out to our place too,' Sophie said.

'Oh, girls, thank you so much. You've made me feel so welcome.'

'We enjoy your company, Alice.'

'So, tonight, who's coming?' Sophie asked.

Callie said, 'Well, it's all of us, including Kent, of course, and Alan Humphreys.'

'Who's Alan Humphreys?' Alice asked. 'I haven't heard

of him.'

'He bought the property on the town side of Jon's, and he's working with the guys today,' Callie said.

'Is he young?' Alice asked.

Sophie and Callie looked at each other. 'Depends what you call young,' Callie said with a cheeky grin.

'Less than forty?' Alice ventured.

'He won't suit. I think he's on the wrong side of sixty. He owns a few properties around the region, and he's only here working to get this one off the ground. He's going to put a manager in. Nice house on it, though.'

'The man's more important than the house,' Alice said.

'And he brought a couple of his stockmen with him. I don't know them, but they'll be staying for the barbeque as well. A couple of young blokes, but I think they are pretty young, as in their early twenties from what I saw when they arrived with him before in his truck this morning,' Callie added.

'Billy's coming,' Sophie said.

'Billy Burke?' Alice said, her heart sinking.

'Billy's older than the other young guys, Sophie, but he's still not what you'd call old.' Callie said.

'True,' Alice agreed.

'That's right. You were involved the day Beau skipped school and ended up out here a couple of weeks ago,' Callie nodded. 'Billy's a nice guy.'

Alice didn't comment.

Callie glanced across at her. 'What do you think, Alice?'

'No cattleman for me. When I get married and have kids, I'll be choosing a professional man. No offence to you girls; I know you both married property owners, but I want someone who goes off to work in a suit and tie, carrying a briefcase.'

Callie and Sophie looked at each other with a frown.

'Why would you want someone stuffy like that?' Sophie asked.

'Security of a profession, I guess,' Alice said.

Sophie placed another finished mask on the table. 'Nothing to do with security, Alice. It's all about love.'

Callie nodded. 'That's right. It's not the *security* of a profession, sweetie. It's how hard a person works. Life on the land is not easy, as I'm sure you know.'

'Yeah, I guess what formed my opinions and my needs was watching my dad lose everything we had,' Alice said.

'How long ago was that?' Callie asked.

'Back in the drought.'

Sophie nodded. 'They were tough times, but we all got through it. We've restocked now, the rains are great, and the property is going well. You don't need a man to go off in a suit carrying a briefcase to provide security. You need a good man with good, solid working ideals. A man who loves you. Doesn't matter what he does.'

'Anyway, come on, girls, enough of that. I'm going to go and put these two down for a sleep,' Callie said. 'What about Ruby Rose?'

'Yeah, Ruby can go down too. I brought the porta-cot.'

'Then we'll start getting this barbeque sorted. You are going to stay the night, aren't you, Alice?' Callie asked.

Alice thought long and hard. Callie had been so welcoming; it would seem churlish to say no, even though the thought of socialising with Billy Burke didn't appeal.

'Of course, I am, as long as it's all right with you. I brought an overnight bag.'

'Great,' Callie said. 'Come on, girls, let's go party.'

'

Chapter 22

Callie showed Alice her room on the other side of a breezeway, which appeared to divide the large house into two separate wings.

Braden was setting up a barbeque outside of the breezeway space, and the boys were running around. Alice was interested to see that Beau was still here with the Cartwright boys, but there was no sign of Billy. Their meeting had ended on an "agree to disagree" note, and she was disappointed that he was going to be there tonight because she would find it very hard to relax when he turned up.

The problem was that not only did she disagree with his attitude and his brusqueness, but aside from that, she was very interested in him. She wondered what made him tick. At times when they'd been speaking over the table in the pub bistro about the various concerns that she had about Beau, she had found it hard to look away as her eyes roved over his face, noting the strength not only in his physical build but the steadfastness and strength with which he held and expressed his views.

She tried to explain to him carefully, without getting him offside or cross, that having responsibility for a twelve-year-old boy involved a lot more than keeping him clean and fed. Although they both agreed that it wasn't his fault that Billy refused to shower, she suggested that perhaps he should see a child psychologist to deal with his stubbornness.

Alice shrugged as Callie shut the door behind her. She put her bag on the bed, unzipped it, and pulled out the summer dress she had packed, followed by the soft pink cashmere cardigan she'd bought in Charleville a couple of weeks ago. Spring was just around the corner, and the weather was balmy. Maybe she should have worn jeans and a T-shirt tonight, but she wanted to dress well because you never know who you'll meet at a big gathering like the Cartwrights were obviously having tonight. Anything was better than going on that online dating thing in a town like this. It would only take one person to see her on there, and the likelihood of that was very high; she'd be a laughingstock.

'What if Gladys got a hold of it?' she thought, imagining what she'd say. Although her friend Beryl had been pulling Gladys into line lately, Beryl had actually stood up and criticised one of Gladys's statements at the meeting last week.

Gladys had flushed, sat down, and busied herself with her sewing, not daring to chip back at Beryl as she was wont to do.

Alice shook her dress and hung it on the hanger that Callie had taken out of the wardrobe for her. She quickly went into the bathroom, washed her face, brushed her hair, and put on a tiny bit of makeup. It was a casual barbeque, but she didn't want to look too dressed down.

A few minutes later, she strapped on her pink sandals, fluffed up her hair one more time with her fingers, and opened the door. She walked down the hall, hearing the sound of voices growing louder as she got closer to the breezeway. She was nervous stepping out there by herself. Eventually, she lifted her pace and stood at the door, looking out into the wide space. The sun was low in the sky, the lights were still not on, and the boys were still running around, playing with the dogs and making lots of noise. She smiled. She wanted Beau to just be one of the kids. If she was right, he looked a little bit cleaner today. His hair was shining in the late afternoon light, and although his shirt was untucked, he looked cleaner than he had the last two times she'd seen him.

She jumped as a voice came from behind her. 'Satisfied, Miss Templeton?'

She turned slowly, the fragrance of subtle aftershave

filling her senses. She looked up into Billy Burke's blue eyes but could not read his expression.

'Satisfied?' she asked, her smile tight. 'Satisfied with what?'

'You were watching Beau very intently,' he said.

'I was watching the boys play, smiling when I saw what a fun time they were having.' There was no way on God's earth she was going to say she'd been looking at Beau's hair and clothes. 'And it's the weekend, Mr Burke. I'm not working.'

'So, have you made your decision about a notification yet?'

She had, but she wasn't going to tell him that. 'As I said, Mr Burke, it's the weekend. If you want to have a meeting with me, arrange a time for next week.'

'Oh, for God's sake,' he said. 'Surely you can give me a simple yes or no. Put me out of my misery, woman.'

'Woman?' she said, her eyebrows arching. 'Isn't that a bit disrespectful?'

'Isn't keeping me hanging disrespectful? Two-way street, Miss Templeton.'

Billy drained the can of beer he was holding, crushed it, and turned away to put it in the bin nearby with the other cans.

Alice waited for him to return and finish the conversation, but her mouth dropped open when he walked outside without looking back at her.

'How rude!' she said under her breath.

She stood there for a moment, seriously considering putting her drink on the table, going up to get her bag, sneaking out the back door, and leaving. Billy Burke had unsettled her; she didn't want to spend another moment in his company, and if he spoke to her like that again, she *would* leave.

As she stood there, debating what to do, Braden approached her, accompanied by an older, short, stocky man.

'Alice, have you met Alan Humphreys yet?' he asked.

'Hello, Braden. No, I haven't.' She turned and smiled at the newcomer, who was obviously the new property owner next door to Fallon and Jon's house the girls had been talking about

'Hello, Alan.' She smiled and took the hand that was offered

'Nice to meet you, Alice. I hear you're moving back to the district.'

She raised her eyebrows. 'Things certainly get around quickly.'

Braden apologised, 'I'm sorry if I spoke out of turn, but Cal told me you're moving back to Augathella to run the local branch of Choice for Youth up here. I thought you might be looking for somewhere to live.

'No, that's fine, Braden, and yes, I am.'

'I told Braden I'm looking for someone to move into my farmhouse,' Alan said. 'Braden said you may be interested.'

'There's not a lot of accommodation in town with all the new families that have moved into the district recently,' Braden said.

'Yes, that's one of the factors that got Bec's application approved for a local branch of CFY for the town.' She turned to Alan, her eyes wide. 'A farmhouse? How far out of town? Do you have more than one house on the property?'

Alan chuckled. 'I do, but my home is down at Narrabri in New South Wales. I bought this one, and I will eventually put a manager in, but at the moment, we're not running much stock, so it will run itself until I find a suitable manager. It's next door to the Ingram's property, not too far out of town. Do you know where they live?'

'I do.' Alice nodded as excitement began to build. She'd been worried about finding somewhere to live and certainly didn't want to drive up from Charleville every day.

The older man scratched his head and frowned. 'I'm not happy about leaving the house empty. I've heard about squatters moving around the state. It's happened a bit in our district, and I was hoping that someone would move in and rent it from me. A very reasonable rent,' he added.

Alice considered his words and nodded slowly. 'Thank you, Mr Humphreys. I'll certainly give it some thought.'

'It'd be an informal arrangement,' he said. 'No lease or anything like that.'

'And how long do you think it would be before you need to move a manager in?'

He shrugged. 'I'm not sure yet, but do have a think about it, won't you?'

Alice nodded again. 'Yes, I will.'

'Thanks.' Alan walked away and headed to the drinks fridge, which had been opened quite frequently over the last ten minutes.

'I'm sorry, Alice. I hope I didn't put you in an awkward situation,' Braden apologised again.

'No, it's okay, Braden, not at all.' She wasn't going to mention Billy Burke, but she glanced over at him. She drew in a quick breath, and her face heated as she realised he was watching her.

Braden's eyes narrowed, and when he turned to see who had made her blush, Billy Burke was leaning against the side wall at the end of the breezeway, watching the boys play football.

'Are you okay?' he asked.

'Yes, I'm fine, Braden. Thanks for inviting me and for the introduction to Mr Humphreys.'

'Our pleasure. It'll be a good night. We've still got a few more coming—a few young ones closer to your age.' Braden glanced at her almost empty glass. 'Can I get you another drink?' Braden asked.

Alice made a quick decision. She avoided looking at Billy Burke and nodded at Braden. 'Yes, please. Another wine would be good. Thank you.'

***

Billy knew he'd had those two beers too quickly, but he

397

was trying to calm himself down. It didn't matter how much he drank as long as he stayed fairly sober because Braden had offered him a place for his swag behind the big shed. It made sense because Beau was staying the night with Rory Cartwright, and it meant that Billy didn't have to drive out again tomorrow to pick him up. They could both stay the night and go home mid-morning. He was sure Braden could find him some jobs to help out with around the property. It was the least he could do to thank the Cartwrights for the way they had welcomed Beau—and him—to their home.

His eyes narrowed as he watched Alan Humphreys talking to Alice. Alan took a step closer to her. Billy felt sick when she smiled at Alan so enthusiastically.

'What are you up to, you old bugger?' he muttered to himself. He turned his back and lifted his beer to take a sip, then remembered the can was empty. It was none of his business what Alan said to her. Alice Templeton was none of his business at all. The only thing he had to worry about was whether she was going to do that stupid notification or not.

He knew he could take care of Beau just fine, and he shouldn't have to prove himself until he'd done something really bad. At least he'd gotten Beau in the shower tonight and put a clean shirt on him. The promise of playing football all night and tomorrow morning had spurred Beau on, and he'd agreed with everything Billy suggested. Not only that, Beau had chatted non-stop all the way from their place out to *Kilcoy Station*, his happiness giving Billy a warm and fuzzy feeling in his chest.

He shook himself mentally. 'A warm and fuzzy feeling in my chest? For God's sake!' he thought.

Chapter 23

Alice thoroughly enjoyed the night. It didn't take long to settle in and feel comfortable with the group of people, although she studiously ignored Billy Burke. He was the one who made her feel uncomfortable. She laughed and chatted with Sophie and Callie, and they couldn't resist making more plans for the upcoming ball.

At the end of the night, it was a typical Australian barbeque. The women headed to the kitchen to put away the leftover food. Alice helped Fallon load the dishwasher while Callie went to settle the twins, who had woken up for a bottle.

To his credit, Fallon's husband, Jon, helped them carry some dishes, and Braden came in and offered to help wash up the trays.

Fallon shooed him out, saying, 'Go and chat to the men.'

Alice looked at Fallon curiously after Braden went outside.

Fallon smiled at her. 'The guys work hard out on the property, and I know even at smoko they don't get much of a chance to yarn.'

Jon chuckled. 'We're usually talking about cattle issues, fertilisers, and feed.'

'Sweetie, you go out with the guys too,' Fallon said to her husband. 'We can finish off here.'

'Did you enjoy yourself tonight, Alice?' Fallon ran hot water into the sink, and Alice picked up a tea towel

'I did,' she said. 'It was good to meet new people.'

Fallon glanced at Alice. 'Billy Burke seems like a nice guy.'

Alice shrugged. 'I didn't speak to him much.' She certainly wasn't going to mention her professional encounter with him.

'Yes, and young Beau has really bonded with our boys,' Callie said. 'It's good to see. I think he may have had a bit of a difficult background.'

Again, Alice didn't comment.

'Anyway, he's settled in, and they've organised a sleepover for the weekend after next. They're all football mad.'

'Good exercise, and good to see them out playing around in the fresh air,' Alice said. 'Too many kids these days come into the centre, and all they want to do is put their heads in front of a computer and play games.'

'We're pretty strict about that,' Callie said, 'although they are allowed to play a little—a few hours a week.'

The last of the benches were wiped down, and the dishwasher was whirring away in the background. Jon had gone back out to the fire to chat with the men, and Fallon yawned.

'I think I'll go out and get Jon moving,' she said. 'It'll be another hour or two, and then Ryan will wake up. I might feed him before we go, and then he'll sleep all the way home. With a bit of luck, he'll stay asleep when we get there.'

Callie nodded. 'Yes, the twins have gone down for the count now.'

'Enjoy your freedom, Alice,' Callie said. 'One day you'll be like this. Your whole life will revolve around sleep time, nappies, washing, and food.'

'Sounds wonderful to me,' Alice said. 'I can't wait for that time of my life.'

Fallon shook her head. 'Don't wish your life away, love.'

'Fallon, if you're heading off, I'll see you at the next meeting.' Sophie and Kent had left earlier as Ruby Rose was being a little bit fractious.

Callie walked over to Alice. 'Alice, would you like to sit and have a cup of coffee with me?'

Alice shook her head. 'No, Callie, you head off to bed,

and I'll head off. Thanks so much for offering me a bed for the night. I really appreciate it. I don't think I would've enjoyed driving back to town in the dark.'

'No, you were able to relax, have a wine or two, and then head off after breakfast in the morning. Make sure you stay, too, because, on Sunday mornings, Braden does a big cook-up—pancakes and everything for the boys. It's the highlight of their week. "Anything better than wheat?" Nigel always says.'

'Thank you, that sounds lovely, but I'll see how I go. We'll see what time I wake up.'

Fallon came over and hugged Alice. 'It's been good to spend some time with you, Alice. I'll see you soon.' She headed up the hallway to get her baby out of the back bedroom.

'Callie, you look exhausted,' Alice said. 'I'll make my way up to my room. I might even go out and grab some fresh air before I go to bed. The stars are magnificent out here. That's about the only thing I miss about being on the land.'

'Okay, Alice, thank you. You sleep well. If you get cold, there's a spare blanket in the wardrobe in that bedroom.'

'I'm fine, thank you.'

'And there should be soap and shampoo in the bathroom.'

Alice loved Callie; she was so kind and welcoming. 'I'm fine. You go and get some sleep, and I'll see you in the morning. If I wake up early, I'll help Braden in the kitchen.'

'Night, Alice. It's been lovely to have you here. I'll see you in the morning.'

Alice took one last look around the kitchen. After the two women had gone and everything was in place, she opened the door that led out to the breezeway and glanced across to the right. There were still three or four men around the fire. The older boys had gone to bed about ten-thirty when Braden had herded them inside.

She was surprised to see Billy Burke still there. Perhaps Beau was staying the night, and he was going to drive home anyway. She shrugged, but instead of going out into the wing of the house, she turned left and took a door she had noticed before, leading to the other side of the yard.

It was a beautiful night, slightly cool but with a promise of spring in the air, which made her think of the ball. They still had so much to do, and the spring ball was only about four weeks away.

After breakfast, she would head back to her hotel room. She had brought her sewing machine from Charleville.

Hopefully, the house out at Alan Humphreys' would be suitable. It would be much better than driving to and from Charleville until she found somewhere to live.

The night was clear, and a beautiful patchwork of brilliant stars covered the sky. In the east, the horizon brightened as the moon rose.

Alice walked over to the fence on the other side of the big shed, climbed up on the bottom rung, and rested her chin on her hands, looking up as the universe swelled around her. She felt insignificant under the vast sky.

The only sounds were the occasional lowing from the cattle in a nearby paddock and the soft rustling of something in the long grass over the fence.

Peace and serenity enveloped her, and she took a deep breath, enjoying the beautiful evening.

She stood there for about fifteen minutes, watching the sky, and then a slight breeze puffed in. She rubbed her arms, jumped down, and pulled her cardigan more tightly around her.

As she turned to go back to the house, she noticed the glow of a cigarette between her and the door to the breezeway, and she hesitated. Perhaps it was Braden. Maybe the other men had gone. She really didn't feel like talking to anyone. She was feeling calm and at ease, and, to be honest, her main fear was that it would be Billy Burke. She certainly didn't want to get into another conversation with him when she was feeling so mellow.

She strolled back toward the door at the back of the breezeway.

'Don't worry, Alice. It's only me.'

'I'm sorry, I didn't know there was anybody out here.'

It *was* Billy Burke.

As she approached, he dropped his cigarette to the ground, twisted his boot on it, then reached down, picked it up, and put it in his pocket.

'That's okay,' she said. 'I wasn't—'

'Couldn't sleep?' he asked.

'No, I just came out to have a few minutes and look at the sky. It's certainly a beautiful night.' She couldn't believe they were having a normal conversation.

'It certainly is,' he agreed.

'What about you? Are you staying the night?' she asked.

'I normally go home, but Beau was pretty keen to stay with the boys, and apparently, there's a promise of a big cook-up for breakfast from Braden. Beau twisted my arm.'

'It's good of you to take that into consideration,' she said.

'He's had a tough time, Alice. It's the least I can do.' He patted his pocket. 'To be honest, it does my head in. I don't usually smoke, but standing out here tonight, watching the interaction of the kids, I realise how much Beau has missed out on over the past few months.'

Alice nodded. 'He did seem to be having a good time. I watched them for a while, too.'

The usual tension between them seemed to have disappeared, and Alice relaxed.

'Do you think you'll stay in the locality long?' she asked.

'To be honest,' Billy replied, 'I don't know. My job is itinerant, and I follow the work, but seeing how Beau has settled since he hooked up with the Cartwright boys and how he's also settled a little more in school, I'm starting to think that I might have to settle here for a while.'

'Is there a lot of work?' she asked.

He nodded. 'I think there are enough properties around,

depending on what time of year it is. I should get enough. If not, I can always resort to truck driving or working in a rural store.'

'But what about Beau?'

'No, I'd only do short trips. I'd make sure I was doing a run that was only between local towns. I did some truck driving for a while.'

'You obviously like working on the land,' she said.

'I love being outside,' he said. 'I couldn't think of anything worse than being stuck in a building or an office all day.'

Alice shrugged. 'I suppose it all boils down to what you're doing and whether you're doing something that you love.'

'Do you enjoy your job?' he asked.

'I do. I've been doing it for a while.'

'And you've always lived around here?'

She shook her head. 'No, I've travelled overseas. I lived in Brisbane for a while.'

'Why Augathella?' he asked curiously.

'I guess it's where my heart is. I always say that where you spend your formative years always tugs you back. What about you? Where did you come from?

'Mount Isa.'

'And you've got no desire to go back to where you grew up?'

'I certainly haven't. There are not very good memories back there.'

He continued speaking but seemed embarrassed. 'Not that I'm whingeing, and don't worry, I don't want to lay my problems on you, but it was tough.'

He talked about Mary and Beau and moving to the Northern Territory.

Alice was surprised by how talkative Billy was; it was as though a different man was talking to her than the Billy Burke she'd known so far.

'Did you always work on the land?' she asked.

'I worked in the mines when I first left uni. Talk about not being in a building—I was underground a lot of the time.'

'Uni?' Alice felt awful for having made a stereotypical judgment.

'Yeah, I did Agriculture as soon as I left school. A few things happened, and I couldn't stay there anymore, so I went to the Northern Territory and started working with cattle. I found what I really love to do.'

'I think that's the life if you can find contentment in what you do every day,' Alice said.

'It is. I was going well until I suddenly had to take care of Beau. Life's been a bit tough since then.' He cleared his throat. 'I need to apologise. I think I've been pretty rude to you, Alice.'

'No, not at all, don't worry,' she said, meaning it. 'I probably wasn't as polite to you as I should've been either, Billy. I'm sorry.'

In the growing light from the rising moon, she saw a flash of a smile. He held out his hand. 'Start again?'

His hand was rough, warm, and strong, and Alice was taken aback as a tingle ran up her arm to her shoulder and a warm feeling fluttered in her stomach.

'A new start sounds good,' she said, clearing her throat and looking down. 'Anyway, I'd better get to bed. It's been nice chatting with you, Billy.'

'And you too, Alice.'

She turned and hurried for the door, knowing that he was watching her.

Chapter 24

'Uncle Billy, wake up, wake up!'

Billy sat up quickly in his swag. 'Beau, what's wrong? Is that you?'

'It is. Can I go riding on horses with Rory and Nigel before breakfast?'

'Riding on horses? You mean—hang on, stay there, don't go away.' He reached out for his jeans, slipped them on, climbed out of the swag, and clipped his belt. He stretched, then rubbed his hands through his hair.

Beau, Rory, and Nigel were standing at the other end of his swag.

'So, okay, tell me what's happening,' Billy said.

Rory stepped forward. 'Nigel and I just go for a ride down to the dam in the morning to give our horses a run, and the dogs come with us. We just wondered; we really hoped that Beau could come for a ride with us.'

'How long since you've ridden, Beau?'

'Uncle Billy! You always forget. I used to ride all the time at home, remember?'

Billy smothered a grin. When Beau used "Uncle," it was usually to get his own way.

Billy nodded. 'I do, mate, but it's been a while. You reckon you'll be okay?'

'It's okay, Mr Burke,' Nigel said. 'We've got a really quiet pony—'

Beau cut in with an expression of disgust. 'I don't need a quiet pony, Nigel!'

'Anyway, Dad's in the shed; he'll sort us out,' Rory said.

'Can I please go, Uncle Billy? Please, please, please,' Beau pleaded.

'I can't see a problem with that. Be careful, mate.' He

reached over and rubbed the top of Beau's head. For the first time, Beau didn't flinch or pull away.

Billy knew how much he owed the Cartwrights. He stood there, the morning chill cool on his bare chest and back.

As he watched the boys run back to the shed, Billy looked around. He had set his swag up between the shed and the fence line of the main paddock. He looked down at his swag and then across to the trough with the tap on the back wall and decided to wash there. Braden had offered him the use of the shed bathroom, but he only needed to use the toilet there; he'd wash outside.

When he left the shed, he walked over, ran the tap, cupped his hands under the cool water, rubbed it over his face, and ran his wet fingers through his hair.

As he turned to walk back across to his swag, ready to put his shirt on and pack it up, his eyes widened as Alice walked around the back of the shed.

She stopped suddenly, and he was pleased to see the colour rising on her face.

When they shook hands last night, he'd been quite taken aback by the zing her fingers had raised on his skin, and he could tell now from the colour on her face that she wasn't immune to him.

'I'm sorry,' she said. 'I didn't realise you were around here. I was going for a walk before breakfast.'

'Not worried at all. Would you like some company?'

'No, no.' She shook her head. 'It's okay, you go and do whatever you're doing, and I'll... I'll go the other way.'

Billy grinned as he watched her retreat.

Chapter 25

The following week raced by as Alice drove from Augathella to Charleville every second day. On Tuesday, she met Alan Humphreys at his house and was pleased to see that it was a nice place to live and that he was keen to let her move in. The rent they agreed on was very reasonable, but he did tell her that there was some stock down the back if she heard noises at night.

'It's okay, Alan,' she said. 'I spent a lot of my childhood and teenage years out on a property. I can look after myself.'

They shook on the deal before she headed back to Charleville that evening, and as soon as Alice got home, she packed up her gear, ready to bring it up in the car the following day. For the last couple of years, she had travelled a lot and lived in small apartments. The only thing that went everywhere with her was her sewing machine, so it didn't take too long to pack everything up. Alan was to leave late last night to head back to his property in New South Wales, so she decided to go by the property this morning and unpack her gear before she went into the youth centre.

The sky was heavy, and the weather had succumbed to a low-pressure system over the weekend, threatening to bring a lot of rain. She thought about the weather and the floods as she drove onto the property. That was one downside: If it flooded, she'd get cut off out here. She'd noticed a couple of creeks on the way out, but there were no cars or trucks to be seen.

She let herself in, looked around, and was very satisfied with where she would be living. From what Alan said last night, he was hoping to have a manager lined up, but they weren't going to start for another six weeks at least, so it looked like she'd have plenty of time to find somewhere permanent to live in town.

Alice had looked at her investment account last night and thought maybe she could soon afford to buy herself some land. A small holding, just to have some space. Maybe on the edge of town. She decided to see the local agent to check what was available and see if she could purchase something and have it settled by the time she had to move out of Alan Humphrey's house. It would be perfect.

On Thursday morning, Alice unlocked the door of the youth centre, pleased to see that the boxes she expected to be delivered yesterday had arrived. She busied herself setting up the new computers and keyboards along the bench that had been built along the back wall of the new centre. The electrician had been there a couple of days ago and had put in four double power points behind it. By the time lunchtime rolled around, Tilly and Jeremy arrived for their afternoon at the school in Augathella.

The door opened as they walked in, and Tilly grinned. 'Wow, you haven't been mucking around. Alice, it looks great!'

Jeremy walked straight over to the kitchen. 'Looks good in here too. You've done a lot of work this week, Alice. You've been busy.'

'Have you found somewhere to live yet?' Tilly asked.

'Yes, I've found a place about ten ks out of town, an old farmhouse on a property. I'm looking after it until the manager arrives.'

'Sounds like you're really settling in here in Augathella,' Jeremy said. 'Funny how we've all come home.'

'Yes, Augathella is starting to feel like home again to me already.'

'So, what's the plan for today?' Tilly asked. 'What time are we supposed to talk at the school?'

'I was hoping you and Jeremy could do it because I'd like to finish off here. We're opening up for after-school sessions this afternoon, and I've been to the butcher to order some sausages and the baker to get some bread rolls. If you guys want to finish at the school, you can come back here, and we can get a barbeque going at about 5 o'clock. That would be great.'

'Sounds good to me. So, we're at the school for the whole afternoon?' Jeremy clarified.

'Yes, they've got you talking to a few different groups, and the school counsellor is there. She's asked that you sit in on the talk she's giving to Year Ten.'

'Busy day,' Jeremy said.

'Do you want a coffee before you go?' Alice asked, heading over to put the kettle on.

'No, it's okay. We'll grab one at Janice's on the way,' Tilly said. 'Looks like you're busy. We'll head off to the school now and come back as soon as the day is over. See you then.'

Alice waved them off and went back to the last computer, loading in some login details for the kids.

The door opened, and she turned, wondering if they had forgotten something. But before anyone came in, the door closed again. She frowned and walked across to the door, opening it quietly. She stuck her head out just in time to see someone race around the back of the building.

Checking that she had her keys in her pocket, she locked the door behind her and headed quietly along the path that led to a grassed area around the back. Beau Burke was there, sitting on a stump next to the barbeque area. His hoodie was pulled over his face, and his shoulders were hunched.

'Hey, Beau, is that you?' she asked.

He turned to her, and his eyes were red. She could see the marks on his cheeks where tears had tracked down.

'Everything okay?'

He shook his head but didn't speak. Alice walked over and sat on the stump beside him. He lifted his arm and wiped the sleeve of his hoodie across his face.

'Can I stay here this afternoon?' he asked.

'Instead of going to school?' she asked.

'Yeah.'

'Is there a problem?'

'I just don't want to go.'

'What would your Uncle Billy say?' she asked.

'He said it was okay. He used to let me stay home when we were at Kununurra when the kids got to me.'

'Something happened at school?'

He lifted his head and looked at her, and it hit her in the chest how unhappy he looked.

'Will you tell me what's happened? I'm pretty sure I can organise for you to stay here today. I might just have to ring Billy and check it's alright.'

'You can't get him; his phone doesn't work right at the back of Jon's property. I tried to ring him to ask if I could go home.'

'I'm pleased to hear that you did that; it's good to get permission to do things.'

'Can I please stay here with you, Alice? Please?'

'Will you tell me what happened, mate?'

'There's a boy in our class, and he's been tormenting me about not having a mum. He's really cruel. Rory was gonna hit him, but I wouldn't let him.'

'But hitting isn't the answer, is it?'

'Probably not. Anyway, that's what I do. I don't like it. I just go—'

'Like the day you came down to Charleville when I met you.'

'Yeah, it was a good day to meet you. I'm happy we're friends now.'

'Okay, thank you for telling me what's wrong. There's only one thing—if you stay here with me today, I'll have to call the school and tell them where you are.'

'That's okay,' he mumbled.

Chapter 26

After the fabulous night she had at the Cartwrights last weekend and a good week with a lot achieved at the new branch of the youth centre, Alice's equilibrium was restored.

Friday night rolled around, and she asked Jeremy and Tilly what their plans were for the night.

'I'm going to have dinner at the bistro at the pub,' she said. 'If you'd like to join me.'

'Would love to, Alice,' Tilly said, 'but we've already made plans for tonight down in Charleville.'

'No problem at all,' Alice said. 'We'll do it another night.'

'For sure, take a rain check.'

Alice was still staying at the pub until she moved out to Alan Humphreys' property. She was taking the rest of her things out there on Sunday afternoon. She hadn't been able to settle all week, and she couldn't put her finger on what was causing her restlessness. Usually, after a day down at Charleville, when she got back to the flat, she would be happy to collapse in front of the television or with a book and a glass of wine after cooking her dinner, followed by an early night. But the past couple of weeks, she'd found it hard to settle. Last night, she'd looked around the hotel room and couldn't wait to get out to Alan's place. Maybe she'd have more to do out there for a night and a weekend, but it was Friday night, and she certainly wasn't going to stay alone in the hotel room.

Surely, there'd be somebody down in the bistro that she knew. She'd been disappointed when Jeremy and Tilly couldn't join her because they were such great company. She didn't feel comfortable asking Bec. Even though they worked closely, Bec was still the boss, and Alice was still a little bit shy. She knew her place in the employment scheme of things.

Today had been quiet at the centre. Everyone was pretty sure that the fundraising from the ball would be going towards the centre, and everyone Alice talked to had agreed it was the best cause. Mind you, she hadn't talked to Gladys, who was still telling all and sundry that they all needed televisions in their rooms at the aged care facility. Tilly had pulled Alice aside and told her to ignore it. She said if Nana wanted her own television, she could well afford to buy one. She said it was just that she wanted to have a say, but she knew her grandmother loved going out to the communal area to watch television with all the other people in the home.

'Just ignore her, Alice. Don't let her get under your skin.'

'Was I that obvious the other day?' Alice asked, pulling a face.

'You didn't say anything, you were very well-behaved. She's always been used to calling the shots. I was really surprised when Beryl stood up to her last week, too. But listen, I'm sorry we can't come tonight. You go out and have a good time.'

Alice had thought about it when she got home and decided she would. She ran a deep bath, grabbed a glass of wine, and sat back in the refurbished bathroom at the hotel. After getting out, drying off, and getting dressed, she realised that she hadn't booked a table. Well, surely she wouldn't need to book a table for one, but being Friday night, though, you never know. It was a bistro with a dining room, and it could be busy, as there seemed to be a lot of functions on these days. Well, if she had to, she could go and get a hamburger—so be it.

She stood at the wardrobe debating what to wear. She reached into the wardrobe and pulled out her dress. Now that the weather was warming up, that would be good with a cardigan tonight. It was a pretty dress with a sweetheart neckline and a swirly bottom, with a pattern of primary colours that sort of looked like flowers but were really just blobs.

She didn't bother much more. She pulled the clip out of her hair that she'd tied up in the bath and ran a brush through it. A smudge of lipstick and a dash of mascara, she slipped on her pink sandals and headed down the carpeted steps.

She frowned as she reached the bottom step that led into the hall that entered the bistro. It was very quiet. They should be open; they opened every night except Monday. She walked along quickly and pushed open the door. To her surprise, the bistro and the dining room were both empty.

She went over to the counter, where a waitress was polishing the cutlery. 'Is there a function on tonight?' she asked hesitantly.

'No, there's a party over at New Life. One of the old folks from the aged care facility is having his eightieth, and Chloe and Rosie offered to cater because they thought it would be more private for them than here at the pub on a Friday night.'

The waitress rolled her eyes. 'The night's gonna take forever to go. There's nobody booked in for dinner. Not one. Most of the town's going to the party. How come you're not?' she asked Alice with a face screwed up.

'Because I don't know many people in town. I'm staying upstairs in the pub until I move out on Sunday.'

The young girl tilted her head to the side. 'Oh, I know you—you're working at that youth centre thing.'

'Yep, that's me.'

'And you're gonna be living at Alan's. Are you Alice?'

'I am. I thought I might meet some of my friends here, but it looks like they might have gone to the birthday party as well.'

'Probably. Even my folks have gone,' the young girl said. 'It's gonna be massive. But don't worry, you won't be in the dining room by yourself. There's one bloke in there already. He put his order in, but Sean had to run down to the New Life Centre because he was helping Chloe with some dish or other.'

'Are there any specials on tonight?' Alice asked.

The young girl shook her head. 'No, just the normal menu.'

'I'll take one with me and look when I sit down. What's your name?' Alice asked.

'I'm Jules, and I'll be looking after you tonight. I'll be your waitress,' she said in a spiel that she obviously polished when the place was crowded.

'Thanks, Jules. I will.'

'Would you like a drink? I'll go to the bar and do one for you.'

'A glass of white wine would be very nice.'

The girl tilted her head to the other side this time. 'Riesling, Semillon, or Chardonnay?'

'Riesling would be fine, thank you.' Alice hid a grin at the eighteen-year-old waitress who knew all the white wines.

'Okay, sit down and here's your menu. I'll be back in a minute to take your order.'

Alice walked slowly to the bistro. Tonight wasn't panning out as she planned. She was sure that someone from the school or one of the properties would've been here tonight, but it looked like she was going to have an early meal and head back up to her room. She let out a sigh. More streaming television. She was never going to meet anyone this way.

She looked over at her favourite table by the window, where at least she could look out on the beer garden and the paddocks. The sun hadn't set yet, and the days were getting longer as spring approached.

She crossed the room, and an amused voice called out to her. 'Miss Templeton?'

Goosebumps ran up her arms. She knew that voice—it couldn't be. . .

She turned slightly towards the side wall, and sure enough, Billy Burke was sitting at the table near the door with an open newspaper in front of him.

A wide grin split his face, and the laughter lines she noticed around his eyes the other evening crinkled.

'Hello, Mr Burke,' she said.

'I thought we agreed to make it Billy and Alice,' he said.

'Well, you called me Miss Templeton,' she retorted.

He put both his hands up in peace. 'I forgot, sorry. But remember, we're friends now.'

A smile crept over Alice's face. 'We are.' She was suddenly pleased she'd put on her prettiest dress and lipstick and brushed her hair.

'Are you meeting someone?' he asked. 'I'm sorry, that's probably none of my business.'

'No,' she said. 'I decided I didn't want to spend the night holed up in my room, getting takeaway and watching television five nights in a row, so I decided to come down and have dinner.' She pulled a face. 'Although I was hoping I'd know somebody here tonight. I mean...' She realised what she said. 'I mean, I thought there might be some groups of friends here having dinner. Apparently, there's some big party on in town.' She looked around the room. 'Where's Beau? Is he okay?'

'Yes, he's fine and as happy as because he's having a sleepover at the Cartwrights.' Billy's eyes met hers, and she found it hard to look away. Without that five o'clock shadow, he looked younger. Her gaze moved down to the snug navy blue T-shirt he wore. Then she realised what she was doing and quickly looked up. A glimmer of a smile tipped his lips as he spoke.

'That's good.' The silence was awkward for a minute as Alice stood there. She looked around again. 'It is very quiet in here tonight.'

'I was thinking the same thing, but it looks like it's going to be a quiet night everywhere in town tonight due to that party. Young Jules there tells me that there are no other bookings. I was pleased to see another customer arrive. And even more so when I realised it was you.' Billy pushed his newspaper aside, and his chair scraped on the wooden floorboards as he stood up. 'May I have the pleasure of your company for dinner, Alice?' he asked.

A strange feeling shimmied down her arms and legs, and she couldn't help but answer quickly. If she had taken time to think about it, she would have said no, and that would have appeared rude. Why should she give up the idea of company and having dinner with an attractive man just because of one difficult encounter? As he said, they had made up and, if not exactly friends, at least they were no longer adversaries. They both had Beau's well-being at heart.

'I would be delighted to have dinner with you, Mr...' she hesitated and smiled. 'Billy.'

He came around and pulled out a chair for her. 'Take a seat, please, Alice. May I get you a drink?'

Chapter 27

Jules came back over but without Alice's glass of wine. 'I came back to check whether you really want wine,' she said, tapping her pencil against the order pad. 'I've picked you as a G&T girl.'

'Do you know what?' Alice said. 'That sounds tempting. I'll change my order. I'm upstairs tonight, so I don't have to worry about driving home. So, yes, please, a gin and tonic.'

'Jules, have you got the orders yet?'

Alice looked past the waitress to the ordering alcove beside the new commercial kitchen. She had to force her mouth to stay closed as her eyes settled on the new chef. Jules simply ignored him.

'Yeah, not bad, is he?' Jules commented with a glance in the chef's direction. 'He could be on one of those TV shows, I reckon.'

'Who is he?' Alice asked. 'I haven't seen him round town before.'

'He's the new chef. Bit of a honey, hey?'

Alice nodded and thought to herself, he certainly is a bit of a honey. A chef—hmmm, that's a profession. Hospitality hours weren't the best, but it's still a profession.

Jules gave a slow grin. 'I can see exactly what you're thinking, but don't get your hopes up, love. He's married.'

Alice tried to compose her features into a serious look. 'What did you think I was thinking?' She blushed as she caught Billy's eyes on her.

'I could read your face, love,' Jules said.

Billy grinned. 'Me too.'

'Okay, I admit it. I was thinking what a nice-looking young man he was and wondering if he was new to town. That was all.'

'Sadly, he's married. His wife's a ringer out at Jon Ingram's place.'

'Interesting combination. Chef and ringer.'

'Like me and my partner,' Jules said. 'I'm an Augathella girl. You're both new to town, aren't you? I didn't realise you were together.'

'We're not.' Alice and Billy said at the same time.'

'Oh, okay. But you are going to sit here?'

Alice hoped Billy didn't see the big wink that Jules sent her way. She nodded. 'Yes, we know each other.'

Billy was looking from one to the other, still smiling.

Jules settled in for a chat and ignored the dagger looks that the chef was sending her way. Alice half expected her to pull out a chair for a minute.

'I grew up here,' Alice said. 'On a property, but now I'm working here and in Charleville, too. I decided to take a room in the pub until I move to a property on Allenvale Road in a week or so. What about you?'

'I grew up here too.' Jules flicked a glance back to the kitchen but kept talking. 'I'm younger than you. My partner came to town. I met him here in the pub one night a few months back. He's a tax agent. He goes around all the small towns. Tax time keeps him busy.'

'Where's he based?' Alice asked.

'Longreach,' she said. 'I guess I'll move there when we get married.'

'You're engaged?' Alice looked at Jules' hand, but there was no ring on it.

'No, but we're going to be. I've made up my mind,' she said, 'to get out of this hick town.'

'It's come a long way since I lived here,' Alice said.

'Yeah, I gotta admit, there's a lot more to do here now, but you know, when you grow up somewhere, you want to go and try something else.'

'Yes, I did that.' Alice was aware of Billy's interest as she spoke.

'Anyway, I better take your order before Robbo loses his cool. He's got a bit of a temper,' Jules said.

Billy chuckled. 'We haven't looked at the menu yet.'

***

'Can I buy your drink?' Billy was still grinning as Jules walked away.

Alice chuckled. 'Thank you, but I'm fine. May I get you a drink when she brings mine out?' She noticed that his beer glass was almost empty.

'Are you going to drink wine with dinner?' he asked.

'Possibly,' she said. 'I don't have to drive tonight. What about you, with Beau?'

'Friday night out at the pub has become quite a habit,' he said. 'A regular date. Braden invites me to stay over, too, but I know he and Callie have got their hands full, and he works so hard. I'm sure they would appreciate having a night to themselves without a third wheel. Besides, I think Beau is a little bit more relaxed when I'm not around.'

'How are you both getting on?' she asked. 'And I'm asking as a friend, nothing official, okay? Don't take it the wrong way.'

'I know. You don't look like Alice Templeton at work tonight.'

'Should I take that as a compliment or not?' Her face reddened as she felt the heat rise into her cheeks. 'I'm not fishing for compliments. Please don't take it the wrong way.'

'You look very pretty tonight, Alice. I find it hard to connect you with the woman with the tight bun and the navy blue suit.'

'I got dressed up that day because I had a meeting down at the council in Charleville. You'll rarely see me in a business suit.' She chuckled. 'You were just lucky, Billy, that you met me that day. Maybe you wouldn't have taken me so seriously if I had a dress like this on.'

'Maybe not,' he said.

'You never know. Anyway, I wasn't digging. Tell me,

how's it going with you two?'

Before he could answer, Jules arrived at the table and placed a large glass in front of Alice.

'Oh, wow, that's a big one,' she said.

Jules winked again and nudged Alice with her elbow after she put the drink on the table. 'I made it a double to save you some money,' she said.

'You didn't have to do that.'

'Well, you don't have to drive home, do you?'

'Thank you, Jules. Put the drinks on my tab,' Billy said.

'So, are you ready to order yet?' Jules grinned and looked back at the kitchen, where the chef could be seen hovering at the small alcove.

'No, give us five minutes, thanks,' Billy said. 'We still haven't had a chance to have a look.' He winked at Alice as Jules walked away.

'Do you work with the chef's wife?'

'I do. Noreen is one of the new ringers.'

'It's an unusual combination.'

'These days, anything goes,' Billy said. 'I've seen lots of different setups as I worked around the properties in the NT and here. Head stockman at the big spread over there was married to the lawyer in town.'

'I guess I'm too judgmental,' she said.

'How long were you on your farm?'

'Mum and Dad passed away and left the farm to me. I sold it because I didn't want to spend my life there. And I couldn't afford the mortgage repayments.'

'Regretting it now a little bit? Do I pick up a hint of nostalgia in your tone?'

'Really, I think that's because I'd like to put some roots down. And I think Augathella will be the place where I do it.'

'When are you moving into Alan's place?' he asked.

'Not sure yet,' she said. 'I've decided to stay here at the pub for a few nights instead of going backwards and forwards to Charleville. Alan kindly let me put some of my things in the shed so I can stay at the pub until I move in.'

'So you can let your hair down tonight. Shame there's no music on. You didn't know about the birthday party either?'

'No,' she said. 'There are a lot of new people in town that I don't know. When I came back from travelling overseas, I lived in Brisbane before I moved to Charleville. I lost touch with a lot of my friends. Since I got involved with the organisation of the spring ball, I've met a lot of the girls again. Some of them I went to school with, but most of them are younger than me.'

'How old are you? I thought you'd not long left school.'

'Ha ha.' She gave him a coquettish look and then put her head to the side and a finger to her cheek. 'Is that a question you ask a lady?'

'Perhaps not. I was curious. You seem to have done a lot. I'm thirty-four, so you don't have to ask me my age,' Billy said.

'Okay, then. I'm almost thirty-three,' she said.

'Well, you certainly don't look it. Tonight, you look about twenty-one.'

'Flattery will get you everywhere, Mr Burke.' It had been a long time since she'd flirted, and Alice was enjoying herself. She took a big sip of her drink. Wow, Jules had been heavy-handed.

As if her thoughts summoned her to the table, Jules came back to the table. 'Have you had a look at the menu yet? Robbo's getting a bit antsy,' she said. 'If he feeds you now, he can have an early night.'

Alice shook her head. 'No, he can't. I'm out for dinner to have a nice meal. I'll probably have an entrée, a main and a dessert, so let the chef know we'll probably be here for quite a while.'

'Well, hurry up and choose so we can at least get started in the kitchen.' As Jules spoke, a group of six older people came through the door.

'Looks like you're going to have a busier night than you

were expecting,' Billy said.

'Bloody grey nomads,' Jules said. 'They always come late. Anyway, I don't mind. I'd rather be busy. Now, it might be wise to have a look at the menu and pick what you want. Otherwise, if these guys get their orders in before you, you might be waiting a while.'

'Are you in a hurry, Alice?' Billy's smile was cheeky.

She grinned back. 'No, are you?'

Alice picked up the menu that was in front of her. Nerves trembled in her arms and legs as Billy held her gaze across the table.

'Would you like to buy a couple of entrées and share them?' Billy asked.

'Sounds good to me. What do you like to eat?' she asked.

'Well, being a long way from the sea, I'm always reluctant to buy anything seafood because it's inevitably battered and deep-fried. Did you see the venison on the menu?'

Alice quickly scanned the laminated menu. 'It sounds good, doesn't it? Okay, I'll order that. And what are you going to order?'

'I think I'll have the deep-fried camembert.' The next five minutes were spent discussing the various options on the menu, and they were totally relaxed with each other by the time Jules came over to finally take their order and deliver another gin and tonic for Alice, as well as a beer for Billy.

'Would you like wine with your dinner?' Billy looked at the schooner of beer that was sitting in front of him on the table.

'What about you?' she asked. 'I certainly can't drink a bottle by myself.'

'Well, I guess if I drink this schooner, I'm not going to be able to drive home for quite a few hours, so why not? What wine would you like, Alice? Red or white?'

'Well, we're sharing the venison and I'm having the steak. I think I'd like to go with red. How about you, Billy?'

'Sounds good to me.'

Alice watched as Jules handed him the wine list, and he looked at it. 'Yes, I've had that one before. Let's go for the Hunter Valley Merlot. Not too heavy. Is that okay with you, Alice?'

'Sounds good.' As Jules took their order and walked away, Alice looked at him curiously. 'You know your wines.'

'One of my hobbies,' he said. 'I'm not just a beer-swilling stockman.' But his tone was light, and she knew he hadn't taken offence.

By the time Jules brought out one sticky date pudding and a pannacotta for Alice, she and Billy were firm friends. She had gone slowly on the wine, but the two strong gins and the two glasses of wine had certainly had an effect and relaxed her even more. She found herself looking at Billy, her gaze lingering each time and enjoying that pleasant feeling running through her bloodstream.

'Just the wine talking,' she chided herself silently.

By the time they finished dessert, there were a couple of glasses of wine left in the bottle, and Jules and Robbo, the chef, were packing up.

'Would you like to go out and sit in the garden and finish the wine?' Billy asked.

'That would be lovely,' Alice said.

Billy picked up the wine and the two glasses in one hand and waited for her to stand. He followed her out of the side door of the bistro into the beer garden with his hand on her elbow. Her skin burned where his fingers gently touched her.

Calm down, girl. It has been a long time since you've been with anyone

Was that the only reason she was having such a physical reaction to his touch?

Then again, if she was honest, she had the same physical reaction every time he looked at her and as he'd told her more about himself over dinner. He was a good-looking man, and she had now decided he was a very nice man. 'Nice is a terrible word,' she remembered her school teacher saying in primary school. Okay, he was a great guy, and she was really enjoying his company.

As they reached the table in the far corner with the best view of the moon over the pub's roof, he put the glasses and the bottle down, but she didn't move, and his body brushed against her. Billy hesitated as he stood back, and somehow, his other hand moved to her, and he pulled her close.

'Thank you for your company, Alice. I really enjoyed myself,' he said quietly as she stared up at him, his features outlined by the soft moonlight.

Alice couldn't help herself. She stood on her toes and brushed her lips against his. 'Thank you, Billy. I've enjoyed myself too.'

'I guess before we sit down and finish that bottle of wine, I better go and make sure I can get myself a room here; otherwise, I'll be camping in the back of the ute.'

Alice didn't hesitate. She'd let too many opportunities pass in her lifetime, opportunities that she regretted. If she had taken them up, who knew—she could be a married woman by now with a couple of kids.

'I have a king-size bed in my room,' she said slowly. 'I'm sure there's plenty of room for two.'

Billy's eyes widened, and a sexy smile lifted his lips.

'Are you sure about that?' he asked, pulling her closer before his lips met hers.

Chapter 28

On Monday morning, Alice was still smiling when she closed the door of her hotel room behind her and headed down to the youth centre.

Friday night had been unbelievable, and there had been no embarrassment when she had woken with Billy beside her the next morning. He'd stayed until mid-morning, and the kiss they'd shared at the door told her how much he'd enjoyed their dinner and the rest of the night.

'I really enjoyed myself too,' she said, her voice a little shy.

'Can I ask you out for a real date next time Beau goes out to stay at the Cartwrights?'

Alice hesitated for only a second, and a smile tilted her lips.

'That would be lovely,' she said, 'but remember I won't be here past Wednesday. I'll be staying at Alan Humphreys' house for a few weeks.'

'Even better,' he said. 'That's not terribly far from where I am at the Ingram's. I can pick you up, and we could come into town.'

What remained unspoken was that they would spend another night together, but Alice crossed her fingers behind her back as Billy kissed her goodbye again.

'I better go,' he said reluctantly. 'I have to pick Beau up.'

Tilly was already in the centre when Alice arrived, and the aroma of fragrant coffee greeted Alice. She pushed the door open, smoothed her hands down her shirt and jeans—she had dressed casually this morning—and stepped inside.

'Well, hello,' Tilly said. 'Don't you look lovely? Looks like you had a very relaxing weekend. You haven't moved out to your new place yet?' she asked.

'No, I went out and had a look, but Alan wants me to wait until new carpet is laid in the bedroom and living room. I said to him it didn't matter, but I'm happy to wait. I'm staying at the pub in town.'

'I thought you might've been at the party on Friday night.'

'No, I didn't know whose party it was,' she said, 'but I had dinner at the pub. It was lovely.' She couldn't help the blush that heated her cheeks.

'Did you see the new chef, Robbo? What a looker.' Tilly pretended to fan herself. 'If I weren't taken, I'd be spending my time there too.'

'He's married,' Alice said.

'Really? What a waste. Okay, take him off your list.'

'He wasn't on it,' Alice said with a secret smile as she crossed the room to the coffee machine. 'What's on the agenda today?' she asked.

The week flew by. The youth centre was busy, and a lot more of the local youth were getting involved as each day passed. The ball was coming up quickly; it was now only three weeks away. Alice had sewing to do each night. They had now made over three hundred masks. Surely that was enough, she thought as she added the last one to the pile at the end of a week of hard work and constant sewing. The committee held weekly meetings now, and progress was made each week. Callie was a great chairperson and managed to keep Gladys Tingle in line, much to Tilly's relief.

'Honestly, she's getting worse as she gets older. Maybe she's learning bad habits in that aged care facility,' Tilly said at morning tea at the youth centre on Wednesday morning. The meeting at Jenna's Tearoom yesterday afternoon had been relatively heated, but Callie had kept the peace.

'Your grandma's all right,' Alice said. 'She's just lonely. She likes to have her say.'

'She certainly does.' But Alice's kindness towards

Gladys Tingle disappeared very quickly at the end of that meeting.

Gladys picked her time very well. She waited till everybody was there and having coffee before Callie started the meeting.

'I hear you had dinner at the pub with Billy Burke on Friday night, Alice,' Gladys said, her lips pursed in disapproval.

Alice was wearing a red T-shirt, and she was sure that her face was the same colour as her T-shirt when everybody turned to look at her. Gladys was the only one looking at her disapprovingly; several other faces had delighted smiles.

It's none of your business, Gladys, Alice thought as she kept a bright smile on her face.

Tilly caught her eye and nodded. 'Aha,' she said.

Gladys picked up on it quickly. 'Aha what, Tilly?'

'Nothing, I was just clearing my throat.'

'And that's not all I heard,' Gladys said. 'The next morning—'

Alice put down her coffee cup with a loud thud on the table. She turned to Callie. 'Perhaps we could get the meeting started now, Callie. We have a lot to get through, Gladys,' she said, her voice tight.

Tilly leaned and whispered in her grandmother's ear, and she obviously said something that made Gladys shut up, much to Alice's great relief.

If Gladys Tingle knew that Billy Burke had been seen leaving her room on Saturday morning—and she was sure he had been very cautious in getting out to his car—then she had probably told the whole town by now.

Anyway, no one could confirm he had been in her room; there were plenty of vacant rooms that night, so who was to say they shared a room? Not that it was any of their business. She'd had a fantastic night, and if anyone wanted to talk about it, she'd be pretty upfront and tell them it *was* none of their business.

After Gladys's interruption, Tuesday afternoon's meeting flew by, and by the time the meeting closed at five p.m. things were sorted.

'The masks have all gone. We need to get another fifty or so made in the next week. Thanks to everyone who volunteered,' Callie said. 'And the ticket sales are going brilliantly. We're up over three hundred now.'

As it was a weekday afternoon, everyone packed up and left quickly, and Alice and Callie were the only ones left. Alice helped Callie carry the empty coffee cups over to the kitchen for Gemma, and Callie smiled.

'I'm pleased to hear that you and Billy had dinner together the other night. It'll be good for him to get to know somebody.' Callie smiled. 'Oh, and just so you know, in case you want to do it again, Beau's staying at our place on Friday night.' Alice put her head down and carried the next cups to the kitchen.

***

'Billy, watch out!' Braden called. Billy pulled up his horse just in time before it stumbled at the end of the creek bed.

He shook himself. 'Sorry, mate, my mind was elsewhere.'

'Beau giving you grief again?' Braden said.

'No,' Billy shook his head. 'He's been great. He's even started calling me Uncle Billy all the time now, not only when he wants something.'

'Everything okay?'

Billy's grin was broad. 'Everything is pretty good.' He had found himself daydreaming over the past few days, and a couple of times, he picked up his phone to call Alice. They had exchanged numbers on Saturday morning because he was going to ring her up and pick a night for them to go out.

When he picked up Beau on Saturday afternoon, Billy was as pumped as Beau was after a whole day of football.

Callie had put her hand on Billy's arm before they headed

to the car and said, 'How about another sleepover next Friday night? It's good for my boys to have company other than each other,' she said.

Normally, Billy would have hesitated, but the thought of another night out with Alice won out.

'That would be great, Callie. Thank you so much.'

'And the same as last week,' she said. 'You're quite welcome to stay the night. If you don't feel comfortable staying in the house, bring your swag.'

Billy grinned as he compared sleeping in his swag at the back of Braden and Callie's shed to sharing a room with Alice Templeton.

'It's good for Billy and me to have some time apart. If that suits you, we'll make Friday night a date.'

'I'll let the boys know tomorrow.'

'Thanks, Callie. I really appreciate it,' Billy said. 'I'll tell Beau.'

He held off ringing Alice until Wednesday morning. She answered quickly, and he wondered if it was because she'd recognised his number.

'Hey, Billy, how are you?' she said.

'I'm great, thank you. How are you?'

'I'm great too,' she said.

'That's good.'

He wondered whether he was rushing too much.

'Did you have a night in mind for us to have the next date?' she asked

His voice held steady. 'Yes, Beau's staying out at the Cartwright's again on Friday night. I was wondering if I could pick you up and bring you into town for a meal.'

She was quiet for a moment. 'Well, look, instead of driving into town and making a bit of a spectacle of ourselves again, how about I cook dinner at my new place? Apparently, Gladys Tingle saw us, or someone told her that we were there. I'll have to have a word with Jules. Plus, it's not so far for you to drive home.'

He nodded, 'Okay, we'll see what the night brings. I'd love to have dinner there, but one more question.'

'Yes?' she asked, her voice sounding worried.

'Can you cook, or do I need to bring a barbeque?'

'I'll have you know that I'm a very good cook,' she said

'They say the way to a man's heart is through his stomach.'

Why did he say that? He was turning into some sort of romancing pansy.

Alice Templeton had been in his thoughts since he walked out of her hotel room on Saturday morning, and no matter how he tried, he couldn't get her out of his head.

Chapter 29

Beau's sleepover at the Cartwrights' became a regular Friday night event, as did Billy's sleepover at Alice's place every Friday night. Alice was walking on air most of the time, experiencing feelings she'd never felt before. She'd had boyfriends before, and she'd gotten over them when they'd moved on, even Rafe, who had held her heart until she'd realised it was a one-sided affair, but the time she was spending with Billy was fantastic. And it wasn't only the physical side of their relationship—it was the kind and gentle man that he was that made her smile and long to spend more time with him.

Billy had opened up about his past, and she learned how he left Mount Isa as a young boy and went to work on the land before he went to university. He'd tried a few other things, he told her, but he hadn't gone into detail because many of their conversations never finished. They ended up in the bedroom, and there wasn't a lot of talking.

The fourth Friday night they spent together was in mid-September, only a week before the Masquerade Ball.

Billy wanted to know what she was going to do when she had to move from the farm. It wouldn't be long before she had to move out because Alan Humphreys had called to say the new manager was arriving soon. She had to decide whether she was going to buy a place or rent again.

But Alice knew she had bigger decisions to make.

As much as she loved spending time with Billy, he wasn't the man she could spend the rest of her life with. She wouldn't marry anyone connected with the land; she'd seen what it had done to Dad. She loved the time she spent with Billy, but there had been no talk of a future, so she didn't have to worry about it.

She shook herself out of her thoughts as she parked at the New Life store, where the ball was being held.

The meeting room at the side of the store was crammed with people. The committee had grown over the past weeks as more volunteers had joined up to help on the night. Callie stood with her hands resting on her pregnant tummy, and Alice hoped that she wouldn't go to the hospital before the ball. Callie had been the glue that held this whole committee together as president, and with her agenda, she had addressed absolutely everything they could think of.

'You're not going to have that baby before the ball, are you?' Alice asked.

Callie chuckled. 'No, I'm just huge. I've still got two months to go yet.'

'You're not having twins again, are you, Callie?' Gladys Tingle asked.

'Thank goodness, no. It's only one baby,' Callie said.

'Must be a boy,' Gladys said.

'Must be,' Callie said with a patient smile.

Alice kept glancing at the time on her phone as the meeting seemed to go on forever. Time dragged on as they discussed all the final details, such as how much milk to buy and what time Chloe and Rosie would be opening up the department store for them to clear the bottom floor to extend the function centre.

Many women had volunteered their husbands and sons to help move the stock and put the chairs in, so there was a sitting room outside of the dance area on the night of the ball.

Finally, just before six, Callie called the meeting to a halt. 'Well, ladies, can I just say what a tremendous job you've all done?'

Gladys Tingle stood up and shook her head. Callie turned to face her, and Alice stared, her mouth open, wondering what Gladys was up to now.

'All of *us*,' the elderly lady said. 'Now, I'd like to say a few words, Callie. I'd like to formally move that we thank

Callie for the wonderful job she's done as president and how she's kept us all on the straight and narrow.' Gladys chuckled. 'Beryl told me how difficult I can be sometimes, and Tilly keeps me in line, too. But Callie, you've done a fine job, and the success of this ball rests on your shoulders.'

Callie smiled and shook her head. 'Thank you, Gladys. It was a group effort, but I've really enjoyed being president. But,' she patted her tummy, 'it will be nice to step down and have a bit of a rest. School holidays start the day after the ball, and I intend on putting my feet up for two weeks.'

When the meeting was over, Alice waited beside her car for Bec to come out to the car park. The car park was almost empty as everyone had left to go home before dark. Spring was almost here, and the air was fragrant with the smell of the roses growing on a trellis at the back of the car park. Not only had Chloe's group provided a store for the community, but they had beautified much of the town with new gardens.

She waved as Bec walked across towards her car. 'Bec, can I have a quick word?'

'Hi, Alice. Hard to believe that was our second last meeting.'

'I'm sure we'll have a follow-up after the ball. I've got used to our afternoon meetings in town.'

'And how lovely was our Gladys this afternoon?' Bec grinned. 'You haven't had any more run-ins with her?'

'Don't talk about it. I'm sure she has spies all over town.' Alice chuckled.

'I was really pleased to hear you've been going out a bit. You've been working too hard.'

'Speaking of that,' Alice said, 'I was hoping I could take a couple of hours off tomorrow afternoon. I need to put together some new furniture that's being delivered. I didn't know it was going to be one of those "follow the instructions to put together" cupboards.' she said. 'Jeremy and Tilly are both happy to stay till five o'clock for the after-school crowd at the centre.'

'Yeah, look, take all afternoon if you want,' she said. 'That's not a problem at all. You've got so many hours up your sleeves, even since the camp.'

'No, I'm not worried about that,' Alice said, 'but a couple of hours would be great.'

'Do you need a hand out there? Can I send Matt over to help you?'

'It's all good. Billy and Beau are coming over to help me with it.'

Bec looked at her with a smile. 'Are you going to the ball with Billy Burke?'

Alice stared at Bec. 'I . . . I don't know. Why?'

'I thought you were a couple these days. Small town, remember, and we do have Gladys, who keeps everyone up to date with what's happening in town.'

Alice folded her arms. 'I don't even live in town anymore!'

Bec chuckled. 'Gladys doesn't miss a trick. So is she right?'

'We've spent a bit of time together.' Alice's face heated. 'I hope that's okay, having time with someone socially,' she said. 'I did start off with Billy in an official capacity.'

'You bring too much of your old job to this one, Alice,' Bec said. 'Remember, they're not clients; they're just kids who come to the centre. How's young Beau going, anyway?'

Alice was pleased to get off the subject of her relationship with Billy. 'By all accounts, he's going really well. Billy told me the other night that he was getting some extra tutoring because he was getting picked on a bit at school. I had him at the centre one day, and I had to ring the school and tell them that was okay. They actually sent over one of the teacher's aides to work with him offsite.'

'They run a good outfit there at the primary school. They wouldn't let anyone fall behind. Anyway, happy furniture making, and I'll see you at our final meeting on Friday afternoon.'

'Thanks, Bec. I really appreciate it.'

Chapter 30

Beau chatted non-stop to Billy from the minute he picked him up at the bus stop at the Ingram's front gate, and he climbed into the ute.

'There's a sandwich and a can of lemonade in the cooler between the seats,' Billy said as Beau clicked his seatbelt on. 'Grab some of that if you're hungry.'

'Why are we going back into town? I could've stayed in there.'

'No, we're going to Alice's place to help her put some furniture together.'

'Oh, cool! I wonder if she's got a computer at her house or maybe a game console.'

'Did you hear what I said, Beau? We're going to help her, not socialise or play games. She needs two men to help her put a cupboard together. You might learn some new skills that don't involve looking at a screen.'

Beau's chest puffed out. 'I can help do that. I'm a quick learner. Coops told me today I'm nearly caught up.'

'That's great. Plus, you're growing like a weed. Some of that food you're eating is finally starting to settle on your bones. You look really good, mate.'

'You know what it is, Uncle Billy?' Beau leaned forward and put his hands on the dashboard as they turned onto the road that led the five kilometres to Alice's place. 'I think it's because I've got friends.'

'And you reckon that might put weight on your bones?'

'No, I think it's because I'm happy. I don't spend all my time worrying.'

Billy lifted his hand off Beau's hair. 'It's good to hear that, mate. Not good to be worrying.'

'I know. I miss Mum, and I'll never forget her. I really wish she was still here, but I guess moving down here has been really good. I've made friends. I've settled in at school really well, and I don't mind having you look after me now,' he said.

Billy's throat closed with emotion. 'Good to hear, mate. I have you for company, too.'

'Is Alice gonna be your girlfriend? Are you going to marry her one day? She'd make a great stepmum, just like Rory's mum. Did you know she wasn't his real mum?' was the next question, and the lump disappeared from Billy's throat as he almost choked, coughing.

'My girlfriend? Where on earth would you get that idea from?'

'Rory told me that he heard his mum and dad talking about you being her boyfriend and her being your girlfriend. Do you like her?'

'Of course, I like her. She's a nice person.'

'Why can't she be your girlfriend?'

'Well, I guess if we both wanted that, maybe she could, but it's early days yet, mate. I don't know her that well.'

'Mum used to say it didn't matter; you just knew the one.'

'The one? Who was she talking about?' Billy asked curiously.

'I always hoped it was my dad, but I guess I'll never find out with Mum gone.'

'Probably not, mate, but listen, if you ever do want me to chase it up, I can do it for you.'

'No. Mum made me promise that I'd forget about it because she said if *she* didn't know, how the heck was I ever going to? How can you not know who gives you your baby?' His eyes were wide.

Billy swallowed again and searched for the right words. 'I guess there are all sorts of things to do with that, mate, but we might talk about this when you get a bit older. You'll understand it better.'

Beau's face was a picture. 'I know what causes it; I've lived on farms all my life.'

Billy choked again. 'Yeah, but this isn't the time to be having this conversation. Look, we're at Alice's house now, and she's just pulled up in the driveway.'

Warmth suffused his chest as Alice stepped out of the car, her jeans snug and tight on her long legs. Her hair was loose on her shoulders, and his fingers itched to run through the soft, silky strands.

He had it bad.

Chapter 31

Alice parked near the shed at the farm, and it was only a few minutes before Billy and Beau pulled up in his ute. She had been sitting in her car, thinking about what Callie had said, but she couldn't quite come to terms with it. She knew what she didn't want, and before this situation with Billy got out of hand, she was going to have to make it quite clear to him.

She knew her voice was stilted as they approached her, and Billy's smile was wide. It still sent that usual mushy, warm, trembling feeling through all her limbs, but she refused to meet his gaze.

'Beau, if I give you my key, let yourself in the back door. I made some cakes last night, so there are some little cakes for your afternoon tea, and there's some chocolate milk on the fridge door. So, go and help yourself.'

Beau took the key from her. 'Thanks, Alice. You're a whiz. Do you have a com—'

'Beau.' Billy's voice held a warning.

Beau disappeared around the back of the house like a shot, and Billy reached over to put his arm around her, but Alice took a step back before he could kiss her.

'Everything okay?' Billy asked, his brow in a frown.

'Yes, yes, yes. I just wanted to have a bit of a talk with you, Billy. I'm a bit worried that I was leading you on too much.'

'Leading me on? What do you mean?'

'I don't want you to think that I'm after anything permanent or anything here.'

Alice looked down, and if she could have seen the look on Billy's face, maybe she would have reconsidered. By the time she looked up, Billy's mouth was set.

'Alice, I don't expect anything of you. I've just enjoyed your company.'

Enjoyed? So it was over already? That was easy, she thought as pain sliced through her chest. He hadn't expected anything of her. Did that mean that with one simple line like that, it was over?

'Anyway,' he said, 'We can't stay long as I have to help Jon with something this afternoon, so we only just came here to help you get that cupboard together.'

Oh. She had cooked dinner for them, but she wasn't going to say that the aroma drifting from the slow cooker in the kitchen had been intended for them, too.

She forced a smile to her face. 'It's in the garage.' She took off across the yard, and Billy followed her.

Maybe it was for the best.

Beau and Billy put the cupboard together and carried it into the living room for her, which only took fifteen minutes. She probably should have left it in the shed because she was moving soon, but she wasn't going to get into a personal conversation with Billy this afternoon.

'Is there anything else you need a hand with?' he asked briskly.

'No, that's all, thank you.'

'Dinner smells good,' Beau said, obviously not noticing the tense atmosphere. 'Are we staying?'

'No, we're not,' Billy said tersely. 'Jump in the ute. I've got to go and help Jon.'

'I thought you said we'd stay here for tea?'

'No, I never said that, mate.'

'You didn't?'

'You can stay for dinner if you like,' Alice said quietly.

Billy replied, 'No need for that. See you around.'

Alice's heart broke as Billy looked at her—really looked at her—and she wondered if she had made a mistake.

'Are you going to the ball on Saturday night?' she asked

hesitantly.

Before Billy could answer, Beau chimed in, 'We sure are! We've got our tickets, and I think Billy was even gonna ask you to come with us. Weren't you, Uncle Billy?'

Billy held Alice's gaze. 'I was, but I guess you would've said no.'

'No,' she shook her head. 'I wouldn't say no. That would be really nice, thank you.' She put her hand on Billy's arm. 'I would like to go with you.'

'I'm not sure if we'll be in town that night, Alice. I'll talk to you later. Come on, Beau.'

Her heart ached as they climbed into the ute and disappeared quickly in a puff of red dust.

***

Billy put his hand to his forehead before he crossed to the sink and rolled up his shirtsleeves.

Alice's words had broken him. He took out his frustration on the pots and scrubbed the bottom of the burnt fry pan until he could see his reflection in it.

Beau walked in and picked up the tea towel. 'Not the best dinner you've cooked, Uncle Billy. If we'd had tea at Alice's, you wouldn't have a burnt pan to scrub.'

'Least of my worries, mate.'

'Why did you tell her you had to help Jon? He wasn't even home. You tell me not to lie.'

'Sometimes it's necessary, Beau.'

Beau shrugged and threw the tea towel onto the bench. 'Must be good to be grown up and do what you want. I'm going to do my homework. You're gonna be hours scrubbing that pan. I can still taste that burnt steak.'

Billy dropped his head into his hands.

Why was he such a coward? What the heck had he been thinking, taking Alice to bed and then thinking he could keep it casual?

She'd made it quite clear that was all she wanted. Where was he going to find the courage to let her go? He couldn't afford to trust what his heart was telling him.

Go and see her. Tell her you love her.

No, it would be easier to move on. He and Beau could move and start afresh somewhere else.

***

Alice put the contents of the slow cooker into containers and put them in the freezer.

Her mouth was dry, and her stomach was churning; she couldn't eat a thing. She knew she'd hurt Billy, and Beau was going to be collateral damage.

Confusion. Panic. Dread.

All the feelings running through her fought for precedence as she closed the freezer door.

More fool her, to blurt out to Billy that there was no future for them. Hell, he hadn't even offered one, and she'd come roaring in making assumptions. All because she was scared.

Now, Alice forced herself to step back and think about what she really wanted. Was it here on the farm that brought her unhappy memories back? Nights when Dad had looked exhausted as he stared out the window waiting for rain, and Mum had tried to tell him everything would be okay. Alice let the memories roll in; she had blocked so many unhappy memories. Tears ran down her face as she grieved for her parents.

But it hadn't been all right, and they had lost everything except the land and the house, which had been pretty much worthless back then.

Alice thought of the nights Billy had spent in her bed and the fun they'd had spending Sunday afternoons with Beau. The feeling that filled her when he'd held her in his arms.

She didn't want to be here without Billy. And Billy belonged on the land. Where did she want to be? Maybe she should move back to the city?

Her thoughts churned as she went to the bathroom and ran a deep bath.

Alice soaked in the hot water, letting it soothe her feelings. She'd fallen for Billy Burke, but there was no future there—not the future she wanted. He was an itinerant stockman with no home and an adopted child.

More fool her to get involved in the first place. Now Alice forced herself to step back and think about what she really wanted.

Could she move away? Or could she live here?

She sighed and closed her eyes.

Chapter 32

Tilly and Sophie had volunteered to help Jenna pack up the coffee cups and plates. Alice waited when Sophie called Callie over.

'Cal, a quick word before you go.'

Alice stood looking out over the paddocks as Sophie's excited voice reached her. The sky was a brilliant soft blue with shards of gold streaming from the low clouds to the west. The flat plains of the western region stretched as far as she could see to the north, broken only by the narrow ribbon of highway. The highway that beckoned to her. Maybe she'd be happier if she left. No matter how much she'd thought over the past few days, all she could think of was leaving Billy—and Beau—behind.

Callie's smile was wide when she approached the door, and they walked down to the car park together.

'You look happy,' Alice commented.

'Sophie's had some news from Jacinta, Kent's sister. Do you remember her?'

'I do. Didn't she work at the primary school for a while?'

'She did. But she moved to Brisbane when she met Ryan again. Maybe the strip show came to town before you moved back to the district?'

'Strip show?' Alice's eyes were wide. 'I don't think I recall a strip show in town?'

'A long story, but a good one with a happy ending. I'll tell you about it one day over a coffee. Ryan was the strip show manager. Anyway, he and Jacinta married a few years back, and she and Ryan have a little girl now. They don't get back here much because Ryan's second in charge of an international medical research establishment in Brisbane. The company has promoted him, and they're moving to Germany for a while.'

'That's a long way from Augathella,' Alice said slowly. 'Maybe I need to expand my horizons.'

Callie looked at her thoughtfully. 'Are you okay?'

'I'm fine. What about you? Are you going back to school after the holidays, Callie?'

'No.' Callie shook her head. 'I have my hands full with the twins. It's getting a bit hard to manoeuvre them now with this one.' She touched her belly.

'You are amazing, Callie,' Alice said.

'I'm not amazing, Alice. I'm just a woman who fell in love, found a family, and then made it bigger. My life is wonderful; I'm just so happy.'

Callie must have noticed the look on Alice's face because she put a hand on her wrist. 'Are you really okay, Alice? I know that you and Billy have been seeing each other.'

'Yes, we have, Callie, but there's no future in it. He's not what I want as a partner.'

'He's not?' Callie asked. 'Are you sure? I've seen the way you look at each other. You've both seemed so happy.'

'He's a really great guy, but he's not the one for me,' Alice said, 'but like I told you at that sewing bee we had at your place that afternoon, I don't want to marry or be with anyone on the land. I saw what it did to my dad. I want a professional man, someone who comes home every night with a briefcase and someone who works until five and has the weekends off.'

'You don't think you're dreaming too much, Alice?' Callie said.

'No, no, I know what I want.'

Callie kept her hand on Alice's arm. 'And you know what I thought I wanted, Alice? I had a great job at a TV station in Brisbane. I had a beautiful home on the river, and I had all the money a girl could need. And you know what? The last thing I ever thought I'd need would be a widower with three young boys way out west, where I would never have dreamed of living. But love has different plans for us. When you meet the person you're destined to spend the rest of your life with, considerations like profession, money, and where you live all become very minor. If you truly love somebody, you will go where they want to go, and they will go where you want to go. Together, you work it out. And if it's the thought of Billy having young Beau that's holding you back, let me tell you that getting readymade sons when I fell in love with Braden was the icing on the cake.'

Alice looked down, her heart heavy.

'Callie, I've told myself all those things over and over again, but I still know what I don't want. It's deep in me; I can't let it go.'

'Perhaps, Alice, if things develop the way that I can see they are, perhaps you need to think about what you *do* want, not what you don't want.'

Chapter 33

Friday night would have been their sixth weekend together, but Alice told Billy she was busy. As well as their regular Friday night date, there had been Sunday afternoons when she, Billy, and Beau went for a picnic. They'd also been to a couple of weekend barbeques at the Cartwrights when she'd seen Callie looking at them thoughtfully. But when Tilly asked one afternoon if she and Billy were an item, Alice shook her head and said, 'No, we're just friends.'

Alice couldn't stand being trapped inside. As the sun set, a warm breeze drifted from the north. She decided to go out and pull the weeds along the front path. Her mind was full of Billy and the disappointment on Beau's face when they left early the other night. The meal she had cooked, expecting them to stay, had lasted her the next two nights, and there was still enough in the freezer for tonight.

She paused, her heart heavy, and pushed herself to her feet. There was a loud noise coming from a long way away. She stood still, as a ball of dust rose in the east. Then she realised the sound was that of an ambulance roaring up the dirt road. Her heart lodged in her throat, and she wondered where it was going because it was undoubtedly in a hurry. By the time she walked to the gate, it had covered the road at tremendous speed, dust kicking up behind it as the siren blared and the lights flashed. It sped past her house in a whiz, disappearing to the west in the direction of Jon and Fallon's property.

She felt sick to her stomach. There were no other properties at the end of that road—Jon and Fallon's was the last one, and that's where Billy and Beau lived, in the house down the back. Someone had had an accident, and the chance that it was somebody she knew, somebody she cared about, someone she had rejected, filled her with fear.

She rushed inside and grabbed her keys, not caring that she was wearing shorts and an old T-shirt with dirt on her knees. She didn't even stop to put on a pair of shoes, only realising her feet were bare only when she pulled up at the gate of Fallon and Jon's property.

She was right; the ambulance was parked outside their big shed. She jumped out of the car, slammed the door, and ran across the dirt to the shed just as Fallon came out of the house carrying young Ryan.

'Oh my God,' Alice said, 'I'm so pleased to see you. Are you all right? Is Jon okay?'

'Yes, he is.'

'Please tell me that Billy and Beau are all right, too?' Alice started to cry, tears streaming down her face. She put her hand up to her face. Fallon came over and put one arm around her shoulder.

'Billy and Beau are fine. It's Noreen. She got caught in the cattle crush and has a broken leg. We weren't sure about internal injuries. That's why the ambulance was in such a hurry. They've decided not to move her until the RFDS arrives The helicopter's on the way.'

'Oh my God, I was so worried.'

'You were worried it was Billy, weren't you?'

'I was. I did the wrong thing. Oh, Fallon, I made a mistake. A huge mistake. I told him I didn't want to see him anymore.'

'And you didn't mean it, obviously.'

'No, I didn't mean it. When I thought it could have been him, I knew. I've been so stupid.'

'Well, you'd better sort it out because he's been grumbling around here like a bear with a sore head since Wednesday afternoon. Even Beau got sick of him and came up and had dinner with us last night. Billy's in love with you, Alice.'

Her eyes widened. 'You really think so?'

'I do, but that's something you have to sort out between yourselves. Okay?'

'I will,' she said quietly. 'Where is he now?'

'He's with Beau, back at their place. Beau got upset when he heard the ambulance—it brought a lot of his sad memories back. I made them a hot drink, and they went home. They've not long been gone. It brought tears to my eyes. Billy had his arm around Beau, and Beau wouldn't let him go. He's a beautiful young man, and I think he's just realising how much Billy loves him.'

'Thank you. I hope that poor young woman is all right. She's the wife of the chef at the hotel, isn't she?'

'Yes, that's the one. Robbo is on his way out now.'

'Okay, now I know you guys are all okay, and there's nothing I can do, I'll go back to my place. Unless I can help?'

'No, it's fine.'

'Okay. Please don't tell Billy I was here.'

'Are you sure, Alice?'

'Yes, I've got a lot of thinking to do.'

***

Billy sat on the front porch of the old house, staring out over the paddocks. It had taken a good hour to settle Beau, and he had gone to bed without any dinner. He cried himself to sleep after having a shower, and Billy sat beside him, his hand on his shoulder, until the young boy drifted off.

As Billy gazed down at him, he could see so much of his sister in Beau's features and a deep sadness lodged in his chest. He thought about moving away, but he knew it would be cruel. It wasn't the right thing for young Beau.

He was settled here, in school, and had made good friends. Billy knew he had as much work as he needed while he wanted it—all he didn't have was Alice.

But he was going to do something about that. If Beau went to school tomorrow, he would go and see her. Beau was his priority at the moment; he had to put his feelings aside.

450

He patted his pocket for a cigarette, remembering again that he had given up smoking. In times of stress, his hand still automatically went there, looking for comfort. He hadn't had a beer tonight either because he wanted to stay awake in case Beau needed him during the night. They had a good heart-to-heart, and Beau had let out a lot of grief he'd been holding inside. It was the most Billy had ever seen him cry.

Billy stood and stretched, his eyes narrowing as he saw the headlights of a car coming up his driveway. His heart started pounding hard as the car moved closer, and he realised it was Alice's small red sedan.

'What's wrong now?' he wondered. The helicopter had gone over two hours ago, and he hoped that Noreen would be okay.

He waited at the top of the steps as Alice got out of the car and walked across to him. She stood at the bottom and looked up at him, and there was enough light for him to see her expression. He wasn't sure who moved first, but they met in the middle, and he put his arms around her, burying his face in her shoulder.

'This is where I have to be.' Her breath warmed his skin as she spoke quietly. 'This is where I want to be.'

'Where, Alice? Tell me.' Billy lifted his head, and her breath hitched as she reached out and touched his face.

'With you. Wherever you are.' Her voice was soft as his eyes held hers.

'And I want to be with you, too. Wherever you are, I can leave the land. I can go back to an office job if that helps you. We don't have to work in the country. Unless you want to stay?'

'I love my job, and I love living in this town. I was wrong, Billy. I want you to do what you love.'

'What I love? I love you, Alice.'

***

Joy, like Alice had never known, flooded through her. She lifted her arms around his neck and pulled Billy's head closer to hers.

'Kiss me.' She pressed her lips against his mouth. 'Kiss me. Please, kiss me.' Warm lips moved against hers, and she remembered the first time he had kissed her the night after they'd had dinner in the hotel. 'Kiss me as if you can't bear to let me go.' An unbelievable feeling ran through her as Billy's hold tightened, and she closed her eyes. As his lips claimed hers, a chuckle came from the porch above them.

Alice pulled back and looked up into Beau's smiling face.

'About bloody time,' he said.

Chapter 34
The Augathella Masquerade Ball

Gladys Tingle stood on the raised stage next to a huge flower arrangement that graced the stage. Chloe and Rosie had donated the floral arrangements for the night, and even though the ball was being held on their premises, they had gone above and beyond. Gladys had never seen flowers like it in her whole life. Not even in Brisbane.

The tables for eight were beautifully decorated, and she was pleased to see the little pink bells she had crocheted were sitting in the middle of each table. Tickets had been sold far and wide, and according to Fallon, who'd supervised the online ticket sales, guests had come from as far away as Longreach and Roma. It was certainly going to be an excellent fundraiser.

Gladys nodded. She could see this ball becoming an annual event on the Augathella calendar, which pleased her as she would miss their weekly meetings in the tea rooms.

Lightness filled her heart as she looked around at the couples dancing on the floor below the stage. Even the band was playing decent music, none of that modern stuff. She closed her eyes and let the music take her back to her teenage years when she met Harry at Cloudland in Brisbane. She had gone from Augathella to Brisbane to stay with her cousin, and that had been her introduction to music and dancing. She'd loved it ever since. She had fallen in love that night, and eventually, her Harry had come home to Augathella with her.

They had had a wonderful life, and she'd loved him dearly. He'd been a fine husband, but sadly, they'd only been blessed with one child. Tilly's father worked in a mine up near Mt Isa; she hadn't seen him for ten years but was thankful for the Christmas and birthday cards she received.

Gladys knew she had turned into a bitter old woman as she'd aged, but over the past few months, spending time with her granddaughter, Tilly, and the younger women in town and her friend, Beryl, she'd felt her heart lighten.

Nowadays, she thought before she spoke. She had said some nasty things and been rude to a lot of people over the years, but now it was time to make amends. She loved living in Augathella and she was enjoying her time in the aged care facility. It was time for her to start living another happy life.

She opened her eyes and smoothed down the skirt of her shantung ball dress. Tilly had taken her shopping in Longreach a few months back, and Gladys had laughed when Tilly held up the ball dress and said, 'This will look beautiful on you, Nana.'

'Don't be silly. I don't need to wear a ball dress,' Gladys replied.

'You do,' Tilly insisted. 'And I've made you a mask to match it. I saw this dress up here last time I was here, and I asked them to put it away. I knew it would fit you.'

'You're a good girl, love. But I can't afford it.'

But Tilly had insisted. 'It's your Christmas present from me.'

Now Gladys looked down at her shantung dress as the purple and pink reflected in the spinning light above the dance floor. She smiled; life had been happier since Tilly had come home, and Jeremy, her young man, was a delight.

Tilly looked stunning in her royal blue ballgown, and Jeremy's bow tie was the same shade of blue.

Everyone had excelled themselves tonight. The men wore dinner suits or good trousers and dress shirts with bow ties, and every woman was in a ball dress. Watching the dancing was like watching a rippling rainbow; even the children were dressed up.

In the adjacent room, there was a second, smaller dance

floor for the children, and when the music volume decreased in the main ballroom, she could hear the laughter and squeals as the children enjoyed the ball as much as the adults.

Even the children wore masks, and there was much hilarity as koalas greeted cockatoos and rosellas played with echidnas. The masks of the adults were much more Venetian, with some faces totally covered except for the eyes.

Callie, Sophie, and Alice had excelled themselves. Even Gladys had to admit that. She reached up and gently touched the beaded purple mask that covered two-thirds of her face. Her eyes were all she needed tonight, and she was having great fun standing up in the corner of the stage behind the flower arrangement, trying to figure out who was who beneath the colourful masks.

It wasn't too hard. She could pick the colour of the men's hair and whether the women were pregnant or not. Callie and Braden were impossible to miss, even though they had huge masks that covered their entire faces. Matching bronze and gold masks—they were very spectacular, she thought, but she tried not to be uncharitable. Callie had made lovely masks for *everyone*, not just her own.

Callie was easy to spot because of her pregnant stomach. The others were easy to pick, too—Amelia Riley, because of her pregnant stomach and dark hair, and her husband, Ben, because he was one of the few men singing along in full voice with the music. She was surprised that someone who sang country and western with Matt Hunter would know the words to these old songs. At the moment, he was crooning, *'It's Amore'*, and he sounded just like Frank Sinatra.

Memories hugged Gladys. That was her old life of many, many years ago, and she and Harry had made a good life in Augathella.

Now that she was in her twilight years—the last time she said that Tilly had tapped her on the wrist and said, 'Nana, you're not in your twilight years yet.'

'Sweetheart, I live in an aged care facility,' she said.

Tilly hugged her and said, 'Well, it's still not your twilight years.'

A couple crossed in front of the stage, and it took her a few minutes to figure out who they were. Then she realised it was Fallon and Jon Ingram. Fallon was pregnant, but her dress concealed her stomach. Their masks were red and blue.

Sophie and Kent Mason twirled across the floor, showing off their dance skills. Gladys was sure they would win the prize for the best mask. Sophie had excelled herself with the ones they wore.

Braden and Callie Cartright danced by sedately because Braden could barely get his arms around his wife; she was so big with her pregnancy.

Goodness, she thought, there was going to be a need for an extension to the primary school with all these pregnant women. Amelia and Ben Foley danced past the bottom of the stage, and Amelia looked up and smiled at her. She was the sweetest young woman.

Next in the dance line were Laura and Dr Harry. Gladys had a soft spot for Dr Harry as he shared her late husband's name. He had always been very kind to her, and Laura, even though she'd been prickly when she'd first come to town, was a lovely person. Laura always called into Gladys' room to say hello when she was at the facility.

Gladys pursed her lips as Beryl swept past in the arms of Ward Whelan, the new butcher in town.

Silly woman; she was old to be dancing.

But Gladys looked down longingly as Beryl smiled. Maybe she wasn't too old to dance.

The tempo of the music changed to one of those modern songs that Gladys didn't know. Many of the dancing couples headed to their table for a rest, but Bec and Matt Hunter moved to the middle of the dance floor. They started doing some sort of rock'n roll dance in the middle of the floor, and two local couples stood back, clapping at them.

Kimberley Calthorpe, who was also pregnant, clapped her

hands and laughed as Matt lifted Bec high in the air. Jenna and Josh Foley stood beside them, and Gladys could hear Jenna's loud laughter over the music.

On the other side of the room were those she still called the newcomers to town, and even though they were newcomers, they'd done an amazing job in the last eighteen months since Chloe and her New Life crew had come to town.

But the couple that made her heart sing were Billy Burke and Alice Templeton. Seeing them in each other's arms filled her with happiness. They'd been inseparable over the last two weeks, and last she'd heard—Gladys folded her arms and nodded—Alice was moving in with Billy and young Beau.

Ward Whelan ran lightly up the stairs to the stage and held out his hand. 'Come on, Gladys Tingle. You can't be a wallflower. I think this dance is mine.'

Fancy a young man wanting to dance with an old lady like her.

Gladys smiled as she took his hand and joined her friends on the dance floor. It was a long time since she'd rock and rolled with Harry, but she'd give it a go.

Soon, Jenna and Kimberley were clapping them. Ward certainly knew his moves, and Gladys dug deep for the energy to keep up with him. They soon had an audience, and the look on Tilly's face made Gladys' night.

'There's no doubt,' she said to Ward as he escorted her back to her table when the band took a break, 'The Augathella Masquerade Ball is a huge success.'

Just after ten o'clock, Callie touched Braden's hand. 'I've had it, love. I cannot dance another step, even though I'm loving every moment of it.'

Braden put his arm around her and escorted her over to a soft lounge near the bar. 'You sit here, and I'll get you a lemonade.'

'Thank you.' Callie eased her feet out of her flat shoes and looked at them with a smile. Shoes she'd bought in

Brisbane before she'd met Braden and their boys. Shoes that had almost been ruined in the deluge of water that had run down the irrigation channel the day Braden had rescued her and her luggage. Her first day in Augathella, and the day that she first laid her eyes on Braden Cartwright. Callie smiled as Petie crept in from the children's ballroom.

'Mummy, can I have a little bit more money, please?' he asked

'Some more money? What do you want that for, sweetheart?'

'There's a girl here from school, and I asked her if she'd like a drink, and she said she would.'

'Of course, sweetheart, that's very kind of you.' Callie reached the small reticule that was sewn on the side of her ball dress. Her stomach was so big that the small purse had slipped around, and she couldn't reach it.

'Can you reach it for me, Petie?' She pointed to the little velvet purse. 'Take a couple of dollars. Will that be enough?'

'That will. Thanks, Mummy. Love you.'

Callie smiled as she watched him run back to the other room. Rory and Nigel were feeling very grown-up tonight, and they looked it when they both put their suits on. Along with Beau Burke, she'd had taken them to the op shop together in Charleville a few weeks ago and managed to find suits that fitted the three of them. She knew that Rory had his eye on one of the girls in Year Six, and she smiled as they danced past the doorway half an hour ago.

Callie sat back and put her hands on her stomach. She closed her eyes and let the love in the ballroom surround her—the love for her man, the love for all their children, and the love of their friends and family, and all the joyous people in this room tonight.

She sent a quiet prayer up to Julia, Rory, Nigel, and Petie's mother. 'I'll look after them for you, Julia, until I take my last breath.'

Braden came back with her lemonade and put his arm

around her. 'Okay, sweetheart?'

'More than okay,' Callie whispered. 'I love this community, and I will never regret the day I came to Augathella.

'And Augathella loves you, just as we all do.

Callie lifted her face for her husband's kiss.

She lived in a wonderful community, and she knew she would never live anywhere else.

THE END

I hope you've enjoyed reading about the Augathella girls and their community.

Come on over and meet the Johnson family in Duckinwilla Creek.

<u>Duckinwilla Days</u>
Coming Home
Secrets and Surprises

<u>*Books 3-7 to follow in 2025*</u>

Also by Annie Seaton
Daughters of the Darling
From Across the Sea
Over the River
By the Billabong_(2025)

A Bec Whitfield Mystery
Bowen River
Shadows on the Shore (June 2025)

Duckinwilla Days
Coming Home
Secrets and Surprises
Books 3-7 to follow in 2025

Home to the Outback *(2025)*

Lucy
Angie
Jemima
Isabella

Porter Sisters Series
Kakadu Sunset
Daintree
Diamond Sky
Hidden Valley
Larapinta
Kakadu Dawn

Others
Whitsunday Dawn
Undara
Osprey Reef
East of Alice
One Summer in Tuscany
Four Seasons Short and Sweet
Follow the Sun
Ten Days in Paradise
Deadly Secrets
Adventures in Time
Silver Valley Witch

The Emerald Necklace
A Clever Christmas
Christmas with the Boss
Her Christmas Star
The Emerald Necklace

The Augathella Girls Series
Outback Roads
Outback Sky
Outback Escape
Outback Wind
Outback Dawn
Outback Moonlight
Outback Dust
Outback Hope
<u>Boxed Sets</u>
Augathella Girls 1-4
Augathella Girls 5-8

Augathella Short and Sweet Series
An Augathella Surprise
An Augathella Baby
An Augathella Spring
An Augathella Christmas
An Augathella Wedding
An Augathella Easter
An Augathella Masquerade Ball
Boxed Set
Augathella Short and Sweet 1-3

Sunshine Coast Series
Waiting for Ana
The Trouble with Jack
Healing His Heart
Sunshine Coast Boxed Set

The Richards Brothers Series
The Trouble with Paradise
Marry in Haste
Outback Sunrise
Richards Brothers Boxed Set

Bondi Beach Love Series
Beach House
Beach Music
Beach Walk
Beach Dreams
The House on the Hill Boxed Set

Second Chance Bay Series
Her Outback Playboy
Her Outback Protector
Her Outback Haven
Her Outback Paradise
Boxed Set
The McDougalls of Second Chance Bay Boxed Set

Love Across Time Series
Come Back to Me
Follow Me
Finding Home
The Threads that Bind
Boxed Set
Love Across Time 1-4
Bindarra Creek
Worth the Wait
Full Circle
Secrets of River Cottage
A Clever Christmas
A Place to Belong

About the Author

Annie lives in Australia, on the beautiful north coast of New South Wales. She sits in her writing chair and looks out over the tranquil Pacific Ocean.

She writes contemporary romance and loves telling stories that always have a happily ever after. She lives with her very own hero of many years and they share their home with Toby, the naughtiest dog in the universe, and Barney, the ragdoll puss, who hides when the four grandchildren come to visit.

Stay up to date with her latest releases at her website: http://www.annieseaton.net

Awards

2023: Winner of the long contemporary RUBY award for Larapinta

Finalist for the NZ KORU Award 2018 and 2020.

Winner ...Best Established Author of the Year 2017 AUSROM

Longlisted for the Sisters in Crime Davitt Awards 2016, 2017, 2018, 2019

Finalist in Book of the Year, Long Romance, RWA Ruby Awards 2016 Kakadu Sunset

Winner ...Best Established Author of the Year 2015 AUSROM

Winner ...Author of the Year 2014 AUSROM Best Established Author, Ausrom Readers' Choice 2017 Book of the Year

466